MALI

Torben Mathiassen

MALI

FORLAGET
PANTANAL

MALI

By Torben Mathiassen

Novel
Copyright © 2022 by Torben Mathiassen
Published by Forlaget Pantanal 2025
Original version: MALI
Printed by KDP
1st edition, 1st print 2025
ISBN: 978-87-94451-02-4
Cover photo: Pobytov / iStock by Getty Images
MALI is translated from Danish with the aid of ChatGPT- 4o

This book is dedicated to my family.

"What you do makes a difference, and you have to decide what kind of difference you want to make."

Dr. Jane Goodall

Prologue

El Niño and its sister La Niña typically occur as weather phenomena every two to seven years in the regions surrounding the Pacific Ocean. Together, they have a significant impact on the climate of countries such as Australia, Indonesia, all of South America, Central America, and the southern parts of the United States.

El Niño occurs during a brief warming of the surface waters in the tropical parts of the Pacific Ocean. When this happens, the weather around Australia, Indonesia, and South America becomes warmer than usual. Paradoxically, the weather in the southern United States is cooler and wetter. When the opposite phenomenon, La Niña, occurs, the surface waters are cooler than normal, cooling down the entire region. The weather in the southern US and Central America, on the other hand, becomes warmer and drier.

Between the two phenomena, there is what is known as the natural state. This entirely natural cycle is one of the most important climate cycles on our planet, and no matter what stage of the cycle the Earth finds itself in, it has consequences for weather conditions somewhere.

Studies suggest that global warming intensifies the effects of the El Niño/La Niña cycle in such a way that Australia, Central America, and the southern United States experience longer droughts and wildfires during La Niña periods, and conversely, severe flooding during El Niño periods. The warmer the global temperature becomes, the more extreme the effects of the weather phenomenon.

There is more uncertainty regarding the effects of warming near the equator, but much suggests that regions in Central Africa, which have been plagued by extreme drought for millennia, will experience significant increases in rainfall. Some previously arid areas are even predicted to become fertile, offering the possibility of cultivating the land.

However, the effects of global warming do not stop there.

The land in the vast tundra steppes of Siberia, Alaska, and Canada is warming even down to the deeper soil layers. Dead animals and plant material that have been frozen in permafrost for thousands of years are being exposed and decaying, releasing significant amounts of greenhouse gases into the atmosphere—gases that further amplify the effects of global warming.

The poles are melting, releasing billions of litres of freshwater into the world's oceans, which are expected to rise by up to seven metres, causing significant flooding of low-lying landmasses all around the world. The Earth's population is gradually being forced to move closer and closer together as flooding renders coastal areas uninhabitable.

The vast amounts of freshwater flowing into the sea also threaten to stop the Gulf Stream, a current that has for thousands of years carried warm water from the Gulf of Mexico up along Western Europe. This current is the direct reason why Western Europe experiences higher temperatures and a milder climate than its geographical location would suggest. If this is disrupted, temperatures in the Northern Hemisphere are expected to drop dramatically within just a few years, which could mark the beginning of a new Ice Age. Hundreds of millions of Europeans, North Americans, and Russians would then be forced southward towards warmer regions.

The melting of the world's third pole, the glaciers of the Himalayas, will also cause extensive climate disasters. Nearly two billion people live in the lowlands at the foot of the Himalayas and are heavily dependent on the rivers that derive their water from the glaciers in the mountains. Initially, the rivers will overflow their banks, flooding vast areas of farmland. Later, as the glaciers are no longer replenished with fresh snow, the river deltas will dry up, creating vast desert environments where nothing can grow. Two billion people will be forced to find new places to live in an already crowded area.

The future climate crisis is predicted to be the largest humanitarian disaster ever, with up to half of the world's population being forced to flee their homes and crowd together on land that is already at its limits in terms of capacity. In a world that is already tense due to religious conflicts, territorial disputes, and economic collapses, such crowding as a result of climate change is likely to significantly increase these existing tensions.

Sixty-eight million people worldwide currently live as refugees or internally displaced persons due to war, religious persecution, ethnicity, or nationality. This is the highest number since World War II. Additionally, nearly 20 million people have been forced to flee directly due to significant climate changes already today.

The threat is real. Somalia, South Sudan, Madagascar, Chad, and Ethiopia are all examples of countries where millions of people are daily threatened by starvation due to prolonged drought periods and failed harvests.

The economy of the world's most oil-rich country, Venezuela, has collapsed due to falling oil prices, poor leadership, and a lack of long-term vision. Inflation is so severe that no one can afford to buy food anymore. Millions of people are forced to seek help in neighbouring countries in hopes of surviving. It is easy to imagine that similar situations could arise in several Middle Eastern or North African oil-producing countries when the demand for oil is expected to fall drastically, as more and more renewable energy sources gain ground in the global community. Saudi Arabia, Kuwait, Libya, and Algeria are just a few examples of oil-producing countries where more than 80 percent of the country's income is directly linked to oil extraction.

Religious conflicts between different faiths have always been a cause of war throughout history. Syria, Nigeria, Yemen, the Democratic Republic of the Congo, and Myanmar are just a few of the countries that are currently deeply affected by religious persecution, forcing millions of people to flee. There is little evidence to suggest that the world's population will become more tolerant or humane as they are packed ever closer together.

None of the millions of people who are currently fleeing their homes due to war, persecution, or climate disasters have voluntarily chosen to throw themselves into the uncertainty of their future fate.

Life as a refugee often creates deep psychological scars for life, and living in refugee camps regularly exacerbates these psychological traumas. Often, the conflicts people are trying to escape from follow them into the camps, where racism, violence, and suicide attempts are part of daily life, even for children as young as ten years old.

The largest refugee camps are typically located in neighbouring countries, where the economy is often sparse. This is reflected in life in the camps, where there is a lack of food, medicine, and sanitary conditions. Conflicts frequently occur in the struggle to secure the most basic necessities of life.

To make matters worse, the tents and huts in which refugees are usually housed are so flimsy that extreme weather risks flatten the camps, creating a catastrophe within a catastrophe. Cox's Bazar camp in Bangladesh, which houses a million refugees, is located on hillsides in the monsoon belt, where cyclones become stronger every year. Flooding and widespread mudslides within the camp are common, and the danger of drowning or being crushed to death while trying to escape is ever-present.

Even within Europe's borders, life in the camps is almost unbearable. In the infamous Moria Camp on Lesbos in Greece, which was designed to house 3,000 people, a devastating fire broke out in 2020, leaving its 13,000 residents with nowhere to live in a state of chaos and deep desperation.

Nearly 90 million people are currently fleeing their homes. This equals one percent of the world's population.

One percent!

One can only speculate about what will happen when this number rises to ten percent. Or twenty!

Part I

Polar bear

1 Magnus

The wind is picking up. It brings the cold with it. At first, it sneaks in like a cool breeze, just lowering the temperature by a few degrees, but soon the chilled air will flow down over the landscape, making it a torment to be outside.

The periods of sunshine from a frost-clear sky are gradually getting shorter and shorter. However, this past week the sun has been out every day, sending its warming rays down over the frozen landscape. Not that the air becomes significantly warmer because of it, but at least it doesn't blow when the sun is out. When the wind comes, the world transforms into an in-hospitable place, where the few living creatures who still endure seek refuge inside frost-cracked houses or in caves that are already covered in ice on the inside after several years of harsh frost.

Most of those who survived the first really harsh winter have long since given up and sought refuge southward, where the sun can still warm the ground, and it is still possible to grow edible and nourishing crops.

I understand them well. We've fought through several truly miserable winters, and the latest nearly killed us all. But taking two children, aged 11 and 15, on a long and perilous journey away from the violent raging of the elements, among thousands of other desperate survivors, is not something one does lightly. It requires courage. I don't know if I dare subject my family to that. But as I now look out over the frozen sea and feel the cold creeping in, I'm not sure if I dare stay either.

I've caught two seals, which I load onto my sledge.

Even though there are not many of us left, there are still too many for the task. The seals are frightened away by the men, who, with spears, harpoons, bows, and crossbows, try to secure the family's survival for a little longer.

Firearms are forbidden. It's not a law, but an unwritten rule, because a shot from a rifle scares the animals away and greatly reduces the chances of meat for everyone.

My dog, Mali, watches me with her large brown eyes. Her blue-speckled tongue hangs slightly out of her mouth, and her breath forms misty clouds in the air as she exhales. Mine does too. It forms tiny ice crystals in my beard.

I am always cold. Even when the weather is good, I freeze. I have on seal-skin boots, a seal-skin hat, and seal-skin mittens, which my dear wife made for me from the skin of one of the first seals I brought home. I'm wearing three fleece sweaters and a large seal-skin jacket over them. Still, I freeze.

The cold seeps through to the marrow and bones.

Winter has loosened its grip, but even though we are deep into spring and summer is on the way, it is still unbearably cold to be outside.

I squat down and hug Mali close to me. I try to absorb some of her body heat. Her fur is soft and airy with a dense undercoat that seems to keep her warmer than my four layers of clothes. She tries to lick me on the cheek, but I won't let her do it. Her saliva freezes to ice immediately and would just give me frostbite.

Mali is an Eurasier, who has saved me more than once in these unforgiving surroundings. She is a faithful companion and my very best friend. She doesn't wander, and I am grateful for that. I would constantly be worried about what might happen to her. Mali doesn't scare the seals either, and she doesn't chase them away. Cautiously, she warns me in time before other people approach. She snuggles up to me at night to keep us both warm, and several times she has even made sure to bring me back safely when I unwittingly stray from the trail in the featureless, snow-covered landscape. Mali is one of a kind, and she is worth all the food she eats, even if it means one more mouth to feed.

"We should probably head back," I say, getting to my feet.

Mali pricks up her ears and wags her large bushy tail, which curls over her back in a beautiful arc. I call her Mali because her reddish-brown color reminds me of the earth in the fertile land of Africa by the same name, and I couldn't imagine a better name for her. Mali, which was once one of the world's driest deserts, but is now a temperate climate zone where agriculture flourishes and food is abundant.

Mali is a distant dream, far to the south.

I have never been there, and the images I've seen come from before this part of the world became nearly uninhabitable. I have no sense of what it's like now, where the cold has only intensified. I don't even know how far south the ice has spread. Radio and TV have long ceased transmitting in the northern regions, and no one travels voluntarily from south to north, bringing back news.

Anyone who is able flees from the north to the south. Not the other way. Never the other way.

"How on earth will I be able to bring my family safely to Mali?" I ask quietly into the air. "It's far too cold to be outside for more than short periods of time."

Mali tilts her head and looks at me intently. She senses that I am in turmoil. She knows all my moods.

"It's far too far away," I mumble, looking once again out over the frozen sea.

The thick, heavy ice sheets are pushing their way inland, packing even tighter together and forming sharp ridges that rise up to several metres in height. Every day, the distance to the open sea becomes longer, and the journey out there is difficult and dangerous. The ice can suddenly rear up beneath you when the pressure of the compacted ice gives way, exploding with a violent force that can swallow a person and crush bones and flesh like a giant meat grinder.

"It's becoming too far for me to fetch food all the way out here. And it's too far for us to walk all the way to warmer lands. We're too late, Mali," I say.

I begin to secure the seals to the sledge.

"We should have left when everyone else left. It's my fault that we're stuck here now. But what could I have done? Emilie and Kristian couldn't manage the journey. Maybe they could now, since they're a bit older? But it's even colder, and we're not getting enough food. We need food to have the energy for the long journey."

I continue securing the seals, all the while berating myself.

Deep down, I know that if we had left with the large migration, Emilie and Kristian likely wouldn't have made it. Maybe Kristian could have, but certainly not Emilie, who was only 7 years old back then.

"But if we stay here another winter, we'll all die," I sigh quietly.

Mali comes over and rubs her bushy head against my leg as if to assure me that I will find a solution. She has complete trust in me.

We have plenty of dry wood to burn, since most of the trees

died in the cold. What once were lush, beautiful, green beech and oak forests are now just grey and mournful testaments to a climate change that is well on its way to rendering the northern hemisphere barren. The trunks stretch naked from the snow, reaching their leafless arms up to the sun in a futile attempt to absorb life-giving warmth. But the winter frost has destroyed any budding hope of seeing the beautiful light green colours when the beech woods burst into leaf in the spring.

However, an abundance of firewood won't get us through another winter.

We're short of food. Quite literally.

With the frost, agriculture died. Growing crops for pig and cattle feed became an impossible task. For a while, farmers tried to import feed from Southern Europe, but as the cold continued to creep further south, that option died as well. And even if they had been able to get enough feed, they wouldn't have been able to heat the barns sufficiently to keep the animals alive in the severe frost. Livestock died in droves. Reports often came in of entire herds perishing on particularly cold winter nights.

When farming died, the food shortage became acute, and soon all other production stopped as the overwhelming common problem became food, or the lack of it. Europe literally ground to a halt within a few years after the frost set in and trapped the northern hemisphere's otherwise industrious and affluent population in a deadlock.

North America and Russia were in the same situation, and the millions of people suddenly in need of food could not be supported by the production in the southern parts of those countries. Not even though the previously dry desert areas of

Africa started receiving more regular rainfall and slowly transformed into fertile, nutrient-rich agricultural land.

The African countries were still struggling with unstable, fluctuating regimes and a general lack of structure and stability in their economies. They were in no way prepared for such a sharp increase in demand for their newly developed agricultural products.

People therefore panicked and began looting the shops and food stores that still had a few scraps left. But no one had enough food to survive the winter that was coming. It was colder and longer than ever before.

Every day, we heard about people dying in the neighbourhoods around our house. Children and adults. No one was spared. The frost and hunger made no distinctions.

It was when people ventured outside in search of supplies to replace the empty pantries that they died. Most of those who went out simply never came back, getting lost in the constant snowstorms. Those who managed to return often had such severe frostbite in their feet and hands that gangrene set in.

There weren't enough doctors to treat all the frostbite cases, and often it was completely impossible for the doctor to reach anyone due to the extreme low visibility and the ever-present risk of getting lost in the darkness.

Many died after a long and painful course at home, by the stove, where the gangrene slowly spread and consumed the patient from the inside.

Winter continued well into the spring.

When the summer sun finally broke through and once again offered its life-giving rays to the long-suffering population, the survivors emerged from their winter shelters. Most were marked on both body and soul after a long and painful fight for survival, watching their loved ones die before their eyes, unable to do anything to help.

I don't know why my own little family was spared when so many others perished in the cold. Maybe we were just lucky. Not that we didn't suffer like everyone else from the cold and the lack of food.

As winter went on, we had to burn more and more of the furniture in the house, until we finally tore up the floorboards in the farthest rooms and burned them one by one. Sitting huddled together by the stove, we watched how the fire greedily devoured the precious wood.

We all feared the day when I would have to venture outside in the winter storms to look for more fuel for the flames, which voraciously consumed everything we fed them.

No one had anticipated such a long and harsh winter, and therefore no one had gathered extra firewood from the surrounding forests.

But we survived.

And even though I'd had a few trips outside to find more wood, I got off lightly.

The last month, we lived off the rats that had sought refuge in the houses in an attempt to escape the deadly winter cold. Instead, they ended their days on a spear over the flames, before we eagerly devoured the meagre meat. The first mouthful took some overcoming. Biting into such a revolting animal wasn't exactly at the top of my wish list. But then again, neither was starving to death.

Soon, we stopped thinking about it. It was food. Protein. Survival.

The great migration began the month after, when people had recovered enough to feel capable of the long journey down through Europe. Thousands of people packed their belongings and began walking south.

Few cars were able to start after such a winter. Summer couldn't thaw the frozen carburettors and batteries. The only sound was the constant dry cough when ignition keys were turned in the faint hope of being the lucky owner of one of the thousand cars that could actually start.

Trains and planes were similarly out of action.

For most, there was no other choice but to walk – on foot. A journey through frost and snow of more than 1,500 kilometres south to an unknown existence.

No one knew what the situation was like further south. Whether the harsh winter had spread even further down into Southern Europe and was also keeping the population there in an icy grip, offering little hope for survival.

It was fearful to see our friends and family members leave the city.

We cried. Convinced that we would never see them again.

My wife took her hand out of her mitten and gently placed it in mine, as if to feel the warmth from another human being.

We briefly discussed whether we should go with them. Fearing we would only send our children to their certain death by cold or hunger on the long journey, we decided to stay.

Only a few families chose to stay in what was now developing into a genuine ghost town, with half-dead, icy winter souls wandering aimlessly.

We've survived four winters since then.

Even though we've been well-prepared and gathered plenty of firewood, and tried to store provisions for the long winter, it's never enough. Each winter is colder and longer than the last, and the wild animals are fewer and fewer. Unless a larger seal herd passes by during the summer, I'm afraid we won't survive the next winter.

Although the northern regions of Norway, Sweden, and Finland have historically been rich in wildlife, and the animals have been able to find food on the great Arctic tundra even in winter, the same animals have not moved further south to Denmark. Not even though the waters around Denmark, the Kattegat, and the Skagerrak are likely frozen over throughout the winter, allowing free passage between the countries.

The temperate zone that has always surrounded Denmark, which was so favourable for lush plant and animal life, has in recent years been replaced by an especially harsh polar climate. Over time, a true tundra environment will likely develop, with particularly winter-hardy plant species such as mosses, lichens, and ferns. But for now, the frost has killed almost all existing fauna, leaving the land as a barren, hard, and almost impenetrable shell that yields nothing edible.

Mali catches my attention as she begins to growl softly. A deep rumble from the back of her throat.

"What can you see, Mali?" I ask, allowing my eyes to scan the land in the direction she is staring.

The snow-covered sand dunes lie deserted, but everything could be hidden effectively in the valleys between them.

I turn around to look for the men still on the ice, hoping to catch another seal. Like me, they will have to turn back soon to avoid being trapped in the impending snowstorm, which I am convinced is on its way.

They are still there – all five of them. So, none of them have managed to sneak past me up into the dunes unnoticed.

The wind picks up, and tiny snowflakes begin to swirl around my head like flies around a lightbulb.

Mali is still staring up at the dunes. Her triangular ears stand upright, picking up sound signals that will forever be impossible for me to hear. She no longer growls.

"Whatever it is, we'd better head home, Mali," I say, running my gloved hand along her back. "We have to go through the dunes, so keep your ears and eyes open."

I fasten the harness from the sledge around my waist, pull my neck gaiter up over my face to avoid frostbite from the biting cold wind, and adjust my sunglasses over my eyes.

I grab my short compound bow, complete with its cables, string, and wheels, and murmur almost inaudibly.

"Come on, let's go."

Slowly, we begin to move, both with our eyes fixed on the dunes.

My quiver hangs from my belt, gently slapping against my leg with each step I take. I have 15 good arrows with hunting tips made of stainless steel, which I can ready on my bow in a matter of seconds.

When the frost set in, I had never shot a bow before, but necessity teaches a naked man to spin. After the first harsh winter, when most others had fled south, I realised I needed to learn to hunt if we were to have any chance of surviving another winter.

I found a deserted hunting and fishing shop and tried to make sense of the many weapons. I first eyed a hunting rifle, but I couldn't find any ammunition. It was most likely locked away in the shop's safe. Instead, I chose a compound bow and found a book on bow hunting, which I also took with me. I spent hours practising hitting my targets until I had mastered the bow well enough to hunt with it.

The sledge runners glide effortlessly across the frozen snow.

The only sound is the crunch of the snow under my boots with every step I take. My ears strain to catch any sound that doesn't belong, but I trust Mali's hearing more than my own. I keep an eye on her constantly, but she remains silent as we slowly pass the many frozen sand dunes.

At one point, I stop at the top of one of the highest dunes and let my eyes scan the surroundings in a 360-degree circle.

The wind has picked up even more, and the skin around my eyes, which is unprotected from the cold, begins to sting. My eyes water, and I try to make out the blurred shapes I see all around me through a veil of tears.

It is easy to hide in the dunes if you don't want to be seen.

Dry grasses poke up in tufts from the snow around me. Snowflakes drift across the landscape, already covering the footprints I've just made.

Mali growls again. A soft rumble deep in her throat.

Her gaze is still fixed behind us in the direction we've just come from.

I still don't see anything.

I wipe my tears away with the back of my gloved hand and fumble for my snow goggles from my pocket. They are essential in this weather, but because they have dark lenses to protect against the glare of the sun off the snow and the risk of snow blindness, I don't see my surroundings as clearly when I wear them. I never wear them when hunting. But when the wind picks up, I have no choice. They protect the skin around my eyes and prevent my eyes from watering, which would leave frozen streaks of tears down my cheeks.

I glance up at the sun, which has now disappeared behind a cloud cover.

We need to find shelter before the storm catches us.

I think of the other hunters out on the ice. They're probably on their way back too, just like me. It's probably one of them that Mali has caught the scent of.

"Come on, Mali," I say. "We need to hurry."

It's impossible to travel far in this weather. I head towards one of the many deserted holiday homes scattered along the entire Danish west coast. Once a popular tourist destination, they now lie unused, decaying surprisingly quickly.

Below the dune area, there is more shelter from the strengthening westerly wind, and without the wind constantly battering us, it doesn't feel quite as cold.

I am momentarily tempted to keep going a little further, but I know that as soon as I'm out of the dunes' shadow, we'll be exposed once more to the polar winds that could freeze me dangerously quickly.

There is no choice. We'll have to spend the night in one of the holiday homes. The nearest one is about a kilometre away. I set off towards it.

As soon as I leave the dunes, I feel the wind's icy grip, and I quicken my pace. The sledge is heavy, and I move only slowly.

I try to work my way to warmth, but it's an art that is hard to master. Too much activity, and I begin to sweat. Sweat is one of your worst enemies. It moistens your clothes and skin, making the cold greedily draw out any remaining heat from your body. But if you don't stay active enough, you won't generate the body heat needed to keep your vital functions going.

Here and there, where the wind has swept the snow aside, the runners scrape noisily across the frozen surface before gliding smoothly over the loose powder that lies like a blanket across the landscape.

I try to avoid the bare patches, as the seals weigh nearly 200 kilos together, and pulling that weight over a rough surface is almost impossible. A couple of times, the sledge gets stuck when one of the runners hits a bare spot. It stops so suddenly that I nearly fall over backwards, and I have to use all my strength to free it again.

Almost at the holiday home, Mali runs ahead, as if to scout the place for potential inhabitants.

The house is empty, just like all the other holiday homes.

You can't live so close to the sea, where the wind relentlessly sweeps in from the ocean and freezes everything in its path. The residents are forced to stay in the town, ten kilometres further inland, even though it means I have to make the trip out to the ice edge to shoot seals. In the town, there is more shelter from the wind, and even though the cold is harsh, we are not as exposed to its chilling effect as if we had settled in one of the abandoned holiday homes.

The two seals on my sledge will provide us with food for two to three weeks, depending on how cold it is outside and how much energy we use to keep warm. We live entirely on the meat and blubber from the seals I catch. The supermarkets have long since been emptied of canned goods, pasta, and other long-lasting foods.

To ensure we survive the winter, we need at least 20 seals in our food stores, plus those we eat during the hunting season.

Since I can only pull two seals at a time on my sledge, I have to make the ten-kilometre journey to the sea and back at least 17 times during the four months that summer lasts. One day out. Shoot two seals. One day back. Five days to help Freja butcher them and pack the meat. And then off again on a new seven-day cycle. Provided, of course, I shoot two seals on each trip.

I dread the thought of being locked inside for another seven or eight months with no chance of going outside, just passively watching our food supplies dwindle day by day, with no way of doing anything about it.

You quickly become alone with your thoughts in such confinement. Even though we're together as a family, that kind of imprisonment is so harsh on the soul that madness seems to be a particularly persistent guest.

A lack of food is a worry we definitely don't need again.

Although I know the summer house and have stayed there before, I glance through the windows before I enter, to ensure there's no one inside that I don't know.

When I think about it, it's actually a silly action. Strangers no longer pass by casually. I haven't seen a new face since the migration south. But once you've experienced what it's like to be locked in for an entire winter and watched the supplies shrink to nothing, you don't take any chances. At least, I don't.

As expected, the summer house is empty.

I leave my sledge outside, grab a few of the firewood logs piled up by one corner of the house, and light the stove.

The five other hunters will probably turn up soon, and each of them will take a bundle of firewood inside, so we won't have to go outside and collect more during the night.

Rarely, I can manage to go out and return on the same day if the weather holds and hunting luck is on my side. However, most of the time, I have to stay overnight on the way. Sometimes I use this summer house, and other times, I can get further inland before the weather forces me into one of the abandoned houses.

Mali settles quickly into her usual spot under the coffee table, unaffected by the gloomy thoughts of survival, hunger, and depression that constantly haunt my mind.

I've been to the summer house so many times now that it no longer feels intrusive to enter someone else's private property.

Each time I break into a house for the first time seeking shelter, it feels strange. It feels like I'm invading privacy, even though the people who once lived there have long since abandoned it. I can't help but wonder if they might come back someday, when the weather changes and releases its frost grip on Denmark. What will they think when they return and discover someone has broken in, burned their furniture, and taken shelter in their home for a short time?

The fire crackles softly in the stove, which under normal conditions is built to heat the whole house but can barely keep the living room warm now.

The door opens as Erik and Svend enter, letting in a freezing cold wind with them.

Mali jumps up from her spot under the coffee table and barks aggressively at the newcomers. Though she knows them, she keeps her distance, only stopping her barking when I tell her to be quiet and lay down under the table again.

"The others will be here soon," says Svend, dropping a bundle of firewood onto the pile Erik just made beside the stove. "They were tying their catches to the sledges when we crossed the dunes."

To avoid leaving the women completely alone in the town, and to not scare the seals too much, we hunt in groups of six men at a time. It's usually the same group of us, so we know each other well and know what to expect.

We make the journey from the town to the sea at least four times each month while the wives stay at home with the children.

It didn't take long before climate change effectively broke down many years of painstakingly built gender equality. Braving the elements several times a month and bringing down animals weighing between 60 and 120 kilos is simply easier for men with larger muscle mass than for most women.

But the women aren't left helpless. Their role is just as important. When we go hunting, they head into the woods a few kilometres away and bring back load after load of firewood.

To survive the winter, we need at least 50 cubic metres of wood, equivalent to 30-40 medium-sized trees, which must be felled, split, and hauled back to the houses on home-built sledges. 300 kilos of wood every single day during the four months of summer.

It's hard work for them, so when we men aren't by the sea or butchering seals, we're in the woods with the women.

Every day during the summer is a race against time to be ready for winter, and honestly, I don't know how long we can keep it up.

We men don't always go out together when we head off on our hunting trips, but the first few weeks after winter has released its iron grip on the country, the weather is very changeable. If we're not careful, we risk getting caught in a snowstorm and losing our way, blinded by the snow masses that fall from the sky. In such situations, it's good to stay together in a group, so we can keep an eye on each other if something unexpected happens.

It was in such a sudden snowstorm that Mali literally saved my life last year.

The weather had looked fine. The sun was shining, and there wasn't a breath of wind, so I decided to head home the same day, after having had good luck hunting as soon as I arrived. I said goodbye to the others and set off on the five-hour journey, pulling my sledge with around 200 kilos of freshly caught seals.

But just an hour into my journey, the weather started to turn, and ten minutes later, I was in the middle of a freezing, roaring snowstorm, where the visibility was so poor I could hardly see my own feet as I walked. I had no idea where I was going. Whether I was following the path or straying off it, beyond the marshes, away from any chance of shelter in one of the abandoned houses along the way.

But Mali knew. She walked closely up beside my leg, making sure I stayed on track. If I veered off too much, she switched sides and nudged me back onto course. For half an hour, I stumbled blindly with Mali pressed against my leg.

I was sure we were going to die in the snowstorm, unable to save ourselves. But Mali kept nudging me forward, and eventually, I found myself in front of one of the abandoned houses I knew well from previous trips, where I had also had to seek shelter.

Had I not had Mali with me that day, I'm convinced I wouldn't be here now. She saved my life.

As if she reads my thoughts, she crawls out from her bed and comes over to nudge her fluffy, soft head into my stomach. I gently scratch behind her black ears and let her give me a wet dog kiss on my cheek.

"There are fewer seals this year than last year at this time," I say, turning my attention to Erik and Svend, who have each pulled out a chunk of semi-warm seal meat. They're placing it on a pan directly on top of the stove.

I reach under my blouse and pull out my own pouch of seal

meat, tossing a piece onto the pan beside theirs, already sizzling in its own fat. We always keep the meat close to our bodies, as otherwise, it freezes when we need it.

"I've been thinking the same," says Svend, taking a couple of large pots, then heading outside to fill them with snow, which we can melt for drinking water.

The wind has picked up even more. It pulls so violently at the door that Svend loses his grip. The wind slams it against the outside wall. Erik quickly goes out and wrestles with Svend for a moment before they manage to free the door from the storm's iron grip.

The snowfall has increased in strength.

"If they're not here within five minutes, we'll have to go out and look for them," says Erik.

He's of course right.

The journey through the dunes, with no landmarks and visibility at zero, could very easily send them in the wrong direction.

But it's not that bad yet.

I'm sure they're right on our heels.

"I'll take Mali and go look for them," I reply, getting up and beginning to put on my neck gaiter, hat, and mittens. My overcoat is still on.

Just as I pull my snow goggles from my pocket, the door suddenly bursts open again, and the last three men tumble in, engulfed in a cloud of snow and cold.

I can tell something is wrong.

"We just saw a polar bear!" exclaims Zaid in disbelief.

2 Freja

Kristian squints one eye as he points his finger in the direction he's aiming. In his other hand, he holds a snowball. Moments later, he hurls it towards Emilie and Fatima, who are huddled together behind one of the frost-covered cars abandoned in the street.

He's moistened the snow with his spit to make it stick together into a snowball firm enough to throw. Later in the year, hopefully, the sun will have managed to warm the frozen ground enough for the snow to melt, allowing them to have proper snowball fights and build snowmen or snow forts. But until then, Kristian has to wet the snow with his spit.

He's already pressing together a new lump of snow, shaping it into another snowball, the perfect size to flush out two younger girls from their hiding place.

The girls squeal with delight as he suddenly dives to the side and flings the snowball forward with surprising agility, even for a 15-year-old. The snowball smashes into one of the car's tail lights with great force, exploding in a cloud of tiny snowflakes that rain down over the two girls' seal-skin hats as they unsuccessfully try to shield themselves by turning their backs.

I burst out laughing at the surprised and slightly bewildered expressions on the girls' faces. Kristian hears me laugh. He stands up and waves at me. I wave back, giving him a warm smile.

"That was quite the trick shot," I shout.

He smiles and begins to run towards me. I watch his sunken

cheeks. We're not getting enough food, and what we do eat is too one-sided. Seal meat keeps us alive, but we're starting to miss the essential vitamins from fruits and vegetables, as well as from sunlight. There's no fruit or vegetables here, and sunlight is scarce for much of the year.

Moreover, Kristian refuses to eat the seal liver, even though it contains a wide range of the vitamins we need to thrive.

"It tastes absolutely disgusting," he usually says, handing his portion over to Emilie, who on the other hand loves the taste and, especially, the scent of freshly fried liver.

"Can we run ahead to Farhana's?" he asks.

"Yes, of course," I reply. "I'm coming too."

I pull my hat down further over my ears, load the axe and saw onto the sledge, and begin the journey down the street to meet Farhana.

We always go together when we head into the forest. It's as if the work feels a little easier when we do it together. Not that we're ever alone in the forest. All the women of the village are out there every single day, along with the men who aren't out hunting.

Imagine that the world has come to this, I think to myself. A global society, with a technological development racing ahead at breakneck speed, and then we're checkmated within a few short years by the chaos of nature.

When the first harsh winter was over and we could finally go outside without the risk of getting lost in snowstorms or suffering frostbite from the bitter winds that continuously swept across the country, it was an overwhelming feeling to see the other survivors again. And to hear about all those who had passed away during that winter.

I vividly remember the tears on everyone's faces as we

walked amongst each other, seeing how emaciated we'd all become. We heard about the suffering people had endured in their desperate struggle to survive the hunger and the all-encompassing cold. So many people had died.

Darwin's famous sentence flickered through my mind for a few seconds amid the emotional chaos in my head: only the strongest survive. The children had survived because their parents had made sure they ate more than they did themselves. The eldest family members, on the other hand, had almost all died, as if they had a silent agreement to sacrifice themselves so that the children and grandchildren could live.

The many deaths, followed by the mass exodus, meant that we're now no more than 40 or 50 people left in the village. To be better able to help one another in case of emergencies, we agreed it would be best if we all lived close to each other. So we moved into Grønnegade and Præstegade in the town centre, where the houses stand side by side, and where the neighbour's wood stove not only heats their own living room but also keeps the end wall of the house *we* live in warm. Furthermore, the many surrounding buildings offer a bit of shelter from the winter storms.

The house we chose for ourselves is a yellow, lime-washed half-timbered house from the 1800s, which had since been thoroughly renovated to meet much higher environmental standards of later times. When we first entered the house on Grønnegade, it felt like we were violating someone else's private property, like stepping into an abandoned world filled with joys, sorrows, hopes, despair, and, in the end, desperation. Just like our own house, it had been completely stripped of anything burnable. Bookshelves, dressers, beds, wardrobes, paintings – everything was gone, consumed by greedy flames desperately fighting a losing battle against the deadly cold. A cold that clings like a relentless grip, constantly threatening to break through the fragile shield of warmth the flames manage to provide.

It's a battle of the elements – David versus Goliath.

At first, I had an irrational expectation that the door would suddenly open, and the rightful owners of the house would stand there, demanding their property back. But as time passed, the house became part of us. It gives us security and comfort. The former owners, of course, are never coming back.

Just as relieved as we were to have survived that first brutal winter, we were equally terrified when the second winter arrived far too soon, and we found ourselves once again trapped indoors. Unsure whether we had enough firewood to last through the winter. Whether we had enough food.

At first, we barely dared to touch our supplies, but as time went on, it became clear that we were much better off this time. So, we increased the rations and burned a little extra wood in the stove.

We realised that we could indeed survive under these harsh new conditions, but it's hard work. Every day is about survival and preparing for the long confinement. Any mistake could prove fatal.

"Slacking only burns your own behind," Magnus always says.

Magnus is my wonderful husband and the father of both my children. Magnus is my soulmate, and without him, I wouldn't have survived this long.

Farhana opens the door after my second knock. She's dressed in homemade seal-skin trousers and a seal-skin jacket. Before stepping outside, she pulls a seal-skin hat down over her black, shoulder-length hair and puts on her warm seal-skin mittens.

"I'm ready," she says, her Syrian accent still faintly present, despite having lived in Denmark for over 15 years and speaking almost fluent Danish.

I've known Farhana and her husband Zaid since they were granted asylum in Denmark, and I was introduced to them as a volunteer network contact, tasked with helping them integrate into Danish society. But it wasn't until the great exodus that we became best friends. Sure, we'd always had a good rapport, but in a busy life with work, school, and family as the main focus, I didn't have much time to form new friendships.

After the exodus, however, we were left behind and soon realised we needed to stick together as a group if we were going to have any chance of survival.

It quickly became clear that Farhana and I worked well as a team, and today we do almost everything together.

We walk in silence, side by side, each pulling a sledge behind us.

The children run ahead, laughing loudly. Once we reach the forest, there's no more time for play. They'll have to help load the sledges with firewood. We need all hands on deck; no one can be spared.

I secretly observe my friend as we walk side by side, each lost in our own thoughts. It's as though these long periods of confinement have changed the way we are together. People don't talk much anymore, but we appreciate each other's silent company all the more. Just being near another person in such harsh, life-threatening conditions is enough to fill our social cup.

Farhana looks surprisingly well. Her eyes are bright, her

cheeks round, showing no signs of vitamin deficiency or lack of food at all. She looks strong, I think to myself, remembering with dread my own reflection from this morning. My eyes were sunken and tired, and my reddish-blonde hair hung limp over my shoulders, greasy and tangled.

I hadn't looked at my own reflection in a long time, afraid of what I might see, but when I saw how well Farhana seemed to be doing, I decided this morning that it was time.

I got a shock.

I don't look anywhere near as good as she does. I look as if I've aged at least ten years over the course of the winter we've just survived.

"You look great, Farhana," I say, offering a tentative smile.

Farhana looks at me, surprised, and smiles broadly, her dimples showing. She doesn't reply but seems to enjoy the compliment quietly.

"What's your secret?" I ask. "Why do I look like something the cat dragged in, while you look like a true desert princess from a Disney movie? How do you do it?"

She stares at me for a moment, then suddenly bursts into hearty laughter. "I'll never get the hang of all these special 'Danish' expressions," she laughs, quickly wiping away the tears that form at the corners of her eyes before they have a chance to freeze into ice crystals. "Something the cat dragged in... I think I get what you mean, but I'd never think to say that myself."

"No, what I mean..." I begin, realising how odd such an idiom must sound to a foreigner.

Caught by Farhana's infectious laughter, I can't help but join in. Before I know it, we're both standing there laughing out loud.

For a split second, I think about how absurd it must look to any passerby—two women wrapped in thick layers of seal-skin in the middle of a deserted street, with abandoned cars, empty houses, and long icicles hanging menacingly towards the ground. In a world that's harsh, cold, and unforgiving, there we are, unable to stop laughing like a pair of silly teenage girls.

The children turn to look at us as if we've gone mad. It's been a long time since they've heard anyone laugh so loudly and for so long.

There's not much to laugh about anymore.

Slowly, the laughter fades.

We embrace, holding each other for a moment in a hug that confirms the other's physical presence.

"So, what's the secret?" I ask again, forcing another short giggle.

We begin walking again. Silence descends over the town once more. The frost has muted all sounds, and we can only hear the drag of our footsteps through the snow.

The children have run ahead and have already reached the end of the road, where they turn right, leaving the town behind, heading towards the forest. When we get there, we'll probably be able to hear the sounds of people already chopping down trees and splitting firewood. The sounds travel easily in the frozen landscape when the buildings don't block them.

As we walk, my thoughts wander to Magnus and Zaid, who set off early this morning with Mali. I hope they have good fortune and return soon.

I don't like being apart. I feel far too vulnerable, and I can't imagine how the children and I would manage if something happened to Magnus. I wouldn't be able to both hunt and gather firewood, and the other families are barely able to provide for themselves. How could they take on the extra burden of caring for a woman and two more children? It frightens me. We are far too exposed.

Farhana breaks the silence, pulling me out of my dark thoughts.

"We make sure to have a bath once a week, all through the winter. You wouldn't believe it, but it really makes a big difference. Just lowering your body into a tub of warm water is one of the most life-affirming things. It really does something good for the soul."

I stare at her in surprise.

We hardly ever bathe, not even in the summer. It's simply too cold, and it's a huge effort to gather enough snow for a bath, melt it, and fill a tub with warm water. I can't imagine what it must be like in the winter when you have to go outside in the deadly cold to collect snow and ice.

"It's a deadly task, and I consider it foolish and an entirely unnecessary risk to expose oneself and one's family to that," I say.

"It was Zaid's idea," she continues. "At first, I was against it, but he insisted. He convinced me that it's important to maintain as many of our old habits as possible, so we don't go mad. He said that a warm bath would be just the thing when winter storms are howling outside, and snow is falling heavily.

"I admit, it was nerve-wracking … No, it was terrifying the first time we went outside to gather snow. I've never been so cold in my life. But when we could sink into a hot bath afterwards and feel the warmth seep into our bones, pushing away all the worries about frost, winter, firewood, and food—just for a little while—it was all worth it."

She pauses and looks at me nervously, as if expecting a scolding. She surely knows how I feel about their dangerous winter bathing, but in a way, it makes sense. And the results are obvious. She looks well. Much better than the rest of us.

"How long do you think we can keep living like this?" I ask instead, letting my gaze wander down the street at the metre-long icicles hanging ominously from the gutters. Every now and then, one breaks off when it gets too heavy, crashing to the ground. When that happens, you better not be standing underneath it—an icy, spear-like shard weighing several kilos, falling from several metres up, could do serious harm.

Farhana follows my gaze and sighs.

"I don't know," she says quietly. "But I know that when we're in a crisis, we have to take it one day at a time. Even though it looks bleak now, there's always light at the end of the tunnel. That's what I learned when Zaid and I fled the war in Syria."

I shrug.

"Who knows?" I say. "Maybe the frost will retreat just as quickly as it arrived. And then, perhaps, they'll all come back?"

We walk in silence to the end of the road, following the children towards the forest.

Soon, we hear the first tree crashing to the ground with a thunderous force. The branches snap like brittle matchsticks as it tumbles through the bare, dense treetops, reminding me of the crackling fireworks of a distant New Year's Eve.

As we approach the forest, the landscape shows the signs of our daily trips to haul load after load of firewood back to our stoves. Tree stumps stand like silent monuments scattered across the landscape. The closer we get, the more densely they're packed together. Short and splintered, they stand as evidence that the forest is not an endless resource.

We find a tree a little further from the group of women, who are already busy swinging their axes. When trees fall, it's best not to be too close to each other.

In our small community, we have no doctor and certainly nothing resembling facilities for surgery if an accident occurs.

Farhana grabs her axe and, with great precision, begins to chip away at the trunk. I watch as she alternates between swinging the axe at a 45-degree angle, first from above and then from below. Like the seasoned lumberjack she's become over the past few years, she fells the tree in just a few minutes. Slowly, it begins to fall in the direction of the notch she's been cutting, her axe blade biting deep into the wood until the remaining part of the trunk is too weak to keep the tree standing. With a crash, it falls to the ground, 15-20 metres long, leaving thick splinters pointing upwards on the opposite side.

Only slightly out of breath from the exertion, steam rises from her nose as her warm breath mixes with the cold air. Large clouds of steam form around her, reminding me of the Valkyries of Norse mythology, as she stands there with her axe in hand, her cheeks glowing red.

Farhana has already been through so much in her short life, I think to myself.

First, she fled the war in Syria, and now she's living like an Inuit, fighting a daily battle for survival.

But she doesn't seem as worried about the situation as I am.

I shake the thoughts away and focus on the task at hand. I take up my axe and begin chopping the trunk into smaller pieces with the same experience and precision that Farhana has just demonstrated. She does the same from the other end, and we slowly work our way towards each other. It's important to keep a steady pace so we don't sweat too much. Sweat can be deadly in the cold.

As Farhana and I chop the trunk into smaller pieces, Kristian takes on the demanding task of splitting them so they'll fit into the wood-burning stove at home. Using a steel wedge and hammer, he quickly splits the wood into eight nearly equal parts, which Emilie and Fatima then stack onto the sledges.

No one complains about the work. Everyone understands the importance of each person's contribution to our shared survival.

My axe tears through the trunk, splinter by splinter.

At first, I was completely exhausted after just half an hour of work, but now I've learned the technique and can work efficiently all day.

My thoughts constantly revolve around our situation. I fear another winter like the first more than anything else. It keeps me going. But I can also feel it breaking me down mentally. What will we do when the forest is empty? The next large forest is far away. What if the seals disappear? They're our only reliable food source. What will we do if we get hurt or fall ill? This situation can't last forever.

All around me, the constant sound of axes biting into hard wood fills the air, only occasionally interrupted by the crash that follows when a tree falls. Afterwards, there's always a brief moment where all sounds seem to disappear, as if we've silently agreed to hold a minute's silence for each tree that falls.

"Let's leave?"

Magnus and I have discussed it over and over. Should we

follow those who have already headed south? Or should we stay and hope we can survive along with the rest of the small community that's remained? That summer will return and push the ice back north again.

"Mum?"

Someone tugs at my sleeve, pulling me back from my thoughts.

"Mum, we have to go!"

Emilie looks up at me with her large blue eyes, her nose and cheeks red from working in the cold. I smile at her.

"What is it, sweetheart?"

"Mum," Kristian says with feigned indignation. "It's not fair that we're working while you just stand there daydreaming! The sledges are full. We need to go home."

I look in surprise at the loaded sledges.

Farhana is already fastening her harness, preparing to use her full body weight and strength to pull the sledge. She looks up and smiles when we make eye contact.

"I think the nice weather is over for now. Look at those dark clouds coming in from the sea," she says, pointing to the west.

I look up at the clear, pale blue sky and the sun, which casts its rays across the landscape from its low position.

I close my eyes and enjoy, for a brief moment, the faint warmth spreading over my cheeks before turning my gaze to the horizon. Large, dark clouds are moving rapidly inland towards us.

I know the wind will reach us first. If we don't want to get caught out in the open by the freezing cold wind, we need to leave now. Worse still, if those clouds bring a snowstorm. Getting lost outside the town, blinded by a whiteout, would be catastrophic. We'd freeze to death in just a few hours.

I think of the men out by the coast as I fasten my harness. Hopefully, they've already found shelter in one of the summer cabins.

I know Magnus doesn't take unnecessary risks. Not after that time he and Mali got caught in a snowstorm. If it hadn't been for the dog, Kristian and Emilie wouldn't have a father today.

I don't know what we'd do without Mali. Some of the remaining people in our small community think she's an unnecessary extra mouth to feed, and she's been a recurring topic of debate. But besides literally saving Magnus's life, she's the only little source of joy we have left in this cold winter hell, something that isn't just about survival. Something that gives us a bit of happiness when she jumps up to play tag with Emilie or Kristian. Or when she curls up next to us in the evening as we gather around the warm stove, demanding a belly rub or a scratch on her back near her tail.

"Let's go," I say, still lost in my own thoughts.

"Is something wrong, Mum?" Kristian asks, concerned.

I haven't responded to his teasing. There isn't much to laugh about these days. But I should still send a playful remark back. Humour is the only thing that keeps us going. Without it, the seriousness would be overwhelming. Without it, we'd constantly talk about the dangerous things. The things that worry us, spiralling deeper and deeper into our inner fears until the worries tie themselves into a knot deep in our stomachs—a knot that sends depressive thoughts like arrows through our entire system, threatening to destroy us one by one, because no one has the energy or mental strength left to survive.

Humour is crucial.

But right now, my mind is blank. I don't know what to say.

"No, no. I'm fine, love. I'm probably just a bit tired. Let's get going before the snowstorm hits us."

Kristian looks at me for a moment, then moves behind the sledge to help push it forward while I pull.

Emilie and Fatima do the same with Farhana's sledge.

Slowly, we make our way out of the forest, pulling the heavily loaded sledges filled with wood—far more precious now than all the foolish consumer goods we used to crave. Electronic gadgets, which are now only useful for their batteries, good for starting a fire when you press a bit of steel wool against both terminals at the same time.

I glance back over my shoulder. Everyone else has also begun the journey home.

Behind me, I can hear Kristian panting as we struggle through the snow. The runners drag heavily over the loose-frozen snow. Further on, where the snow has been compacted by the many feet trampling back and forth between the forest and the town, it will slide a bit more easily. But right now, until we reach the trail, it's hard work.

It's a sad childhood, I think. There aren't many playmates, but then there isn't much time for play either. No school. No future.

I glance towards the horizon. The clouds have come dangerously close, and fast.

"Kristian, push! The storm is near!"

As if to emphasise my words, the first cold gust of wind hits the back of my neck. Five minutes later, the snow begins to fall upon us like needle-sharp spikes, piercing any exposed skin.

We stop briefly to wrap our scarves tightly over our faces before continuing towards the shelter of the town.

We've only been exposed to the biting wind for a few minutes, but I can already feel how it's draining all my energy, leaving my legs tired and heavy. Slowly, bent forward, we struggle through the blinding white blanket of snow.

I consider leaving the sledges behind and coming back for them after the storm passes.

Through the howling wind, I hear Farhana shout.

"We're almost there. Just a few hundred metres more."

I look up and squint. I can just about make out the far end of the long row of terraced houses where we live. Ours is number 12 in the row.

I lean forward in the harness.

The storm has caught up with us with the speed and force of a proper autumn gale heralding the arrival of winter.

We need to get to shelter as quickly as possible.

3 Magnus

"A polar bear?" we exclaim in disbelief, speaking over one another.

We all stare at Zaid.

"Are you taking the piss?" I ask, glancing at Mikkel and Jørgen.

The snow clings in large frozen clumps to the beards of the three newcomers, a sign that the snowstorm has arrived quickly and with fierce intensity. We all have full beards now. They protect against the wind and cold. At first, I had to get used to it, as I had never had a beard before, but now it feels like the most natural thing to have.

Mali stops barking and settles back under the coffee table with a contented sigh once she recognises the three men as familiar. She doesn't seem particularly on guard anymore, but I can't help but think about her reaction out in the dunes, where she had caught the scent of something she didn't like. It was clear. The scent of a polar bear?

The situation feels utterly surreal. Polar bears don't belong in Denmark. As far as I know, there have never been any naturally occurring here, so hearing three grown men claim to have seen one honestly feels a bit absurd. But then again... our whole new existence is absurd. A few years ago, no one could have imagined that today we would be fighting for our lives in a cold so extreme, the likes of which are only seen in the Arctic.

"Bloody hell, yes," Mikkel responds energetically. "Right out where the ice ends. We'd just come ashore when I looked back and saw it crawling out of the sea, shaking itself so that the water sprayed in huge cascades around it. There's no doubt. It was bloody well a polar bear! A real, proper polar bear! Imagine if it had come ashore while we were still standing there," he finishes, seemingly unconcerned, pulling his sealskin anorak over his head and tossing it into the corner behind the door.

Mikkel is the youngest of us. More than ten years younger than I am. I think his enthusiasm reflects equal parts immaturity and ignorance.

"If it really was a polar bear you saw..." I begin, but don't finish the sentence. "Are you sure it wasn't just a large seal climbing onto the ice? I mean, where would it have come from? There are thousands of kilometres to where they live. And even if the ice had frozen solid all the way from Greenland to Scotland, there's still hundreds of kilometres of open sea between England and Denmark."

I don't want to believe what I'm hearing. I simply can't handle any more life-threatening challenges, and in some way, I'm trying to deny the truth.

Deep down, I know they're telling the truth. But I'm not ready to admit it yet. We're in a situation where I'm desperately struggling to survive in an environment I still haven't fully adapted to. And now, on top of that, we'll have to watch our backs with every step we take.

"It wasn't a seal," Zaid mutters quietly, fishing out his bag of seal meat from under his jumper.

He reaches for a fork, spears a well-cooked piece of meat from the pan, and hands it to me, making room for his own.

"While we were standing there, looking out over the ice, it started trotting quickly inland, right towards where we were standing," he continues thoughtfully, spearing another piece of meat and handing it to Erik. "The sledges with our seals are still out there on the beach. We didn't dare risk dragging them through the dunes with that beast lurking around."

"Speak for yourself," Mikkel interrupts, laughing smugly. "You should've seen Zaid and Jørgen's faces when the polar bear started trotting towards us, like a tsunami roaring in from the sea."

He winks knowingly at me and continues.

"It's just a big dog. Toss it a bone, Zaid, and you'll have a guard dog, just like Magnus."

"You're being an idiot, Mikkel!"

I cut him off sharply, giving him an irritated look at the same time. I'm not in the mood for Mikkel's stupid remarks.

I hold his gaze for a moment until he shrugs and slumps into the sofa near the life-giving warmth of the wood-burning stove.

Silence descends among us.

Each of us processing the new information. The latest development in our already hopeless situation, where only the strongest survive.

The strongest!

Are we even strong enough to survive under these conditions?

Polar bears are.

But are humans?

Without thinking much about it, I take a bite of the seal meat. The characteristic, slightly sharp flavour spreads across my tongue, pulling me back from my deep thoughts.

"What do you think it's doing now?" I ask.

"It's probably looking for food, I reckon!"

It's Jørgen speaking for the first time since the three of them arrived at the cabin. His voice is deep, and he always speaks so softly that you have to strain to hear him when he finally does open his mouth, which rarely happens.

"We've all seen that there are fewer seals this year. Why should it be any different further north? Seals are the polar bear's main food source, so maybe it's just followed its food supply south. I don't think it's come from England, Magnus. I think it's more likely from Norway. Contrary to what many people think, polar bears are marine mammals, and they move just as well in the sea as they do on land. There have been multiple sightings of polar bears up to 100 kilometres from land. But it's still at least 100 kilometres of open sea between Denmark and Norway. Which tells us that large parts of the Skagerrak must be frozen over. So it's had to walk at least part of the way. And that hasn't happened since the last Ice Age, 12,000 years ago."

Jørgen looks thoughtfully at each of us in turn, letting the weight of his last sentence sink in.

"So maybe the polar bear is actually the least of our problems," he continues. "If we are truly entering a new ice age, it's not something that's going to end any time soon. We can't just bundle up in our houses around the woodstove and hope that if we can survive a few more harsh winters, the warmth will eventually return. If it really is a new ice age, we should expect it to trap Denmark in a biting cold for thousands of years to come.

The last ice age lasted 55,000 years, and although humans lived in Europe, and at times even in Denmark, we are neither physically nor mentally prepared to live under such conditions today. Many animals have already disappeared. Even though new ones might arrive from the north, as the polar bear suggests, it's doubtful we could survive long enough to evolve into a true hunter-gatherer society. Our flora and fauna aren't adapted to such cold conditions, so we can't rely on gathering roots, berries, nuts, or edible plants for survival either.

And if it gets as bad as it did 22,000 years ago, we might even face the possibility of Denmark being covered by a thick layer of ice. And there's no way we could survive here if that happens."

"What are you saying?" I ask. "Do you mean we should throw in the towel and follow the others south? Because I'm not sure that's even an option anymore. If we were going to leave, we should have gone when they did. The cold is worse now than it was back then. We only have a few months to make the journey before winter returns."

I speak quickly, unconsciously revealing that this is something I've been thinking about for a while. There's a brief pause before Zaid quietly breaks the silence with his distinctive Syrian accent.

"And now, with a polar bear as a travel companion."

"What's the likelihood it'll settle here?" Erik asks, addressing Jørgen, who has already earned the title of polar bear expert.

Jørgen scratches his beard thoughtfully for a moment before answering.

"If it's followed the seals here, I see no reason why it would leave before its food source is depleted. Even though we've been talking about fewer seals this year, there are still enough for us to survive on. The same goes for the polar bear, I suppose. The bigger question is, how long before we can expect more than just this one?

Humans have lived alongside polar bears for thousands of years. But certainly not without risk. A hungry polar bear is aggressive and not easily frightened off. And forget about trying to outrun one! Over short distances, they can reach the speed of a galloping horse, and with a sense of smell that can detect prey from kilometres away, I'm seriously concerned about the journey back to town. Especially when we're dragging heavily loaded sledges of freshly caught meat behind us."

"Then we'll just have to kill it," Mikkel interjects with the carefree bravado of youth. "There are six of us against one bear. With our weapons, we wouldn't even need to get close. Kill it, and let's move on. Besides, I wouldn't mind a warm polar bear skin for the boy back home."

Mikkel's son was born the year before the great migration, making him the youngest member of our small community. He would never have survived the journey south, which had been a key factor in his family's decision to stay. Unlike the rest of us, Mikkel seems to thrive in these harsh surroundings. He rarely lets the challenges get to him, making him a huge motivator for the rest of us. But he's also a constant source of frustration and worry as he repeatedly pushes the boundaries we've set for our survival.

Outside, the wind has picked up violently, developing into a full-blown snowstorm. The dark clouds have once again blocked out the sun, which we can feel inside the house. Instead of being barely warmed by the sun's weak rays, the house is now fully exposed to the biting cold wind that relentlessly assaults the windows, shutters, and roof.

The creaking of the timber and the howling wind are deafening, stifling any desire for further conversation.

The woodstove, originally intended as a supplement to our

primary electric heating system, isn't enough to heat the house. We all sit on the floor, huddled together as close to it as possible, trying to soak up every bit of warmth. Every now and then, Erik opens the door and adds another log, which the fire greedily devours.

Mali crawls out from under the table and nestles against me, resting her head on my lap.

And so we sit in silence, waiting for the storm to pass.

I think of Freja, Kristian, and Emilie. I'm not worried because I know that everyone in our little colony looks out for one another. But I don't like being separated from my family.

Even though we spend the whole winter cooped up together, and you'd think we'd welcome some time apart when we can get it, it doesn't work that way. On the contrary, the struggle for survival has brought us closer than ever. We rely on each other in a completely new way, especially mentally.

Perhaps Freja and I could survive alone if it were just about physical endurance. But being confined for so many months, unsure if the food and firewood will last throughout the winter, alone with your own thoughts—that's not something I would wish on anyone. Even with family by your side, it's incredibly hard. It requires 100 percent focus on and understanding of each other. The days are long, and time passes excruciatingly slowly. It's easy to fall into arguments. But it's absolutely crucial that we can pull each other up if one of us falls into a mental pit. That we remain fully aware of each other's needs while also giving space to be ourselves. And above all, we must trust one another and keep each other mentally stimulated when we have no one else to communicate with.

After the first winter of confinement, we had a serious discussion among the remaining people about whether it would be more sensible to stick together for the next winter, rather than staying in small family units. But it's crucial that we get through the confinement without driving each other mad. There's no room for internal conflicts because they spread like ripples in water. Before long, our little community could split into even smaller groups that can't agree on the smallest details.

We didn't want to take that risk.

So, we live as family units, just as we always have. We help each other in the summer and wish each other luck as we huddle separately through the winter. It works. And it brings us closer as families.

Freja has become an extension of my soul and mind. No one knows me better than she does. She knows what I'm thinking and feeling before I even realise it myself.

Kristian and Emilie are more than just my children. They are my best friends and my source of mental stimulation as we spend the winter delving into various subjects of general interest. Mathematics. Geography. Politics. Literature. Biology. English. Danish. They crave knowledge, which breaks up the monotony. It gives us something to do.

The town's abandoned library contains untold resources for mental enrichment, for both adults and children. We make sure to stockpile books in our homes before winter traps us indoors once again. Non-fiction and novels pile up, their numbers slowly dwindling, book by book, as the long winter drags on.

● ● ●

I wake up to Mali licking my nose.

The cabin is cold, so I grab another log and place it in the wood stove. The fire hasn't gone out, meaning someone kept it going through the night.

I glance around at the sleeping faces and notice Mikkel is missing. I quickly confirm that he's nowhere else to be seen in the small cabin. He must have gone outside, where the storm has passed and the sun is once again shining in a clear, frosty sky.

At some point during the evening, we must have drifted off.

I pull two pieces of seal meat from my bag and place one on the hot pan atop the stove. The fat immediately sizzles, filling the small cabin with its rich scent.

Mali watches me closely, knowing the other piece is for her. I slice it into bite-sized chunks with my knife and feed them to her one by one, as I wait for mine to cook through. As always, she whimpers expectantly between each bite.

After we've eaten, I put on my wool coat and step outside to answer nature's call.

The others are still asleep.

The cold hits me hard as soon as I open the door. It's even colder than yesterday, as though the storm swept away what little warmth the sun had managed to spread over the land, before losing its battle once more to the harsh wind, snow, and frost.

I wrap my scarf around my face and head towards the dunes.

I only think fleetingly of the polar bear, trusting that Mali will alert me in good time if there's any danger.

The snow from the night lies in deep drifts that Mali bounds through with playful energy, while it swirls lightly aside as I drag my feet through it. The sun's rays aren't warm enough to melt the snow crystals, so the snow remains light and fluffy.

I find a lookout point and climb to the top, surveying the surroundings.

Down on the beach, I spot Mikkel, returning to the cabin, pulling one of the abandoned sledges behind him.

I call out to him and wave when he looks up and sees me. The sun is behind me, so he raises a hand to shield his eyes and waves back with the other.

"One of the seals is missing from Zaid's sledge," he says when we meet at the base of the hill.

His breath rises in large clouds from his mouth and nostrils, matching the rhythm of his heavy breathing.

"But the snow has covered all tracks to and from the sledges, so it's impossible to tell which direction the bear went. I haven't seen any sign of it, and I've been standing watch all morning. Maybe it just saw our sledges as an easy meal and kept moving, wherever it's heading..."

Mali approaches Mikkel briefly, greeting him, but doesn't let him pet her. She's too reserved for that. She's independent and only truly gives herself to her immediate family.

I don't respond. Instead, I ask him a question.

"Was it you who kept the fire going through the night?"

Mikkel turns his back to me, looking out in the direction from which he came.

"You all fell asleep so quickly," he says. "I couldn't stop thinking about the bear and what Jørgen said—that we might be heading into a new ice age. It makes sense, doesn't it? I mean, the Gulf Stream stopped completely a few years ago, and since then it's just been getting colder and colder, with no sign that it's started up again, has there? We've never had as many seals in Denmark as we've had these past few years, and when polar bears start arriving at our latitude, it must mean it's become too inhospitable further north, even for a seal or a polar bear that's built to survive in a polar climate."

He turns back towards me, studying me carefully before continuing.

"We can't travel south! We can't, Magnus. Little Kasper wouldn't survive the journey. He's too young! He wouldn't make it, and we can't protect him. But if we stay here, what chances do we have? Tell me that."

It's clear Mikkel has been thinking deeply about all this while he's been tending the life-giving flame in the stove. The laid-back attitude he usually exudes is gone. It's as if he's aged ten years overnight.

I feel for him. I've had all the same thoughts myself. But unlike me, the full weight of the situation has hit him while the rest of us slept.

I place my hand on his shoulder.

"I know, my friend. I know. None of us wants to leave, but staying doesn't seem to be an option anymore either. I'm afraid I can't tell you what's best for you. I'm just as unsure. The only thing I do know is that if we're going to leave, we need to do it now, so we have the entire summer for the journey. We can't wait much longer."

I grab the handle of the sledge.

"Come," I say. "Let's see if the others are up."

● ● ●

The group agrees to help Zaid shoot another seal to replace the one the polar bear took, before we turn back towards home.

We all prefer to stick together, given the new situation.

There is a small group of spotted seals on the ice, close to where the ice edge meets the sea. It's still too early in the year for us to be seen as a potential threat, so they let us get fairly close before a couple of them react by heaving themselves over the edge and disappearing into the deep blue-black waves of the sea. The rest remain, lazily watching us. Like us, they enjoy the sun and have no intention of getting stressed unnecessarily. Later in the year, once they've been hunted often, they might be less inclined to let us get close, but right now, with the sun finally breaking through and the winter storms subsiding, we have easier access to a quick hunt.

Mali and I keep a bit of a distance from the others. I've told them about her behaviour on the dunes the day before, and we agree that it's best to make use of her keen senses to keep an eye on the polar bear while the others hunt.

We have stopped halfway between the ice edge and the shore, although I don't know where we'd flee to if the bear were to appear from the land side. But at least we'll get a head start, allowing us to prepare a joint front should it attack us.

I reflect on how quickly our reality has once again changed as I watch Svend line up his harpoon on a large bull, lying protectively between the hunters and the group of grey-spotted seal cows.

The seal keeps a watchful eye on the men, who are slowly closing in to within shooting range. The moment Svend prepares to fire his harpoon, the seal warns the others, causing the entire group to immediately move towards the ice edge. With surprising agility, they make their way across the few meters of ice and plop into the water, one by one, disappearing out of range of our weapons. Only the large bull holds its ground against the hunters, snarling loudly and baring its sharp teeth in a threatening gesture.

Hunting seals isn't really that difficult. Often, you can get very close to the group and fire your weapon before they even realise the danger, disappearing like dew in the sun. Usually, this allows you to take the first seal before the rest are gone, but since they can only stay underwater for a maximum of 20 minutes, they soon resurface not far from where they dove. With some luck, they'll haul themselves back onto the ice a couple of hundred meters further down the ice floe.

It's best if you can find one of their breathing holes between the ice edge and the shore, as they tend to pop up through these after being scared into the water. Then you just have to sit and wait for them to stick their heads out.

The bull's snarl shifts immediately to a long series of howls as Svend's harpoon pierces the skin and embeds itself deep into the animal's gut.

Hunting with a harpoon doesn't provide particularly precise aim, but on the other hand, you can attach a line to the spear, which means you won't lose it if you miss, and it ensures that you can hold the animal in place when it tries to escape after being hit.

I don't have that advantage with my compound bow, so I must focus before every shot, making sure it hits precisely and kills the animal instantly. The bow allows me to hunt from a distance and still have good fortune.

Svend grabs the line and holds on tight with his free hand. The bull alternates between roaring loudly and howling in pain until Erik reaches it and swings his baseball bat in a practiced blow to the back of its head, silencing it instantly.

The whole thing takes only a few seconds, but I'll never get used to the piercing cries of a wounded animal.

"Well done, Zaid, it's served," Erik laughs.

He turns to Zaid, who raises his right fist for a high-five, which Erik returns in an extravagant gesture.

"But you'll get to butcher it yourself," he continues, making a solemn bow towards the dead seal.

"Of course! Thanks for the help, guys."

Zaid draws his knife and crouches beside the dead animal, expertly cutting into the spotted seal's belly and breaking it open, spilling the steaming entrails onto the ice.

I watch the ice around Zaid turn red with the blood of the dead animal. The sweet, metallic smell reaches my nostrils, even from this distance, and I remember what Jørgen told us the evening before.

How long will it take before the scent reaches the polar bear's sensitive nose?

I again sweep my gaze over the ice and the open sea. I can see the small heads of the frightened seals popping up to the surface a couple of hundred meters out. They watch us curiously, as though they haven't yet realised that their leader, their protector, has lost its life to a species higher up the food chain. For the next few days, they will experience confusion and loss, with no one at the top of the hierarchy, and the protection of the group will be minimal. Afterward, the younger males will begin internal struggles, until one can assert itself over the others and claim the title of new leader of the group. Until then, the group members are exposed and particularly vigilant against anything perceived as potentially dangerous.

But for now, their attention is focused on land. On us.

For a moment, I feel guilty, but it passes quickly. Seals are our only source of food, and we must do whatever it takes to survive.

I turn and let my gaze sweep over the dunes stretching along the coastline as far as the eye can see. The frozen landscape lies desolate.

The sun is still high in the sky, but even though it sends warmth across the landscape, it has little warming effect since the snow effectively reflects the heat away from the surface, the so-called albedo effect. The lighter the surface, the harder the sun has to warm the earth and melt the snow.

Researchers talked a lot about the albedo effect before the climate crisis. That the albedo effect was an uncertain factor in climate models that could accelerate the onset of the catastrophe. The argument was that the ice around Greenland was melting at an unprecedented rate, partly because the snow on the ice sheet had turned black due to air pollution, thus trapping heat from the sun's rays instead of reflecting it away, as ordinary white snow would do. And partly because global temperatures had risen so high that the ice sheet that formed in winter was no longer thick enough to hold up throughout the summer.

The result was that the ice melted rapidly, and billions of litres of fresh water flowed directly into the North Atlantic, mixing with the warm saltwater brought up by the Gulf Stream from the Gulf of Mexico.

The remaining salty water would sink to the bottom and flow back southward as a deep current. A kind of pump mechanism that kept the Gulf Stream running year after year.

Eventually, the increased mixing of seawater with meltwater from the ice sheet diluted the salt content so much that the pump mechanism, which had kept the current flowing for thousands of years, simply collapsed.

The consequences were far more dire than even the most pessimistic climate scientists had predicted.

The climate changed drastically almost instantly!

The first winter after the collapse, the average temperature fell by five degrees. The next year, by ten degrees.

In summer, the land dried out as the rain failed to fall.

Before we knew it, all food production had come to a near halt.

Our ability to adapt to the new climate conditions was laughably ineffective. The climate was changing simply too quickly. It got even colder, and most of the precipitation we now get falls as snow. Snow that settles as a white blanket over the landscape, further intensifying the albedo effect. The sun's rays are reflected away by the white surface, so the earth is only sparsely warmed, and the cold continues to intensify year after year.

I think back to the group's conversation the previous evening.

I'm no longer in doubt that we are well on our way into a new ice age. Helped along by humanity's completely uncontrolled release of nitrogen into the atmosphere over many years.

All the climate summits attended by world politicians in good faith have had no effect whatsoever. No politician was willing to take more responsibility for the climate than what was politically popular with the public. And since it was the public's votes that guaranteed re-election after the end of a term, any initiative that put restrictions on our excessive consumption of the earth's resources was doomed from the start.

Now it's too late. There's nothing we can do to undo the mistakes of the past.

It is painfully clear that humanity is just a small, arrogant piece in nature's great cycle, despite our frequent delusions to the contrary. Just because we are equipped with a unique ability to think, process information, and create complex things out of the earth's basic elements, we immediately believe that we are the rulers of the world. That we are the ones who control the course of events and decide which species will survive and which must go extinct. That we can adapt nature to our needs rather than adapting our ways to nature's biological barometer.

Nature struck back.

First in the form of numerous small warnings, which were sent ahead, but ignored.

Smaller outbreaks of the Ebola virus emerged from the rainforests of Central and West Africa, as they were felled in our endless pursuit of exotic wood species for our living room or terrace floors. Or to make way for new agricultural land to meet the world's ever-increasing demand for meat.

Ebola outbreaks, which killed thousands of people as if to warn us against continuing the intense clearing of the world's lungs.

Plant material and dead animals that had been frozen in a permanent state in the Siberian and Canadian tundras thawed and decayed. Enormous amounts of greenhouse gases were released into the atmosphere, contributing to a violent escalation of global warming.

At the same time, so-called "zombie bacteria" were revived from the thawed carcasses, infecting local livestock with a deadly anthrax infection. Thousands of reindeer perished, and soon local populations died in droves after consuming the infected animals.

Several global pandemics of coronavirus broke out. Pandemics that killed millions of people worldwide as a warning against our steadily growing population and population density. Still, there was no effect.

The world's population continued to rise exponentially, and we kept gathering in megacities that just kept growing. The number of cities with more than ten million inhabitants grew explosively worldwide, leading to significant challenges in terms of sanitation control, hygiene, lack of clean drinking water, and handling disease outbreaks.

In many areas, droughts became so pronounced that massive, uncontrollable wildfires erupted, with catastrophic consequences. Entire communities were consumed by flames. When the forests were burned down and no network of roots remained to hold the soil, violent mudslides often followed when the rains finally came. Mudslides that, without warning, swept over and buried the cities and communities that had miraculously survived the wildfires.

Yet, we still didn't listen.

Now, nature has deployed its heavy artillery.

Climate change, which we can no longer ignore as if nothing has happened.

Humankind has been brought to its knees. Put in its place with a clear message: We are not the rulers of the world, but merely humble guests on the blue planet.

• • •

I spot the polar bear at the same time as Mali begins to growl deeply from her throat. A few hundred metres down the coast, it suddenly comes charging out from the dunes at high speed. Purposefully, it leaps directly onto the ice, seemingly unaware of us. Yet.

Its white fur camouflages it effectively against the snow-covered surface of the ice.

I watch in fascination as it quickly covers half the distance between the shore and the ice edge. In one powerful, agile movement, it lifts its entire front half a metre and a half into the air, then slams its front paws hard down onto the ice beneath. Even from a distance, it's clear that this is a muscular and terrifying animal.

I stand completely frozen to the spot, watching silently as the bear hammers a hole into the ice beneath it until it can pull a paralyzed seal out of the breathing hole it has just opened.

With a powerful bite across the animal's neck, the bear kills its meal. The blood spreads steaming around its nose, staining its fur red.

The entire episode lasts no more than a couple of minutes.

I am at once full of admiration for the bear's hunting skills and terrified beyond reason by the same. If it can so efficiently scent out and precisely locate a seal beneath the ice, then we stand no chance of evading it if it takes an interest in us. We are not equipped to live in harmony with such a well-trained predator, so perfectly adapted to life in the Arctic. The challenge of adapting ourselves to the polar climate, which has rapidly encapsulated our part of the world, is already proving difficult enough, without the presence of such a creature.

A moment later, it sees us.

It raises its head and sniffs the air, but perhaps thinks that we do not pose a threat to its prey, for soon it redirects its attention back to the seal on the ice before it.

Mali no longer growls. Instead, she softly whimpers, as if she fully understands that she stands no chance against the white giant, should it come to a direct confrontation. I pray that it will never come to that, but at the same time, I think to myself that it is probably a naive wish, especially if more polar bears follow the first.

"Come," whispers Jørgen softly, and pats me gently on the shoulder.

The others had just finished loading the dead seal onto Zaid's sledge when the polar bear attacked, and now they've caught up with me.

"Let's pull back carefully, now that it's focused on its prey."

We move slowly in the direction of the coast, away from the polar bear, all the while keeping a watchful eye on it.

I notch an arrow on my bow, so I'm prepared in case it does become interested in us. I can hear the other members of our small hunting party doing the same, as we quietly create greater and greater distance between us and the bear.

For a brief moment, Mikkel and I exchange glances. He looks scared; yesterday's arrogant attitude has completely disappeared. His eyes flicker nervously, and his skin is pale. His thoughts are undoubtedly circling around the untenable nature of the whole situation, which has only just become clear to him. I understand him well. He has a responsibility for his child, but whatever decision he makes, it comes with great danger and uncertainty for the future. I feel the burden myself and have done so for a long time.

The journey back to the town is largely in silence. Each of us is consumed with grim thoughts, while we take turns casting

fearful glances behind us, afraid of spotting the polar bear following us. The snow crunches beneath our feet with each
heavy step we take.

The sledge harness rubs against me, and I unconsciously adjust the straps over my shoulders at regular intervals.

The sun warms my cheeks and briefly nourishes a faint hope
that warmer weather is on the way. I know it's a false illusion,
but my body craves warmth so much that, for a moment, I let
myself be seduced by it.

Zaid and I walk ahead. Behind us, Jørgen and Erik follow,
then Mikkel and Svend, who bring up the rear. Mali stays
close to my left leg. Occasionally, she nudges my knee with her
snout if I've been silent for too long, expecting to receive a few
encouraging words or a couple of affectionate pats on the
back. Then she looks up at me with her brown eyes and lights
up in a big carefree smile. She, of all of us, is completely unaffected by the situation. As long as she has us, her little family,
she is happy.

After we've been walking for a couple of hours, I look up
from the snow in front of my feet and briefly observe Zaid's
face. Brown-tinted snow goggles cover his eyes. A thick black
beard covers his naturally brown skin on his cheeks and chin,
and with a large scarf wrapped around his neck and a heavy
seal-skin hat pulled well down over his forehead, it's immediately difficult to interpret his facial expression.

Zaid is normally a quiet man, one who rarely uses large arm
gestures. He is the thoughtful type who thoroughly weighs up
the pros and cons before making any major decision in life.
Having had his entire livelihood uprooted when the war
broke out in Syria, and being forced to place his fate in the
hands of strangers, had been an incredibly boundary-pushing

experience for him. But that was precisely what he and Far-hana had had to do when the fighting between rebel forces and the Sunni militant group Daesh broke out in their hometown in Syria.

A few days after the first shots were fired, the entire neighbourhood had been levelled to the ground, and they had nowhere to retreat to. The family's home had literally collapsed around them when a bomb detonated outside their front door.

The town was quickly transformed into huge piles of rubble. Beneath every mound lay the bodies of friends and family members who had been caught in the bomb rain, including both of Zaid's parents and Farhana's eldest sister. Farhana's brother-in-law had been dug out of the rubble, badly wounded, 22 hours after the bomb exploded, but without the possibility of being admitted to a hospital and receiving professional medical help, he died just a few days later.

The story is not easy to tell. We've pieced it together bit by bit, as Zaid or Farhana have gradually lifted the veil on the horrific experiences that no one should ever have to endure.

These two thoughtful and kind-hearted people, whom we have gradually begun to regard as our closest friends, had been forced to flee when Daesh took control of what was left of the city. A flight that could cost them their lives and was therefore accompanied by severe psychological consequences.

They have occasionally spoken in fragments about the many fearful thoughts and the constant feeling of helplessness that haunted them throughout their month-long flight under harsh conditions. But neither of them has ever shared in detail how they fled. What experiences they were subjected to along the way. Or how they were received and helped by strangers they had no choice but to trust, fully aware that they could be betrayed at any moment.

I pull my own scarf down so that it no longer covers my mouth.

"Zaid?" I ask, pulling him out of his thoughts.

My voice is hoarse, and I clear my throat a couple of times before continuing. I know that what I'm about to ask him will not come easily. But I have to ask.

"When we get back, could you and Farhana tell us a bit more about what we can expect from a life on the run?"

I don't explain my request. I'm afraid the decision of whether we stay here or move south is imminent. And that Zaid and Farhana are the only ones in our community who have the faintest idea of what it means to flee for one's life.

Their experiences might be decisive, I think.

I don't elaborate on my request because I'm certain that Zaid is grappling with exactly the same thoughts, and that his decision must be even more difficult than mine, precisely because he has tried to flee for his life before.

Zaid lifts his snow goggles up onto his forehead and studies me for a long time before answering.

"We'll come over tomorrow. Then we can talk about it," he says, before pulling his goggles back into place without further comment and disappearing again into his own thoughts.

No one says anything more for the rest of the journey.

The polar bear doesn't appear again. I think it must be full from its meal. But it lingers in my thoughts as yet another piece in the puzzle that is shaping our lives.

I feel relief when the furthest houses of the town finally come into view on the horizon.

The sun is setting behind us.

By the time we arrive, darkness will have fully engulfed us, but the sky is clear, and the moonlight reflecting off the snow will provide enough light for us to still orient ourselves.

I miss Freja. I need to talk the whole situation through thoroughly with her.

4 Freja

We leave the sledges behind as soon as we find shelter among the buildings and hurry off towards our respective homes. I hold Kristian and Emilie by the hands so they don't fall behind. Between the houses, the wind swirls in powerful, unpredictable gusts that can easily knock a child over.

I tighten my grip and pull the children towards the middle of the street when icicles start breaking off the rooftops and flying unpredictably around. Out here, there's less shelter, and we're once again exposed to a veritable onslaught of needle-sharp ice crystals. It hurts, and we try to turn our faces away from the wind as we stumble through the snowdrifts.

Farhana and Fatima make it home before us. Out of the corner of my eye, I see them disappear through the door into the safety of their house. I instinctively envy their feeling of security. For a brief moment, I consider following them and seeking refuge in their home, but our own house is only four doors down the street, so we push on.

A second later, I lose my grip on Emilie as a particularly strong gust of wind suddenly tears at us, throwing her off balance. She lets out a scream as she falls into the drifting snow swirling around us. As I turn to help her up, I spot several other townspeople struggling forward, bent against the wind, further down the street. A wave of worry hits me—will they all make it home safely? The tension in my stomach tightens another notch, leaving a sharp sensation in my gut.

We are far too vulnerable, I fleetingly think, as I pull Emilie back to her feet and rush down the street. We are far too vulnerable. The thought clings to my mind like a tick in a dog's ear, surfacing more and more often.

It feels like an eternity since we set off from the forest, but finally, we reach our house and step inside the warmth. There's nothing left but embers from the logs I put in the stove this morning, but compared to the temperature outside, it feels like paradise.

My skin tingles and stings where it was exposed to the bitter wind and the relentless assault of snow crystals. My childhood's romantic associations with snow and outdoor play are nothing like the reality of an Arctic snowstorm, where temperatures drop well below minus 40, and storm-force winds make it feel like minus 60 or worse.

Though it's spring, the cold still bites. The weather has become even more erratic in recent years, as if winter is desperately clinging on with the last of its frozen grip, refusing to give way to spring.

In a few weeks, the weather will hopefully stabilize, with more days of clear blue skies and a sun high in the sky. By then, temperatures can reach five to ten degrees Celsius during the day and hover around freezing at night—right until autumn arrives abruptly and far too early, bringing with it a merciless plunge in temperatures, fierce winds, and heavy snowfall, forcing us to huddle inside by the fire for the long months ahead.

I open the stove door and place a few logs inside from the woodpile stacked along the outer wall of the living room. When winter begins, the pile covers all the walls of the room from floor to ceiling in two rows, but now only a few cubic meters remain.

Soon, the warmth spreads in wonderful waves, keeping the cold at bay. We stand together for a long time until our chilled bodies stop trembling, and the pain in our skin subsides.

I watch Emilie and Kristian as they take off their outer clothes. Their cheeks grow red as the warmth penetrates their skin. Emilie finds an old Harry Potter book and settles down in front of the stove. She opens it and begins reading, seemingly unconcerned about the storm outside.

Not so long ago, getting children to read was a growing problem. I remember a time when everyone consistently had their noses buried in some electronic device, playing pointless games or watching equally pointless videos of dancing dogs or cats, people falling over, or others foolishly seeking attention by filming themselves climbing high buildings without safety nets.

None of that exists anymore.

Board games and books are the only forms of entertainment we have left. Two things that have entertained humanity for countless years and have once again proven their worth as valuable pastimes. The digital age turned out to be just a fleeting bump in the road.

I ask Kristian to fill the soup pot with ice. The children's main task, after we finish chopping wood, is to keep our supply of ice chunks topped up.

While they work, I stack wood along the walls of the house or help Magnus butcher the seals he's brought home.

In winter, when snow falls thick and often, it's easy to get drinking water just by filling a pot with snow from outside the front door. But as winter wanes and snow becomes scarcer, we have to go further from the house to find enough clean snow to melt for drinking. When the sun shines, it's a welcome chore, as everyone needs to stretch their legs after being cooped up for so long in winter's icy grip. But on a day like today, when the storm rages and it's dangerous to stay outside for long, we must rely on other methods. That's why we always melt more snow than we need, so we can freeze the excess water into ice chunks to use when the weather prevents us from venturing far outdoors.

The tub of ice chunks stands in the room furthest from the stove, where the temperature rarely rises above a few degrees Celsius.

Kristian disappears into the adjacent room and remembers to close the door behind him to keep the warmth from escaping.

While he's gone, I cut a lump of half-frozen seal meat into smaller pieces. I brought it inside this morning before we left, but it's still not fully thawed.

Behind the house, we have a shed we use for storing meat. Our supply is nearly depleted now, but by the time winter returns, it will be overflowing again with both frozen and dried meat.

We dry all the meat during the first half of the year, except for what we eat immediately, because the temperature rises above freezing at the height of summer. If it isn't dried, there's a risk it will spoil before we can eat it. As soon as the temperatures drop again in late summer, we freeze the meat without further processing, as that's the best way to preserve the nutritious fat.

Kristian returns and places the pot, now filled with ice chunks, on top of the stove. Besides being our only source of heat, the stove also serves as our cooker.

"I'm worried about Dad and Mali," Kristian says.

I pull him close and kiss the top of his head.

"Dad won't take any unnecessary risks after what happened last year when he and Mali got caught in that snowstorm out in 'no man's land.' You don't need to worry about them."

I try to sound reassuring, but deep down, I share his anxiety. I don't like it when we're apart. Magnus is the rock we all cling to when things get tough. He's the one who keeps his cool when everything seems hopeless. He's my safety, my haven, my soulmate.

Emilie puts her book down, gets up, and squeezes in between us.

I never really know how much she takes in from everything going on around her when she's lost in a good book, but a good group hug rarely escapes her attention.

I love my children so much, and it breaks my heart that the world they're growing up in has become so barren and joyless. Stripped of all life-affirming experiences. They are forced to live in a world where everything revolves around sheer survival.

What does their future look like, I wonder? Will they ever experience the joy of opening presents on Christmas Eve?

Will they ever know the thrill of falling in love? The security of starting a family without constantly worrying whether their loved ones will survive another day?

Will they ever get to experience taking life for granted?

The water on the stove begins to boil.

I let go of the kids and drop the seal meat into the pot. I prefer to boil the meat. It makes it more tender, and afterwards, we can use the broth as a warm, nourishing drink when we're out in the forest.

●　●　●

I lie awake long after the children have fallen asleep, my mind swirling with dark thoughts. Outside, the storm still rages. Everything that could possibly be torn loose has long since been swept away by the countless storms that came before. A large part of our summer is spent repairing whatever has been damaged by the winter's relentless tempests.

I listen to the children's soft breathing, hardly noticeable due to the howling wind outside. I envy them their carefree existence. They aren't weighed down by daily worries like we adults are. They don't remember the time before the cold really took hold, so their frame of reference is limited to the time when we've had to adapt to this Inuit-like way of life.

But it's not really fair, I think, scolding myself. They have their worries too. It's not fair to say their lives are carefree — far from it. But they don't have the same awareness that this isn't the only kind of life out there. That life here was very different when Magnus and I were children.

Of course, we've told them stories about life before the catastrophe. But it's one thing to hear a story, another to have lived that life — only to now be trapped in Mother Nature's furious attempts to restore the Earth to the state in which we received it. Back to the starting point.

It's the simple things I miss the most. The things I once took for granted. Being able to hop on my bike and ride to the beach without worrying whether the weather might suddenly change. Taking a walk in the woods, meeting other dog owners for a chat while the dogs play, enjoying the scent of spring flowers mixed with the earthy smell of decaying leaves and twigs on the forest floor.

Who would have thought? I chuckle quietly in the dark. Imagine, I miss the smell of damp forest floor. But then it hits me—Emilie and Kristian will never get to experience the incredible diversity of smells and sounds in a living forest.

A tear escapes from my eye, rolling down my cheek and onto the pillow. My quiet chuckles turn into soft sobs as more tears follow. I let them flow freely, muffling my sobs into my sleeve so I don't wake the children.

I feel sorry for myself. I feel sorry for Magnus, for my children. I hate what our lives have become. I hate that our future has been stolen from us. I hate that we're reduced to struggling through this life, day by day, without knowing how long we'll have to keep fighting. How long we can keep fighting, before Mother Nature decides there's no room for us in her new world order. I hate the uncertainty that constantly surrounds us.

I wish I could see Emilie and Kristian grow up, get an education, find a job. Fall in love and start a family. Enjoy the taste of a freshly pulled carrot or a just-picked apple from their own garden. Anything other than this frozen hell we're trapped in now.

As I lie there, listening to the storm gradually subsiding, a thought starts to take shape in my mind.

It's not that we haven't talked about it before. But maybe we've reached a turning point? Maybe we're already backed into a corner, out of options?

Maybe it's time for us to head south too? But how far south will we need to go? We have no idea how far the cold extends.

● ● ●

Half of the logs are scattered in the snow around the abandoned sledges outside the house. The storm had tossed them about like dead leaves. Farhana and I stand on the street, shivering in the cold, until we begin to gather the logs and stack them back onto the sledges.

Because of the storm, there's extra work to do today. Before we can start on the task of felling more trees, we need to bring yesterday's logs home and stack them inside so they can dry. Luckily, with the children's help, it goes quickly. They're ready and waiting as we haul the heavily loaded sledges, and without hesitation, they get to work straight away. They know the routine and understand we can't afford delays. Any delay must be caught up on as quickly as possible.

I glance at them out of the corner of my eye as we walk back and forth from the house with armfuls of frozen logs. My children have become strong—much stronger than most children their age. But that's what our life demands. It demands strength from all of us.

You get used to the physical labour quickly, although the muscles ache at first when we finally get back outside. Even our best efforts to stay in shape during the winter confinement can't quite match the raw strength we build up through the hard summer work.

The sun shines once again in a clear sky. Its rays reflect sharply off the windows of the abandoned buildings that aren't boarded up to keep the heat in. The sun glistens cheerfully off the small icicles hanging from the rooftops like tiny jewels. It's just warm enough to melt small amounts of snow, but still cold enough for the droplets to freeze again quickly, forming new icicles that grow larger by the minute.

I squint as I step outside into the bright light. Inside, the house is lit only by the flames in the wood-burning stove, so the contrast between the darkness and light is overwhelming.

I stand still for a moment, letting my eyes adjust to the light, and then notice the sledge is already empty.

Kristian comes up to me and slips his hand into my glove. His hand is wonderfully warm.

"Mum, why were you crying last night?" he suddenly asks, looking at me with concern.

I stare at him in surprise for a moment before I respond. His beautiful brown eyes seem deep and intelligent, as if they hold much more wisdom than they should at his age. His face, framed by a grey sealskin hat, is usually pale from the lack of sunlight, but now his cheeks are flushed pink from the hard work.

"I'm sorry, did I wake you?" I ask gently.

"No. I think it was the storm that woke me. But then I heard you crying," he replies softly.

I look down at him and try to keep my voice steady. "You don't need to worry, Kristian. I was just missing your dad," I say, and while it's not entirely true, it's not completely false either.

I don't want to burden him unnecessarily. We normally try to be open with each other, even insisting that no one keeps their feelings to themselves. It's crucial that we don't feel alone with our problems and that we can rely on each other for support. After all, we only have each other. But Kristian is still only 15, and I don't think he needs to share in my worries until I've had a chance to talk things through with Magnus.

"I'll get used to him being away for several days at a time again. That's all it is," I add, giving his hand a squeeze inside the glove.

He holds my gaze a little longer than usual, then pulls his hand away without saying anything more. I can see that he doesn't fully believe my explanation, but he doesn't push it. Instead, he starts gathering up the icicles scattered on the pavement, which we save for later use.

Shortly after, Emilie comes over and wraps her arms around me. "I miss Dad too," she says. Her innocent trust makes me smile faintly. She believes every word I say, without question.

"When will he be back?" she asks.

"He should be back this afternoon," I reply, pulling her into a tight hug. I hold her so close that she eventually wriggles out of my embrace.

● ● ●

"I have a headache."

Emilie lies between two grey-spotted sealskins, as close as she can get to the wood stove without burning herself. She's wearing a grey sealskin hat and looks just like a seal pup, with shiny eyes and pale cheeks, gazing up at me. She's shivering from the cold.

"And I'm freezing."

She pulls the blanket right up over her ears, so only her nose and eyes are visible, as if to emphasise the truth of her statement.

Kristian is engrossed in a new book. Judging by the title on the cover, it's about humanity. *Sapiens – A Brief History of Humankind*, I read, mumbling the words softly to myself.

Humanity. His next debate topic, until he finishes this book and starts on a new one.

Kristian gently scratches his nose as his eyes move from side to side. He often sits like that, absorbed in his book, while the index finger of his right hand scratches the tip of his nose with calm, unconscious movements. His scruffy dark brown hair hangs partly in his eyes, but it doesn't seem to bother him. Even so, I decide he needs a haircut once I've seen to Emilie.

"Let me feel you," I say, sitting down in the blankets beside her.

I place my hand on her forehead. She feels warmer than usual. I slide my hand under the blanket and touch her chest.

"There's no doubt," I say worriedly. "You have a fever."

The skin on her chest feels burning hot, no doubt made worse by her cuddling up under the sealskin. We rarely get sick, though. I believe the cold kills most bacteria and viruses. Those that survive have a hard time spreading, as there are so few people in our small community, and we almost never have direct contact with anyone outside our immediate family. When one of us does fall ill, though, I can't help but feel afraid.

We don't have access to antibiotics, so if the illness turns out to be particularly aggressive, we have no choice but to hope the body's immune system can fight it off on its own.

In this regard, I am the family's protector. I'm the one who fusses over the sick, who fights alongside them. Whether it's Magnus, Kristian, or Emilie, there's no difference in the care. Once one of us is sick, we all catch it quickly, and if we all get sick, we lose at least a week of preparation for the next winter.

Under no circumstances will I allow anyone who is ill to ignore their health and carry on working with the illness raging under their skin. It's too risky and just another way to get yourself killed.

I wish I could give Emilie a cup of hot chocolate, but all I have is the broth I'm boiling meat in.

I gently stroke her cheeks as I look at her lovingly. She's inherited my steely blue eyes, but right now her pupils are so large in the glow of the wood stove that they almost appear brown.

"I'll warm some broth for you," I say, standing up to place the soup pot on the hotplate of the stove.

"I'm not hungry. I'm cold!" she snaps, raising her voice.

"The soup will warm you up again, my love!"

"When is Dad coming home with Mali? Mali can warm me," she says, hinting at how she and Kristian often cuddle up with the dog through the night to share her body heat.

Magnus should be home by now, I think anxiously. Where could he be?

"It's too late now," I reply offhandedly, trying to hide my own nervousness. "They probably won't be back until tomorrow. The storm must have delayed them."

Or maybe there are no more seals?

Magnus mentioned after the last trip that there were fewer animals than last year.

Or perhaps the seal colony has moved further away, meaning the men need more time to track it down?

Maybe there's been an accident?

Maybe one of the men has been injured, and the others have to stay back to tend to him?

There are many reasons they might not be home yet, but I

can only think of the worst ones.

Stop it, I tell myself, annoyed. Why do you always have to imagine the worst?

Because Magnus would never stay away from his family longer than necessary. Something must have happened out there.

The soup starts to boil.

I ladle some into a mug and hand it to Emilie.

"Here, drink this. Please," I say softly. "And I'll read to you from your Harry Potter book while you do."

Emilie loves when Magnus or I read to her. She cuddles up under the blanket, resting her head against our chest as she listens to our quiet, soothing voices.

"Okay," she responds quickly, flashing me a cheeky grin.

She takes the mug and holds it to her lips, sipping cautiously at the warm broth.

"Where's the book?" I ask, settling into the cosy seating area Magnus built during the first winter, around the wood stove.

In truth, it's just a backrest made from disused radiators, arranged in a large square around the stove, except for a small opening in one corner so we can easily get in and out. The floor and sides are covered with a thick layer of sealskins, making it both soft and warm to sit or lie on.

The construction helps to trap the heat from the flames in a smaller area. When it gets really cold, we can even cover it further by draping a sort of hanging roof over the top, leaving only the wood stove exposed in a one-metre radius. Inside this "den" is where most of our activities take place during the winter when we're not outside in the spring and summer. We eat there. We read there. We play there. And we sleep there. In winter, we're only briefly interrupted by the need to go outside, prepare food and drink, or feed the ever-hungry stove with logs from the stacks that line the walls from floor to ceiling.

Emilie reaches under the blanket and pulls out the worn book.

I turn to the page marked with a carefully folded dog-ear and begin reading from the start of a new chapter. Emilie snuggles up to me, quickly getting lost in the wonderful adventure of Harry Potter and the Goblet of Fire. She sips her warm drink as she listens.

I can feel the heat from her small body, even though she's shivering with cold.

5 Magnus

Now they've been warned. There's nothing more we can do. It's not our responsibility if they don't believe us or take the threat seriously.

Yet, I'm furious.

The same reaction everywhere: childish arrogance, pride, and dismissal of the real danger the polar bear poses to our community. If it were simply a case of a bear wandering too far south, into a climate unsuitable for its survival, I could maybe understand their lack of concern. But that's not the case at all.

Mikkel, Zaid, and I have just left the house of the last of the six members from one of the two other hunting groups that we took it upon ourselves to warn before they set out for the coast.

"I wonder if the others had better luck," mutters Zaid.

"I don't know," I reply, irritated. "But if they don't take the threat seriously and the bear catches them by surprise, I don't need much imagination to guess what happens then."

We're making our way down the alley that connects Præstegade to Grønnegade. The cobblestones under the snow are uneven, and there's a risk of slipping if you're not careful where you step. Right now, though, that's the least of my concerns.

"It's irresponsible," I fume. "It's not just themselves they're putting at risk. It's the whole community. Who's going to feed their families if they die? Or if they're badly injured? Who's going to make sure they have enough meat to get through the winter? The women can't fetch firewood and hunt at the same time."

Though my anger is directed at the men who literally laughed in our faces, I'm also filled with frustration at how vulnerable we are.

"Maybe they just need some time to process the news," interrupts Mikkel. "Remember, I also didn't take the whole bear situation seriously at first, until we discussed it more in our group..."

"They haven't seen it with their own eyes, like we have," adds Zaid. "If there's one thing I've learned about human nature, it's that most people, consciously or not, ignore warnings about danger until they experience it themselves. To place your fate in someone else's hands requires trust—trust that those people are truly capable of protecting you and your interests. Be it politicians, leaders, or even your closest friends, you have to believe that their knowledge and experience surpass your own. We're all novices in this life. Forced to take things as they come and face challenges head-on. Give them time, as Mikkel suggests. I'm sure they each listened to what we had to say. When they meet tomorrow before heading to the coast, they'll discuss it and take precautions along the way. Our warning has been heard—that's what matters. And it's all we can do for now."

I have a lot of respect for Zaid. His wisdom and understanding of human behaviour often calm me when I get carried away by my own impulsive thoughts and actions. He and Mikkel are probably right.

We walk on in silence, with Mali bounding ahead of us, just as eager to get home as we are. The moon shines brightly in a sky full of stars, providing enough light for us to find our way through the narrow streets.

The three of us live at the same end of Grønnegade, so we walk side by side. We're tired after the long journey home, and we should've been back home with our families hours ago. I'm sure they're worried, but we all felt the need to warn the other men before they went to bed for the night. Our families would just have to wait a little longer.

Maybe that's part of the reason I'm so frustrated with the scepticism we were met with. I should have been home with my own family instead.

As we walk, I glance up at the starry sky and reflect briefly on how, once upon a time, people could navigate using the stars. But that knowledge has long been lost to most, replaced first by drawn maps of roads and landscapes, and then by digital satellite-based navigation systems.

The maps are still useful as long as the landscape's contours remain visible beneath the snow and ice. But the digital devices have lost all utility due to the lack of power sources to recharge them.

As I've thought many times since the world changed, the digital age, in so many ways, reduced humanity's ability to live in harmony with nature. Basic observational skills, essential for survival—like identifying the cardinal directions or predicting the weather by observing cloud formations—have long been replaced by satellite-based guidance and forecasts.

Our dependence on electronics has left us almost unable to navigate with something as simple as a drawn topographical map.

I decide that tomorrow I'll stop by the town's abandoned library and find some books on navigating by nature's elements. Who knows? It might be worth rediscovering this old skill.

Right now, though, none of that matters. I just look forward to getting home to Freja and the children and holding them in my arms again.

It feels like ages since I set out with Zaid, Mikkel, Jørgen, Erik, and Svend, even though it was only yesterday morning.

First, though, I need to get the seals into the cold room—the room we also use to store ice blocks and cold water. The nighttime temperatures are still too low this time of year to leave them outside overnight if I want to process them in the morning.

We left the sledges at the entrance to Grønnegade. When we find them again, we stand together for a brief moment, patting each other on the shoulders as men do, before we head our separate ways.

Zaid promises again to stop by tomorrow evening with Farhana, once the day's tasks are done.

"We've got important things to discuss," he mutters, before heading off home.

I grab the harness and drag my sledge around to the back of the house, where I can haul the seals inside through the courtyard. There, they can stay in near-freezing temperatures until Freja and I have a chance to butcher them together tomorrow afternoon.

Mali is already sitting impatiently, staring up at the door handle, when I step into the courtyard. She ran ahead, eager to reunite with the rest of her family. Her whole body is quivering with anticipation, and her ears are pricked forward, straining to catch the slightest sound from inside.

Inside, I find Freja leaning against the backrest in the sleeping area, with an open book resting on her lap. Emilie is snuggled up to her shoulder, wrapped warmly in furs and a hat. They're both fast asleep, having dozed off between pages 121 and 122, judging by the numbers at the bottom of the book.

Kristian is lying on the other side of the woodstove, where it's quieter, reading his own book while Freja read aloud to Emilie. He, too, is fast asleep, though he managed to set his book aside before drifting off.

I smile warmly, glad to see them, but at the same time, I'm a bit disappointed that I didn't make it home before they fell asleep. I don't have the heart to wake them, even though I long to hear their voices. Life here is hard enough, with all the chopping, splitting, and stacking of wood, so they deserve all the rest they can get.

Mali, however, doesn't possess the same amount of respectful restraint as I do. Before I can stop her, she's snuggles up to Freja, enthusiastically licking her nose until she sleepily pushes her away.

Mali jumps back a step, her bushy tail wagging playfully as she stares expectantly at Freja. When she doesn't move, still deeply asleep, Mali bounds forward again, licking her nose once more. This time, she paws at Freja's arm repeatedly until Freja finally opens her eyes. She's greeted with a flurry of excited, wet kisses from a spotted dog tongue.

I can't help but laugh as Freja tries to escape the impromptu face-wash while simultaneously trying to free her arms from the blankets so she can hug and pet Mali's thick fur.

"Come here, Mali," I chuckle. "Let Mum sleep. She's had a hard day."

Mali looks at me curiously, then gives Emilie a quick lick on the cheek before moving on to Kristian, offering him the same gentle greeting. When neither of the children stirs, she circles three times, then clumsily drops down beside Kristian and soon drifs into a deep sleep. Moments later, she is snoring loudly.

I have already removed my boots and outer layers. The room iss freezing, so I grab a couple of logs from the pile against the wall and feed them into the stove. Once the fire is going, I crawl over to Freja, eager to get under the blankets with her.

"Emilie's sick. She's got a fever," Freja murmurs sleepily, kissing me on the lips. Her lips are soft.

"Is it serious?" I ask, a familiar worry settling in. The last thing we can afford is for any of us to come down with something serious, like pneumonia.

"She's not coughing, but she's burning up and shivering, even under all the blankets," Freja replies, still drowsy, as she adjusts Emilie's position, tucking the covers tightly around her. She check her forehead again before settling down next to me. We both slide under the blankets, our children sleeping peacefully a few metres away.

Freja doesn't seem too worried, which usually means things aren't too bad. When she isn't anxious, I can relax as well.

"Did it go well?" she ask, pressing her back against me, her warmth immediately soothing.

"You're home late," she adds.

"We'll talk about it tomorrow," I say, pulling her closer. I kiss her earlobe, feeling a desire rise within me like molten lava, spreading heat through my body. Soon, the cold is the furthest thing on my mind.

"Is there something else on your mind?" she teases, as she feels me grow hard beneath my thermals. She shifts her hips back, grinding against me playfully, and before I can respond, her hand slides into my trousers.

Keeping our intimate life alive is a constant balancing act, especially with the children sleeping so close. It is important not to lose touch with each other, but at the same time, we would never want the kids to wake up in the middle of something and find us like that.

Sometimes we sneak into the next room, but it is nearly freezing in there, and it is hard to stay in the mood when your teeth are chattering.

Tonight, though, we stay where we were, moving slowly, quietly, until we've drained the last of our energy.

We fall asleep, half-naked, wrapped together under the blankets.

● ● ●

During the night, Emilie starts coughing. At first, it's just a minor cough, but by early morning, it has turned into full-blown coughing fits, preventing her from sleeping. After each fit, she sits there gasping for breath, tears rolling down her cheeks.

Freja takes her onto her lap, trying to keep the blankets wrapped around her frail body to stop her from getting cold. Emilie quickly pulls them off again, complaining that it's far too hot, even though there's nothing but embers left in the stove, and the temperature in the room can't be more than ten degrees.

She breaks into another deep cough, which wakes Kristian.

"What's going on?" he asks, looking sleepily out from under his blanket, which covers most of his head.

Mali, still lying beside him, lifts her head sharply when she hears his voice. She sticks her wet nose into the opening of the blankets and gives him a lick on the nose, a good morning greeting.

"Mali!" he exclaims, pulling her in for a big bear hug. "Dad, when did you get home?" he asks, his head buried deep in the dog's soft fur.

"Last night, after you were all asleep. Emilie's not feeling well."

"So, she won't be helping with the firewood today?" Kristian asks. His question sounds innocent enough, but I know my son, and I know that's not what he's really asking. He's wondering if his own workload will be heavier now, since they'll be short one pair of hands to load the wood onto the sledges.

It's clear he's not fully awake yet. Normally, he knows that when I'm home, and with Zaid's help, we have two extra pairs of hands for our little woodcutting team. Even if Freja stays behind to look after Emilie, we'll still have enough manpower to get the day's work done faster.

"You can relax, my boy," I say, sitting down beside him. I pull the blanket away from his head, revealing his tousledge brown hair and one ear.

"We're not going into the forest today. I've brought two seals home that need dealing with. I've got a couple of other tasks for you instead."

I reach for his book to see what subject has currently captured his interest. He props himself up on his elbow, looking at me expectantly.

"What jobs?" he asks, clearly relieved at the prospect of a day off, even if it's only a half-day. None of the tasks I have for him will be as tough as splitting wood all day.

"First, I'd like you to fetch a couple of the ice blocks I brought in from the sea and set them to boil. We need more salt for the dried meat."

"Okay," Kristian replies. "That's not so bad."

"No, it's not," I confirm. "And then I'd like you to run over to the library and find a few books for me. Some about navigating by nature. Think you can find something like that?"

"Of course!" he exclaims, excited.

Kristian loves the library. It's a sanctuary for him, a place where he can be alone, losing himself in random books and magazines while gradually building up a collection of interesting topics to bring home. The large, dark rooms, with their mazes of dusty bookshelves, make him feel as though he's completely alone in a strange world, where it's easy to forget the reality outside. Often, he loses track of time, and Freja or I have to go and fetch him.

"But why do you want to learn how to navigate by nature?" Kristian asks.

"Ah, don't you think it's a useful skill to have?" I reply evasively. Truthfully, I'm not quite sure why I want to learn it myself. Instead, I get up and grab another couple of logs for the stove. I poke at the embers with a fire iron, spreading them out so they'll catch onto the new wood more easily. For a moment, I enjoy the warmth from the embers before closing the door again.

"But first, get that saltwater boiling," I remind him. "And don't stay out too long! You're responsible for the salt while your mum and I prepare the meat for drying."

Making salt is a time-consuming process. The saltwater needs to boil all day, with the water evaporating slowly, leaving the salt as crystals at the bottom of the pot. As the water evaporates, you have to stir more and more frequently to prevent the salt from burning. Eventually, when it reaches a thick, porridge-like consistency, it's poured into a tray to dry at lower temperatures until the last of the water evaporates.

The space on the floor under the stove's opening is ideal for drying the salt, and it's usually ready for use the next day. Ten litres of seawater yield about half a kilo of salt, so the process is far too slow to use the salt as a preservative. Its sole purpose is to add flavour to the dried meat.

"What about me?" Emilie interrupts, immediately launching into another violent coughing fit. Her body convulses as she struggles to catch her breath between each cough.

"You're going to stay under the blankets and rest, so you can get better," Freja says, running her fingers gently through Emilie's light hair in long, loving strokes.

"That sounds boring," Emilie replies, once the coughing subsides. But she still snuggles herself back under the blanket.

Her eyes are glassy, and her breathing is laboured. There's no doubt about it, I think anxiously. She's come down with pneumonia.

● ● ●

The knife slides easily under the skin around the flippers.

I make sure to keep it sharp, so skinning the seals goes faster. I begin by cutting the skin free all the way around each of the four flippers and around the animal's neck. Then I follow the cut I made out on the ice, when I opened it up and removed the innards, so the incision now runs in a straight line from the cross-cut around the back flippers, all the way up to the similar cut around the neck.

Between the skin and the meat, the seal has an eight-centimetre-thick layer of blubber, which helps it stay warm in the icy water, where it spends most of its life. This layer of blubber clings to the inside of the skin and is easy to cut free along the entire body, revealing the characteristic dark red meat underneath.

The meat's particularly dark colour comes from its high myoglobin content, which binds oxygen as a kind of oxygen reserve in the muscles.

I work quickly and with focus, using the knife. Freja helps me pull the skin aside as I cut it free. We're both wearing large sealskin mitts, which make the work much harder, but the risk of frostbite is too great if we take them off. Once the meat is separated from the skin, we take it inside, where it's possible to process it without needing the big mitts, but until then, we work directly on the snow in the courtyard to minimise the blood getting inside.

I haven't yet told Freja about the encounter with the polar bear. I'll wait until we're inside, away from the bitter cold.

After about ten minutes, the skinned, bloody carcass lies in the middle of the skin, which is spread out around it. The blubber and snow are streaked with its blood.

At first, I was disappointed by how little meat there is on such an animal, compared to how big and heavy it is to drag home. The majority of its large body volume is simply blubber. But the meat is rich in nutrients, and we quickly realised that we don't need as much of it as we would if it were ordinary beef.

We can also thank the seal meat for the fact that our vitamin deficiency isn't more severe than it is.

We always make sure to keep a large portion of the blubber to fry the meat in or to add to the soups we so often make.

Sometimes, we even cut it into cubes, salt it, and fry it in the pan as a sort of snack. The texture is strangely tough, like chewing on cartilage, and at the same time, it's very fatty, so when we have actual meat to eat, the blubber doesn't rank highly on either mine or Freja's wish list. But we force ourselves to eat it, because we need the extra calories.

It's quite the opposite for Kristian and Emilie, who've both been served these snacks for as long as they can remember, and who eat them with great delight.

Apart from its high caloric value, the blubber also has a decent burning value. With a bit of practice, it can be used as fuel in a kind of oil lamp. Chunks of blubber are placed in a flat clay dish, where a wick made of moss is wrapped around a cone-shaped stone so it doesn't drown in the melted blubber. As the blubber burns away, it's replaced with new chunks.

It sounds pretty simple, but it took us a long time to figure out how to make the wick so the lamps wouldn't smoke heavily or get drowned in blubber. When we finally found the solution, however, it made a huge difference to our comfort in the winter darkness. Now we have light to read by, and lamps we can carry with us when we move around in the dark inside the house.

It almost felt like we had reinvented the candle when we finally managed to make a lamp that could stay lit for a whole evening.

Freja and I free the rest of the body from the skin still attached to the animal's back. Then we carry it inside before starting on the next seal. We leave the skin and blubber for later.

All in all, the seals we've caught have more blubber than we can use, and while the skin is highly valuable protection against the icy wind or as blankets for insulating the house, we don't clean every skin. Cleaning, curing, and preparing the skin so it can be used as blankets or clothing is a long and laborious process. We prefer to delay that work until the winter, when it can be done in the warmth around the wood-burning stove, when there's little else to do.

These two skins, I'll take with me next time I head to the coast and leave them somewhere along the way.

Inside the cold room, it feels warm compared to outside.

The work of separating the meat from the skin takes no longer than 20 minutes for both animals combined. I've built up a good routine by now and know exactly how best to go about it; but it's so bitterly cold outside that even 20 minutes of work is pushing the limits of what we can endure, when the job doesn't involve hard physical activity.

We go into the living room to check on Emilie. She's sleeping soundly under the blankets.

The pot of saltwater is bubbling away on the wood stove.

Kristian is still at the library. He's taken Mali with him, which I think is a good idea. With her by his side, he's less likely to lose track of time, as she demands attention if no one has spoken to her for a while.

As the cold stiffness in my jaw begins to wear off, I move behind Freja and wrap my arms around her.

"We've encountered yet another challenge," I say.

I try to sound as casual as possible, but it's hard to keep my worries from showing.

Freja turns her head and looks at me questioningly, so I continue.

"When Mikkel, Zaid, and Jørgen were on their way back to the cabin for shelter from the storm, they suddenly saw a polar bear climbing up from the sea."

"A polar bear?" she exclaims in surprise, staring at me with a barely suppressed smile, as if I'm trying to spin her a tall tale.

For a brief moment, I feel angry. The men's reaction the night before is still fresh in my memory. But Freja knows me well enough to tell when I'm joking and when I'm serious. The smile fades as quickly as it appeared, and my anger dissolves like mist in the sun, as the information slowly processes and takes root in her mind. The expression in her steely blue eyes shifts to one of deep concern. She immediately grasps the implications of this new information.

I love her for that.

I love her for many reasons, but right now, I especially love her because she understands so easily and doesn't doubt the seriousness of what I'm telling her.

She's taken off her hat. Her long hair hangs messily around her shoulders.

"But how can you hunt safely with such a creature roaming around?" she asks, worried.

At the same time, she remembers that the next hunting party had already set off towards the coast earlier that morning.

"What about the other hunters? Has anyone warned them?" she asks.

She always thinks of the others first. If anyone understands that our community and its members only survive by sticking together and helping one another, it's her.

"We split into two groups and went out to warn them last night when we got home," I reply. "That's why I got back so late."

I tell her about the reactions we encountered from the other families. Like me, she becomes angry when she hears about the lack of understanding of the gravity of the situation.

"Does no one understand how vulnerable we are?" she fumes. "We don't need any more challenges or worries."

I see tears welling up in the corners of her eyes, so I tighten my grip and pull her closer to me. She turns around in my arms and buries her face in my woollen jumper, starting to sob quietly.

I can feel her body trembling.

I say nothing.

No false words about how everything will be fine.

No one here needs false illusions, not under the circumstances we live in. In our situation, we have to face reality as it is.

Before I can say more, I hear Freja mumble softly, still with her face hidden in my jumper, so I have to strain to hear her voice.

"We have to head south," she says.

Unsure if I heard her correctly, I pull her away from me to arm's length and study her face closely.

Her cheeks are wet from tears streaming down. It's been a long time since I've seen her cry, I think fleetingly. She's grown tough over the last few years, but as I look at her now, I see a woman on the verge of breaking down.

I feel sorry for her.

Her voice is barely a whisper as she repeats herself.

"We have to head south, Magnus. We can't survive here. We can't."

I realise that she's been grappling with the same thoughts as I have, and that she's come to exactly the same conclusion.

If we are to survive another winter, we must leave Denmark and seek out warmer places.

As if to underscore the point, Emilie starts coughing violently under the blankets. I pull them away from her face to give her some fresh air.

She feels warm. Even warmer than before. Freja and I exchange worried glances as the coughing fits slowly subside.

She wakes just long enough to see that we're both in the room before closing her eyes again and drifting back to sleep.

Freja decides to stay with her, while I return to the cold room and begin preparing the meat for the drying process.

When Kristian returns, she'll likely join me again, but until then, I work alone.

Like with the salt production, drying meat is a simple but time-consuming process. The meat is sliced into thin strips, which are then placed in a brine of melted blubber mixed with salt to absorb the flavour. Afterward, it's hung on a rack around the wood stove, where the heat draws the moisture out of the meat overnight.

It sounds simple, but it takes a long time to cut the meat into thin slices and hang it up on the rack once it's absorbed enough.

As I work, I wonder how we'll manage a journey south.

What about food along the way?

Where will we find shelter from the storms that can rise out of nowhere?

And what about fuel to keep us warm?

How much can we take with us from the start, and how much might we find along the way?

The thoughts whirl around in my head, making me dizzy.

I'm scared. Scared to leave. But I'm also scared to stay.

● ● ●

When Kristian and Mali finally return from the library, the first batch of meat is already hanging to dry on the racks around the wood stove, and the pot of saltwater is still boiling on top. Half of the water has evaporated, and salt crystals are starting to form at the bottom of the pot.

The smell of drying meat slowly fills the room, and Mali, in an unguarded moment, lets herself be seduced by the aroma. While Kristian proudly displays the books he's brought home, she sneaks behind the stove. Out of sight, she deftly swipes a couple of slices of meat from one of the racks. It's only when she tries to take the third piece that we catch her, as the meat is stuck, and the rack rattles across the tiles when she pulls at it.

"Mali!" I shout in surprise when I spot her.

Of course, she should have something to eat, but not the meat I've so painstakingly cut and hung up to dry. In the cold room, I have a bowl of raw meat and fat meant for her. Mali looks at me with an innocent smile, as if to praise me for both my skills and the delicious taste. Her big tail wags enthusiastically, and her tongue hangs panting from the corner of her mouth. The salted, dried meat has made her thirsty. I find it impossible to be angry with her, so instead of scolding, I scratch her behind the ears.

She gazes at me expectantly. It's her usual mealtime.

I fetch her bowl and give her what was originally intended for her, minus the amount of meat she's already stolen. We can't afford to waste anything.

Outside, darkness is beginning to fall, casting long shadows down the streets. It won't be long before Zaid and Farhana arrive.

I'm not entirely sure what I expect from the conversation. The situation today is very different from the war they fled. I think I just need to hear that what we're contemplating isn't hopeless. That there's a way through all this despair and we can make it out successfully on the other side.

Perhaps they'll tell us we're fools to even consider it, and maybe they'll be right. But aren't we even bigger fools if we stay in a place that threatens our lives every day?

I need us to make a decision soon.

But if we're in a situation where the choice between staying or fleeing is even a matter for long deliberation, is it really a life-or-death situation?

The crucial point, I think, is that the prospect of improvement is becoming less and less clear.

There's no sign that the cold will retreat or even stabilize. Quite the opposite. Year after year, winter sweeps over us with renewed force, like an avalanche that drags everything with it, gaining momentum the further down the mountain it goes. Just as people at the foot of the mountain are forced to flee to avoid being buried under the snow, we are forced to flee to avoid being frozen alive.

I sigh in resignation and sink down into the blankets next to Kristian. He's already settled comfortably, his nose buried deep in *Sapiens*.

Humans. An incredible species, which has managed to adapt to life on Earth far better than any other creature before it.

"How's the book?" I ask.

He looks up and answers me with a question.

"Did you know that humans lived here during the last ice

age?"

"Yes," I reply. "I did. Humans have always been good at adapting to extreme conditions. Think about how people have lived in Siberia for many years, where winter temperatures drop to minus 50 degrees. And on the other end of the temperature scale, people have adapted to life in the Sahara desert, where it gets as hot as plus 50 degrees. That's a difference of 100 degrees between these two extremes."

"As much as boiling water!" he exclaims with childlike enthusiasm.

"Yes, that's one way of looking at it," I laugh.

"We're doing pretty well, too, aren't we, Dad?"

The question catches me off guard, and I don't answer immediately. What's behind this question right now?

Neither Freja nor I have shared our thoughts with anyone else before, and Kristian was at the library when Freja and I finally opened up about it.

Kristian watches me, waiting. His deep brown eyes hold my gaze intensely, very unlike what most other children his age would do. He's growing up fast, I think.

"What are you thinking?" I ask, once again avoiding answering directly.

He glances over at Freja, who has just gotten up to stir the pot of saltwater, as if to ensure the conversation stays between him and me. He waits to respond until she's back under the blankets with Emilie, reading aloud from her book.

Emilie has slept most of the day. She woke when Kristian came home and is now alert enough to focus on the story. She's still very warm, and I suspect it's only a matter of time before she drifts back into the healing rest of sleep.

Outside, the sun has now completely set, giving way to the

moon and another starry night, and it's starting to feel colder inside the house. The chill seeps in from all sides, despite our frequent trips to feed the wood stove with logs.

I shiver and pull the blankets tighter around my shoulders.

"While you were away, Mum seemed more worried than usual," Kristian says quietly, making sure Freja doesn't overhear.

He speaks softly, so I have to focus to hear him over the gentle bubbling of the saltwater pot, the crackling of the fire, and Freja's steady voice.

"Almost like she's giving up," he continues. "Last night, she cried all night, but she won't tell me the real reason. She just says she misses you, but I know that's not the whole truth. I think she's giving up on everything. And then when you got back, you asked me to get books from the library. About navigating nature. Why is that suddenly so important?"

He stops and looks at me, expecting an answer. There's a brief pause before I pull him closer, so he's sitting with his back against me. I wrap my arms around him, hugging him with my warm sealskin blanket.

I rest my chin on the top of his head.

We sit like that for a while, silent, until I finally respond. He's more observant than Freja and I give him credit for, I think to myself.

Of course he notices when our moods shift. It's only natural, given how close we live to one another. It's naive to think otherwise. He deserves to know the truth before Zaid and Farhana arrive. He's part of the family, and of course, he should have a voice in whatever decision we make, whatever that may be.

I take a deep breath and reluctantly begin to share with him the concerns Freja and I have been wrestling with.

"But we've managed so far," Kristian protests.

"That's true," I whisper softly into his hair. "That's true. We have managed so far. But how long can we keep going? That's the crucial question we have to keep asking ourselves."

We're interrupted by a knock on the door.

Mali immediately jumps up and barks aggressively, running ahead to the front door.

Zaid and Farhana are standing outside, stamping in the snow with their daughter Fatima. Despite living just a few houses down the street, they're bundled up in thick jackets, hats, gloves, and scarves covering their faces.

The cold outside is brutal.

The moment I open the door, the freezing air rushes into the room. I feel its merciless bite on the parts of my cheeks not covered by my thick, bushy beard.

The door handle inside freezes over and pinches my skin as I touch it to close the door behind them.

"Emilie has pneumonia," I say, nodding subtly in Fatima's direction.

I don't want her to get infected.

"It's probably best if the two girls don't sit too close to each other tonight," I suggest.

Shortly after we settle in the living room, gathered around the warmth of the wood stove, there's another knock at the door. It's Mikkel, his wife Anna, and their son Kasper.

How old is he now, I wonder as I catch sight of him hiding behind his mother's legs, pressing his face into her sealskin trousers as if that would make him invisible to the rest of us. Is he five now? Six? It's a miracle he's survived his early years.

I usher them inside quickly and shut the door behind them

before the warmth escapes.

I look questioningly at the new arrivals. Mikkel hangs back a bit, looking like he's been caught somewhere he doesn't belong.

I smile and give Anna a brief nod. She looks a bit embarrassed.

I don't recall ever exchanging more than a couple of words with her. She strikes me as someone very introverted, quite the opposite of Mikkel, who can be a bit of a loudmouth. She seems more like the nerdy type, with thick-rimmed glasses perched on a freckled, upturned nose. Her golden hair falls loosely in natural curls over her shoulders, framing a face with skin that's somewhere between pale and pink.

A very charming girl, I think to myself as she smiles back at me, revealing dimples in each cheek. But not the sort of girl I'd immediately associate with the kind of mental strength that both Freja and Farhana seem to have.

Freja joins us and hugs them both.

"What brings you here?" she asks, sounding genuinely pleased to see all three of them.

Mikkel clears his throat before answering.

"Well, I overheard you asking Zaid if he and Farhana could talk a bit about what it was like fleeing Syria. And I thought maybe it wouldn't be a bad idea to listen in, if that's all right with you?"

His eyes dart around nervously as he speaks, like someone unsure of his place.

I instantly understand what he's getting at. He's reached the same conclusion that's been simmering in my mind for some time now, accelerated by the arrival of our unexpected guest on the coast.

They'll want to join us if we decide to head south!

I stare at him, surprised, for a long moment before responding.

I have no doubt Mikkel can make the journey south. He's proven his strength on many occasions during our hunting trips.

But can Anna make it? She doesn't seem particularly strong. And what about Kasper? He's still just a little boy.

"Of course, you can stay and listen," I say, motioning them towards the sofas where we're now sitting, tightly packed.

No harm in that.

The saltwater in the pot has finally evaporated enough that the thick, briny paste can be poured out to dry into usable salt crystals. Before sitting down beside me, Freja lifts the pot from the stove and spreads the paste in a thin layer on a baking tray, which she slides into the gap between the floor and the stove.

Mali has curled up next to Emilie, who's fighting to stay awake, curious about why so many people have suddenly gathered in our home. However, she drifts off to sleep before the conversations even begin.

No one seems to doubt why we're gathered here, but no one wants to be the first to open up the wounds that Zaid and Farhana have worked so hard to heal.

We sit in silence for a long time, each lost in thoughts. Zaid stares blankly into the flames behind the stove's blackened glass door.

I have no doubt he's reliving every nightmare from their long trek north to escape the horrors of war.

Farhana leans against him, also lost in thought, biting her lower lip, visibly moved by sad memories.

So much of their lives was left behind—abandoned in favour

of a hope for safety, where the future seemed open and full of possibilities, rather than reduced to ashes by the religious fanaticism and narrow-mindedness of others.

I feel for them both and decide, then and there, that I won't force them to dig up their painful memories.

The situation is what it is, and it shouldn't be fear of what might lie ahead that determines our future. Either we believe we can survive here, or we don't, and then we must figure out what to do.

Without further introduction, I begin to speak. Slowly, and without addressing anyone in particular.

"We need to make a decision," I say. "Freja and I have reached the point where we no longer believe there's a future for us here."

I pause briefly and look around at the others. Mikkel meets my gaze and nods slightly, as if to confirm he's hearing what I'm saying.

He's taken off his hat. His blond hair is flat and a bit greasy. His son is asleep, his head resting on Mikkel's lap. His breathing is heavy.

Anna sits beside him, lost in her thoughts, twirling her long red hair around her fingers. I'm not sure she's heard a word I've said, as if she's subconsciously trying to block out all the bad and retreat into herself. A bit like Freja when she gets lost in thought, letting her mind wander.

"Zaid," I say.

He lifts his head, taking a moment to focus his eyes on me.

"You and Farhana have been our friends for many years now. I respect your views, but I won't ask you to relive your memories. You don't deserve that. What I do need, though, is your perspective on our options. Is it time to follow those who fled before us in the hope of finding a better life elsewhere? Is it even realistic?"

I try to say it as casually as I can, but I can hear the nervousness in my own voice.

This is the moment of decision. Tonight, we make our choice.

"I've spent most of today and all of yesterday on the way home thinking," Zaid replies, his deep voice resonating. "I've weighed the pros and cons with Farhana. Because I agree with you, Magnus. We are at a crossroads. If we're going to leave, it has to be now. We can't wait much longer if we're to reach safety before winter. But it's not just about deciding whether we leave this year. I fear that the decision we make tonight will also determine our future opportunities.

If we choose to stay, I think we'll miss the chance to leave next year. Or the year after that. Winter grows longer each year, and summer shorter. We barely have enough time to get as far south as we need to, to reach safety, even now."

"How far south do you think we need to go?" I ask.

Zaid leans back, wrapping his arm protectively around his wife. He takes his time before answering.

Kristian and Fatima sit close together, listening intently. They are fully aware that our future will be decided today and are determined to be part of it.

Fatima is 14 years old, and it's already clear that she will grow up to be as beautiful as her mother. They are just friends for now, but I've seen Kristian steal longing glances at her on more than one occasion.

"We need to go all the way down to the Mediterranean," Zaid finally responds. "I can't imagine these cursed winters reach as far south as Italy, southern France, or Spain. So if we're to plan for anything, we have to aim for getting there. If we're lucky, we might find help before then, but since we have no way of knowing for sure, it's best to plan as if the Mediterranean is our goal before winter returns."

"We must have a goal," Farhana interjects in agreement. "If you don't have a goal, you'll get lost along the way."

She takes a deep breath before continuing in a whisper.

"Only those with a clear goal make it."

Tears well up in her eyes. She blinks rapidly and wipes them away with the back of her hand.

"That's true," Zaid confirms. "A goal is crucial. So many of our friends and acquaintances disappeared into refugee camps because they had no definite end point for where they were going. Many were content to seek asylum in the first safe country they reached, whether it was Turkey, Hungary, Greece, or Italy. It didn't matter. But the refugee camps in those countries were enormous, and the conditions were horrible. We haven't heard from any of them since, and we fear they've perished, along with many others, inside those camps.

No one who enters one of those camps ever gets the chance to rebuild their life. Calling them refugee camps is nothing but political propaganda for the international community. An illusion meant to make it look like the country is helping the needy. In reality, they're massive prison camps where you serve a sentence for a crime you never committed, with no end in sight.

It's soul-crushing.

Many who survived the war either go mad or die of hunger or disease behind the thick barbed wire fences of those refugee camps."

"Avoid refugee camps at all costs. That's what's important!" Farhana mutters, interrupting Zaid's heated speech.

He leans back in resignation, sighing in frustration.

All of that is in the past now, just one of countless humanitarian disasters that have occurred around the world since then.

Silence settles over us once again.

I wonder if there's anywhere left in the world where we can build a new life.

"If the goal is to reach the French Mediterranean coast before winter returns, then we've got a long journey ahead of us," Mikkel suddenly says, speaking up for the first time. "It's at least 1,500 kilometres, so even if we walk 15 kilometres a day, pulling sledges with food and the supplies we need to survive the journey, it would still take us more than three months to get there."

"We have five months from now until the winter forces us back indoors," I reply. "But May can be unpredictable. There could be days when we can't even step outside because of storms. And what about September? The autumn storms are coming earlier and earlier. Can we really count on being able to travel through part of September as well? If not, we might be cutting it close."

"Is it even realistic to reach the French Mediterranean coast?" Mikkel asks, sounding resigned. "Maybe there are other destinations, not as far away, where we can take shelter for the winter and then continue south in the spring? What about Italy or Croatia? How far are they compared to France?"

"In terms of distance, there's not much difference," I answer. "But to get to Italy or Croatia, we'd have to cross the Alps in Switzerland or Austria, and surely we can expect extreme cold there too? The safest route is definitely to aim for Provence in France."

"You're right," Zaid rumbles. "Provence must be our goal."

"Hold on a minute," Kristian protests loudly. "Does this mean you've just decided, on behalf of all of us, that we're going to risk our lives and head south? Dad, you always say we have no idea what things are like further south. Who says it's any better there?"

"That's true, Kristian," I reply. "We know nothing for certain. The only thing we do know is that we can't stay here."

"But we've managed so far," he insists fiercely. "Why couldn't we keep surviving here? You can't all just give up!"

"Kristian, my dear," Freja answers sadly. "None of us are giving up. Quite the opposite. Staying here would be the real surrender, in my opinion. Fleeing south means we still want to live. It shows we believe we still have a chance of survival, if only we take it. Southward, there's still hope!"

6 Freja

Now that the decision to head south has finally been made, I feel both relieved and terrified at the same time.

Relieved at the prospect of escaping the claustrophobic winter storms. I look forward to being free from the ever-present fear that constantly lurks in the back of my mind.

Thankfully, there have been no confrontations yet between the polar bear and the men from the various hunting teams, but in recent weeks, everyone has managed to catch a glimpse of it. So far, it's kept its distance, which reassures many in our community that there's nothing to fear from that end.

Maybe they're right.

Polar bears usually hunt far out on the ice, far from human civilization. Why would it take an interest in us unless there's a severe lack of food? When the sea ice retreated, it meant fewer hunting grounds for the polar bears, leading to numerous confrontations between them and humans in areas where their worlds collided.

On the Arctic islands of Svalbard and Novaya Zemlya, the invasion of polar bears was once so intense that the Russian government even declared a state of emergency on the islands. The bears even went as far as entering people's homes in their search for food.

Back then, the situation was different from what it is now.

The sea ice is much more widespread than it has been in years, creating ideal living conditions for the great predators far out at sea.

Perhaps the fear of more polar bears coming is unfounded.

Yes, I'm definitely relieved we've decided to leave. But at the same time, I'm terrified.

The uncertainty is the worst part. What will we face when we're out there, all alone in the frozen landscape, far from everything and everyone?

We're just ten people setting off. Six adults and four children. No one else, apart from those gathered in our house that night three weeks ago, is convinced that leaving is the right decision.

However, Jørgen and Svend agree that heading south is the only right choice for us. But the two of them are in their mid-sixties. Neither of them feels physically capable of enduring the hardships of such a long journey.

"If we go with you, it's uncertain how long it will take before one or both of us starts succumbing to the strain," Jørgen had said. "We'd only slow you down instead of being a help. We'd rather stay here and see how long we can hold on."

As much as I want them to come with us, I can't help but respect their decision. Considering their age, either scenario is likely a short dance with death.

I understand why they prefer to stay where they are rather than tempt fate and potentially spend their final days in inhuman conditions, exposed to the elements.

Erik and his wife Henriette, like several others, are convinced that the risk of perishing on the journey is greater than the risk of staying. That it's already too late to leave.

That's fear talking.

I can't blame them for being scared. The risk of dying during the journey is indeed high, but unlike what they feel, we're convinced that the risk of staying is even greater.

Others still cling to the hope that the weather will soon improve. That talk of a new ice age is doomsday nonsense and that it's just a matter of surviving a few tough years until both they and nature have adapted to the new conditions.

Ten people are leaving, and 36 are staying behind.

The past three weeks have been spent preparing for the journey.

Now that we're no longer facing the prospect of surviving another winter here, there's less need to gather firewood, and the time is mainly spent preparing dried meat for the journey south.

It's anxiety-inducing not to go into the woods anymore because it also means the decision is final. If we change our minds later, the chance to gather enough firewood for another winter will be lost.

To be ready for the journey, we must focus solely on gathering food for the trip. We can't expect much luck hunting along the way, so the need for dried meat is enormous. Magnus, Zaid, and Mikkel are constantly going back and forth between the sea and our home.

For our own little family, we usually need about five kilos of raw seal meat a day to maintain our weight during winter. On the journey south, where we'll use a lot of energy walking, pulling sledges, and keeping warm, the four of us will need at least one and a half times that amount.

This means we'll need nearly the same number of seals we typically require to survive the seven-month-long confinement of winter just to keep going on the four-month journey to southern France.

Survival is, to some extent, a matter of numbers.

The body needs a certain number of calories to keep functioning. At the same time, there's a limit to how much weight

Magnus can pull on the sledge from the coast to home, so we can't expect to have enough meat ready until early June, which is also the absolute deadline for departure to ensure we arrive before winter returns in early October.

We'll need around 900 kilos of raw meat for the journey.

Fortunately, dried meat weighs only half as much as raw meat, which makes the numbers work out in terms of the maximum pulling weight we can each manage during the trip.

Magnus is used to pulling about 300 kilos. I can pull half of that, and Kristian can probably pull about the same. In total, 600 kilos, including meat, sledges, and extra skins to keep warm.

Firewood is my biggest concern since we simply don't have the strength to carry the hundreds of kilos of wood we'll need along the way.

Mikkel, who is probably the most optimistic of us all, is convinced that there are plenty of trees along the way that we can chop down for firewood.

Anna, who's turned out to be a girl full of worries, naturally thinks the opposite. She believes we should expect that most of the trees have already been burned by other people in their efforts to stay alive.

The more I get to know these two people, the more amazed I am that their marriage seems both solid and happy, despite their starkly different personalities. But maybe that's what makes it work so well? Anna holds Mikkel back when he gets too eager and throws himself into bold, sometimes rash, projects.

On the other hand, Mikkel, with his ever-positive nature, helps lift Anna up when she withdraws and is weighed down by fears over life's everyday struggles, big and small.

Magnus is also convinced that firewood won't be our biggest problem along the way.

"There must be plenty of dead trees along the roads and in the fields across Denmark and Germany. As long as we stick to the roads, we can chop down what we need each day along the way."

He argues confidently in his well-meaning attempts to ease my anxiety.

"You're probably right that around the towns, it's more scarce when it comes to wood. But just like we still have wood available here in the nearby forest, I'm convinced we won't be in need along the way. Don't worry!"

I love Magnus with all my heart, and I appreciate all his efforts to reassure me when I'm anything but calm. But he's more impulsive by nature than I am and tends to take things as they come.

I, on the other hand, need to feel certain before I throw myself into something that could end up costing me and my children our lives. It's not enough for me to *believe* that we won't freeze to death on the journey.

I need to know for sure. But there's no way to calm myself, because we won't know if there's wood to be found until we're out there, battling snow, wind, cold, and exhaustion.

That terrifies me!

● ● ●

The dried meat hangs like wet socks on racks around the three free sides of the wood stove.

The large quantities of meat we need to prepare before we

leave, and the frequency with which Magnus brings home dead seals, make it difficult to keep up.

The meat hangs in more rows than is optimal for good drying. The meat hung in the outermost rows, furthest from the direct heat of the stove, dries very slowly. So, once the inner rows are dried, we move the meat from the outer rows into the inner ones before hanging fresh meat on the outermost racks again.

Kristian and Emilie are working diligently, fully aware that our survival depends on having enough food for the long journey.

Kristian is still not convinced that it's better to leave than to stay, but he no longer opposes our decision. I'm sure the fact that Fatima is also leaving plays a big role in his active involvement in the work, even though he'd prefer we all stayed where we are.

He's still just a big child and hasn't yet fully developed the ability to grasp the consequences of staying. And who could blame him? Most of the adults around him aren't convinced of the wisdom of our decision either, and this, of course, strengthens his doubts.

I watch him covertly as his nimble fingers shift the meat from the outer rows to the inner ones. His medium-length hair now covers his ears completely. I still haven't cut it. I now think it's better to leave it, as it will protect his ears from the cold when we leave.

"I'm hungry," he suddenly exclaims and, without warning, throws one of the half-dried pieces of meat onto the scorching cast-iron top of the stove, where it immediately starts sizzling in its own fat.

"Kristian!" I snap irritably. "Use a frying pan, so you don't have to clean the whole stove afterward."

Cleaning the stove means letting the fire burn out and waiting for it to cool down enough to touch without burning yourself. For that reason, we usually do the annual cleaning in the summer when the outside temperature is warmest, not now, in early spring, when it still only creeps up to between five and ten degrees below zero during the day.

"Does it even matter?" he replies defensively. "We're leaving in a month anyway! What difference does it make if the stove's dirty or not?"

He glares defiantly at me. For a moment, I meet his glare without saying anything. I'm completely unprepared for such an outburst, which clearly isn't about cleaning the stove or hunger, but something else entirely.

"If something's bothering you, I think you should tell me directly instead of expecting me to guess what you're thinking," I reply calmly, holding his gaze. "But first, please take the meat off the stove before it burns. It doesn't smell very good!"

"Forget it!" he mutters dismissively, turning to scrape the meat off with a fire poker.

It lands on the floor between the drying racks. Kristian makes no move to pick it up, and I remind myself to set it aside for Mali when she returns later today with Magnus.

"Kristian, my darling. Tell me what's really troubling you, and we'll talk about it."

He whirls around to face me.

"I just don't think we should leave," he bursts out. "I think we should stay here like everyone else. You and Dad made the decision without me and Emilie, even though you always say we should make decisions together. And I don't want to leave!"

So he's still not fully at peace with the idea of leaving, I think to myself.

"I understand if you're scared, Kristian. I am too. But I'm even more scared of staying here."

I sigh wearily. We've had this same conversation countless times since that evening, but Kristian stubbornly sticks to his point.

"What will we do if the seals suddenly disappear?" I remind him. "Then it'll be too late to head south."

"Why on earth would the seals disappear?" he asks sarcastically, not expecting an answer. "Seals are adapted to life in the Arctic. They love the climate here. It's more likely that more seals will come here than that they'll disappear."

"Even if you're right, we have another equally serious problem," I challenge him. "There's not enough wood left in the forest to provide firewood for more than a few more years, and then we'll be forced to move anyway. By then, it'll probably be even colder than it is now. How easy do you think it will be to find new housing somewhere with enough wood to last for many years and near the coast where the seals are? The time we spend finding this paradise on earth, moving in, and settling down will take away from the time we have to gather supplies for the winter."

I'm growing tired of repeating myself to Kristian and all the other sceptics in town, but Kristian is my son, and I want him to understand Magnus' and my point of view.

We have to stick together because, as a family, we only have each other.

"How long do you think your father can keep making the trip back and forth to the coast if it gets even colder than it is now?" I continue, raising my voice just a bit. "Not to mention that there's a bloody polar bear out there now. What will we do if Magnus gets hurt? No one else has enough food to share with us."

"What about me?" Kristian cuts in sharply. "If Dad can't hunt, I can do it."

"And who will help me chop wood while you're at the coast?" I ask.

I avoid pointing out that, for one thing, he hasn't yet learned to shoot with a bow, and for another, he doesn't have the strength to pull a 300-kilogram sledge ten kilometres through snow, wind, and extreme cold.

I don't want to hurt his pride.

"What's the risk of someone getting hurt on the journey?" he asks, changing his tactic. "What about Emilie or Fatima? I don't think they're strong enough to make it. What will we do if something happens to them out there in the middle of nowhere? Then we'll really be on our own."

"Why wouldn't Fatima and I be strong enough to make it?" Emilie suddenly pipes up, looking up from her Harry Potter book, which she's been engrossed in throughout the entire discussion.

She's recovered now. The pneumonia lasted only a short time, though she still has some violent coughing fits now and then.

"Don't listen to him, Emilie. Of course, you're strong enough to make it. If you weren't, we wouldn't even be having this discussion, because we'd be staying here. But you *are* strong enough," I assure her. "And it's better to seek out life than to sit and wait for the cold to slowly finish us off."

I'm losing patience. The last thing we need is for Kristian's fear to rub off on Emilie, making her afraid to leave as well.

We can't let ourselves be ruled by fear, because fear paralyses us, and then we'll never escape from here. But we also can't be reckless and walk into something that leads us to certain death.

I feel like we're standing at a crossroads between these two extremes, and I'm constantly gnawed by uncertainty about whether we've made the right decision.

"Kristian," I say, turning to him again. "We're leaving. Your father and I have made the decision, and it's not up for discussion. We're going as soon as we're ready, and we will all survive the journey until we find help further south. I promise you that!"

"How can you promise that?" he asks, trembling with anger. "None of us know what's waiting out there. You can't possibly know!"

"Fatima is excited to leave," Emilie chimes in. "She says she can't wait to go somewhere warmer and try all the foods she's never tasted before."

Kristian looks at her in surprise.

"She's excited?" he asks, sceptically.

"Yes. She says the journey will probably be tough, but the reward will be so much greater. Her parents say there are loads of juicy fruits like apples, oranges, dates, and nuts, and plenty of delicious fish in the sea for us to eat."

Suddenly, Emilie turns towards me.

"Mum, have you tasted apples?"

"Yes, I have," I answer, once again feeling regret over the limited diet my children have grown up with.

"You have too," I continue. "But you were probably too little to remember."

"I remember," Kristian says. "But I've almost forgotten what they're like. They're crispy and juicy, aren't they?"

"Yes, that's right," I reply.

I look over at Emilie and blow her a kiss, which she catches in her hand. In an instant, she's turned the conversation into something positive about leaving.

"Oranges are sweet and even juicier than apples," I continue. "So juicy that it's hard to keep the juice from running down your chin when you eat them."

"Farhana says dates are like little jewels of the desert, and once you start eating them, you just can't stop," Emilie giggles. "I'm mostly excited to taste those."

"What else has Fatima said?" asks Kristian, who seems to have calmed down now.

Relieved that the crisis seems to have passed, I leave the two of them to talk more about all the exciting things they'll experience once we've arrived.

It's important they can see a goal on the other side, and it seems that Zaid and Farhana have been good at setting out those goals in a way that makes sense to the children. There's no need for me to intervene further. I'd probably just downplay the importance of new food experiences, and I must avoid that at all costs if that's what will help everyone stay positive about leaving.

I put on my thick fur coat, open the front door, and step outside onto the main street, where a cold wind is blowing from the west. The loose snow, not yet packed by our feet, drifts in small white clouds across the road.

The sun is hidden behind a grey blanket of clouds, which threaten to release their load at any moment. It's too cold for any precipitation to fall as rain. It's more likely to be icy sleet mixed with hail, stinging and pricking the skin.

I shiver and pull my hat down tightly over my ears before heading down the street to visit Farhana.

The meat from the latest seals Magnus brought home has already been cut into smaller pieces and is sitting in brine, waiting for space to free up on the drying racks around the wood stove.

There's no other urgent task right now, so I decide to check on how things are going at Farhana and Fatima's house and see if there's anything I can help them with in their preparations for the journey.

I admire Farhana and Zaid. Setting out on another flight for survival takes courage and mental strength beyond anything I can imagine. It would be perfectly natural if Farhana needs a shoulder to cry on, and now that Zaid is still away on the hunting trip, I want to offer mine if she needs it.

As I walk the short distance down the street, I look up at the sky again and let my thoughts wander.

It's been a long time since we've seen birds flying freely above our heads. We see them occasionally on the warmest days of summer, when insects swarm over the few ice-free patches of lakes. Then come the few insect-eating migratory birds that still find it worth the journey all the way to Denmark to breed, but their numbers are dwindling. Summers are becoming too short and too cold for the chicks to grow strong enough to fly south. We live on the edge of the birds' map, I think to myself, just as I reach Farhana's door.

She looks relieved when she opens the door and sees me. Her eyes are red, and it's clear she's been crying.

Before I can say anything, Fatima rushes out of the open door. As she passes me, she asks if she can visit Emilie and Kristian. Without waiting for a reply, she runs down the street in the direction I've just come from.

"What's going on?" I ask, confused, as we sit down wrapped in blankets.

Farhana and Fatima don't usually argue, but then again, Kristian and I don't usually either. We're all wearing our nerves on the outside these days.

"I don't know if I can do it again," Farhana sobs, breaking down.

She hides her face in her hands and begins rocking back and forth like a frightened child.

"I try to be strong for Fatima, but I'm so scared I just keep snapping at her."

I put my arms around her and rest my cheek against her sleek, black hair. I don't say anything, because nothing I could say will outweigh the memories she's reliving and her fear that they might happen again.

She's scared. She's as scared as I am of having to flee. But she's also scared of staying. Unlike me, though, Farhana has experience with both, and though I feel sorry for her, it strengthens my belief that what we're doing is the right thing. She would never put herself or her family through the same horrors again unless she were truly convinced that the alternative was worse.

I shudder at the thought of what lies ahead.

But we have no choice.

I just want my children to experience the joy of taking life for granted. They deserve that.

7 Magnus

Now that the decision to leave has been made, I feel as though a huge burden has been lifted from my shoulders. I'm not afraid of the journey, because unlike the girls, I'm used to walking the ten-kilometre route between the town and the coast. I know how to survive the cold and predict sudden weather changes that might require us to find shelter as quickly as possible.

Besides, we have Mali, who is incredibly skilled at staying on track, even when visibility is disastrously poor. What worries me the most is whether we'll make it all the way to Provence before winter returns. Emilie and Fatima are one thing, but Kasper is only six years old, and I highly doubt he'll be able to walk the entire way on his own. Mikkel is as strong as an ox, but can he really manage pulling his own heavily loaded sledge *and* Kasper at the same time when the boy gets too tired to keep going?

We have plenty of worries. I try not to let them get to me too much, but it's not easy. Not when it's not just my own life at stake, but also that of my family and friends.

I stop at the milestone that marks three kilometres until we reach the town centre. Mali looks curiously at me as I shrug off the harness from my shoulders and stretch my back to ease my overworked muscles. The many trips back and forth with heavy sledges over the past weeks are taking their toll. Normally, after a long winter break, it's better to rebuild muscle gradually, but this year, due to the decision we've made, that hasn't been possible. We're all feeling the strain now. Hopefully, we'll manage to build enough muscle to handle the journey without sustaining injuries along the way.

Worries! No matter how much I try not to dwell on them, they constantly confront me.

"Let's take a break, guys!"

Zaid and Mikkel, who've already passed the milestone, stop and look back, then silently shrug off their harnesses too. Like me, they stretch their backs thoroughly before leaving their sledges where they are and returning to the milestone, where there's an old bench we can rest on. Mali sneaks behind the milestone, where there's more shelter from the wind, and lies down against its back to catch her breath.

I notice that the back of the large milestone is greener than the other three sides. The snow-covered fields lie desolate, and along the field boundaries, the wild hedgerows stand tall and naked—something I hope will be widespread throughout our journey south. I'm still counting on them to provide us with burnable material on a daily basis. The hedgerows are a mix of trees and low bushes, originally intended to provide Denmark's wildlife with the best possible conditions.

"I can't help but think how harsh it must be even further north," says Mikkel. "Do you think the native Inuit have survived until now? I once saw a programme on TV about how they adapted to life on the northernmost coasts along Alaska's Pacific shore and Canada's and Greenland's Atlantic coasts. The land was covered in snow for up to ten months a year. It's that programme that's kept me going until now. I thought, if they can do it, so can we. Here, after all, we're more or less snow-free for three months of the year, and we have wood to burn, whereas they had to keep the fire going by burning bones and blubber."

"What made you change your mind then?" Zaid asks.

I look at him in surprise, as he sits hunched forward, elbows resting on his knees, staring blankly into space, as though his thoughts are somewhere else entirely. A cold breeze blows, causing his breath to condense into tiny droplets that drip from his nose and freeze into small crystals on his black moustache, slowly growing larger and larger.

Unconsciously, I brush my mitten across my own beard, which is just as full of ice crystals as Zaid's. The touch causes them to fall into the snow on the ground.

"It was the day after we first saw the polar bear. Do you remember, Magnus?"

I don't reply, just nodding slightly, unsure of where I fit into the story, but he doesn't elaborate.

"I realised how vulnerable we are out here, all alone."

Mikkel starts to say more but then changes his mind and falls silent. I look at him, silently encouraging him to continue, but he just shakes his head.

Five minutes later, I assume he's said all he wanted to. I get up and begin putting on my sledge harness. Mali soon stands by my left leg, ready to continue the journey home to our waiting family. Just as I'm ready to set off, Mikkel suddenly starts talking again.

"Anna suffers from anxiety, and on top of that, she sometimes has severe depressive episodes where she can hardly get out of bed. It's worst in winter when she doesn't see any sunlight."

Zaid and I stare at Mikkel in surprise.

Even though we've been hunting together for years now, I suddenly realise we know almost nothing about each other.

Everything revolves around survival. Nothing else!

Once Mikkel starts, he talks quickly, as if he's desperate to get everything off his chest before we embark on the long journey together.

"When people decided to head south, I raided all the pharmacies in town for anything that contained Benzodiazepines for acute anxiety attacks and Fluoxetine for depression. While you all were stockpiling antibiotics, I was stockpiling antidepressants. But we're running out of medication, and honestly, I don't know what to do when it's gone. I have no idea what other types of medicine might work, or how to dose them, if there's even anything left at the pharmacies.

She's always taken Fluoxetine. We know that drug, and we know it works.

The risk that she'll shut down completely and not be able to care for Kasper when I'm out hunting is far too great if the medication doesn't work properly. That's a risk I can't take. I won't take it! Maybe I can find some more of the familiar medication in the pharmacies in neighbouring towns, but when it's used up, then what? She needs a doctor.

The day you were all discussing polar bears and how vulnerable we are out here, all I could think about was Anna and her medication. I'm not worried about the polar bear, but it made me realise that this isn't just about me and what I can handle.

We couldn't have gone south earlier because of Kasper, and now we're practically forced to, even though he might not yet be strong enough for the journey."

Mikkel pauses briefly before continuing.

"For God's sake, I don't even know if Anna is strong enough for the journey. What am I supposed to do if she has a panic attack halfway through and refuses to keep going?"

There's a moment of silence, where none of us know what to say or how to react to this unexpected outpouring of emotion.

We all clearly have our individual struggles to deal with. The mind is a powerful travel companion. It can either be your friend or your worst enemy in the battle for survival. Nature doesn't care whether you're in control of your mind or if your mind controls you. Out here, only the law of nature reigns, and in nature, it's the strongest that survive! That much is crystal clear to all of us. If it wasn't before, it certainly is now.

In a family where two out of three members couldn't survive on their own, the mental strength of the third is tested to the limit.

I can't help but admire my younger friend for having carried such a burden for so long without buckling under the pressure.

Zaid, still sitting on the bench next to Mikkel, puts a protective arm around his shoulders.

"My friend," he murmurs. "You're not alone. The three of us are in this together. We'll get your wife and son to safety. I promise you that." He looks up at me. "Isn't that right, Magnus? There's no need to worry. We'll make it through, all of us."

"Like the three musketeers," I reply with feigned cheerfulness, even though a voice deep inside me questions whether we can really keep that promise.

There's a devil sitting on my shoulder, refusing to let me rest in the belief that everything will go smoothly.

As so often before, there's not much more we can say or do to encourage Mikkel, or anyone else in our situation for that matter. We've long since accepted that any reassurances that everything will be fine and that things will improve with time sound hollow and are hardly worth the respect we afford one another.

Empty promises. Nothing more.

"Let's go home," says Mikkel, standing up.

In doing so, he signals that the conversation is over. He's said what was on his mind, and there's no point in talking further about something we can't change.

As I pass Zaid and Mikkel's sledges, I glance briefly at the dead seals lying there with their glossy black eyes and beautiful grey-speckled fur. Their stiff whiskers jut out from their snouts like bristles.

Not long ago, I would never have considered shooting these lovely sea dogs. They remind me too much of real dogs. But boundaries are crossed when you're pushed to the brink of what you can handle.

A shiver runs down my spine as I briefly wonder what personal limits we might be forced to face in the near future.

I push the thought away and try to distract myself by thinking of Freja's naked body. It's not rational, I know. But I've found that for me, it's the best way to divert the negative thoughts that so easily arise on the long trips between the town and the coast.

Even if I try to occupy myself by planning different projects in my head, I somehow always end up back at the thoughts I'm trying to escape. But not when I think of my beloved wife's soft curves. Then I'm able to concentrate, and my imagination becomes so vivid that it's sometimes hard to wait until the kids are asleep in the evening before making love to her after I've returned home.

She usually calls it the hunter's wife's reward for gathering firewood while the hunter is out on the hunt, referring to the stereotypical Stone Age gender roles that we've so quickly re-instated as something perfectly natural.

When I think about it, we're having sex much more often now, when our freedom is more restricted, than when our sex life had to compete with all sorts of other activities like daily exercise, walking the dog, watching TV in the evening, the internet, mobile games, and so on. Sex is a great distraction from all the negativity.

I only realise we've passed the town sign when Mali brings me back to reality by gently nipping at my left knee. She wants to be let loose so she can run ahead, home to her family. I never keep her on a lead, but she knows she's only allowed to run home when I give her the command.

"Looking forward to seeing them again?" I ask, bending down to stroke her along her back. "Well, go on then."

She wags her whole body, happy for the attention, but she doesn't run off. She's still waiting for the proper command. I only give it when I say the word "free," at which point she bolts down the streets of the town like a shot, heading towards our home.

Before long, she'll be scratching at the back door with her paw, patiently waiting for someone to open it and let her inside into the warmth.

Sometimes, Freja or Kristian come to meet me when Mali has announced my arrival. Then Mali leads them back to me, jumping and dancing around us when the whole family is finally reunited.

To my great disappointment, I make it all the way home without meeting anyone along the way.

When I open the door, I see Fatima, Emilie, and Kristian sitting close together on blankets around the wood stove. Freja is nowhere to be seen.

Emilie looks up and, with exaggeratedly clear enunciation, greets me.

"Good evening, Your Royal Highness. Welcome back from your long journey. Her Ladyship is visiting the exiled desert princess, Fatima's royal mother. Shall I send the noble knight Kristian to escort her safely back to your stronghold?"

When she finishes, she blinks dramatically three or four times and gives me the biggest smile she can manage.

I burst out laughing and can barely manage to stammer a "Yes, please, I'd greatly appreciate that," before collapsing in giggles and having to sit down in the blankets with the girls.

The noble knight Kristian immediately dashes out the door.

Children's adaptability is remarkable. Even under such harsh and inhumane conditions, their imaginations somehow always manage to distract them and, for a moment, take the focus off the grim reality we live in.

Being able to slip relatively easily into another universe, where snow and cold no longer threaten to take your life, is, in my opinion, one of the best tools we have to maintain a healthy and strong mental state.

Their imaginary worlds prevent them from sinking into a dark hole where desperation and despair threaten to drown them in their own fear. As long as their imaginations continue to flourish in their young, still-developing minds, I'm fairly confident that they'll be alright for some time yet.

The day our children are no longer able to lose themselves in a parallel fantasy world is the day I dread the most. Because it would mean that I've failed to protect my family and that the world has become such a harsh place that the question of whether life is even worth fighting for anymore must start to press.

I haven't even taken off my outerwear before I collapse on the sofa. The difference in temperature between outside and inside makes me drowsy. I close my eyes for a moment, just to blink away the fatigue, but I must fall asleep instantly, because suddenly I wake to the sensation of Freja's soft lips on mine.

She kisses me gently.

I must have slept soundly, because when I open my eyes and look around the room, Kristian and Emilie are fast asleep, each wrapped in their own skin.

Fatima is nowhere to be seen; she must have gone home.

I blink in confusion and try to focus on my wife. She's sitting next to me, running her fingers lovingly through my stiff hair.

"You were sleeping so soundly after Kristian brought me back that I didn't have the heart to wake you," she says, smiling so that her dimples show.

"Isn't it rather warm in here?" I ask, suddenly feeling sweat trickling down my back under my clothes.

"Not really," she replies. "You're still wearing your outdoor clothes. That's why I woke you."

She starts unbuttoning my jacket and pulling it off me. It's so warm and snug that I immediately begin to feel cold as soon as my half-sweaty body is no longer protected from the cooler room temperature.

I'm still a bit groggy, so I let her pull my sealskin trousers off as well, after which I start to shiver uncontrollably.

I quickly burrow under the blankets.

Soon after, I feel Freja's bare skin against mine as she slips under the covers and presses herself tightly against me.

I'm still shivering, but soon her skin feels burning hot against mine.

She caresses my chest until I stop shaking. Then her hand starts to move lower. Lovingly but insistently.

She wants her reward for keeping the dried meat production going while I was away.

The hunter's wife's reward.

She rides me hard and long under the blankets, and when we're both sated, she stays on top of me.

She keeps me inside her until she falls asleep, as if to hold onto my full presence.

Before we venture into the unknown, fleeing the cold.

Part II

Summer storms

8 Freja

The weather gods are against us.

As a bad omen, the sky opens its floodgates early in the morning on the day of our departure. It envelops us in a freezing inferno of sleet and hail, relentlessly lashing the landscape with such force that we can barely see the other side of the street. It's utterly impossible to stay outside. We take turns opening the front door every so often, hoping to see the storm pass, but it continues all day without any sign of letting up.

In no time, the streets are covered with a thick layer of packed ice, growing thicker by the minute. In the backyard, our loaded sledges disappear under a white blanket, which we will have to chip off before we can leave. The dried meat is well protected under a layer of sealskin, so there's no risk of it getting damaged, as long as we can keep the skin reasonably dry. That's usually not a problem in freezing temperatures.

Later in the afternoon, Magnus opens the front door once more, hoping for a break in the horizon, but closes it again despondently as the storm seems to rage on with unchanged ferocity. He's barely outside for half a minute, yet his hair and beard are already coated in ice crystals, which melt and fall to the floor when he runs his hand through them.

"We'll have to postpone our departure until tomorrow," he mutters resignedly.

He opens the stove door to throw in another log. A spark flies out, burning his hand as he irritably tosses the wood into the embers with too much force. He instantly pulls his hand back, briefly rubbing away the sting, but otherwise doesn't seem to be too bothered by it.

"We've had clear skies and no wind for the past two weeks straight," he grumbles, not addressing anyone in particular. "And then, on the very day we're supposed to leave, the heavens suddenly open up."

I don't respond. When he's in that mood, it's best not to comment further and just let him calm down on his own. A day more or less probably won't make a huge difference in the grand scheme of things, but I understand his frustration. The last several weeks have been spent preparing for this very day, and we've all been eagerly watching the weather improve day by day. We've been fully convinced that we'd manage the journey.

Perhaps it's for the best, I wonder. Maybe we all need to be reminded that for the next three or four months, we'll be outside almost constantly. The weather is unpredictable and deadly if we don't take great care.

Kristian and Emilie are reading their books, unconcerned. It's their last chance to read for a long time, since we had to cut books from our luggage to keep the overall weight down. Right now, they see the storm as a welcome delay, allowing them to finish the books they've already started. For a few days, tensions were high—especially for Kristian—when it dawned on them that they wouldn't be able to bring reading material on the journey.

The storm traps us indoors for five whole days. The sledges have now completely disappeared under a thick blanket of snow, something we normally only experience in the autumn, just before winter returns.

This is the first time we've encountered such a violent storm this late in the year, having just entered the first of the summer months.

All four of us oscillate between desperation at not being able to leave as planned and doubts about whether our venture is even possible. Are we, as many in the village have constantly warned us, already too late? Is summer already over? If that's the case, we're in serious trouble, as we don't have nearly enough food or firewood to survive a winter that starts already in June. Neither do those staying behind in the village, for that matter. There simply hasn't been enough time to prepare.

Could this be the end of all life at these latitudes?

I wonder if Farhana and Zaid are managing to keep their spirits up. And Mikkel and Anna? We have no way of staying in touch while the storm rages, so we have no idea how our fellow travellers are holding up.

Can Anna avoid slipping into one of her panic attacks, where she freezes completely and becomes unreachable by reason? With this storm fresh in her mind, I wouldn't be surprised if she's now too frightened to come along.

When Magnus came home and told me about their struggles, I suddenly saw the couple in a new light. The inner strength Anna must possess is immense if, despite our harsh and uncertain living conditions, she has managed to keep her illness at bay. To not simply give in to the anxiety that must constantly nag at her mind.

I resolve to do everything within my physical power to ensure we all make it through alive, and that Anna gets the help she needs.

If we even manage to leave at all, I sigh quietly.

I glance over at the front door, where the sound of hailstones still beats against the wood and the shuttered windows. My thoughts swirl endlessly, while time drags on at a snail's pace. The waiting is unbearable.

It feels almost like that first winter, when the uncertainty of whether we would survive or die constantly hung over us like a heavy burden. A storm like this one, at this time of year, brings those cursed thoughts rushing back.

As if sensing my frustration, Mali suddenly rises from the blankets where she's been sleeping soundly for the past few hours. She stretches, then jumps up, placing her front paws on my shoulders to lick my nose. As if trying to reassure me that everything will be okay.

I wrap my arms around her and bury my face in her thick fur, while she energetically keeps licking, now moving to my ear.

Suddenly, I start laughing. Instantly, I feel the weight of all my negative thoughts lift from my shoulders, just as my ear gets more and more coated in dog slobber.

After a while, I gently push her down to the floor, where she pants with her tongue hanging out, smiling at me to make sure I'm alright again. Then she trots over to the living room door and starts scratching at it with one paw.

She hasn't been out to relieve herself all day, so I get up to let her out into the backyard, rubbing my ear dry with my sleeve as I go.

When I open the door, I have to help her over the slick wall of ice that's built up almost halfway across the doorway.

Mali quickly disappears into the howling storm to do what she needs to. The wind blows straight against the front of the house, so I have to shut the door behind her as ice crystals whip into my face, forcing me to close my eyes. The cold is so brutal that I already feel the first tingling signs of frostbite on my exposed cheeks after just a few seconds.

Mali's thick undercoat is warm and effectively shields her from the cold, while her outer fur repels rain and sleet. But even she must feel the unforgiving temperatures outside, as it's not long before I hear her scratching at the door to come back in. Her fur is already covered with a centimetre-thick layer of snow, which she shakes off in large cascades the moment I close the door behind her.

Magnus appears in the doorway from the living room.

"How's it looking out there?" he asks.

I sense the defeat in his voice and decide to sugar-coat the truth a little.

"I think it's eased up a bit. Maybe it's the end of the storm passing over us now. The last flick before the sun returns to-morrow morning."

I try to sound optimistic.

I can't know it as I say the words, but along the coastline, the sun is indeed starting to spread its faintly warming rays over the snow-covered landscape. The storm is on its way out, and seals have already gathered in large groups, hauling them-selves up onto the ice floes to enjoy the first touches of sunlight in days.

The polar bear, who had sought shelter from the storm in the dunes, has shaken the ice from his fur and now stands atop the highest point, savouring the scent of his larder. He's hungry and already in the process of selecting his next meal.

● ● ●

I wake to the sound of someone knocking at the door.

Confused, I sit up and look around. Everyone else is still asleep, even Mali. She's curled up close to Kristian, snoring softly.

Did I dream it? I stay seated and listen.

Only the faint crackle of the fire and Mali's snores break the silence.

The knock comes again.

This time, Mali wakes up and starts barking, though sleepily, without much effort.

At first, I'm surprised that someone has braved the storm to knock on our door.

Has something serious happened?

Is someone ill?

When the knocking sounds a third time, Magnus wakes up.

"What's going on?" he asks drowsily, pulling his blanket aside to get up.

"I think there's someone outside the door," I reply.

I should hurry to open it, to get whoever it is away from the storm, but for some reason, I'm frozen in some sort of shocked paralysis.

The storm.

I listen again to the quiet, now interrupted only by Mali's occasional barking. I can no longer hear the storm's fierce grip on the roof or the hail and sleet lashing against the windows.

It's eerily quiet outside.

Magnus opens the front door, and sunlight floods in.

I'm blinded and can't see who's standing out there.

The storm has finally passed, I think to myself, feeling a brief rush of joy. But it's soon replaced by a nervous tightening in my stomach, because this also means it's time to leave.

"I was beginning to think that storm would never end."

Zaid's deep, cheerful voice carries in from outside, filling me with relief. They're clearly doing well.

At the sound of Zaid's voice, Mali stops barking and trots over to the doorway, tail wagging, to greet him.

Zaid is crouching on top of the ice, more than a metre above floor level.

A broad smile spreads across his black beard as Mali jumps up, briefly acknowledging his presence. He knows that's all he can expect from her, as someone being not in her immediate family. He also knows it's more attention than any total stranger would ever receive from her.

● ● ●

It's hard work digging the sledges free.

The ice is tightly packed on all sides and above, so it takes a long time to clear them enough to pass a rope through the runners, front and back, and lift the sledges out of the holes.

We have three sledges ourselves, Zaid and Farhana have two, and Mikkel and Anna have the same. Seven sledges in total, each carrying between 150 and 300 kilos of supplies, all of which need to be hoisted up onto the ice.

The ice has become the new surface we're moving on, high above the usual street level. Right now, it's quite solid after five days of constant icefall and temperatures well below freezing. But as soon as the sun warms things up for a few days, it will start melting, leaving hidden holes beneath a thin crust, making the surface dangerously treacherous. There's a high risk of falling through and breaking a leg if we're not extremely careful.

"Lift!" Mikkel grunts as we try to heave Magnus's large sledge up and out of the hole.

Zaid and Mikkel are lifting one end together, while Magnus and I each take our individual end of the rope tied to the rear runners.

I'm not as strong as the men, so when we lift, the sledge tips towards me and scrapes against the edge of the ice, where it gets stuck. It's too heavy for me. I don't have the strength to both hold it and push it free again, so as I try to give it a good kick with one foot, I lose my balance and fall flat on my back. The rope slips from my hands as I fall, causing the sledge to swing towards Magnus and dig deep into the ice on his side.

Zaid, lifting diagonally across from me, loses his balance on the slippery surface and has to let go of his end of the rope to avoid being pulled into the hole.

The result is the sledge crashing sideways back down to the bottom with a loud thud.

"Is anyone hurt?" Magnus exclaims in alarm.

He's by my side before I fully realise what's happened.

He looks into my eyes with concern.

A broken foot or even just a toe would be disastrous at this point — not just for me, but for the whole family.

"I don't think I'm hurt," I reply with relief, glancing nervously at the others. "What about you?"

Magnus, Mikkel, and Zaid all shake their heads.

Everyone's fine.

"We need to be more careful," Magnus says, kissing me on the lips. "Even though we're behind schedule, it's better to take a little longer to get ready than to risk anyone getting hurt."

He stands up and looks down into the metre-deep hole, where the supplies have come loose and are now scattered across the bottom.

"Let's dig it out," he says determinedly, and starts pulling bags of dried meat out of the hole.

With everyone's help, we finally manage to lift the sledge and repack it, the last of the seven to be loaded.

At last, after what feels like an eternity, we're ready to depart.

Even though the evening sun still hangs high on the Danish summer sky, it's too late in the day to set off now.

I shudder at the thought that from tomorrow morning, our fate will truly be in the hands of Mother Nature's unpredictable and capricious mood, where autumn storms can suddenly appear in summer and bury us all under a metre of ice.

Whatever happens, I hope and pray that the humanitarian spirit of helping those in need is still intact wherever we go, because we'll need all the kindness we can get as we start over with not a penny to our name.

9 Magnus

The women are crying as we say goodbye. All the other men have already gone to the coast. They are five days behind on their winter preparations due to the storm, so only the women and children have come to wave us off.

We assure them we will arrive safely, but without any way to send word when we get there, I suspect our reassurances will remain just that.

The uncertainty about our future fate brings the most tears to the eyes of those who stay behind. For our part, it's the opposite. All of us who are leaving are convinced that those left behind have nothing to look forward to but a slow, freezing death.

My heart is a tight knot in my chest.

We see them standing at the edge of the town, watching us until we reach the southbound road that none of us has followed for years. There hasn't been any reason to; the seals are west, and the forest lies to the east.

No one speaks.

It feels as though we are abandoning our friends, knowing full well that nothing within our power can change the fate that awaits them. In my imagination I imagine them shutting themselves inside their homes as winter comes, but by the time spring breaks again, none of them will be alive.

How many winters can they survive yet?

If it's possible, we'll send a rescue team back to fetch them once we arrive. That's a promise we've made.

Heavy-hearted, I'm not sure how likely that really is. If it had been possible, I imagine we would have been evacuated long ago.

I try to push the gloomy thoughts away from my mind. Better to focus on our own challenges, which seem large enough.

The sun shines for the second day in a row. The top layer of ice we walk on has turned into a five-centimetre-thick slush, which soon seeps into our boots, making our feet both wet and cold. This could become a major problem along the way. If we aren't able to dry our feet and boots at night, we'll be forced to stop before we've even really begun.

The so-called trench foot, which claimed the lives of some 80,000 soldiers during the First World War, is a condition where the feet first become numb. They are then attacked by a red, itchy rash or turn blue from poor blood circulation. If the feet aren't kept dry and warm after the first symptoms appear, open sores and gangrene will soon follow.

"Let me know if at any point you can't feel your feet anymore," I say, looking to Kristian, Emilie, and Freja. "That means it's time to seek shelter for the night and dry our boots."

They all stare back at me with wide eyes and nod solemnly.

"No matter what time of day it is," I continue. "That goes for all of you."

I make eye contact with each member of our group.

Everyone knows the risk of trench foot. After all, we've lived in the cold for years now. But I don't want anyone playing the hero just because we need to cover a certain number of kilometres per day to reach our destination before winter overtakes us again. The storm has already set us back, and the icy, cold slush only slows our progress further.

We all have homemade spiked shoes to help us keep our

footing on the slick surface, but even though the sledges glide so easily across the ice that I can barely feel the 300 kilograms on it, it's still heavy work trudging through the slush.

Zaid and Farhana walk side by side in front of Freja and me. Behind us, the four children trudge along together with Mali, while Mikkel and Anna bring up the rear, ensuring no one falls behind.

Despite the melting sun, the air is still freezing cold, and we've all pulled our hats down snugly over our ears.

As far as the eye can see, the ice stretches out, reflecting a flickering light that, over time, becomes quite irritating, even though we're all wearing dark ski goggles. It's tempting to walk with my eyes closed, but I need to keep a watchful eye on the treacherous holes under the ice's surface. They can be hard to spot until it's too late.

Before we've gone far from the village, Mali starts falling behind. The damp slush is clumping into big balls in the fur around her paw pads, making it hard for her to move forward. I have no choice but to tie her on top of my sledge after cleaning her them.

The group continues moving while I take care of Mali, and I have to walk briskly to catch up. Just as I get back into my place in the column, Zaid's deep voice suddenly breaks the silence.

"The difference between being a war refugee and a climate refugee is that this time we had time to say goodbye and plan our departure. None of us are in immediate danger of dying right now, but we likely won't survive in the long term. The end result is the same."

I'm not sure who the comment is directed at, if anyone. No

one reacts, and most likely, it's just a conversation Zaid is having with himself in his own head, with part of it spilling out as words we can hear.

Freja and I exchange brief glances.

Water is squelching in my boots. At first, the feeling irritates me, but over time, I get used to it. I'm also not freezing my toes, as I would have expected. The constant movement keeps the blood circulating in them and warms the water inside my boots. As long as I keep moving, I don't think the cold will be a problem.

It's only when we take a short break after a few hours of marching that it becomes uncomfortable. My toes stiffen, and they're already starting to hurt a little by the time we set off again. The stiffness and pain persist only for a few minutes until my toes are back in motion and warmth has returned to the outer joints.

"I think we should slow down a bit," Mikkel calls out from his position at the back a short while later. "Not everyone's used to this pace."

I turn and discover Kasper and Anna walking side by side, a little behind Mikkel.

It's clear that the sledge's weight is giving Anna more trouble than it is for Freja and Farhana, even though it's still sliding relatively easily through the slush. She leans forward into her harness as if she has to put more weight into the pull, but she doesn't seem too exhausted.

Kasper plods along beside her. His short legs are struggling to lift his feet clear of the slush, so he's wasting a lot of energy kicking his legs through the muck. Water splashes up around him in small, sparkling, colourless cascades with each step he takes through the water.

"Zaid! Hold up!" I shout forward, and the column immediately stops.

The milestones along the road are buried deep beneath the ice, so I can't say for sure how far we've come. I doubt we've covered more than six or seven kilometres since we set out this morning, which is about one kilometre per hour. We're moving more slowly than I'd like, but the conditions are far from ideal. To reach our destination by October, we need to walk nearly 15 kilometres a day!

Under ideal conditions, that's entirely possible for an adult, but as the recent storm has clearly shown, we can't expect to cover that distance every single day. We estimate that the unpredictable weather will prevent us from staying outdoors about 20 percent of the days we have available. This means the actual distance we will need to cover each day is more likely to be 18-20 kilometres.

We still have many kilometres to go before we can afford to stop for the night.

I dread whether Kasper will truly be able to keep up all the way to Provence.

"Maybe Kasper should take a break on top of your sledge, Mikkel? The sledges are gliding more easily on this surface than we're used to, so I don't think the extra burden will affect you much."

Mikkel glances at me for a moment and nods.

"You're right," he says. "It won't make much difference to me. I'm not sure why I didn't think of it myself."

He turns resolutely to the boy.

"Come here, Kasper," he says, reaching out to help his son up onto the sledge's load.

Kasper gratefully settles into the thick sealskins with a leg on either side.

After about half an hour, he starts complaining about cold feet. Another half hour later, he can no longer feel his toes. None of us had considered that putting him on the sledge with wet boots would speed up the onset of hypothermia in his feet. The lack of movement in his toes simply reduced blood circulation and heat flow.

Not even 10 kilometres from the village, and we're already forced to stop for the night to warm the boy's feet.

It's not Kasper's fault, of course, and I don't blame him. I blame myself. If we're to reach our destination safely, we can't afford mistakes like that.

I know better.

Mikkel knows better.

Zaid knows better too.

We're used to the snow and frost, and we should have thought to wrap the boy's feet in warm blankets instead of leaving him in wet boots.

Abandoned farmhouses are scattered along the roadside, and it's not hard to find an empty house with a wood stove. We choose a small, whitewashed farmhouse between two barns. At some point, it likely housed a small herd of cows, pigs, and chickens.

The garden and the immediate surroundings have been stripped of all trees, but further out into the fields, I can see the tops of some trees poking through the snow.

"If we can't find anything to burn inside the house or in one of the barns, we'll have to go out and chop down one of those trees," I say, pointing with my whole arm towards the treeline.

Zaid and Mikkel follow the direction of my arm and nod in agreement.

The door is locked when we try the handle. Even though the previous occupants must have fled the house to escape the cold, they still took the time to lock up behind them, as if it were just a temporary evacuation. Understandable, I think. It's the same hope we've clung onto until now.

It's been a long time since I've felt guilty about breaking into someone else's home for shelter, so when Mikkel kicks the door open with a solid thud, I don't give it a second thought. It's become our right in our fight for survival.

The house is of the old-fashioned type, with wood-burning stoves in both the living room and the kitchen. Everything that could burn has apparently long been fed to the flames by the previous inhabitants. The house contains no furniture, no paintings, no interior doors, skirting boards, or kitchen cabinets. Only the carpets remain, and I catch a glimmer of hope that there might be wooden floors underneath. I bend down and pull up a corner of the carpet, only to discover it's laid directly on a concrete floor.

Anna and Farhana are busy getting Kasper's boots off, while the rest of us search the property for something to start a fire with.

I pause briefly on my way through the kitchen just as Anna pulls off his innermost socks. His toes and most of the tops of both feet are noticeably paler than the rest of his feet. The skin looks more stretched than it does on the heel, where it's wrinkled like a prune from prolonged exposure to moisture.

Anna examines his feet with a worried expression but breathes a sigh of relief when she feels the skin is still relatively elastic. This indicates only a superficial frostbite, a first-degree frostbite, which can still be serious though, if not treated.

"Can you feel anything when I touch your toes?" Anna asks,

rubbing them between her fingers.

Kasper shakes his head silently. Tears well up in the corners of his eyes as he presses his lips together so tightly they, too, turn colourless.

"We need to get the blood flowing again," says Farhana, grabbing the other foot and beginning to massage it between her strong hands.

I leave the women and Kasper to themselves.

Soon enough, when the blood begins to flow freely, he'll experience intense pain in his toes until they return to normal body temperature.

I feel sorry for him.

I wonder if this thoughtlessness on our part—on my part— might make Anna regret our journey and refuse to continue?

I hope not.

Kasper isn't my responsibility. I know that. Mikkel and Anna should have thought to wrap him up dry, but I still feel a great sense of responsibility.

Freja always tells me not to carry the weight of the world on my shoulders, but I can't help it. That's why I know I'll feel a deep sense of guilt for any misfortunes that happen along the way.

Mikkel comes running into the house with an armful of old planks. He passes me in the doorway just as I step outside.

"The roof has collapsed on the far side of the left barn," he exclaims excitedly and hurries into the kitchen.

He rushes to light the woodstove, eager to get some warmth going for his son's feet.

I find Zaid, Freja, and Kristian out in the barn, where the roof has indeed collapsed, likely after the owners of the house abandoned it. The weight of several tons of snow over the years has been too much for the old rafters, which have eventually given way, bringing the ceiling down with them. Broken beams, old planks, and crumpled metal roofing sheets lie scattered across the floor.

All three are busy pulling planks aside and breaking them into smaller pieces that will fit into the woodstove. It'll take a lot of planks to warm the room enough to keep us through the night.

Kristian smiles when he spots me.

"We're lucky, Dad," he says, throwing yet another piece of wood onto the pile with energy. "I was the one who found it."

"Well done, Kristian," I reply, giving him an encouraging pat on the shoulder.

I start carrying wood into the house as well.

Soon after, we're sitting around the two warm stoves, with our bare feet as close as we can get without burning them.

When I take my boots off, I'm shocked to see the condition of my feet, which have taken on a fungal texture after being wet for so long.

I carefully inspect Freja's and the children's feet for any blisters or open wounds but find nothing to worry about.

Freja checks mine, with the same result, and after some time with our feet near the warmth, our skin is as smooth and healthy as usual.

The three of us sit in the living room with Zaid and Fatima. Fatima has positioned herself right next to Kristian, listening intently to his youthful excitement as he recounts how, without much hope, he'd decided to investigate the barn for anything that could burn. Inside, he'd stumbled across a real treasure trove.

In another time, Kristian's story wouldn't have raised an

eyebrow, but nowadays, entertainment options are severely limited, so even small, trivial stories are told and retold with great success.

I watch the two teenagers.

I don't think Fatima is filled with romantic feelings for Kristian just yet, not in the same way that he clearly is for her. She looks up to him as a kind of heroic figure. That much is clear. As someone who's taken on greater significance for her than if she only saw him as Emilie's older brother. Romance is probably still an unfamiliar feeling for her, but it won't be long before that changes.

Kristian enjoys the attention and finishes his story with great enthusiasm.

Farhana and Anna have managed to rub warmth back into Kasper's feet out in the kitchen. When the blood begins flowing into his toes, he cries in pain. Anna cries too, but from relief that he only had a scare.

"I hope this icy slush doesn't continue too far south," I say to Zaid, who has been relatively silent until now.

He stares into the flames for so long before replying that I begin to doubt if he heard me. While I wait, I fish out a couple of pieces of dried meat from inside my anorak and give one to Mali, who is lying beside me with her head resting on my legs. She sniffs it cautiously before taking it in her mouth and noisily chewing on its tough texture.

With my sharp knife, I cut the other piece into smaller, bite-sized chunks, which I share with Freja. I'm hungry, and the salty taste feels satisfying.

"You two should make sure to eat something as well," I hear her say to Emilie and Kristian. "We've got a long day ahead of us tomorrow."

Obediently, they both take out a piece of dried meat from their own spotted anoraks. I can't help but smile when I see Kristian, like me, cutting his piece into smaller chunks, which he offers to share with Fatima. Just a few days ago, he would have done exactly as Emilie does—sticking the end of the meat into his mouth and gnawing on it until it frayed.

At long last, Zaid replies.

"It's hard to say. If we're lucky, it might stop after just one or two days' march. But given the strength of the storm, I think we should be prepared for it to stretch well into Germany. For now, it's still relatively easy to cross, aside from the discomfort of wet boots. But in a few days, once the sun has had a chance to dig deeper into the ice, we'll be wading through knee-deep slush, which I imagine will make it much harder to pull the sledges through. If you ask me, we don't have time to stick to 18-20 kilometre days as long as the surface is still walkable. When the slush gets deeper, we might not manage more than ten kilometres a day at best."

"Twenty kilometres at a maximum speed of two to three kilometres an hour means at least eight hours of hard walking," Freja chimes in, her internal calculator already working at full speed. "We also need time to find firewood for the night and to recover for the next day. Is it even possible for us to cover more distance than that without physically breaking down?" she asks.

"I don't know," Zaid answers. "Let's assume the slush continues for at least another 100 kilometres. If we also assume that the weather will prevent us from walking every fifth day on average, it would normally take us at least six days to cover that distance, if we manage 20 kilometres a day. If we can't cover more than ten kilometres a day, we lose another week on top of the week the storm has already cost us. So we're suddenly two weeks behind before we've even properly begun."

I let the truth of Zaid's words sink in.

A week's delay for just 100 kilometres.

What do we do if the storm stretches even further? 200 kilometres? Or 300? In that case, we'd quickly lose an entire month and wouldn't arrive until the end of October, when the autumn storms are at their worst.

I shudder at the thought.

I have no illusions that we'll be able to survive an unprepared winter on our own, even if we're as far south as Geneva or Lyon by that time.

"I can pull the sledge for more than eight hours," Kristian interjects, sitting up straight. He glances at Fatima from the corner of his eye. Is she impressed by his youthful bravado?

She's still staring at him with her hazel eyes, full of admiration.

He smiles shyly, trying to sound confident at the same time.

"I'm sure you can," I reply, playing along with his act. "You're strong."

Zaid catches my eye discreetly and gives me a knowing wink. He's also noticed Kristian's budding admiration for his daughter.

"But I'm not sure Emilie, Kasper, and Fatima can, even though they don't have sledges to pull," I add.

"We'll just have to take it one day at a time," I say, turning to Zaid. "If we go as far as the weakest among us can manage, physically, then we can't do much better than that."

"I know, my friend. I know."

• • •

The overnight frost freezes the top layer of water into ice during the night. By the time we are ready to continue early in the morning, the surface ice lies smooth and mirror-like, with a centimetre-thick crust that breaks as soon as we put weight on it. Beneath the crust, the water is still liquid in a five to six centimetre-deep layer, sitting on top of the more solid ice beneath.

For the first few hours, Zaid and I lead the way, side by side, breaking the crust for the others.

It's heavy work, as we have to lift our feet high with each step to free them from the icy edges of the holes made by our wet boots. As soon as we place weight on the foot that first lands on the crust, it cracks with a snap.

It's impossible to find good rhythm.

Our sledges break up the ice further behind us, creating a wide trail that makes it slightly easier for the others to follow. However, the trail is filled with broken ice fragments, which slip under their feet as they step on them, despite their homemade spiked shoes.

We move painfully slowly. The children, in particular, struggle to keep their balance, and they take turns falling into the wet layer beneath. Thankfully, the sealskin that all our outerwear is made from doesn't absorb much water, so only a limited amount of moisture gets through to the skin.

Mali no longer needs to be tied onto the sledge, as the snow and ice are frozen solid and no longer clump to the fur on her paws. At first, she walks eagerly on top of the ice crust, which is strong enough to hold her weight spread across four legs. However, it's so slippery that she struggles to get a firm grip, and after an hour's walk, she comes over and nudges my knee. She wants to ride on the sledge again.

By late morning, the slippery surface nearly causes a catastrophic accident.

Zaid and I need Mikkel and Freja to take over at the front, as the unnatural walking rhythm is taking its toll on the muscles around our hips. We step aside to let them pass between us and wait until everyone has gone by, so we can form a new rear guard.

As Farhana passes Zaid, she impulsively tries to give him a quick kiss on the cheek, but as she steps aside, she loses her footing and falls sideways in front of the sledge, which continues sliding forward on the mirror-like surface.

Kristian, walking just behind her, instantly reacts and grabs hold of her sledge, bringing it to a sudden stop just a few centimetres before the metal runners hit her shins.

However, Kristian's sledge behind him keeps moving, as a heavily loaded sledge on ice can usually only be stopped by slowing down over a long distance. It slams into the back of his calves, pushing him forward until its front runners hit the back of Farhana's sledge. It finally stops, with Kristian trapped in the small gap between the two sledges.

Apart from the shock and a small bruise on the back of Kristian's leg, both fortunately escape unharmed.

It could have been much worse.

Zaid and I both praise Kristian for his quick thinking. At the same time, I feel a huge sense of relief that he didn't get hurt himself.

Had I been able to see his face behind the dark ski goggles, I would have seen the fear in his eyes, mixed with a certain pride at being the hero of the day for the second day in a row.

Another story to bask in glory around the woodstove tonight, when we've settled in yet another abandoned house.

He deserves it, I think. If it hadn't been for him, the heavy sledge would likely have passed over Farhana's legs, resulting in a broken shin.

Freja fusses over him, as a mother would, and Kristian awkwardly tries to free himself when he notices that Fatima is watching him.

After the accident, we continue our progress, rotating teams at the front to act as ice-breakers.

Even though the sun is high in the sky, it provides no warmth. The ice crust doesn't melt noticeably during the day, and it remains an exhausting ordeal to break through it.

Mikkel takes a double shift at the front after Freja swaps places with Anna after about an hour. Then comes an hour with Farhana and Kristian, after which it's Zaid's and my turn again.

I'm very impressed by Kristian's endurance. He's becoming a strong young man. His years of cutting wood have given him a powerful and well-developed muscle mass, especially compared to when I was his age, spending my days on video games, TV shows, fizzy drinks, and crisps. It won't be long before he starts asserting his right to take a more active role in the decisions we'll have to make along the way.

Aside from the crunching sound of ice breaking under our feet and sledges, it's deathly quiet. There's no wind howling in our ears. It's been a long time since I last heard the roar of a machine, and birdsong is just a faint memory in my mind. Everything is desolate and abandoned, leaving us with the impression that we are the last people alive.

Despite our slow progress, I'm full of positive energy because we've finally taken the initiative to save ourselves. The decision had been weighing on me for so long, and now it's finally been made. We've taken matters into our own hands, and we're finally making an active effort to save ourselves.

Kasper's feet seem to have recovered well. He bravely pushes through the ice without complaining or showing discomfort. Anna watches him attentively. Every time he slips on the ice, she stops, concerned, to check if he's hurt.

Emilie stays close to her mother all day, as she has been used to during the past years of daily woodcutting. She looks longingly after her friend, who, following the morning's rescue, doesn't leave Kristian's side. She hates that Fatima has become so obviously full of admiration for her older brother that she hardly has time for Emilie anymore, leaving her feeling all alone.

We walk through a small village, the first since we left our own.

I'm not surprised to find it deserted, but I'm still struck by how many people stayed behind in our village in comparison. Abandoned cars are parked along the main street, wrapped in such a thick layer of ice that only the rooftops are still visible.

"The ice layer is much thicker here than it was at home," mutters Zaid as we pass the roof of yet another unidentifiable car.

"We're moving towards the centre of the storm," I confirm.

"That's good," he says. "The big difference in the ice thickness over such a relatively short distance suggests that the storm's extent is smaller than feared. Maybe not much more than 150-200 kilometres in diameter."

"Maybe," I reply evasively. I'm not convinced he's necessarily right.

"It's simple maths," he continues enthusiastically. "We're about 20 kilometres from home. The ice layer is 40 centimetres thicker here than it was there, which means it increases by 40 centimetres for every 20 kilometres. So 70 kilometres north, it must be more or less ice-free, and surely the same applies to the south?"

Everything can be calculated mathematically. We do it all the time. Freja more than others. We calculate how many kilos of meat we need, how many cubic metres of firewood per day, how many kilometres we can walk per day.

Simple linear calculations that are so crucial to our survival.

I'm not sure, though, that a storm's spread can be calculated linearly. In fact, I'm a little surprised that Zaid, usually such a thoughtful man, lets himself be convinced so easily.

We all need positive news to keep our spirits up. Maybe that's his real intention? To try to keep everyone's morale high?

Farhana always says that if it weren't for him, she would have given up long time ago.

"I hope you're right," I mumble. "At this pace, we'll never make it."

The windows of the houses we pass are all boarded up in an attempt to insulate against the cold. Some of the boards are cracked by frost. Behind them, you can see remnants of fabric stuffed into the gaps by the people who lived there, trying to insulate their homes further. It hasn't helped much. The battle was lost, and those people gave up long ago. I wonder if they survived long enough to flee south.

By the time exhaustion overwhelms us in the early evening, we've just passed a high road sign indicating that we're only 25 kilometres from home.

Twenty-five kilometres in two days, when we should have covered 40.

At this pace, we'll need at least a month longer than we can afford.

The conditions are far from favourable.

● ● ●

Two days later, we cross the border into Germany.

I glance up at the blue border sign with all the yellow stars, indicating the country's membership in the European Union. Or rather, it *was* a member of the European Union.

The Union that had ensured equal political rights, economic stability, and a united international trade front for more than 440 million European citizens. The Union that had given small European countries a voice in international affairs and mediated conflicts between nations to maintain peace. The Union that collapsed when the crisis truly hit, and it became clear to everyone that solidarity ends just when it is needed most. You help your closest first—your family. Then your friends. Your neighbours. The resources you have are shared with those you feel the closest connection to. Despite the Union, nationalism became too strong, and the sense of unity that Europe had prided itself on for so many years evaporated like dew in the sun when it was needed the most.

The ice we're walking on is now like knee-deep slush.

The sun has regained some of its usual summer strength, pushing back the frost during the day. Hats have been packed away, and the gentle caress of the light breeze is a balm for the soul after so many days of storms and frost, so late in the year.

I've taken off my ski goggles and stand for a moment, squinting up at the sun, enjoying its warm embrace on my bearded face. As I stand there, I can forget time and place for a moment and let my thoughts drift back to my carefree youth.

Back when summer meant sun, beach, cold beer, and flavourful ice lollies. When women lay scantily clad on the beach, getting white bikini lines on sun-bronzed skin, while us young lads queued up for the chance to rub their glistening bodies with UV-protective suntan oil.

Climate change had meant we were blessed with four months of uninterrupted sun and summer heat. It wasn't like that in our parents' time, when summer was an unpredictable affair with fluctuating temperatures, rain, and wind. Farmers longed for the good old days, when drought didn't threaten their harvest every year. But the rest of us enjoyed life and silently thanked the climate sinners for their contribution to the Danish tropical summers, year after year.

In the evenings, we watched the news reports about large migrations around the world, without a care. The poles were melting. Vast areas were suffering from drought. Others were being flooded. There was nothing we could do about it anyway, we claimed. The world is ever-changing, and as long as the masses stayed far away from our borders, we didn't really have to consider anything seriously.

Nature was just tidying up, we said. Where it was most needed.

We shouldn't interfere.

We were arrogant. We deliberately ignored the fact that these were people in need, fleeing for a better life. Fleeing for their lives.

We weren't alone. A growing number of Danes saw the problems associated with climate change as self-inflicted. That countries around the equator weren't properly prepared to face the challenges wasn't our fault, after all. These people had made their bed and now had to lie in it.

As long as we had our own security, life was wonderful. Deep down, we knew, of course, but it was easier to pretend we didn't. Sure, plenty of climate activist groups emerged, solemnly proclaiming they were fighting for a better planet, but the efforts were half-hearted, and the results were severely lacking.

Now, we can no longer pretend. The truth has caught up with us and left a bitter taste behind.

The criminals have been judged guilty, and the guilty have become victims, now forced to join the world's growing number of climate refugees.

Freja suddenly stands beside me and slips her arm through mine. I lean slightly to the side and kiss her gently on the forehead. She's sweaty, but as long as the wind stays calm and the temperature remains above freezing, it's not critical.

It's unusually hard work pulling the sledges through the slush. We plough through, struggling with every step. The days when the sledge glided smoothly over the ice disappeared along with the return of the warmth.

"Four days, and we're already a day and a half behind," she says, gazing out over the landscape ahead.

It looks just as desolate as the land we've already passed through. There's no immediate sign of any improvement in the ground's firmness.

Freja pops a piece of dried meat into her mouth and chews slowly.

We're eating more than planned because we're burning

more energy than expected. I worry we might run out of food long before we reach our destination, but I quickly dismiss the thought. I have to stay optimistic.

"Are you holding up?" I ask her, alluding to the heavy load.

My own shoulders and back are aching, and I imagine she must be suffering the same.

"Right now, I wouldn't mind having the frost back," she says, giving Mali a piece of meat. She swallows it without tasting it.

"Careful what you wish for," I reply.

These days, wishes like that come true far too easily.

"I know," she says. "But at this rate, we'll wear ourselves down long before we're halfway. Kristian will never admit to it, but I can see he's struggling. And Emilie too."

"Maybe we should take a day's rest to regain our strength," I suggest. "It's better to be another day late than to not be able to continue at all."

She nods thoughtfully. Our slow progress worries her, but she agrees with my assessment.

"I heard Anna ask Mikkel earlier if it wouldn't be better to turn back to the village," she says after a brief pause. "I think she's digging deep into her reserves right now. We all are. Maybe you should talk to Mikkel and see what he thinks? Get his assessment. He knows her better than anyone. If they turn back, they're doomed, and we both know it. If he thinks she needs a day's rest, then we'll take it."

"You're right," I say. "I'll talk to him now."

Mikkel and Anna are standing a little off to the side. She's leaning against him, her back to him, nestled in his embrace. He rests his chin on the top of her head.

They're clearly enjoying the sun. It looks peaceful, and at

first glance, there's nothing to indicate a crisis brewing.

Kasper is lying flat on his stomach on Mikkel's sledge, his arms and legs spread out like a baby koala clinging to its mother's back.

"Keeping your spirits up?" I ask as I approach.

They both open their eyes and look at me for a moment. I can see the exhaustion in Anna's eyes, the dark rings beneath them standing out starkly against her pale skin. We're all suffering from dark circles under our eyes, especially in the spring, due to a combination of lack of sunlight and a monotonous diet. When fatigue sets in, they become even more pronounced than usual.

"It's tough," Mikkel says. "It is for all of us. That cursed storm hit us at the worst possible time."

"It did," I agree. "We're about 50 kilometres from home now. Zaid is convinced we'll be out of this terrain in three or four days, once we reach the edge of the storm's reach. Right now, it's melting quickly. We can hope the ice will have melted away completely when we get to the last 20 kilometres of the storm's extent, where the layer is thinner. If that's the case, we'll be through it in two or three days."

Mikkel pulls Anna even closer, as if she's a good luck charm that can make the prophecy come true.

"Two or three days," Anna murmurs softly, addressing Mikkel. She sounds worn out. "At this pace, we're at least five days away from home." As Freja hinted, this isn't the first time this topic has come up.

"What can we expect once we're out of the area?" Anna asks.

"We have to believe the snow will melt away as it usually does," Mikkel says. "Once the snow is gone, we'll move much faster. And with a fraction of the effort we're putting in now.

Turning back would be suicide."

"Mikkel's right," I agree. "It would be a death sentence."

My last remark risks opening a door we all try to keep tightly shut. It's the door that, if we step through, confronts us with the loss of the friends we left behind. Friends we know deep down we'll probably never see again, because death will claim them far too soon.

"Freja and I suggest we take a day's rest to recover our strength," I say. "Everyone's exhausted, and we think it's better to gather strength now, before we're completely worn out."

Mikkel replies quickly.

"I think that's a good idea. Let's rest and get back on our feet before we continue."

He gratefully accepts the lifeline I offer him, nodding in thanks. Anna is probably even closer to the edge than I imagine. This only confirms that it's absolutely the right decision, despite the pressure we're under.

She doesn't react, but I sense the relief surge through her as I leave them to inform Zaid and Farhana.

On the German side of the border, we find a solitary, abandoned house hidden behind a cluster of downy birch trees, which have so far survived both the frost and the firewood stove. Downy birch trees are highly resilient to extreme cold. They are widespread throughout most of Northern Europe, Siberia, and Alaska and were among the first tree species to take root in Denmark after the last Ice Age. The trees in front of the house are bare, but small buds on the branches hint that it won't be long before the pale green leaves emerge and once again cover the white trunks. To survive the frost, the tree drains its trunk of water before winter, greatly reducing the risk of frost bursting the cells in the wood. This way, the tree avoids freezing to death, but the longer the winter lasts, the greater the risk of the tree dying from dehydration instead. Strong winds and heavy snowfall can then cause branches or trunks to snap, inflicting severe damage on the tree.

However, these trees still stand tall and strong, and I feel guilty that we have to cut them down in order to survive the cold of the night. When all life around you withers away, you appreciate all the more the plants that still defy the cold year after year and refuse to give up. The Danish national tree, the beech tree, was not quite so hardy. Sensitive to prolonged drought, the trees quickly died as the frost set in and winters became longer. Much of the logging the women carried out in the village was from dead beech trees that had already succumbed during the first years of harsh frost.

The house doesn't appear to have been lived in for quite some time. There are no makeshift shutters nailed to the windows, and the wood panelling inside, halfway up the walls in the hallway and kitchen, is still intact. We deliberately seek out older houses, as more modern homes have had to forego wood-burning stove installations in favour of more CO2-neutral building regulations.

Before long, we have dismantled the interior wood panelling. Door panels, skirting boards, and part of the ceiling boards are ripped apart and placed in the stove. With a bit of luck, we can spare the birch trees outside, even though we plan to stay here for two nights.

We set our wet boots to dry. Our feet continue to suffer from the damp conditions inside our boots. They're not exactly frozen, but the skin has taken on a spongy appearance that no longer disappears overnight, even though we dry our feet thoroughly. Both Kasper and Emilie have developed painful blisters between their toes, where skin has rubbed against skin hour after hour, day after day. The blisters are undoubtedly caused by the persistent moisture in their boots. Freja cuts thin strips of soft sealskin and places them between the children's toes, hoping this will ease the skin and prevent the blisters from worsening.

Because of the cold, they don't feel much discomfort from the blisters while moving during the day, but in the evening, when the warmth of the stove is allowed to heat their skin, it's a different story. The burning sensation is especially intense where the skin has split and the flesh beneath is exposed.

Tonight, we all feel equally tired and disheartened. It's hard to imagine an end to the mire we've been stuck in for the past few days. Zaid stubbornly insists that we'll soon reach the edge of the storm's reach, and then we'll be able to pick up speed.

It turns out he's right. Two days later, we suddenly find ourselves looking at large patches of bare earth and asphalt amidst all the white.

We burst into loud cheers and embrace each other as if we've already reached the end of our long journey. The extra day of rest did us good. Now we have the strength to keep going, though it's still tough. I guess the daytime temperatures are now around ten degrees, while at night, it's still well below freezing.

Since the storm passed, the wind hasn't picked up to much more than a light breeze, so the biggest challenge has been the thaw and the vast amounts of melting ice.

As the days go by, the ice disappears too. Eventually, we're forced to stop and modify the sledges with the wheelchair wheels we brought from local care homes back home.

This isn't a new technique for us, invented for this journey, but born out of necessity when we had to transport seals from the coast after most of the snow had melted during the summer.

The modification is quick. We had previously installed axle holes on either side of the sledge, both at the front and back. The snap-lock axles of the wheels fit into these holes, so that when the wheels are clicked into place, the sledge runners now hover about 25 centimetres above the ground.

The biggest problem is lifting the heavy sledges high enough to click the wheels on, but with everyone helping, it's a minor issue.

The sledge now has four wheels with puncture-proof tyres and is easy to pull behind us on the snow-free roads.

If you've never lived for months on the ice and snow, it's probably hard to understand the significance that dead grass, ghostly trees, bare earth, exposed asphalt, visible road signs, and budding birch trees can have on your morale. Just the colours, after all that blinding white, are enough to stir a feeling of happiness inside you.

For a moment, you forget time and place.

Mali runs joyfully, marking her territory everywhere, sniffing excitedly at everything above street level. She's been tied to my sledge for a whole week, so the freedom must feel wonderful. A big smile is plastered across her doggy face from ear to ear as she bounds from Freja to Kristian and then to Emilie and me, showing her joy at finally being set free.

She rewards me with playful nips on the knee before leaping off again to enjoy her newfound freedom.

Emilie laughs out loud at Mali's antics and momentarily forgets the pain between her toes as she chases after her across the fields by the roadside.

The blisters haven't had enough time to dry out and form new skin, so both Emilie and Kasper still suffer from them. Kasper has even developed new ones. The sealskin strips between their toes have spread their toes so much inside their boots that now blisters have formed on the outsides of their little toes as well.

Unlike Mali, the children's freedom has become more restricted, as they're mostly forced to ride on the sledges to avoid worsening their condition.

I'm no longer worried about frostbite on their toes due to lack of movement, as the daytime temperatures remain well above freezing.

In the following days, we manage to keep up a brisk pace. I reckon we make up a few kilometres each day, but without GPS, we can't be sure, so we rely on instincts and the experience from many walks between the coast and the village, as well as the maps we brought from the library before we left.

The carts roll easily on the asphalt, and the aches we had started to feel in our shoulders and backs after pulling the sledges through thick slush for days are easing day by day.

Spirits are high. Even Anna seems to have regained her optimism. There's a shared budding belief that we'll make it.

Until, suddenly, the weather changes. Almost out of nowhere, a low-pressure system forms above us. A storm is rapidly brewing, and before we know it, snow is falling so thickly that we can't see even a metre ahead. The temperature plummets, and with the storm-force winds, the summer-like feelings of the past few days vanish in an instant.

We're on a desolate stretch of road, where houses are few and far between, so there's nowhere nearby to seek shelter.

We're forced to stop and put on hats, gloves, ski goggles, and outerwear before the cold can tear at our exposed skin.

Emilie's outerwear is packed under the skins on Freja's sledge, so I help her down from mine and send her down the column to meet up with Freja, who is bringing up the rear.

Mali appears at my knee almost immediately. She knows that one of her most important tasks lies ahead. She must lead us to the nearest house for shelter, as we humans are practically blinded by the fierce snowstorm.

We set off once everyone has put on their outerwear.

The wind cuts through to the bone. I can tell that if we don't find shelter soon, we are in serious danger of freezing to death.

We make sure to stay close enough together that we can still see the person in front.

I walk at the front with Mali. Kristian follows right behind with Fatima by his side. I can't see him, but I can faintly hear his voice through the howling wind as he shouts that he's ready.

Now it's up to him to stay so close to the back of my sledge that he doesn't lose sight of it. If he does, he and the rest of the group might end up wandering blindly for hours without ever finding shelter.

Before long, the contours of the road are blurred. It's impossible to spot the driveways to the few houses that must line the route.

Mali is our best, and perhaps only, hope. She tracks ahead of me and corrects my direction at regular intervals when I get too close to the ditches along the road. It would be a disaster if the sledge's wheels went over the edge, causing it to topple into the ditch.

I trust her sense of direction and immediately adjust my

course whenever I feel her gentle nudges against my knee, steering me away from the side she wants me to avoid. Inside my ski goggles, I stare into a white, impenetrable curtain of snow pouring down over the landscape. I desperately try to catch a glimpse of a house nearby, but I can barely see my own feet.

The asphalt we're walking on has absorbed just enough heat from the sun that the snow settling on the road becomes thick and wet. Under different circumstances, it would have been perfect for snowball fights or building snow forts. But right now, it's a problem, as the surface beneath our feet has turned as slippery as soap.

My steps become short and tentative, and despite the seriousness of our situation, I can't help but think of the classic Disney scene of Bambi slipping on ice, which used to air on TV every Christmas when I was a boy.

The ski goggles don't cover my entire face. I feel the frost biting at my nostrils as I breathe. In the rush, I didn't put on a scarf, so I have nothing to protect my mouth or nose. Soon, I start to feel the first prickling sensations on my lips, signalling the rapid approach of frostbite. I try to hold my hat tightly against my cheeks to protect my ears from the cold, but it's hard to keep a grip on the hat while maintaining my balance on the icy ground.

The wind chill is so intense that I feel my energy draining with every step I take.

When Mali eventually starts nudging me more persistently to the left, I'm so exhausted that I barely register her touches at first. Lost in my thoughts, I've unconsciously shut off all external stimuli as a way to cope with the discomfort.

But Mali doesn't give up. She starts biting my knee repeatedly until my instincts finally kick in and I respond to her efforts.

Could she have found a house?

I still can't see more than a metre ahead, so it's impossible to say for sure, but I trust her and decide to follow her lead. I pause briefly before leaving the road to make sure Kristian is with me. He comes up beside me, and I gesture with my hands that we're turning off. He nods in agreement.

We continue walking for what feels like an eternity. I'd expected us to step onto an open courtyard, sheltered by a house and maybe a few outbuildings, but soon it dawns on me that we're walking down a long gravel driveway.

I have no idea how long we've been going. Five minutes? Ten minutes? Time stretches out painfully slow as we inch forward in desperation to find shelter. Perhaps it's not as long as it feels?

Suddenly, Mali brings me to a halt. She tugs at my trouser leg. We've arrived. She's found our safe haven.

I glance around and can just make out the faint outline of a black door through the falling snow on my left. I quickly shrug off the harness from my shoulders and reach for the door handle. It's unlocked, and I rush inside, escaping the storm.

Kristian, Fatima, and Mali are right behind me, followed by Farhana, Zaid, Mikkel, Kasper, and Anna.

As Anna closes the door behind her, being the last to enter, my stomach clenches in dread as I realise Freja and Emilie are nowhere to be seen.

A surge of panic washes over me.

I rush back outside. The snow immediately envelops me, blinding my vision. I run up and down the road, frantically calling out for Freja and Emilie in turns.

Have they gone too far? Have they passed the house?

My voice is swallowed by the storm's roar, so deafening they probably wouldn't hear me even if they were just 20 metres away.

It slowly dawns on me that they likely didn't follow us down the gravel driveway. They're still out there somewhere, lost on the main road, alone and at the mercy of the raging snow-storm.

10 Freja

I'm in the process of putting on my thick sealskin jacket, hat, gloves, and ski goggles when Emilie suddenly breaks through the falling snow and stands in front of my sledge.

"Dad sent me down here," she says, looking at me with her big, ice-blue eyes.

She's shivering violently in the cold, and her lips have already lost most of their usual red colour.

"My outer clothes are under the cover on your sledge," she continues through chattering teeth and starts pulling at the protective blanket, which lies over the sledge like a heavy, snow-white layer.

I can barely hear her, as the wind howls so fiercely in my un-protected ears. The cold stings my earlobes and fingers as I fasten the last buttons on my coat, but I prioritise helping Emilie retrieve her outerwear before finishing dressing myself. She struggles to free her jacket from the heavy sealskins, so I tuck my gloves and hat under one arm and hurry over to assist her.

As I pull the hat down over her ears, I don't think to hold onto my own, which is still clamped under my arm. I drop both the hat and the gloves into the snow, where the wind im-mediately catches the lightweight hat. Before I can react, it's swept away by the wind into the swirling snow.

Panicking at the thought of losing it, I quickly bend down to grab the gloves before they too fly off. My ears are burning. It won't be long before frostbite sets in if I don't get them protected from the wind and cold.

"Stay here," I shout as loud as I can and rush off in the same direction as my hat disappeared.

I'm completely blinded by the blowing snow, but I have only one thought: to get my hat back before I lose both ears. I stumble forward without any clear direction, trying to catch a glimpse of something dark fluttering in the wind.

The snow stings and pricks at the exposed skin on my face. I haven't had a chance to pull up my scarf to cover it yet. The pain is almost unbearable, and I try to shield my ears and cheeks with my gloves as I press on.

I quickly lose track of how far I've wandered from the sledge and Emilie. Suddenly, I trip over a stone at the roadside and fall headfirst into a small thicket that stretches as far as I can see in both directions—not far at all.

As I push myself free of the branches, my eye catches a dark object caught in the bushes about a metre to my right. My hat! It's followed the same path as I have and got stuck in the same bushes.

Gratefully, I pull the hat free and tug it firmly down over my ears. They hurt so much that tears well up in my eyes.

When I turn around, I realise I've wandered so far away from the sledges and the others that I can't even make out their outlines through the curtain of snow. Panic rises again, but I force myself to take deep breaths and stay calm.

My fall has disoriented me, and I'm no longer sure of the direction I came from. I freeze, desperately scanning for something that might help me figure out where to go to get back to Emilie and my sledge.

The wind lashes mercilessly at my face.

I'm about to turn my back to it when it strikes me—the hat must have been blown in the wind's direction, meaning the sledges must be straight upwind. Relieved by this realisation, I bend slightly forward and begin walking back against the strong wind. Frozen snowflakes sting my face, threatening to tear the skin from the unprotected parts.

Before long, to my great relief, I spot the outline of my sledge and Emilie, who is standing there, peering out into the snow curtain, looking for me. When she sees me, she begins waving her arms wildly. I can clearly see the panic in her movements, as she shouts something I can't hear. She keeps shouting and pointing in the opposite direction, towards the front of the column, until I reach her.

"The others have gone!" she screams in panic, tugging at my coat.

She throws herself into my arms, sobbing uncontrollably.

"They've left, Mum! I couldn't see you, and I didn't know what to do."

It takes a moment for me to fully grasp what she's saying.

Gone?

Who's gone? I think, knowing that no one in the group would leave anyone behind to face their fate all alone under these conditions.

I peer ahead, towards the next sledge in the column, but I can't see it. I push Emilie slightly to the side and walk a few metres forward. She follows me closely.

"I was scared you were lost too, and that I was all alone," she sobs behind me.

I hear her, but I can't respond or comfort her, as it suddenly hits me what she meant by *the others have gone*.

The others *have* gone.

Magnus has abandoned us!

They've left us completely at the mercy of the storm, with no one or anything to guide us to safety.

I feel anger flare deep inside me, a burning sensation that, in stark contrast to the cruel cold outside, starts in my toes and quickly rises until it reaches my brain and explodes in a verbal outburst, mingling with the howling wind and fading into the snow's muffling blanket.

I turn around and see Emilie staring at me, wide-eyed, as though I've lost my mind. My anger is instantly replaced by an overwhelming surge of maternal instinct. I will do anything to protect my child. I pull her close, and we stand there in each other's arms for a long time as I let my thoughts race.

We have no choice but to start walking in the same direction as the others and hope that we either catch up with them or don't miss the house they might have found shelter in.

"How long ago did they leave?" I ask.

"I don't know. You were gone for what felt like forever. I didn't think you were ever coming back."

I crouch down and look as deeply into her eyes as I can, holding her face between my hands.

"That must have been a horrible feeling, sweetheart," I shout, trying to make myself heard over the storm. "But I'm here now, and we will find the others. I promise. But we have to stick together and not lose sight of each other. Can you help me with that? Stay close to me and never let go of the sledge."

Emilie nods seriously.

"I promise," she replies bravely, pausing briefly before continuing, tearfully. "When they shouted if we were ready, I called back that you were missing, but they left anyway. Why did they do that, Mum? Why didn't they wait for you to come back?"

"Maybe they heard your voice but couldn't make out what you said, so they thought we were signalling that we were ready to go," I reply. "It's hard to hear anything over the storm. I'm sure they didn't leave us behind on purpose. As soon as Dad and Kristian realise we're not with them, they'll definitely come back to search for us with Mali. We just need to keep walking in the same direction as them. Everything will be fine. Come on, let's get moving so we don't fall too far behind."

I try to sound confident, but deep down, I'm just as scared as Emilie. I'm having to push myself hard not to fall into a consuming, self-destructive panic attack. The truth is, if we don't find shelter soon, we're doomed. The likelihood of us dying right here in the middle of a desolate road in northern Germany feels dangerously real.

I have to keep a clear head, even though what I really want to do is sit down and scream as loud and as long as I possibly can. Instead, I fasten myself into the harness and prepare to move on. Emilie holds tightly onto the sledge behind me, and slowly we set off. I pull the sledge up to speed, and we move forward, hopefully following the same path the others took. The snow has already erased any tracks they may have left behind.

I try to stay in the middle of the road, but visibility is so poor that it's difficult to navigate. We haven't gone far when I feel the ground change beneath my feet and realise we've drifted too far to the right, heading into the verge. I try to steer us back, but two of the sledge's outer wheels have already slipped off the road, making it impossible to pull it back onto the asphalt. We have no choice but to keep going along the right-hand edge, where it's nearly impossible to spot any sheltering buildings on the opposite side of the road.

As we walk, it feels like the wind has grown even stronger. Blasting from the southwest, it whips straight into our faces, forcing us to turn our heads away from it. Every 20 steps, I force myself to look up, hoping to catch a glimpse of some building in the distance, but the wind bites so fiercely at my skin that I have to turn away after just a few moments.

The cold drains my strength so quickly that my legs feel like they could give in at any moment. Under normal circumstances, I would be clear-headed enough to realise that our chances of survival would be much higher if I abandoned the heavy sledge and continued without it, but my brain is shutting down so much that all I can think is that the sledge is necessary because it's what Emilie holds onto to avoid losing me. So, we trudge on slowly, the sledge dragging behind like a heavy anchor in the wind.

Every now and then, I reach back to make sure Emilie is still with me. She slips a few times in the snow but manages to pull herself up and keep going, determinedly staying on the sheltered side of the sledge. We don't see a single building where we could take cover.

I briefly wonder where Magnus and Kristian might be, but my mind is no longer functioning clearly. I picture them sitting safely at home in the village, warming themselves by the stove.

I don't know how long or how far we've walked when my legs finally give up, and I collapse into the snow. The sledge behind me rolls slowly forward until it bumps into my back and comes to a stop. I barely register it. The pace is slow, and it doesn't hurt. I try to pull myself up, but I'm so drained of energy that it's impossible. Instead, I remain where I've fallen, snow rapidly piling onto my shoulders.

I feel Emilie beside me, but I can't hear what she's saying. She's trying to help me stand, but I'm like a heavy rag doll, limp and unresponsive, and she doesn't have the strength to lift me. Suddenly, she's gone again.

I sit alone in the snow, feeling life slowly drain from my body, pulled out by the icy storm. I lie down and close my eyes. My thoughts seem to be blown away by the wind, and I feel an indescribable calm spreading through me. I no longer feel the cold or the wind tearing at me.

"Mum! Wake up!"

Somewhere far off, I hear a voice calling, like a distant echo.

"Mum! Come on. Wake up!"

The wind tugs even harder at my clothes, and I grow irritated that I can't just sleep in peace. But I open my eyes anyway and see Emilie sitting next to me again. I smile weakly at her and try to say something, but no sound comes out of my mouth.

"Mum, come here," she shouts. "We're more sheltered from the wind under here."

She pulls at me. I struggle to understand what she's saying until I finally realise she wants me to come under the sledge. With one last effort, I manage to drag myself beneath it, and immediately feel relief from the storm's merciless assault.

The last thing I remember is Emilie curling up next to me. She wraps us both in a heavy sealskin blanket before my eyes close again, and I drift into sleep. I wake briefly a few times, dimly aware that the storm is still howling outside as I slip in and out of consciousness, unsure of what is dream and what is reality.

At one point, I feel Emilie in my arms, huddled against my chest. I feel the warmth of her body, and I pull her closer to me before falling back into unconsciousness.

I dream of a polar bear breathing into my face and lying down on top of me with all its weight, but I don't feel afraid. There's something comforting about the bear. In the dream, I'm a little girl, snuggling trustingly into its thick, soft fur. The warmth from it spreads slowly until I'm drenched in sweat, but I can't escape its embrace. The polar bear is protecting me and won't let go, even as I struggle violently. Instead, it starts licking my face as if I were its cub in need of a bath.

It disturbs my sleep, and I try to push its head away, but that only encourages it more, and then it starts calling my name.

"Frejaaa. Frejaaa. Wake up!"

It shakes my limp body with its big paws.

I open my eyes and stare into Magnus' bearded face.

He looks worried, but then suddenly breaks into a huge smile.

I'm confused. Where's the polar bear, and how did it turn into Magnus? I glance around in bewilderment and am immediately rewarded with a thousand kisses from a warm, wet dog tongue.

Mali?

"She's awake, Emilie!" Magnus calls out.

He gently pushes Mali away and strokes my hair lovingly. I focus on his face, which is no more than 30 centimetres from mine.

Above him, I see the underside of the sledge. I vaguely remember crawling under it and Emilie wrapping me in blankets.

I'm warm now and try to free myself from the blankets, but I'm lying on my side, and the polar bear seems to have settled in behind me. I can barely move, squeezed between it and Magnus, who is pressing in from the other side.

I elbow the bear repeatedly in its thick stomach, as hard as I can, trying to get it to shift.

"Hey, easy now!" it grumbles with a deep, familiar voice.

It moves away from me a bit, giving me more space. I wriggle onto my back and free myself from the blankets, trying to shake off some of the excess heat.

Then I remember how cold I had been earlier, and I can't understand how I could feel so warm now. Am I dead? The thought flickers through my mind, and I turn my head, curious to see the polar bear that has apparently decided to befriend me.

To my surprise, it's Zaid behind me instead. He's smiling too. Suddenly, out of nowhere, Emilie flies at me, throwing her arms around my neck.

"Oh God, Mum! I was so scared you were going to die," she cries, tears streaming down her cheeks.

"Emilie, my darling! What happened?" I ask. "The last thing I remember was the freezing cold, and that I couldn't stay awake. Where are we?"

"Your daughter saved your life," Zaid says, his voice full of admiration. "She showed incredible bravery and quick thinking in impossible conditions."

"When you were on the brink of succumbing to hypothermia, Emilie did the only thing she could," Magnus continues. "By covering the open sides of the sledge with sealskin, she created a small shelter underneath, where you could both lie protected from the storm. Once Mali found you, we were able to heat the space quickly with our body warmth."

I look at Emilie with admiration and pull her close, feeling incre-dibly proud of the person she has become at such a young age.

"When we realised you weren't with us when we arrived at the house, Zaid and I rushed out to search for you together with Mali," Magnus explains. "If it hadn't been for the dog, we might never have found you, as visibility was so poor we couldn't even see across the road. But Mali wasn't confused for a second. While we had turned off the main road, you had continued on for quite a distance. The sledge was completely covered in snow by the time we found you. If it weren't for Mali, we would have passed right by without noticing either of you.

When we looked inside, we saw you and Emilie huddled together. Emilie was awake, but you were completely unconscious. We quickly realised you were severely hypothermic, so we all laid down, one on each side of you, with Mali near your head, to warm your body. There was just enough space for all of us, and we stayed there the entire night until you finally started moving again this morning."

As I listen, a pounding headache begins to spread behind my eyes. I must have winced in pain because Magnus stops talking and looks at me with concern.

"Are you okay?" he asks, reaching for the water bottle Zaid hands him. "Here, drink some water. You need it."

I take a few sips and feel the cold water slide through my throat. As I start drinking, it's like my body is screaming for more, and I can't get enough. I gratefully drain the bottle and hand it back to Zaid, empty.

"Thank you," I say, turning my attention back to Emilie.

"And what about you? How did you get so strong?"

"I don't know," she replies earnestly. "I guess I've just grown up surrounded by the cold."

Zaid laughs and ruffles her hair.

"As far as we can tell," he says, "the fact that Emilie was sheltered from the wind by the side of the sledge while you faced it head-on made all the difference."

"Do you think you can stand up?" Magnus asks. "The sun's shining again, and it might do you good to warm up in it and get your blood circulating."

The water has revived me, but it's agony to move as I crawl out from under the sledge. I squint up at the bright sun, which has broken through the clouds, shining through a large blue gap in an otherwise grey sky.

It's only lightly windy, but it's enough to make me start shivering again as I painfully pull myself to my feet.

Mali circles around my legs. When I look down at her, she immediately breaks into a wide grin. She jumps up, paws out, expecting a hug, which I gratefully bend down to give her.

I don't know what we would have done without her.

"Come on, let's get you back to the others. They must be worried sick. Kristian wanted to come with us to search for you, but I told him to stay behind and help get the fire going for when we returned. He wasn't too happy about that."

Supported by Magnus' strong arms, I move slowly. Each step sends waves of pain shooting through every corner of my body, places I didn't even know existed.

Zaid pulls my sledge, and Emilie and Mali walk at a calm pace beside it.

Back at the house, Kristian throws his arms around all of us the moment we step through the door. He's thankful to see us alive.

Farhana kisses Zaid all over his face, clearly just as worried about him as Kristian was about us.

The story is retold for all who haven't heard it, and Emilie is hailed as a hero. To Kristian's irritation, Fatima sits right beside her, eager not to miss a thing, but he can't really blame her. He's obviously just as impressed by his little sister's bravery.

I'm utterly exhausted, and it's not long before the warmth of the fire lulls me to sleep. I drift off to the sound of voices retelling our tale, over and over, until every detail is covered, and all questions answered. The pain in my muscles eases as I take in water, energy, and warmth, but I still feel weak and doubt I'll be able to continue tomorrow, even if the snow melts under the returning sun.

Mali doesn't care about stories. She senses I'm unwell and curls up close to me, as if to protect me in my frailty.

• • •

We decide to stay in the house until I've recovered enough to pull the sledge without difficulty again. I'm concerned, as it delays us by several more days, but at the same time, I have to accept that I was close to death, and a full recovery isn't something that happens overnight.

Anna, on the other hand, seems quite content that there's no rush to move on. She's enjoying her time with Kasper, sitting outside during the day and basking in the sun when it occasionally breaks through the clouds. She keeps mostly to herself, only speaking with Mikkel and Kasper, but it's clear to everyone that she's in no hurry to leave the house.

The blisters on both Kasper's and Emilie's toes also heal during these days, so in that sense, the delay is a blessing in disguise.

Farhana and Emilie dote on me constantly. They make sure I'm served warm soup and seal meat, along with fresh water regularly throughout the day. I must admit, I enjoy the attention, and much of my relatively swift recovery is due to their care. I also sense that the bond between Emilie and me has strengthened even more after the incident.

Kristian, however, is quickly becoming a young man who sees himself as an adult—a man whose role is to make big decisions for the family, despite his still quite young age. He spends more and more time with Magnus, Zaid, and Mikkel, trying to distance himself from the women, though he can't quite help stealing glances at Fatima.

By the time I'm finally strong enough to continue, we've lost another week. We simply have to pick up the pace if we're going to make it safely before winter is upon us again.

But just as we've packed the sledges and are ready to head off, Anna refuses to leave the house. She feels it's too risky to carry on, and nothing we say can change her mind. The more we press her, the more she withdraws, completely refusing to discuss it. Mikkel tries to reason with her, but it's clear that our presence is only making things worse, both for her and for him. Before we know it, she's sitting there hyperventilating and complaining of chest pains that come and go.

I've never witnessed someone having a panic attack before, but it's evidently extremely distressing for her.

I stand by, unsure of what to do, feeling helpless as I watch. When she suddenly faints and stops breathing, I fear her heart has stopped. But Mikkel remains remarkably calm. Sure enough, after only 10–15 seconds, she gasps awake and begins hyperventilating again, only to faint once more shortly after.

"Can you find something for her to drink?" Mikkel asks Kasper.

Kasper stands by, looking concerned, though he must have seen this before. He nods and returns moments later with a filled canteen, handing it to his father.

When Anna wakes up again after fainting for the third time, Mikkel is ready with her head in his lap. He tries to get a benzodiazepine pill into her mouth and makes her swallow it with some water, all while she continues to hyperventilate.

"There we go," he says soothingly once she finally swallows the pill. "It won't be long before you calm down."

She glances up briefly and gives a faint nod.

"My heart hurts," she complains, clutching her chest with both hands.

They remain on the floor like that for the next ten minutes or so, until Anna's breathing slows enough that she's no longer at risk of fainting again.

When Mikkel finally stands up, he drapes a blanket over her, and Anna lies there with her eyes closed. Soon, she's peacefully snoring, as though nothing has happened.

"I'm afraid we'll have to wait until tomorrow to continue," he says, as he starts gathering blankets for himself and Kasper. "The pill will keep her relaxed for the next five or six hours. Afterward, she'll be so physically exhausted that she won't be able to pull her own sledge."

"What happens if she doesn't get that pill?" I ask.

"Then this could go on for hours, which is extremely uncomfortable for her. She'll have chest pain and feel like she's dying.

But I'm running low on them, and honestly, I don't know what I'll do to help her when they run out."

"We'll pass through Hamburg in a couple of days," Magnus says. "What if we search a few pharmacies there and see if we're lucky enough to find something you can use? It shouldn't delay us much."

Mikkel nods thoughtfully.

"Yeah, let's try that," he replies, though he doesn't sound optimistic. "But I fear most of it will already be gone. After all, it's been years since pharmacies received their last supplies."

11 Magnus

If we had previously felt alone in a desolate world of frost and cold, it was nothing compared to the sensation that greets us as we walk along the empty streets of Hamburg. The metropolis, once home to Europe's third-largest industrial port, lies utterly abandoned.

As we find ourselves once more on one of the more than 2,000 bridges that cross the many branches of the Elbe in the city centre, I let my eyes wander along the canal's banks, as I've done countless times before.

The result is every time the same. The ice that had covered the canals in a metre-thick layer all winter has only just begun to thaw in a narrow strip along the riverbanks. When waves from the sea further away ripple through the canal system, the water gently laps in the openings. They are still not large enough for seals to emerge, so the canal appears totally devoid of life.

Still, I imagine the water teeming with fish beneath the ice, and I get an overwhelming urge to stop and try to find an opening big enough to cast a line.

I haven't tasted fish in years. In my mind, I dream of varying the monotonous diet of tough, dried seal meat with freshly caught fried fish that melts in my mouth.

Maybe I should try my luck fishing this evening before we settle down for the night, I think to myself. Then I begin to wonder how we might actually catch fish deep beneath the ice without any fishing gear. Back home, we didn't fish, as it wouldn't have provided enough food relative to the time spent. But now, while we're on the move, there's no harm in trying to supplement our monotonous diet, as long as it doesn't cause further delays.

Despite being completely cut off from the world for several years, there's still something strangely futuristic about being confronted with the deafening silence in what was once a thriving metropolis.

The inhabitants fled long ago.

Like a ghost town, it engulfs us, full of empty buildings and abandoned vehicles, with hundreds of avenues showing clear signs that the inhabitants were desperate in their search for anything burnable.

Though Hamburg, with more than a quarter-million trees in its urban landscape, had always been known as a green city, the trees could never have provided enough warmth for its nearly two million residents when the deep freeze truly set in. Now, only stumps remain where the trees once stood. Here and there, someone had tried to dig up the roots to burn them too, but I imagine their efforts were futile. The frozen ground would have yielded nothing.

The city's inhabitants must have been forced to flee years ago.

It suddenly hits me how many millions must have walked the same route as us in recent years. All with the same end goal. The migrations must have been enormous. Hamburg, Bremen, Hannover, Düsseldorf, Cologne, Dortmund, Bielefeld, Münster, Bonn. All of them walked the route before us.

Not to mention all the Danes.

Thirty million people. At least.

How many have survived?

How many lie dead along the way, overcome by the effort? By hunger? The cold?

I stare up at the buildings, some rising ten or fifteen storeys above me.

How many lie dead and frozen inside the many abandoned apartments around us? I shudder at the thought, and suddenly it feels as if we are being watched from the shadows. I feel oddly observed, but everything is eerily still.

I glance at Mali, who is trotting happily beside Emilie and shows no signs of being on alert. If there are people nearby, she hasn't picked up their scent. This reassures me enough that I decide not to share my worries with the others.

We're nearing the city centre. Doors have been forced open into shops, windows smashed. The shelves are empty. We haven't yet spotted a single pharmacy, which prompts Mikkel to break the silence.

"Didn't Hamburg's citizens need medicine?" he asks sarcastically.

He tries to sound unconcerned, but I can hear a note of despair behind his forced cheerfulness. The burden on his shoulders is heavy. He has clearly pinned his hopes on the city providing what he needs to ease the weight a little.

"The main station is just ahead," I say, pointing forward. "Surely, there's a pharmacy in there?"

When we step into the entrance hall, we are met with a chaos of broken glass and non-flammable shop fixtures scattered everywhere. Someone has thoroughly ransacked the place in their desperate search for something valuable to help them survive a little longer. Across the large building, there are signs of big bonfires that suggest the station once served as a temporary refuge for some of the city's residents. Probably the

196

city's homeless.

As we gradually push deeper into the building, all my internal alarm bells start ringing. At the same time, Mali begins to growl softly, though her attention doesn't seem focused on anything specific.

What aren't we seeing?

I stare cautiously into the dark corners of the building, but no matter how hard I strain my eyes, I can't spot anything alarming.

Yet all my senses scream.

"There!" Mikkel shouts, startling me.

My thoughts jump back to the mission at hand.

"Down there at the end. The pharmacy!"

Mikkel quickens his pace.

"What's that smell?" Farhana asks as we approach.

The smell!

That nagging sense that something isn't right. The smell is disgustingly foul here, and it grows stronger the deeper we go into the building.

I don't like it. Not just because it smells bad, but because the odour suggests life.

Life that is hiding from us.

In a world of frost and snow, I've learned that most of the truly foul smells are man-made. Human waste. But the smell usually dissipates quickly, either encased in frost or eroded by time.

Here, however, the stench is sharp. Sickening.

"Does it smell rotten?" Farhana asks, trying to identify the odour.

The stench is pervasive. It's hard to pinpoint where it's coming from.

Mikkel, Anna, Zaid, and Freja disappear into the pharmacy.

I glance briefly through what used to be a large shop window, now shattered into a thousand pieces on the floor. The steel shelves I can see are all empty. I doubt there's anything of value for us in there.

I have an overwhelming urge to scream that we should leave, but I try to muster patience as Mikkel and Zaid disappear into the back room, where medicine is normally stored. Meanwhile, Mali sneaks cautiously towards the escalators leading down to the tracks below. Her hackles are raised, and she's growling softly. Her tail is no longer curled proudly over her back as it usually is. Instead, it trails warily just centimetres above the ground.

Kristian makes to follow her, but I place a hand on his shoulder to hold him back. "Wait for Zaid and Mikkel," I say. "I've got a bad feeling…"

He nods and calls for Mali, who stops with her eyes fixed on the escalator. Kristian calls again, but she stubbornly stays where she is. Her behaviour is making us both nervous, so I reach for my bow, nocking an arrow, and call out for Zaid and Mikkel. Moments later, they reappear at the door to the shop.

"There's not even a pack of condoms left in there," Mikkel exclaims, attempting to make light of the hopeless situation.

He's never had much sense of timing.

"There's something going on over by the escalators," I interrupt him. "Look at Mali. She won't take her eyes off it."

Zaid notices that I've got my bow in hand and an arrow ready. He says nothing but pulls out his own bow. Mikkel looks surprised at us both but soon finds his harpoon.

Side by side, we cautiously move towards the escalator, each armed with our respective weapons. The stench grows stronger as we approach. Mali sneaks along with us, growling deep in her chest.

I keep my eyes fixed ahead.

Alert.

I have no idea what we might encounter when we reach the top of the escalator.

"God, it stinks!" Kristian exclaims behind me. He's holding his knife up in front of him, ready to use it if necessary.

From the top of the escalator, you can see a large section of the platform below. It consists of 10 to 14 rows of parallel train tracks. I breathe a sigh of relief as we reach the top and find no one lying in wait to ambush us. Neither on the escalator nor further down on the platform. Still, to be sure, I let my gaze sweep quickly across the large area.

Mali continues to growl. She's also surveying the area but makes no move to head down.

Something about the scene feels wrong, but my mind doesn't register it until I hear Kristian's shocked voice beside me.

"Are those bodies?"

● ● ●

Freja and Farhana appear and squeeze in between Zaid and me. They've seen us lower our weapons and concluded there's no danger. A moment passes, then we hear a startled gasp from Farhana before she spins around and buries her face in Zaid's fur coat. He wraps his arms around her in a protective embrace, pulling her close. His eyes meet mine, and I see the sadness in them. If he could, he would have shielded her from all the horrors of this world. I'm sure of it. But he can't. It seems Allah has other plans. Their fate appears predetermined, and it's filled with death.

"*Jahannam,*" he whispers in Arabic.

Hell.

I feel Freja grasp my hand.

I intertwine my fingers with hers, grateful that she's still with us. That I haven't already lost her to the cursed winter cold like so many of those lost souls down on the train tracks.

Side by side, they lie. The dead.

Across the platforms, along the tracks for their entire length, out of the departure hall and further into the open.

All 14 tracks, filled to the brim with tightly packed, dead bodies. They lie so close together that the tracks are no longer visible beneath them. A few are wrapped in sheets, stained brown by decomposition fluids, but most have been laid down naked, robbed of their dignity due to the survivors' need for warm clothing.

All in various stages of decay.

From where we stand, there's no sign that any new bodies have been added recently. Not after the winter we've just endured.

A dark, sorrowful feeling rises within me, gripping my heart as I gaze at the countless dead bodies.

I think back to the large funeral pyres we were forced to build after the first harsh winters. The ground was too hard to dig, so we had no choice but to burn the dead in massive bonfires. We used large, precious amounts of firewood from the forest, but we couldn't just leave them lying above ground.

In the big cities, they didn't have that option. They didn't have enough firewood. And since they couldn't bury them, they had to gather the dead and lay them to rest in open halls like what we're witnessing now.

The harsh frost and short summers must have slowed the decomposition process because, though most of them have been lying there for years, few have completely broken down. Now that daytime temperatures are rising above 5-8 degrees Celsius, decomposition is starting again. And with it comes the horrific smell.

Mali has stopped growling and has begun to whimper softly instead. She scratches at my leg, trying to get my attention. When I look down, she immediately jumps up on her hind legs, wanting to be held. She can feel the sadness that has spread among us too.

Anna calls out to Mikkel.

"What's happening?" she asks. "Can you see anything?"

She, Kasper, and the girls are still standing in front of the pharmacy. They don't yet know that the train station has been turned into a massive mausoleum, and that we're standing in the middle of it.

Mikkel turns and walks back to her.

Shortly after, we hear Anna's shrill voice. "Ugh, for heaven's sake! Are you saying we're walking around breathing in rotting corpses? You can't be serious, Mikkel!"

Before Mikkel can respond, she grabs Kasper and dramatic-ally pulls him towards the exit, back the way we came.

Mikkel stands there for a moment, watching her. Then he shrugs, resigned, and prepares to follow her. She's left her sledge behind, so he has to painstakingly tie it to his own and pull them both at once.

Emilie stares at me. "Is it true that there are dead people down there?" she asks anxiously.

"They've turned the station into a graveyard," I say, nodding. "They had no other choice for their dead."

"There must be thousands of people down there," Freja says, her voice trembling. "So many dead."

She's on the verge of breaking down, so I put my arm around her comfortingly and begin to follow Anna and Mikkel.

"How can Anna be so heartless?" she asks. Tears are now quietly streaming down her cheeks.

I don't respond. My mind is empty of words.

I help Freja into her harness, then put on my own.

On the way to the exit, I glance back. Kristian has his arm around Fatima. She walks quietly beside him, her head resting on his shoulder. Not because of the budding love between them, but because of the need to feel life close by.

When we get outside, we find Anna and Mikkel further down the street, arguing loudly. Anna refuses to eat any more of the dried meat and insists on leaving the sledges behind. She claims the meat is no longer fit for human consumption because it's been exposed to billions of bacteria from dead bodies.

"Then we'll get there faster," she shouts.

"No, we won't. We'll starve along the way," Mikkel shouts back.

"We'll die anyway if we eat it. It's dead people, Mikkel. It's decomposition bacteria. If you eat rotten food, you get sick and throw up. So what's the difference? Tell me that!"

"So what do you plan for us to live on if we leave the food behind?"

"I don't know," she screams. She starts breathing faster, short, jerky gasps that signal another panic attack is looming. "But I refuse to eat contaminated meat. And so does Kasper."

The boy, who had been standing quietly in the background until now, looks up, startled at hearing his name mentioned. Unwillingly, he's being held hostage in his mother's power struggle with his father, and it's clear he's uncomfortable with the situation.

Freja notices it too and goes to hug him. She crouches in front of him, trying in vain to distract him while his parents continue arguing.

At last, Zaid, usually so calm, snaps. Without warning, he suddenly erupts into a stream of words directed straight at Anna. The words tumble out in broken Danish, which only gets worse when he's upset.

"For God's sake, Anna, when will you finally learn to keep your mouth shut? We are here for you. To find medicine for you. To help you! Because we respect that you have an illness that needs treatment. Respect, Anna. Respect for each other. Sick or healthy. Alive or dead. White or brown, it doesn't matter. We owe it to each other to respect one another. We have to stick together! It's the only way we can survive. By standing together and respecting each other.

Those people in there, they're all victims of this cursed climate change, which we humans caused because we have no respect for anything. Not for each other or the world we live in. And you, Anna. You still don't get it! None of us are obligated to help you, but we do it out of respect for your illness. Out of respect for you. For your son. And for Mikkel. Because you belong together as a unit, and none of you, none of us, deserve to end up like those in there. Not after everything we've already been through.

So now, shut up! And eat the damn meat like the rest of us. Because you owe us that. If you get sick, we all get sick. But if you don't eat, and the meat's fine, then it's only you who'll get weak. And then you'll become a burden none of us deserve to bear! Now, kindly shut up so we can move on and try to find more pharmacies and medicine for you."

Just as abruptly as he started, Zaid falls silent again. He's said what he needed to say, and without another word, he starts moving, pulling his sledge south.

We all stare after him, surprised, then glance at each other.

Farhana smiles, pleased, and suddenly Freja begins to giggle.

Before long, the two women are laughing with such infectious joy that, for a moment, it sweeps away all the bad feelings. Even Anna smiles shyly. She's no longer hyperventilating. Instead, she stares in amazement at Zaid's back as he moves farther and farther away from us. Without a word, she puts on her harness and slowly starts to follow him, dragging her sledge and all the meat behind her.

We pass several pharmacies, but with the same disappointing result. All of them are completely emptied of everything that once sat on their shelves. There's no point wasting any more time, and we decide to press on as far as possible before darkness falls. With no burnable materials in sight for miles around, we're looking at a freezing cold night.

We need to get out of the city and back to the countryside as soon as possible, where, hopefully, there's still something burnable in the woods and hedgerows. I give up the idea of trying to catch fish. It's far more urgent that we find a place to sleep, sheltered from the wind and weather. Here, between the tall buildings, it's less windy, but it's as if the cold radiates from the walls, stored up in the steel and concrete skeletons, accumulated and held over the many frosty days of recent winters. It's bitterly cold, and none of us are eager to spend the night inside one of the surrounding buildings. Who knows what else might be lurking in there, waiting for us?

On the other hand, it's also clear we can't survive outdoors. Ahead of me, Freja is scanning the area from side to side, also keeping a lookout. She's recovered surprisingly quickly after her near-death experience just a week ago. I watch her with pride as she walks. I can faintly make out the contours of her body under her leather clothing. Despite working hard, pulling a heavy sledge behind her, her hips gently sway from side to side. I wonder, somewhat wistfully, when I'll again get the chance to enjoy my wife's wonderful body. I catch myself longing for the intimacy that arises between us when desire is given free rein.

Desire is a strange thing, and maybe it's different for men than for women, but I almost always find peace by thinking intimate thoughts about my wife, even when, just moments before, we were inhaling the stench of thousands of rotting corpses and a melancholy mood was spreading among us. She is what keeps me going, more than anything else, when the effort becomes too much. Just like on my trips back and forth between the coast and the village, I now use memories of her naked body to push away the torments that my brain and body endure as we wander through Hamburg's deserted streets. By thinking of her breasts, I manage to keep the sight of the dead at a distance.

The smell of decaying bodies lingers in my nostrils like a permanent reminder, one I'm sure will haunt me for the rest of my life, but by thinking of Freja's soft bottom, I can trick my brain just enough not to let it bother me too much. It's a simple trick. But it works.

We pass a freight train terminal surrounded by warehouses painted in bright colours: red, blue, yellow, and green. The colours form a striking contrast to the otherwise predominantly grey and brown tones of the terminal. The platform, the tracks, and even the freight cars, abandoned in long rows on dead-end tracks, are a jumble of concrete and rusty iron structures. All the freight cars have been broken into, and whatever contents they once held have long since been looted. Graffiti adorns the sides of most of them.

On one of them, I read the word *secrets* written in white letters along the side, as a reminder of all that is hidden from us in the surrounding buildings, things we cannot see. The word sparks a chain of thoughts, which eventually form into an idea in my head.

"What if we spend the night in one of those freight cars?" I ask aloud, not addressing anyone in particular.

Freja turns to look at me as if I've gone mad.

"Think about it," I continue. "First of all, we know they're empty. There are definitely no more unpleasant surprises inside them—we can see that from here. Secondly, they're small enough that our combined body heat should raise the temperature by at least a couple of degrees, unlike if we stayed in a house or an apartment somewhere."

"Like when Emilie saved me by making a little shelter under the sledge," Freja nods in agreement, at the same time pulling Emilie close for a grateful hug.

Emilie looks up at her mother with wide eyes. "I think it's a good idea," she says.

"I agree," Zaid adds.

I look over at Mikkel, who also nods.

"What about the sledges?" Farhana asks.

"We'll park them outside," I reply. "There's no one left in this city anyway, so I'm not worried about anyone stealing them. And if there are still people here we haven't come across yet, Mali will warn us in time."

"Well then, let's settle in," Kristian exclaims, already heading for the nearest freight car. He's eager to show off. "Come on, Fatima, if we take the spot furthest inside, there'll be less draft from the door."

I can't help but smile. Love truly is a powerful force. It can flourish even under the harshest conditions. Fatima shyly looks at her father, who nods approvingly, and then she slowly follows Kristian.

The freight car turns out to be surprisingly comfortable. As soon as the door is closed, and we've set up a thick layer of sealskin on the floor, it never gets unbearably cold, even though the temperature remains below freezing for much of the night. By lying close together, we avoid the danger of freezing.

As I lie there with Freja's body pressed close to mine, I think that Kristian must be experiencing the happiest moment of his life. I imagine him lying there with his arm protectively around Fatima, while she snuggles up to him with her back turned, soaking up his body heat. Zaid is lying on her other side, so I'm sure neither of them would even dare consider kissing.

I pull Freja even closer.

She turns her head, letting me kiss her earlobe. "He'll remember this night forever," she whispers, as if she can read my thoughts.

The night passes uneventfully. I sleep soundly until Mali wakes me early the next morning with a few half-hearted barks. Mikkel, who's lying closest to the door, jumps up and slides it open, only to find the sunlit area outside the car as empty of life as it was last night when we settled in. The sledges remain untouched, just as we left them. I think Mali must have been dreaming, perhaps a nightmare about dead souls wandering restlessly through a deserted concrete city.

Who knows? She doesn't growl or bark anymore. Instead, she stares intently at Freja, as if to say, now that we're up, surely it's time for breakfast. Her tail wags, curled up tightly on her back, vibrating with excitement. When Freja shows no sign of getting up from the furs just yet, Mali whines impatiently and tugs at her arm with her paw until Freja finally gives in, laughing as she turns around. Freja affectionately ruffles the dog's scruffy head between her hands.

"Alright, you impatient little thing. Let's go and find something to eat."

Mali immediately wriggles free and jumps gracefully out of the freight car. Outside, she dances around in circles happily, until Freja takes the meat from her sledge and gives her the pieces that make up her breakfast. A few seconds later, Mali has swallowed three whole strips of meat. She looks around to assess where her best chances of getting more might be. Just then, Emilie holds her own ration in her outstretched hand, and before she can take the first bite, Mali is sitting by her side, eyes locked on the meat in her hand.

Emilie teases her. She pretends to offer a piece, but as soon as Mali opens her mouth to take it, Emilie quickly pulls her hand away. Then Emilie takes a bite herself and laughs loudly. Mali watches forlornly as the meat disappears bite by bite, but she doesn't move from Emilie's side until the last piece is gone.

If anyone were watching us from the shadows, it would be

hard to believe we're actually refugees, forced to flee because the conditions further north have become too extreme to survive. So far, we've been able to create a tolerable existence. We've been able to plan our journey, which is more than many others have had the chance to do. We have plenty to eat, warm furs, and good spirits, and as we sit there, enjoying the warming rays of the sun, we look more like a group of campers than refugees.

But it's not the summer months that make life in the north unbearable, I think sadly. It's the winter. Before we know it, it will be upon us again, and we won't survive unless we've found help further south by then. Our fate hangs by a thread. Back home, we wouldn't be able to survive much longer, but down here, we'll make it if we can find someone willing to help us through the first winter.

12 Freja

We are slowly moving further and further south. At long last, the summer has grown strong enough to displace the winter cold, at least for a while. Even at night, the temperature no longer falls below freezing, and the farther south we go, the less we feel the icy, treacherous westerly winds that have dominated our lives for so many years. Since Hamburg, the weather has been better than feared, and we've only had to take shelter from storms on a few occasions. At last, we are making progress faster than anticipated. Exactly how much faster is hard to say, but I'm certain by now we must have gained at least one of the lost weeks.

We are all exhausted, even though the sledges are getting lighter as we consume the meat we brought with us. The food is dwindling at an alarming rate. I worry we may have miscalculated and not brought enough to get us all the way to southern France. I can see from both Kristian and Anna that they are visibly struggling under the weight of the sledges. I feel it too, of course — the fatigue.

Even though the sun rises early, and it's already light before five, I now find it harder to open my eyes in the mornings and prepare myself for another day on the move. Kristian, who tirelessly tries to impress Fatima, will never admit he is worn out, but it's obvious. Sunken cheeks. Dark circles under his eyes. A short temper. Little dissatisfied sounds when he stretches his aching body every time we take a break. All these are small signs that he is struggling to keep up.

Magnus notices, of course. Discreetly, he makes sure that we eat more from Kristian's sledge than from mine, and more from mine than from his own. He manages the weight reduction in a way that best matches how exhausted each of us seems to be. The weight of his own sledge remains almost unchanged well into Germany. Only when Kristian's sledge is nearly empty does he begin to take meat from his own. But only for himself. The rest of us continue eating from the remaining supplies on my and Kristian's sledges.

I admire Magnus's strength. The endurance he has built up over the many trips between the coast and the village is impressive. But I worry he is sacrificing himself more than is wise for our sake. He still seems to have plenty of energy left, though, enough to ensure Kristian's pride remains intact, so he doesn't lose face in front of Fatima. I love him for that.

It's important to me that we try to maintain some semblance of normal social interaction, as it would have been under normal circumstances, even though we've been driven from our home. Our mental health is crucial to our survival. That's my mantra. Mental strength is just as important as physical strength. Once the mind gives up, the body soon follows, but if the mind stays healthy, you can endure anything—so long as you get enough food, drink, rest when you're tired, and shelter when bad weather strikes.

Even Mali no longer seems to have endless energy. It's becoming rare for her to forage ahead of our small group. Instead, she walks quietly most of the time beside Magnus, as she's used to doing on the trips between the coast and the village. In the evenings, she quickly settles down and snores loudly in competition with Kasper. He too is struggling, even though he spends most of his days being transported on Mikkel's sledge.

Mikkel, however, seems unaffected by the hardships or the extra 20 kilos of Kasper's weight. He seems completely unfazed by our situation and the uncertainty of the future, but it's clear he's deeply concerned about Anna's mental state. He talks to her constantly, tirelessly keeping her brain occupied with mental tasks. All this is to prevent her from sinking into her own dark, brooding thoughts, which could trigger another anxiety attack. Ordinary discussions, which they've had hundreds of times before, are re-examined from every possible angle. In Danish, English, and German, just to meet the need to focus intensely on the subject, even though it's no longer new.

Mikkel skillfully avoids talking about the future. Even though it might be tempting to paint a rosy picture of life south of the ice boundary, the uncertainty about what awaits us when we arrive could be enough to block all positive thoughts in her mind. The risk of her shutting down is high.

I am deeply impressed by the love and care he shows her, but at the same time, it isolates them from the rest of us. They rarely participate in discussions about our daily challenges. I don't blame him, as he's just doing what's necessary to keep his small family going. Family is all we have.

Emilie sticks close to my side. It's as if the bond between us has grown even stronger since we were left alone in the snowstorm. She showed such courage and quick thinking, displaying a maturity far beyond her years. Even though we can't blame anyone for what happened, it feels like she and I have made an unspoken pact not to lose sight of each other again.

No matter what happens, it will happen to both of us, together. At times, she's so exhausted that she has to ask for a ride on the sledge because her 11-year-old legs are about to give up. She insists on riding on my sledge, so as not to lose sight of me, fully aware that it drains my strength. Maybe that's why she only reluctantly asks for a lift. For the most part, she bites through the pain and keeps going on her own two feet.

The fatigue and the close bond between us mean that she and Fatima no longer talk much. Neither of them has the energy for play. Fatima mostly walks in silence, lost in her own thoughts. Kristian's repeated attempts to catch her attention only occasionally get her to break out of her shell, and even more rarely does she reward his efforts with one of her enchanting smiles. When it does happen, Kristian noticeably gains energy for a short period until she, once again, unconsciously ignores his awkward advances.

At one point, it becomes too much for Zaid, who asks Kristian to ease off on the flirting for a while. Whether it's to protect his daughter or because he can no longer bear to see Kristian make a fool of himself, I don't know, but I'm grateful for the intervention. There are limits to how much humiliation a mother can watch her son endure.

Kristian protests loudly with the indignant attitude of youth. Of course, he doesn't understand Zaid's plea. Farhana and I exchange knowing glances but say nothing more. By the next morning, Kristian is back at it full force, like a stag in rut. In that respect, teenage boys are incorrigible, climate crisis or not.

We are still dependent on lighting fires in woodstoves in the evenings. Even though it's summer, the nights are still cold, so every evening we need to find an abandoned house with a stove and combustible materials nearby. After Hamburg, we avoid the big cities. Instead, we stick to the smaller country roads, where there are still remnants of surrounding forests and older houses with chimneys on the roofs.

We haven't encountered any other people yet, and although we sometimes spot a flock of migrating birds high in the sky, none of them show any sign of settling near us. We seem to be completely alone in a world devoid of life. It's dystopian and rather surreal when you've grown up in a world where the population density grew larger every day.

"People must have moved south along with the animals when it got really cold," says Farhana one evening. We are sitting around the woodstove in an abandoned half-timbered house on the outskirts of Cologne.

She and I are the only ones still awake.

"We were probably just lucky that a large colony of seals settled nearby, so we could survive on them for so long," I say. "No one who lived further inland would have had the same opportunity. If it hadn't been for the seals, we wouldn't have survived the winters either."

The warmth from the stove pricks my cheeks. I move back a little.

"We mustn't forget all those who left after that first harsh winter. If they hadn't abandoned the village, there wouldn't have been enough seals or firewood for all of us. I think our little colony was unique in that sense—we've done the impossible. We've defied the odds and survived when everyone else gave up."

"How far south do you think we'll have to go before we meet people again?" Farhana suddenly asks, looking at me with a nervous gaze.

Once again, I get the sense that she's desperate to share her painful memories with me, but behind her hazel eyes, she battles inner demons that stubbornly refuse to let the secrets out.

"I don't know," I answer softly, scooting closer until I'm sitting so close to her that I can feel the warmth from her body. I gently rest my head against hers. We sit like that for a while, in silence, each lost in our own thoughts.

I wish I knew the magic words that could unlock those memories. Keeping so much pain inside, with no one but Zaid to share it with, can't be healthy. But I'm out of ideas on how to get her to open up, so instead, I continue where we left off.

"I think we'll have to go far," I say. "If even the animals no longer come here in the summer, it's because the winter has driven them so far south that they can't make it back before the cold forces them to migrate again."

"I hope it's far," she whispers so quietly that I have to strain to hear.

"Let's hope it's not so far that we can't make it there before the frost is upon us again," I reply.

She doesn't respond.

"Do you regret coming with us?" I ask after a pause.

"No... I don't know. I don't think so. Maybe."

"We can't survive back home," I insist.

"No."

"We need help."

Suddenly, she lies down, resting her head in my lap.

"Who's going to help us?" she asks in despair.

"There must be aid organisations out there that will help us through the first winter once we get there. After that, we'll just have to try and build a new life for ourselves, as best as we can."

"No one will help us!" she cries out. "You don't understand! No one wants to help us. Refugees are unwanted, no matter where we go." She starts to sob quietly.

I can feel the trembling in her body as I gently stroke her hair, trying my best to comfort her. But nothing I say or do will be able to ease the deep pain she carries within. The best I can do is listen to her fears.

"When Zaid and I left our life in Damascus, there was nowhere else to flee but Lebanon. Because of our Shia Muslim background, we were in danger of being killed by the Sunni Muslim rebel forces if we stayed in Syria, even though we didn't take part in the conflict ourselves. There were no refugee camps in Lebanon, but the country was collapsing under the weight of the refugee crisis, and the economy was so shattered that there was no help to be had. We had to work peeling garlic for local Lebanese restaurants just to earn enough money to pay the rent for the tin shack we shared with two other families. It was literally nothing more than some wooden pallets with corrugated metal sheets laid across them in a barren field, but the rent still took everything we earned from the garlic. We had no money left for food, and the hunger stripped the flesh from our bones in no time. The landowner didn't care. He insisted that if we wanted to stay on his land, we had to pay the rent.

There was no other work available. The Syrians were already taking all the jobs from the Lebanese. They undercut the wages, so the local Lebanese soon became just as desperate as the rest of us. No one was making money, and tensions quickly escalated to a point where everyone feared being attacked over a crust of mouldy bread.

One night, a fire broke out in the camp. No one knows for sure, but rumours said it was the local Lebanese who set the shacks on fire to drive us away. In desperation, the Syrians attacked the residents of the nearby village, and soon the police forces arrived in large numbers, throwing people into jail. They hit the rioters hard on the head with their batons. If they were still moving, they were dragged into the police vans and driven away. Those left lying on the ground were either already dead or dying. We had no medicine or doctors to care for them."

Farhana has suddenly decided to open up at last, and now the words are pouring out of her. I listen intently, afraid that if I interrupt, she'll close up again. She's still lying with her head in my lap, staring vacantly into the flames in the wood stove, while her words flow out.

"When Zaid saw the conflict escalating, he told me we had to leave before one of us got caught in the violence. Our shack had burned down, and the prospect of getting food and water was now almost non-existent, so at the height of the unrest, we fled once more. We had only the clothes on our backs. Everything else was either buried under the ruins in Damascus or had burned along with the shack in the field. So, we just started walking, literally with nothing.

Empty-handed, we slowly moved west. We had no destination. We only knew we had to get away from there. Without anything to drink under the scorching sun, it didn't take long before I was so thirsty that I couldn't even produce spit to swallow. My throat felt like I had swallowed a razor blade. Zaid desperately tried to get one of the passing cars to stop, but they just drove past as if we were invisible.

We were emaciated. Clearly dehydrated. And still, no one stopped. Finally, late in the evening, a shiny red Toyota pulled over to take us with them. The driver was a fat, smiling man, dressed in the traditional white Arab robe with a red-checked headscarf wrapped around his head. He gave us water to drink and dates to eat. The water was lukewarm, but it revived me surprisingly quickly. As we drove, he and Zaid talked about our hopeless situation—no money, no food or water, and nowhere to go.

The man kept staring at me in the rearview mirror. I remember thinking that he would crash the car because he was looking at me more than at the road ahead.

'I can help you get to Europe,' I suddenly heard him say to Zaid.

We'd been driving for about half an hour by then. All that time, he'd been staring at me in the rearview mirror, licking his thick lips lustfully.

'How?' Zaid asked. 'We have no money.'

'I'm sure we'll find a way to solve that problem,' the man said, winking lewdly at me through the mirror.

Three weeks later, we were on an overcrowded boat in the middle of the Mediterranean, heading for the Greek part of Cyprus.

Until then, we had been living in the man's house. We ate his food. Drank his wine. Slept in his soft, clean beds. And at night, I gave in to all his sexual desires while Zaid lay in the next room, covering his ears, tears streaming down his face.

That was the payment for getting to Europe. Nightly escapades with a wealthy, middle-aged, overweight Arab.

Of course, Zaid was strongly against it from the start, but we were desperate, and it was the only way we could escape to a more bearable life in the promised land of Europe. We had no money, no papers, and we couldn't survive on our own."

I'm shocked.

Never in my wildest imagination had I envisioned anything like what she is now telling me. It's no wonder she fears meeting other people.

And she's not even finished with the story...

"I can still smell the sickly sweet scent of his cologne at night, when I lie awake, unable to sleep.

He was always clean and polite. He never physically harmed me, but mentally, I was completely under his control. If I didn't comply, we'd end up on the streets quicker than I could blink three times – left to fend for ourselves again, with no hope of anything but a slow, painful death from hunger.

So, I shut my eyes and pictured Zaid's face in my mind as the man panted and grunted on top of me, until he finally reached his climax inside me. With each passing day, it took him longer and longer to finish, and eventually, it took so long that he had to give up due to sheer exhaustion. I could tell he was more embarrassed about not being able to finish than he was about forcing me to have sex with him every single night.

From his perspective, we had entered into a perfectly legitimate agreement. Sex in exchange for him paying the smugglers. It was as simple as that.

The next day, he drove us to the beach after dark. To a place north of Tripoli. There, he handed us over to a small group of shouting men, brandishing weapons, who herded us into a small motorboat. We were placed on the floor, which was covered with several inches of seawater.

Beforehand, the fat Arab had slipped a thick wad of cash into the hands of the man who was apparently the leader. Payment for taking us aboard. He had also arranged fake passports for both of us and given Zaid $1,000 to ensure our safe passage, wherever we ended up.

Bribery runs in the blood.

The men sailed us far out to sea until we met up with a larger barge, drifting slowly on the waves. The barge was already packed with people, and there was hardly any room for us when we climbed aboard. The sea was perilously close to the edge, but the leader reassured us that everything was as it should be.

Then they quickly sailed away, back in the direction we had come from.

We were now on the boat that was meant to take us to Cyprus.

The moon was clear in the sky, so I could see the worried faces of my fellow passengers, all of them Syrian refugees like us. Men, women, and children.

No one spoke.

We'd been told not to talk, as sounds carry quickly at night, and we couldn't risk drawing the attention of the Turkish coast guard. If they found us, they'd just sail us back to Lebanon.

Instead, most of us mumbled frightened prayers under our breath, while the helmsman quietly steered us further into the darkness. What he navigated by, I have no idea, but he seemed sure of his course.

Throughout the night, more motorboats appeared. Each time, they brought new passengers, who were loaded onto the barge. Eventually, the boat was so full that we couldn't even stretch our legs. The water was just a few centimetres below the edge, and the waves washed over the sides so often that we constantly had to bail out the water with our hands.

I have never been more afraid of dying than I was during those days and nights on that boat.

Without food or water for several days, we were all so exhausted that by the time we finally approached land, no one had the strength to bail out the water anymore. The boat capsized in the waves, and panic broke out as everyone scrambled to save themselves. I have no idea how Zaid and I managed to make it to shore, but suddenly I found myself alive on the beach. We were surrounded by bodies – children and adults – drifting in the waves that monotonously lapped over the stones.

There were other survivors sitting on the beach, staring blankly into the distance. People who had lost everything. Their homes. Their belongings. Their memories were taken from them. And now, their families too."

Of course, I'd heard the stories of the many boat refugees crossing the Mediterranean in fragile vessels. Boats that weren't even designed to carry half the number of people crammed into them. But never in my life did I imagine that Farhana was one of them.

My heart aches as I listen to her dramatic life story. I'm at a loss for words and can do nothing but listen. Listen and gently stroke her hair. To show her that she is loved.

I make a promise to myself, here and now, that no matter what happens, I will always do everything in my power to protect Farhana from any more of the world's cruelty. Just as I would protect my own family.

"Cyprus was also drowning in refugees, and just like in Lebanon, we quickly realised that we were unwanted there as well. The authorities ignored those of us who didn't cause trouble or weren't in such bad shape that, in the eyes of the international community, they couldn't refuse to help. The rest of us were left to fend for ourselves.

We weren't even registered, as the rules in the EU required. If we weren't registered, we didn't exist. Even if we wanted to apply for asylum, there was no one to take our application.

We saw the weakest among us being taken to refugee camps, where they were given a little food and a tent to sleep in. If any of us mentioned the word asylum, they simply said they didn't have time to deal with our case until they had helped the weakest. But more weak people kept arriving, so there was never any time.

We quickly realised that begging on the streets would also be our fate if we stayed in Cyprus.

We couldn't survive on the streets, Freja. Zaid is an engineer. He had a good job in Syria. We had money and a big house. Food on the table every day. If we had had a choice, we would never have left the life we had there, but the bombs and the looming threat of genocide against the Shia Muslim minority forced us out.

So, when we met other Syrians talking about going to Denmark, because they had family there and had heard that Denmark helped all refugees, we decided to follow suit. With the fake passports in hand and the last bit of money from the Arab, we bought two plane tickets to Copenhagen.

In Denmark, they registered us. They took our asylum application, and we were seen and heard. But it quickly became clear that we were unwanted here too. In the media, they called us 'opportunistic refugees' or 'welfare migrants' because we had travelled through several safe countries where our lives weren't in immediate danger.

But tell me, how were we supposed to survive on the streets of Cyprus? Or in Lebanon? Alongside thousands of other refugees? You can't!

In Denmark, we received help from the authorities and could begin our lives anew. For that, we will always be grateful. We received Danish language lessons, and because Zaid is an engineer, he was offered a job. Engineers were in short supply in Denmark, so it didn't matter that he was a refugee, even if we were generally unwanted.

But unwanted, we still were. The media wrote about it every single day. Social media was ablaze with hateful comments telling us to go back where we came from because there was nothing here for us.

Of course, there were exceptions, like you and Magnus. But even though you took us in as a friendship family, there was always a polite distance. You might not have realised it, but that's how we felt. The Danish social distance towards foreigners is well known among immigrants who move to Denmark. It's a massive barrier to becoming integrated into society. It was a barrier that only broke down when the frost came, and we all became more dependent on each other, regardless of skin colour, religion, or country of origin.

No matter where we end up, Freja, whether it's France, Spain, or Portugal, we will, by definition, be unwanted. No one truly wants to help refugees because there's no financial benefit in doing so. We are an economic burden that no one wants to bear.

It's a truth I've learned the hard way.

There's no reason to believe that this mentality has changed just because we're moving from one European country to another. Solidarity doesn't extend beyond our own back yard.

If you want help, you have to be able to offer something in return. But refugees have nothing to offer. All we can do is receive. Beg for help, even though we've likely spent our whole lives being used to providing for ourselves."

• • •

Emilie squeals with excitement as we spot the geese that had just passed us high in the sky making their descent to land on a medium-sized lake ahead on the meadow.

It's the end of August, and we're only a few kilometres from the Luxembourg border.

"Canada geese," Kristian declares confidently, revealing just how much time we've actually spent learning new things over the past few years. Having grown up in a time when almost all wildlife had migrated south, he had never before faced a live goose.

I decide to test him, even though I can't verify his answer.

"Why do you think they're Canada geese?"

"Look at the large white cheek patches," he replies without hesitation. "With those, the only species you could confuse them with is the barnacle goose, but the barnacle goose is much smaller. Those are definitely Canada geese."

I'm impressed. Not only does he have an insatiable thirst for knowledge, but his powers of observation and memory for details are top-notch.

We stop and watch the large, noisy birds land surprisingly gracefully in the lake and on the meadow around it. One by one. There must be around 100 geese, filling the air with their life-affirming noise, honking loudly in a high-pitched, nasal tone.

Mali trembles expectantly, her ears rigidly pointed forward, trying to catch as many of the sounds as possible. Her bushy tail vibrates intensely, almost as if it has a life of its own. There's no doubt that she would love to be allowed to chase after them and scare them back into the air. But she's so well trained that she doesn't stray from Magnus's side until he gives her permission.

"They are beautiful," says Farhana.

"They sure are," grumbles Zaid, calmly reaching for his bow from the sledge. "Let's see if they taste as good as they look."

"Good idea," Magnus agrees, grabbing his compound bow and quiver. He skillfully nocks an arrow and draws the bow, ready to shoot as soon as he has his target in sight.

"You'd better stay here, Mikkel," Magnus teases good-naturedly. "I don't think anyone's ever succeeded in hunting geese with a harpoon."

"That's probably true," Mikkel laughs. "But no one with my talent has tried before now. Just wait and see. You'll regret your arrogance when you're standing empty-handed after shooting all your arrows into the lake, and I reel in a fat goose, perfectly skewered by my sturdy harpoon."

"If that happens, Zaid and I will eat its feet," Magnus laughs.

"The feet?" Mikkel asks, cocky.

"Webbed and all," Zaid confirms seriously.

"It's a deal then. Let's get going!"

Farhana and I shake our heads in resignation. Men will be boys, no matter their age.

We settle down in the grass, leaning back against my sledge, watching the three men sneak closer to the geese, moving against the wind.

Kristian grumbles loudly that he doesn't have a weapon. It doesn't sit well with him that Fatima won't get the chance to see him as a provider. But when she takes his hand and pulls him around to the other side of the sledge, out of sight, it doesn't take long for him to fall silent. I can clearly hear the sounds of kissing that follow.

Harmless, I think, pretending not to notice. Let them have their private moment in peace.

Farhana hears it too. She takes my hand in hers and smiles knowingly. Together, we sit with our fingers entwined, feeling peaceful for the first time in a long while, watching our men on their very first goose hunt. The three of them spread out in a fan shape, each covering as wide an area along the lakeshore as possible. Mikkel is in the middle with his harpoon, as there's no risk of losing his arrow if it flies into the water.

When they're within shooting range, Magnus is the first to take aim. I catch myself holding my breath until he releases the arrow. What a welcome change it would be to have fresh goose breast roasted over the fire. My mouth waters just at the thought.

The arrow leaves the bow silently. A second later, it pierces one of the many geese grazing peacefully on the meadow. It drops dead instantly. A few geese flap their wings briefly, rising about a metre off the ground before settling back down a few metres from their fallen companion.

Emilie clasps her hands and softly cheers beside me.

Mali springs up from her position between my spread legs, ready to dash down and help find the dead goose for Magnus, if I were to allow it. She's not a hunting dog, but she finds it fun to help out. To her, it's a game.

Magnus and Zaid each take down two more geese before Mikkel scares the entire flock into flight by skewering a goose out on the water. The goose doesn't die immediately but flaps noisily around while Mikkel firmly grips the line on the other end. For a moment, it tries to take off but then falls back with a loud splash. At that instant, the rest of the flock takes off in one coordinated movement, quickly distancing themselves from the hunters' deadly arrows.

I hear Anna burst out in laughter as Mikkel struggles to grab the goose at the end of the line.

Kasper rushes off to help his father, so I take the opportunity to release Mali as well. She races off like a rocket. Long before Kasper has covered half the distance, Mali is joyfully bounding around Magnus, sharing in the excitement as if she herself had brought down the birds.

That evening, everyone is in high spirits.

Six large geese, each weighing about five kilos, are ready to be plucked, gutted, and roasted over the fire. It's hard to believe that we're finally going to taste something other than dried seal meat. I'm as excited as I was as a little girl around the Christmas tree, and when I later bite into the first piece of crispy roast goose breast, tears stream down my face.

It's the best thing I've ever tasted.

Some cry.

Others laugh.

Emotions run free.

For the first time in a long while, there's a glimmer of hope.

We'll be alright!

Later that evening, Mikkel throws two crispy roast goose feet into the laps of Magnus and Zaid.

"There you go. Enjoy. I hope it'll taste as good to you as it will for me to watch you eat your words… and goose feet."

"What do you mean?" Zaid asks with mock confusion.

"I speared a goose with my harpoon, so now you two have to eat its feet."

"Well, that's not quite accurate," Magnus corrects him teasingly. "The deal was that if we'd shot all our arrows into the lake and you were the only one to get a goose, then we'd eat the feet. But that's not how things turned out, is it? We still have all our arrows, and between us, we took down 80% of the geese. So, you can eat your own feet."

He tosses the foot back to Mikkel.

"You're absolutely right, Magnus," Zaid laughs, tossing the other foot in the same direction.

"I knew I couldn't trust two old men," Mikkel laughs loudly and takes a big bite of the webbing on one foot, chewing dramatically.

Anna stares at him in shock, while both Magnus and Zaid roar with laughter. Moments later, Magnus reaches for the other foot and repeats Mikkel's feat. He passes the rest to Zaid, who, without hesitation, follows suit.

Soon, we're all howling with laughter.

For once, survival isn't at the forefront of our minds.

It may have been a harmless game, played in good spirits, but for me, it meant much more than that. For me, this incident during our long escape represents a silent bond between the three of them. The three men stand together no matter what. Shoulder by shoulder. They trust each other.

It's the same kind of bond that formed between Farhana and me that night when she finally ripped off the band aid and shared her painful story with me. We forge invisible ties that make us stronger and prove that none of us stands alone. That we have each other's backs.

As I reflect on this, I catch sight of Anna on the other side of the stove.

Perhaps with the exception of her.

If it weren't for Mikkel, she'd be completely alone.

Maybe Farhana is right when she says that help only comes to those who have something to offer. And Anna offers nothing; she only takes.

I feel sorry for her and decide, here and now, that I will try to be there for her a little more from now on, no matter what I think of her personality.

No one should be left behind. No one. Together is the only way we'll survive.

● ● ●

During the night, the rain begins.

Not just a bit of drizzle or light showers that stop as quickly as they start. No, this is the onset of the autumn rains, which, as we are soon to learn, will fall heavily and persistently all the way down to the Mediterranean. The rain pounds so hard against the roof of the house we've sought refuge in that sleep becomes utterly impossible. I lie awake for a long time, listening to the monotonous drumming of the rain. It's been a while since I last heard rain fall, and I welcome the sound as a pleasant change from the brutal snowstorms back home.

When daylight finally breaks through the grey clouds, there is still no sign of the rain letting up. On the contrary, it continues to pour down all day with varying intensity, and by the time we settle down again in the evening, it's still raining, showing no signs of stopping anytime soon.

The temperature drops to just above freezing.

Combined with the drastically increased humidity, it suddenly feels bitterly cold inside the house. We need more firewood, but no one is particularly eager to go out and chop trees in this weather. After just a few seconds, you're soaked to the skin, and the clothes will take hours to dry by the warm stove. Even Mali doesn't want to go outside, not even to relieve herself. She just stares at me when I open the door for her, as if I've lost my mind, then indignantly turns around and settles back down on Emilie's fur rug.

The next morning, the rain has finally eased enough for us to decide to move on. If we are to reach our destination before the winter cold sets in, we can't let the rain keep us trapped inside for too long. We're still behind schedule, and we can't afford any more delays.

We decide to leave behind the four sledges that Anna, Farhana, Kristian, and I have been dragging all the way from Denmark. There isn't much food left anyway, and what remains can easily fit on the men's sledges. I'm not thrilled about the added burden on their shoulders, but it will help us travel faster, so I reluctantly agree. We're all showing signs of exhaustion, and truth be told, my own strength is nearly gone. I have open sores on my shoulders from where the harness rubs against my skin. For weeks now, this has been severely hindering me. The tree-felling has made me strong, but my endurance is truly being tested.

Halfway through September, we approach the city of Dijon in France.

It rains almost constantly, and our clothes are soaked through. When the downpour gets too heavy, we take shelter in yet another abandoned house along the way, but time slips by too quickly, forcing us to continue even as the rain pours down. Everything is wet, and it's nearly impossible to get a fire going, so our clothes never fully dry. Before long, we're all drenched and chilled to the bone.

The cold feels different from what we're used to because our skin never gets the chance to dry and warm up. Back home, the cold bit into your skin, almost like it was burning you, but it stayed on the outside of your body. Here, the cold seems to come from within, freezing our muscles into stiff knots that cramp up with the slightest wrong move.

I'm growing anxious that we still haven't encountered any other people. How much further south do we have to go before we find life? There must be people somewhere. Where have they all gone?

I'm convinced that if we don't find help soon, none of us will survive much longer.

Kasper, the brave little boy, sits all day quietly on top of Mikkel's sledge, hiding under a thick layer of sealskin. He manages to stay reasonably dry in there, but his lips are blue, and he shivers uncontrollably from the cold. Emilie is still fighting, but even she needs to be carried more and more frequently.

We are all hypothermic.

Exhausted. Depleted.

When we finally reach the sign for Dijon, we're met by a solid double row of barbed wire fences stretching as far as the eye can see, east to west.

"It was put up recently," Magnus observes, tugging hard on it to test its strength.

"In the last couple of years at least," Mikkel confirms, puzzled. "What's this about?"

"They're trying to keep us out," Zaid mutters hopelessly. "This fence is here because they've been overrun by refugees, no doubt about it. This is to stop more from entering France."

"But we're already in France," Mikkel protests.

"This must be the new border," Magnus replies. "North of here, survival is impossible. We've reached our goal." He turns around with a huge smile. "We've reached our goal, friends!"

He shouts his joy into the empty streets, grabbing me and lifting me into the air, squeezing me tightly. His joy is infectious, and I start laughing with him. Soon, Kristian and Emilie join in, their laughter blending with ours. Mikkel and Anna kiss and unwrap Kasper from his blankets.

"We made it, Kasper. We've reached our destination!"

Fatima dances around Kristian, who spontaneously reaches out and kisses her on the lips. She shyly lets him, nervously glancing out of the corner of her eye to see if her parents are watching. They aren't. They're the only ones not sharing in the joy, standing a bit off to the side, looking sadly at the fence.

Fatima pulls away from Kristian and walks over to them.

"What's wrong?" she asks, concerned. "Aren't you happy?"

Magnus sets me down and goes to lay a hand on his Syrian friend's shoulder.

"What's going through your mind, my friend?"

"Unwanted," Farhana whispers sorrowfully, letting a tear roll down her cheek.

I know exactly what they're thinking. The fence represents every-thing refugees have experienced and perhaps still experience every day; the feeling of not being welcome. The fence isn't meant to keep anyone in. No one travels from south to north. The fence is indeed there to prevent us from entering the country, despite Europe's tradition of open borders.

Without the sledges and the children, and if we were in better physical shape, we might easily have scaled the two rows of fence, which stretch four or five metres into the air. But we are exhausted, and climbing over it would mean leaving behind our remaining supplies. Not to mention, I can't imagine either Kasper or Emilie climbing all the way to the top, getting through the rolls of barbed wire without getting stuck, and safely making it down the other side.

"Can you see anyone over there?" Zaid asks.

"Not for miles," Mikkel replies, scanning the deserted streets leading into Dijon.

"That's because this is the outer border," Zaid concludes. "No one lives here. We still need to go further south. We have to get to the other side."

"We can't," I snap irritably, wiping a raindrop from my nose with the back of my hand. "We can't climb over and leave our things behind. Who knows how far we have to go before we find people who can help us? And how are we supposed to get the children and Mali over? We just can't!"

"Then we'll follow the fence until we find an entrance," Zaid grumbles resignedly. He looks worn out. Aged at least ten years during the journey.

I wonder briefly what I must look like but quickly push the thought away. We have bigger problems to deal with.

"Which way?" Mikkel asks, looking both directions.

"West," Magnus replies. "At least that way, we'll be heading towards Spain instead of Switzerland. I imagine the Alps are suffering terribly from the cold too."

Everywhere, the fence is solid. There are no holes or signs of weakness from previous attempts by others to break through. It effectively blocks all unauthorised entry, and as we follow the fence for hours, we slowly start to lose hope.

Dejected, we find yet another abandoned house and settle in for the night. The next day, we continue kilometre after kilometre until, by the afternoon, Kristian suddenly stops.

"I can see someone!" he exclaims excitedly. He points straight ahead.

Sure enough, a couple of hundred metres in front of us, there is movement along the fence where it crosses the A6 motorway towards Paris.

A checkpoint?

They don't notice us until we are about 30 metres away. Five border guards, armed with loaded machine guns, turn around in shock as they finally see us. They're all dressed in dark green military uniforms, large black winter boots, and fur hats with earflaps.

One of them shouts something in French, but when we don't respond, he repeats it in English.

"Stop!"

I'm so relieved I could cry. At last, we've arrived at a place where there is still some form of civilisation.

Help is within reach.

In my rush of joy, I push aside everything Farhana told me about being unwanted. I embrace the moment and convince myself that everything is fine, that we're saved.

"Where are you coming from?" asks the man who speaks English.

"From Denmark," Mikkel replies, stepping forward to shake his hand.

The soldiers instantly step back, raising their machine guns threateningly, pointing them straight at Mikkel's face.

"Step back!" the man shouts in English.

Mikkel jumps back, shocked, hands raised.

"We mean no harm," he says, bewildered. "Don't shoot. We just need help."

The man scrutinises us, one by one, with narrowed eyes.

He finally stops at Mali, locking eyes with her as she lets out a low growl from deep in her chest.

"Denmark, you say? I didn't think there was anything left up there but ice and abandoned cities…"

"There soon won't be," Magnus confirms. "There's a small village still holding on. But it's only a matter of time if they're not rescued soon."

The man shifts his gaze away from Mali, staring blankly at Magnus. He says nothing for a long moment. He doesn't smile, nor does he show any sympathy, despite the fact that we're clearly on the brink of our endurance.

The guns remain trained on us, with no sign that the soldiers intend to lower them.

"What do you want?" the man finally asks.

"Help," Magnus answers. "We won't survive another winter out here on our own."

"Help?" the man repeats sarcastically. "What makes you think there's any help to be found here?"

I feel the knot in my stomach tighten again.

Farhana is right. There's no help for us. We've come all this way for nothing.

Doubt bubbles in the back of my mind. Should we have stayed at home and waited for death to catch up with us there? Anger surges through me. This man is unbelievably arrogant. After everything we've been through, how can he treat us like this? There must be rules, even now. Even in times of crisis, there must be some form of law and order!

"That can't be right!" I shout angrily. "We've always helped each other in Europe. And now you're saying we can't apply for asylum in France?"

The man slowly shifts his gaze from Magnus to me.

He stares at me with malice for a moment, a faint, cruel smile curling the corner of his mouth.

"Asylum, you say? Is that what you want? To apply for asylum?"

"Yes, for God's sake!" Mikkel blurts out. "We want to seek asylum."

"Well, now, that's a different matter altogether," the man replies with barely concealed irony in his voice.

He and the other soldiers suddenly step aside, gesturing for us to enter with sweeping arms.

"Leave your weapons behind. You can't keep those. And leave the sledges too, but you might want to take the blankets on top."

For a moment, we exchange confused glances until Mikkel slowly begins walking past the guards, holding Anna in one hand and Kasper in the other. Once they've crossed the checkpoint, Zaid, Farhana, and Fatima follow, then Kristian and Emilie.

Mali doesn't move. She keeps her eyes locked on the English-speaking soldier, who, by all appearances, is the leader. She growls a warning.

Magnus takes my hand, and together we pass through the checkpoint. It feels nerve-wracking, like handing our fate over to strangers we're not sure we can trust.

Suddenly, I hear a series of loud bangs behind me. I spin around in fright.

Gunfire?

Smoke rises from the muzzle of the man's machine gun.

"Oh, by the way, dogs aren't welcome," he says gruffly, slamming the gate shut behind us.

Part III

Unwanted

13 Magnus

The world-renowned and long-deceased author, Jack London, once said, "A bone to a dog is not charity. Charity is a bone shared with a dog when you are just as hungry as the dog."

I have never considered Mali to be charity, even though it was clear that others in the village did. Mali is family.

Even when we were forced to eat rats that winter, at the beginning, when hunger nearly killed us all—even then, we shared with Mali without complaint. A piece of breast for Freja. A thigh for Emilie. Another thigh for Kristian. A fillet for myself. Innards and tail for Mali. The distribution felt natural, and although our stomachs screamed for more and our bellies cramped in painful spasms, no one looked longingly at the portion that went to Mali. She had as much right to it as we did. Neither more nor less.

If it hadn't been for the dog, I probably wouldn't have survived on my own when I got lost in the snow. If it hadn't been for Mali, we might never have found Freja and Emilie when they got lost in the snow. If it hadn't been for Mali, our family as a whole might not exist today.

All of this flashes through my mind in a split second as my brain tries to make sense of what I'm seeing. I don't understand the scene. A bushy, reddish-brown clump of fur lying completely still on the asphalt on the other side of the fence. Is it an animal?

A few wet strands of fur stir faintly in the wind, but it's raining again, so the fur is heavy and soaked. Thick blood spreads slowly from the animal, but soon the rain dilutes it so much that it blends into the asphalt, adding to the confusion between what I see and what my brain registers. What kind of animal is it, and where did it suddenly come from? Is it a fox? What was it the man said just before he closed the gate behind us?

Suddenly, I hear Freja scream in panic. A moment later, Emilie's higher-pitched voice joins in, just as urgently, just as desperately, just as full of anguish.

I turn my head, confused, as if in slow motion, staring in shock at them as they cry out in unison.

What are they shouting?

Mali?

I focus again on the animal on the asphalt.

Mali?

Only then do I realise that the man with the gun has shot her. Murdered her right before our eyes.

Out of the corner of my eye, I see a sudden movement. Moments later, I watch as Kristian throws himself at the man with the gun, catching him off guard and making him step back two paces. With arms and legs flailing, Kristian tries to hit him in the face and kick him in the groin all at once.

The man raises his gun defensively in front of him, trying to keep Kristian at bay, but when that fails, he suddenly swings the butt of his rifle, striking Kristian hard across his right cheekbone, knocking him backwards with blood streaming from a gash under his eye.

The sight of Kristian falling to the ground, struck down by the arrogant Frenchman, snaps me back to reality. I barely have time to think before I throw myself at him with a ferocity that leaves little to be desired from Kristian's rage.

The man swings the gun at me, but he misses, and I manage to land a solid punch on the bridge of his nose, sending blood spurting. Before I can land another blow, I'm tackled from behind by two other guards.

They pin me to the ground on my side, raining kicks onto my stomach, back, and legs.

In the distance, I hear the women screaming. I think it's their cries that make me ignore the pain and fight back with everything I've got. I grab hold of one man's foot as he kicks me in the gut again, yanking hard enough to make him lose balance just long enough for me to roll into his other leg and knock him down.

Suddenly, Mikkel joins the fight, throwing himself at the other man. He grabs him in a bear hug, locking his arm tightly around his neck in a chokehold, pulling him away from me.

Before I can do anything else, there's another deafening bang from a gunshot.

Mikkel roars in pain, releasing the man and falling heavily to the ground.

Everyone freezes instantly. The women's screams stop as abruptly as they began.

The man with the gun has recovered from the punch to his nose. To prevent the situation from spiralling further out of control, he's shot Mikkel in the thigh, effectively putting an end to our fight. After all, we didn't make it all this way, through frost, snow, and storms, risking our lives, just to be killed by the first border guard we encountered.

"That's enough," he yells, pointing the barrel of his gun at Zaid's head.

Until now, Zaid had kept quietly in the background.

"The dog couldn't come with you," the man continues, "because there's already barely enough food for everyone in the camps. People would fight over it and tear it apart alive just for a little more to eat. Killing the dog now was the most humane solution, whether you like it or not!"

Blood trickles from his nose and into his mouth as he speaks. He wipes it away irritably with one gloved hand.

"Now, if we're done with this nonsense, can we get on with registering and sorting you out? And we should probably get that one patched up too." He gestures dismissively at Mikkel and barks a few quick orders in French to two of the other guards.

They immediately bend down over Mikkel, helping him to his feet before dragging him towards the guardhouse.

Anna and Kasper follow.

Still seething, I force myself to stand. The pain is certainly there, but it's not unbearable. The thick layers of clothing have protected me, and I don't think I've broken anything.

I quickly check the cut under Kristian's eye. It's shallow but will need a few stitches from the repair kit Freja always carries with her. He's already got a large bruise from the rifle butt, evidence of the man's utterly unacceptable behaviour.

There must be someone above him we can complain to? Someone he's accountable to.

"I'll kill him," Kristian mutters through gritted teeth.

"Then you'll end up in prison," I respond wearily. "We didn't come this far just to end up in a French prison for murder."

"But he killed Mali," Kristian insists stubbornly. "An eye for an eye."

"I know exactly how you feel. I'm furious too. And heart-broken, all at the same time. Mali was our best friend. Part of the family. But we need this man's help to survive, whether we hate him or not. Without him, we're done for. So we'll have to swallow the pain as best we can."

Suddenly, I start to sob softly over the loss of my beloved dog. Kristian sees this, and soon he joins in. I pull him close, and together we cry over all the injustices in our lives and the fresh loss of a dear friend.

Freja and Emilie join us, and before long, we are all standing there, crying our pain out in each other's arms.

● ● ●

"Names and nationality?"

"Magnus. This is my wife Freja and our two children, Kristian and Emilie. As I said earlier, we're from Denmark."

"I didn't ask where you're from. I asked about your nationality. There's a difference."

"We're Danish."

The man writes down the answers on a piece of paper in front of him.

It's not much warmer inside the cabin than it is outside, but at least it's dry.

The man sits on an old, worn-out faux-leather office chair that creaks loudly every time he moves. He provokes me endlessly, but I hold myself in check. Partly because we need his help, and partly because there are two guards behind us with loaded weapons.

Our friends are being held in the adjacent room until it's their turn to answer questions.

One of the soldiers has patched up Mikkel's gunshot wound

as best he could.

"Just until he gets to the hospital," he had said.

"Age?"

"My wife and I are both 45. Kristian is 15, and Emilie is 11."

"Religion?"

"Religion?" I repeat, questioning. "What does that matter?"

The man doesn't respond but simply looks up from the paper, irritated, and waits impatiently for my answer. It's written on his report form that he must gather information about our religious affiliation, and if it's written there, he asks, no matter how relevant it may be.

I shrug indifferently.

"None."

"Atheist?"

"You could call it that."

"That applies to all of you?" he asks, looking at my family.

They all nod in agreement, and he scribbles down the answers.

"Why are you seeking asylum?"

"Why?" I exclaim sarcastically. "As I said outside, before you shot our dog, it's no longer possible to survive up north."

"Didn't you also say there are still people up there? Some who've chosen to stay behind and are still alive?"

"Yes, but I don't think they'll survive much longer without help. Maybe a few more winters at most. It's unbearably cold up there, and there's almost nothing to eat except seal meat. But the seals are in decline, too. Can't you send someone up to get them?"

"Why didn't they come with you?" he asks, blatantly ignoring my question.

"Some didn't feel they could make the long journey on foot

through frost and snow because of their old age. Others still cling to the hope that it's just a phase and that the winter will soon release its grip."

"But not you?"

I look at him, puzzled. I don't understand the question.

"You don't think it's a phase? That we'll soon return to normal conditions?"

"No. If we did, we wouldn't have set out on such a long and dangerous journey, would we?"

The man is getting on my nerves, and I have to make a real effort not to get even more hostile.

He remains unfazed. It's clear he's experienced in his line of work. No doubt he's had thousands of similar conversations with thousands of other desperate families before us.

"But you weren't in immediate danger when you left?"

"Of course, we were," I blurt, struggling to sit still in my chair.

What is he getting at?

"Besides being cold and food being scarce, you don't exactly look emaciated. You must have managed to get something to eat?"

"Yes, we were fortunate," I reply, repeating myself yet again. "Our village wasn't far from the sea, where a colony of seals had settled. And we had plenty of firewood from the forest next to the village. But as I said, the forest disappeared day by day in the flames to keep us warm, and the seal colony grew smaller and smaller. More are being hunted than join the group. It's just a matter of time before the resources run out."

The man stops and stares at me for a long time with an inscrutable expression. After an agonisingly long pause, where he doesn't break eye contact for even a second, he suddenly asks a new question.

"Aren't you, in reality, what we call welfare refugees? Migrants, if you will?"

I look at him, shocked. I try to find even the slightest hint that he's joking. A warped, but still just a sarcastic comment intended to lighten the mood. But there isn't the faintest trace of humour on his lips, and I soon realise that the question is seriously meant.

"Welfare refugees?" I ask, indignantly. "Would you care to explain what you mean by that?"

He leans back in the chair, which creaks ominously under his weight, before replying in the most patient tone he can muster.

"Well, there's no indication that you were forced to flee. No one was after you, trying to kill you. You had enough to eat You were able to adapt and survive life in the cold."

"Yes, up until now!" I snap, seething with anger. "But how much longer would we be able to survive? Are you even listening to what I'm telling you?"

The man smiles patronisingly and leans forward in the chair again, articulating his next words with exaggerated care.

"But you didn't flee because the cold threatened to kill you right then and there. And the seals are still there. So, it's not like the food's completely gone. On the contrary, you had so much that you brought ample supplies with you. Those sledges out there are packed with meat. So forgive me if it's hard to believe your claims that your lives were in immediate danger. It seems far more likely that you're here to take advantage of the French people's generosity. Isn't that what this is really about? You just want to freeload off France?"

"You know what?" I shout angrily. "Call it whatever you like! What difference does it make what you believe? You weren't there, so you have no idea what the conditions are like up north. We've risked our lives to get here. Now we're here, and we need help!"

Freja remains unusually silent beside me. I imagine she's too shocked to take part in the conversation. Her eyes are wet, on the verge of spilling over. I take her limp hand in my lap and give it a squeeze. She doesn't respond.

"Well, the difference is quite significant, actually," he says with a smug grin. "You're not entitled to seek asylum. That right is reserved only for those who can be classified as true refugees in the strictest sense of the word. And according to the UN Refugee Convention, that applies solely to people fleeing conflicts, violence, persecution, or human rights violations. These people are protected under international law and can apply for residency under asylum rules. In other words, they have a legal right to stay in France, and we are obligated to care for them.

This right and obligation do not apply to climate refugees, who, from a legal standpoint, are merely migrants seeking a better life elsewhere and are therefore here illegally."

I'm stunned. Have we really travelled all this way for nothing? It makes no sense. What about all those who left before us? The landscape we just passed through was completely deserted. Where have they all gone?

"But don't lose hope just yet. We're not barbarians here in France. We acknowledge that life up north is hard. For heaven's sake, life is hard right here." He stomps the floor with his boot as if to emphasise his point.

"So, what now?" I ask. "Are you going to send us back? Did you kill our dog for nothing?"

He leans back, chuckling in a nasty, spiteful way. There's

something about him that gets under my skin in a way I can't quite describe. He's arrogant, yes. He's despicable in his entire attitude. But there's something else. Something more undefinable.

Hatred?

"No, we certainly won't! How would that look to the outside world if we started sending people back where they came from, only for them to freeze to death in six months? No, that won't do! Even though you technically don't qualify as recognised refugees and therefore have no social or economic rights in this country, we still have an obligation to care for you, as you fall under what we call 'other protection needs.'"

"And what does that entail?"

"Well, we'll put you up in one of the camps and, of course, provide you with a tent to sleep in and some food so you can survive until conditions improve up north. Financially, however, there won't be anything to gain. So everything you might need beyond the tent and the blankets you'll be given on arrival at the camp—you'll have to barter for or find some other way to acquire. But they'll explain all that at the camp. It's outside my remit. My job is just to register you and get you safely sent to the correct camp, which will probably be in Spain. So, you've still got a long journey ahead of you."

"Spain??" Freja and I exclaim in unison.

She obviously hears what's being said, even though she mostly looks like she's withdrawn into herself.

The soldier looks at us, surprised.

"You've really been cut off from the world," he exclaims loudly.

Then, to our surprise, he takes his time explaining further, almost as if we're schoolchildren being taught one of the many implications of the refugee crisis.

"Due to the enormous migration pressure France has faced in recent years, the camps here have become so overcrowded that they simply cannot take any more people. Yes, it's slowed down now—you're actually the only ones we've received so far this year—but millions upon millions have arrived before you. From Germany, England, Ireland, Denmark, the Netherlands, Belgium, and so on. We're talking about hundreds of millions. No, more—over a hundred million.

Everyone has to pass through France to get to Spain or Portugal, so those two countries have received almost no migrants in comparison. Some, of course, have gone towards Italy and Greece. I'm not saying we've handled all of Northern Europe's migrants alone, but we've definitely taken more than our fair share.

The pressure on the French camps eventually became so severe that there was a real risk they would physically collapse. If that happened, hordes of desperate people would storm into society, doing more harm than good. Just imagine the chaos that would follow. Law and order would instantly break down, and nothing would function anymore.

Thankfully, Spain and Portugal understood the risk and agreed to ease some of the pressure on France, which is why we're now sending more and more migrants to camps on the Iberian Peninsula."

"Okay, but I honestly don't care where you send us, as long as we can stay together," I say, cutting him off mid-sentence. I'm getting thoroughly fed up with listening to this Frenchman, and I just want to get moving as quickly as possible. Far away from the latent malice I can sense lurking just beneath the surface.

He clears his throat briefly.

"Well, that's the thing. The man next door with the gunshot wound in his leg—we can't exactly send him on to Spain, can we? How would that look? No, he and his family will stay in France. At least until his leg heals. As for the other family, the ones with Arab backgrounds—they'll automatically be separated from the white families. Experience has shown there are far too many conflicts in the camps when we mix Arabs with white people. So Muslims are housed in one camp, and Christians and atheists, like yourselves, are placed in another. It's not my idea; that's just how it's evolved over time. For safety and peace."

Kristian, who has been silent until now, simply glaring at the Frenchman with all the anger his teenage body can muster, suddenly snaps awake.

"How will I see Fatima again?" he asks anxiously. "If she's sent to a different camp than us?"

The Frenchman slowly shifts his gaze, locking eyes with Kristian. A malicious smile spreads across his face, revealing a row of yellowed teeth in his upper jaw.

"You'd best forget about her as quickly as possible, my little friend, because you won't be seeing her again any time soon."

● ● ●

Mikkel groans loudly in pain as he hauls himself up the two steps and into the dark green military vehicle that will transport us to our as yet undefined destinations. We are seated in three rows at the back of the bus, and the soldier assigned to escort us locks us in behind a sturdy metal grate. He sits up front, where he can talk freely with the driver. Both are carrying Beretta 92 pistols visibly at their hips.

On the wall separating the driver from the cabin hang four Benelli M3 shotguns, locked behind a grille similar to the one that separates us from the soldiers.

There's nothing inherently wrong with us being transported in a military vehicle with loaded weapons within the soldiers' reach, but I feel deeply intimidated being locked up, as if we were dangerous terrorists. As if we were planning to blow up the presidential palace.

I try not to let it get to me and focus instead on saying goodbye to my good friends, who have been such a big part of my life over the past few years. We promise each other that we will reunite when things improve and when we no longer need the French or Spanish authorities' help to survive.

Kristian and Fatima sit close together in the back seat, holding hands as the military bus rattles along the deserted country roads. Both are crying endlessly at the prospect of losing contact with each other before their relationship has even really begun. They kiss each other passionately, not bothering to hide it from the rest of us.

Zaid sees it but discreetly looks away. Of all the challenges we face in the future, his daughter's first love is the least of his concerns. Why shouldn't he let her enjoy the last bit of time with Kristian?

I stare out through the rain-streaked windows, absent-mindedly watching the empty buildings flash by. I know I should use our last moments together to say everything that remains unsaid between friends, the very foundation of a lasting and trusting friendship. But I feel trapped in my own grief over the loss of Mali and filled with anxiety about how I will ensure my family's safety going forward. Can that even be done, surrounded by thousands of others in the same situation, all just trying to get through the days, stay warm, and eat when food is served?

Zaid says life in the camps is worse than we can imagine, and that there's no way to mentally prepare for the horrors that await us when we arrive. I think he's exaggerating. As far as I know, he's never been in a camp run by the UN or the authorities of a European country, where human rights still mean something. Surely, the conditions can't be compared to those he knows from Lebanon or has heard about from Turkey, where refugees were practically left to fend for themselves.

I do, of course, remember the stories about the refugee camp in Calais, France, where nearly 10,000 refugees and migrants gathered on the coast in hopes of reaching England. The hygiene conditions became so bad that it was outright hazardous to stay there. The authorities eventually cleared the camp and relocated people to centres across France. But I also don't think you can compare that unofficial camp, which formed when refugees and migrants simply settled by the coast, with the more organised camps in Spain. There, they've realised that people need help to prevent them from rioting or flooding into local communities, where they would take jobs from the locals, beg, or turn to crime. That would only reduce the willingness of those who could help, or their ability to do so, due to limited economic and physical resources.

Surely, lessons have been learned from past mistakes?

The bus comes to a hissing stop, pulling me out of my thoughts. I focus my eyes on the movements outside in the rain. We've been cut off from the world for so long that even limited activity feels overwhelming. Armed military personnel stand guard outside a large tent camp filled with green tents bearing the distinctive Red Cross logo.

People are rushing back and forth between the tents, hunched over to shield themselves from the rain, which is pouring relentlessly over the landscape. The camp is surrounded by a tall wire fence, just like the one we encountered at the border. You can only come and go with the guards' permission.

A middle-aged male doctor with a grey beard and wearing a white lab coat emerges from the camp. He stops at the guards, showing a card that must be his pass. He holds an umbrella over his head, and the water trickles off the sides and into the neck of one of the guards, who has stepped partially under the umbrella to examine the pass more closely. It doesn't seem to bother him much, though, as he stands motionless until the inspection is done and he allows the doctor to pass.

The doctor walks straight to our bus and knocks on the door without hesitation. "You have a new patient for us?" he says in English as soon as the door opens. He doesn't waste time on pleasantries.

I can see he looks tired. The driver doesn't respond, just points to the back towards us. The soldier up front stands up and starts unlocking the gate. He gestures silently to Mikkel, indicating that he should get up. This must be the hospital where Mikkel, Anna, and Kasper are getting off. Mikkel rises with difficulty, clutching the wound that is clearly causing him a lot of pain.

"Another gunshot wound!" the doctor exclaims indignantly. "It's been a long time since we've had new patients from your area up north. What are you doing to those poor people up there?" he asks the soldier. "Are you shooting them all? I can hardly imagine how many didn't make it past you alive..."

"Cut the accusations," the soldier growls irritably as he slides the gate aside for Mikkel. "You just do your job, and we'll do ours, okay?"

The doctor doesn't reply but glares at him, clearly not the first time they've had this exchange.

I stand up and hug Mikkel as he passes my seat.

"I'll see you at the camp when you're patched up. Take care, my friend. I'll be waiting for you."

I assume Mikkel and his family will be taken to the same camp as us once there's no visible trace of the border guards' violent actions, but of course, I can't be sure. I can't bear the thought that this might be the last I see of my younger friend, so I pretend it's just a minor formality.

"Thanks for everything," he says, giving me a few hearty pats on the back.

That's all we need to say or do. We both understand the meaning. Maybe we'll meet again, but if we don't, we've at least enjoyed each other's company while we could.

In the meantime, the doctor has called for a couple of orderlies who bring a stretcher, and Mikkel lies down on it. I sit silently in the bus, watching them hurry through the rain back into the hospital camp, soon disappearing from sight. Anna and Kasper quickly follow, hand in hand.

"Do you think we'll ever see them again?" Freja asks sadly, leaning her head on my shoulder.

"I hope so."

"I hope they find some medicine for Anna."

"Yeah," I reply. I hope so too, though deep down I know the chances aren't great.

14 Freja

In Lyon, our small group is separated once again. Without the chance to say a proper goodbye, my family and I are herded into a closed freight carriage. Apart from a few open-barred windows high up near the roof, it resembles the one we slept in while in Hamburg.

Zaid, Farhana, and Fatima are led away, and I barely manage to shout a farewell before my friend disappears from sight.

Desperate, Kristian tries to follow after Fatima when he realises she's not allowed to board the carriage, but he's stopped and restrained by two armed guards. To them, a Danish teenage boy's first love means nothing.

He cries and yells at them to let him go, but it's no use. He is not allowed to leave the carriage.

The train carriage is fitted with 27 rows of hard wooden benches with short backs and no cushioning. We're forced to the very back and told to sit on the last row.

Kristian pleads with the guards to let him stay with Fatima. Their faces remain expressionless as they stand against the wall at the far end, staring blankly at us. They don't take their eyes off us for a second, as though we are France's number one enemy.

Which, perhaps, we are, I think sadly. Us and all the other hundred million refugees who came before us.

A hundred million.

It's hard to imagine so many people crammed into various camps across France, Spain, and Portugal. How can they even have space for that many?

By now, I've become so used to counting and planning everything just to survive that my mind often wanders automatically into pointless calculations. If the population density were the same as it was in the Netherlands before the crisis, how many people could the three countries even hold together? There were around 400 people per square kilometre in the Netherlands back then. With the same population density and half of France's habitable land left, the country could accommodate a total of 120 million people. Sixty million more than its original population! So maybe it's no wonder they felt the need to push some of the burden onto Spain.

Once my brain starts wandering into these mathematical paths, I tend to get quite practical and don't let my emotions get in the way. Perhaps that explains why I so easily fall into this exercise.

Spain's geographical area is about 500,000 square kilometres. That means there would be room for 200 million people in Spain alone, or roughly 150 million more than its population. Portugal, by the same measure, could accommodate 25 million more than its own population.

So, space isn't the issue. And while the Netherlands had a relatively high population density by European standards, they still managed to build a functioning society. The same goes for city-states like Singapore and Hong Kong, whose population density was 16 times higher than that of the Netherlands.

So why shouldn't it also be possible in Spain, France, and Portugal?Even though it sounds like a lot of people, an extra 100 million shouldn't be completely unmanageable if production and logistics are scaled accordingly. Of course, Rome wasn't built in a day, but it still gives me hope for the future.

Without realising it, I've been holding my breath, and I catch myself letting out a long, relieved exhale.

Until it suddenly hits me: the population of Northern Europe was far greater than 100 million people.

In Britain and Ireland alone, there were more than 70 million people. Where are they now? Are they all dead? How many Brits are trapped on their own side of the Channel? How many died trying to cross it, now lying lifeless on the seabed or washed up on the shores?

The thought makes me feel sick. Suddenly, I'm nauseous and feel like throwing up.

Most people from the northeastern side of Europe have likely fled toward Greece and Italy, as the border guard told us. But logically, that would make up at most half of the remaining European population. For most others, it wouldn't make sense to go in that direction.

And what about the Norwegians and Swedes? How many of them have managed to escape the cold even further north and cross the Skagerrak or Øresund on their way to safety?

Magnus and I have, of course, talked about all of this hundreds of times before, but it's only now that the reality truly sinks in.

I suddenly remember all the bodies on the railway tracks at Hamburg's central station. Unable to stop it, I vomit in an explosive stream of sour, foul bile that splashes onto the floor and the bench in front of me.

Magnus turns his head in alarm, studying me closely. "Are you sick?" he asks, concerned.

I shake my head weakly, closing my eyes behind my warm mittens, which I've held up to cover my face. I try to take deep breaths, struggling to regain control of my thoughts. Trying to get as much oxygen into my lungs and up to my brain as possible.

The guards stand motionless at the other end, staring at us impassively, as if my health means nothing to them. Maybe it doesn't. Their only task is to ensure none of us escape before we reach our final destination in Spain, preventing us from mixing illegally with the French population.

Their unrelenting stare starts to get on my nerves. I feel like a condemned prisoner, whose only crime is to be part of the group that destroyed the world's climate. But they belong to that same group too. The only difference is that we were unlucky enough to live at the wrong latitude when the disaster struck.

I feel Magnus's warm hand on my forehead. He's checking if I have a fever. I don't. I'm just overwhelmed by the events of the past 24 hours. I've tried to stay strong for Emilie and Kristian, but now, all my emotions are finally catching up with me. I start to cry. At first quietly, but soon the tears flood out, and I sob so hysterically that the children stare at me, frightened.

I curl up into Magnus's protective embrace. Emilie places her little hand on the back of my neck, stroking it soothingly, but I'm too broken to appreciate her loving gesture.

"He shot Mali," I sob.

It's the first time I've actually said it out loud—the loss of our scruffy family member.

He shot Mali.

"Will we ever see Farhana and Fatima again? Why are we being treated like this? Why, Magnus? What did we do?"

"I told you we should've stayed in Denmark," Kristian bursts out from the other side of Emilie. "We never should've left. On the very first day after we arrive, we lose Mali. We might never see Fatima and her family again. And what about Mikkel? He got shot too. What a great welcome we've had! Brilliant decision to leave our house back home. For this!"

"Kristian! That's enough!" Magnus cuts him off angrily. "The decision's been made. It's too late to undo it, and blaming us for everything that's happened won't help anyone. Nobody could have foreseen this."

"Zaid told us! He said to stay away from the camps."

"Yes, he did. And yet he came with us. Do you know why? It wasn't for the company, I can tell you that. He and Farhana have been through the uncertainty and humiliation of fleeing from their home before. You don't go through that again unless you're absolutely convinced it's the only option left.

If we'd stayed home and carried on as before, we might have survived for a couple more years, but no longer than that. The forest would be gone. The seal colony would have disappeared. Wiped out. And it would be too late to move south. We'd be dead before we even reached the German border. We'd be trapped in our own home, with no heat and no food. We'd freeze to death long before winter was halfway through. Just like all those who died in that first harsh winter. But maybe you don't remember that? Would you rather die passively than try to reach out for the lifeline that's being held out in front of you, no matter how fragile it may seem?"

Magnus is hurt.

It took me many years to realise that when Magnus is upset, he doesn't react by crying, but by lashing out. He isn't angry with Kristian. On the contrary, he's frustrated by having been forced to subject his family to all these dangers and hardships, without being able to protect us from them. It wounds his pride, even though it's abundantly clear to everyone that the entire situation is completely beyond his control. There's nothing he could have done differently.

Kristian looks away. He doesn't reply, choosing instead to remain passively silent.

I can sense that he hasn't fully given in, but that he's wise enough to realise that continuing the argument is pointless. He's clearly becoming a young man who is starting to form his own opinions and views. It likely won't be long before he really begins to challenge Magnus as the head of the family, as young men always do when they grow up and go through puberty. There's nothing unnatural about it, but it's crucial for our cohesion, especially in these uncertain and harsh circumstances, that youth and age don't clash too much. Youth's eagerness and the wisdom of age don't always harmonise as they should.

In truth, Magnus and Kristian are incredibly alike. Although Magnus is far more considered now than when I fell in love with him over 20 years ago, he's still impulsive and often acts before thinking—especially if he feels wronged. In that way, Kristian is growing up to be a near-exact copy of his father.

Suddenly, we hear a noisy group of people approaching outside the wagon's closed sides. Soon after, the door opens and a flood of refugees in tattered, filthy clothes comes pouring in. The garments hang loosely around their emaciated bodies. They keep coming until every available seat is filled, and even then they continue to squeeze in. Eventually, the carriage is so overcrowded that you can't even raise an arm without bumping into someone else.

The stench from so many people is indescribable. It's obvious that they've been cut off from basic sanitary conditions for quite some time.

In front of me, an elderly woman has sat down in my vomit. Her coat is already caked with mud, and a sharp odour of stale sweat and urine clings to her. Her long, greying hair is greasy, shining with the evidence that it hasn't been washed in ages.

Once the carriage is packed to the brim, I hear the door scraping along its tracks until it closes with a crash.

The air immediately turns claustrophobically heavy, despite the open windows near the roof. I struggle to breathe and have to force myself to inhale deeply, slowly, in an effort to calm down and get enough oxygen into my lungs with each breath.

Emilie looks at me in panic. She's grown up with plenty of space around her. The fear of being trapped at the very back of the wagon, with so many people blocking the way out, threatens to send her into a panic attack, like those we've seen Anna have on several occasions during our journey. Emilie starts hyperventilating, taking shallow breaths, so I guide her to breathe like I do—slow and deep—until her breathing gradually returns to normal.

The heat from the crowd of bodies quickly raises the temperature inside the wagon. I start sweating profusely in my seal-skin coat. Sweat runs down my forehead, stinging my eyes, making them red and blurry, so the surroundings become hazy. Underneath my clothes, the sweat irritates the open wounds on my shoulders that still haven't healed, even though I haven't pulled a sledge in weeks. Thick scabs cover what were once open, weeping sores, but the scabs keep cracking open, causing small bleeding spots. It's as if they refuse to fully close. The lack of vitamin C and the prolonged physical exertion I've put my body through likely play a significant role in the slow healing process. There isn't much I can do to change those conditions, so I have to grit my teeth and do my best to keep the wounds clean to avoid infection.

I try to distinguish the languages being spoken around me. Most people are Germans, but there are also a few Dutch among them. I don't hear any Scandinavian languages or English among the cacophony of voices, which eventually dies down as the train finally starts moving.

As we pick up speed, the wind soon blows in through the open windows. Fresh, cold air mixes with the stuffy, foul-smelling, hot air inside the wagon, making it easier to breathe again. Along the way, I observe my fellow passengers. Most of them begin nodding off shortly after we depart. Wedged tightly between each other, they sit upright, heads lolling strangely with the train's movements as it rattles along the old, worn-out tracks.

Everyone is wearing old, worn-out clothing. Some have holes at the elbows, others are filthy like the woman in front of me. A few appear to be in decent physical shape, but most are malnourished and show clear signs of being in a state of deterioration.

I wonder how long they've lived in the camps in France to reach such a low point? At the same time, I'm deeply horrified at the condition most people seem to end up in during their stays in the camps, which we haven't yet experienced ourselves.

A woman about my age scratches her scalp with a hand that's just little more than bones and loose skin. As if she can feel my gaze on her, she suddenly turns her head. Her neck is so thin it looks as if it might snap under the weight. Our eyes meet for a few seconds before she lets out a resigned sigh and turns away again. Beneath all the grime, behind her translucent skin and lifeless grey-blue eyes, I see a woman who was once beautiful. A woman who likely received plenty of positive attention from men but has now succumbed to hopelessness. A person who has given up on life, merely following along and letting others dictate her path.

I wonder what she saw in my face?

I lift one hand in front of my eyes and study it closely. Even though I'm thin, I'm not exactly gaunt. And while I'm clearly missing certain vitamins in my body, I'm not malnourished. My muscles are strong, visibly defined under my clothes after years of felling trees and the past months of dragging a heavy sledge.

Did she see a reflection of her own former self, how she looked before she was forced to flee?

I shudder at the thought and once again promise myself that I will never give up like her. My children and my husband need me to stay strong, healthy, and well. I can't allow myself to fall into ruin, because a chain is only as strong as its weakest link, and only together can we stand firm and survive our grim fate.

I think of Farhana and her sorrowful life story. Both she and Zaid kept their heads above water, despite a fate determined to drown them in misery, and they came out stronger on the other side. She's my inspiration, and should my family, for some reason, not be motivation enough to keep fighting, I at least owe it to Farhana. I promised her that we would stick together, no matter what happened along the way, but we've only just arrived, and we're already separated. Will I ever find her and her daughter again? And Zaid?

I'm exhausted.

The train's rhythm is soothing, and despite the cramped, uncomfortable conditions and my aching back from the lack of proper support, I'm slowly lulled to sleep. I drift in and out of consciousness and only wake when the train screeches to a halt in the middle of the night, waking all passengers.

"What's happening?" Emilie asks sleepily.

"I don't know, sweetheart," I reply honestly. "Maybe we've arrived?"

Magnus tries to find space beside me to stretch his sore muscles, which results in loud protests from the men around him, who seem small and frail compared to Magnus's muscular frame.

We sit still for a long time in the darkness. There's no light inside the wagon, and although I can see the moon through the open windows near the roof, only a little light comes in.

The heat and stifling sensation quickly return as the air inside is no longer being mixed with the cooler air from outside.

After a while, I hear the doors of the other wagons opening and closing one after the other. At first, the sound is distant, but it gradually works its way closer and closer until suddenly, the door to our wagon is flung open, and three Spanish-speaking soldiers leap into the doorway. They carry lamps, and the harsh light painfully blinds our eyes so we can't see anything.

I hear the soldiers counting quickly in Spanish, and once they finish, the door is shut and locked again.

Darkness falls immediately. We sit quietly, listening as the soldiers move through the remaining wagons, and then the train suddenly starts moving again, continuing through the night.

"That was probably the Spanish border control," Magnus mutters quietly after we've been travelling for another 20 minutes and the train shows no signs of stopping again.

"They're probably making sure that France isn't sending more refugees than what's been agreed between the two countries."

"I feel like cattle being sent to the slaughterhouse," I whisper back. "A commodity."

Magnus takes my hand in his.

"Maybe that's just how unwanted people are treated," I continue sadly. "When they need to be transported or housed in large numbers without putting more of a financial burden on society than absolutely necessary. You'd think humanity would have learned from the mistakes of the past, but as soon as something threatens our quality of life, we'll stop at nothing."

The train rattles on for more than 12 hours before we finally, bruised and battered, reach our destination, a place just outside Madrid. Here, we are introduced to what will be our new home. The place Zaid and Farhana had warned us about; the camps.

Or more specifically; the *Shangri La* camp.

15 Magnus

"Try down by the Gaza Strip," the man replies dismissively. He's lying on the camp bed closest to the tent entrance when we poke our heads in to ask if there's room for a family of four. His dark green eyes are deeply set in a gaunt face, covered in week-old stubble. His upper lip and one nostril are covered with a red and yellow oozing cold sore, clearly untreated. He's not the first person we've met here carrying around open, infected wounds

The damp and unhygienic conditions provide the perfect breeding ground for fungal infections and itchy rashes. The entire camp is a large, soggy swamp in the middle of the Iberian plateau, La Meseta, about 150 kilometres southwest of Madrid. The rain falls relentlessly, turning the ground between the makeshift walkways into muddy puddles.

Along these walkways, thousands of large, rectangular white tents have been set up, originally designed to house UN staff in disaster zones. Now, they've become home to the many refugees from Northern Europe. Each tent was intended to comfortably accommodate 15 people, but due to the overwhelming number of refugees, each of them now holds at least 50. Space is scarce in every tent we peek into in our efforts to find shelter from the rain. The canvas is soaked through, and it often drips from large, green-mottled patches in the roof. The atmosphere inside is at best damp, at worst downright unhealthy, with airborne spores from mould floating freely in the air we breathe.

"Gaza Strip?" I ask, giving him a puzzled look.

"The western end," he answers irritably, pointing with his entire arm in a random direction that could just as well be east.

It's not easy to find our bearings among the many identical tents, which form a huge maze within the enclosure. It seems almost impossible to tell which way is which, especially when I have no point of reference.

The man turns away, lying with his back to me as if to emphasise that his helpfulness has reached its limit.

I look around in vain, hoping to catch the eye of someone who might offer some assistance, but no one seems particularly interested in me. In the end, I have no choice but to turn back and step outside the tent, where Freja, Kristian, and Emilie are waiting patiently in the rain.

I shake my head, feeling defeated. I've already lost count of how many tents we've tried to find shelter in, but each time, the answer has been the same. They're full to bursting. If there's any space left at all, you might be lucky to find one free sleeping spot, never four.

"Someone suggested we try down by something he called the Gaza Strip. In the western end."

Freja gives me a questioning look. I shrug, just as baffled by the answer as she is.

"It'll be dark soon," she notes, glancing up at the solid grey sky.

It stretches across the horizon as far as the eye can see.

"I know. Let's see if we can find this Gaza Strip. So far, we haven't had much luck going from tent to tent, so we might as well see if the man was right, that there's available space there."

Freja bends down and once again picks up our meagre belongings, which consist of the seal-skin blankets we brought with us, some grey woven cotton blankets, and four empty plastic water containers we were given upon arriving at the camp.

"Which way is west?" she asks, looking around, disoriented.

Despite the rain, there are plenty of people outside on the walkways, weaving in and out of each other. Children and adults. Women and men. All of them gaunt and filthy. They move quickly through the rain like silent shadows, rushing aimlessly between the many tents. No one seems to notice us, merely pushing past from both sides as we stand there in the middle of the walkway, an insignificant obstacle.

I pull Emilie in front of me to protect her from the many nudges and bumps from people who don't even look up when they run into us.

There are 20 tents on each side of the walkway we're standing on now. 40 in total, with 50 people in each. Altogether, 2,000 souls. How many parallel walkways have we already passed, I wonder, feeling disillusioned. Ten? Fifteen? From what I can see, we're not even a tenth of the way into the camp. I shake my head in shock as I realise this camp alone must house several hundred thousand people.

We slowly begin to move with the flow of people until we come across a crosswalk leading us further into the camp. The closer we get to the centre, the denser the crowd becomes, until eventually, it's so packed it's almost impossible to squeeze past one another.

I grip Emilie's hand tightly as I try to create a path for us to follow, but as soon as I pass through, the opening closes behind me again. I constantly lose sight of both Kristian and Freja.

"We'll stay on this walkway as long as we can," I shout over the noise of the crowd. "No one turns onto another walkway unless we all agree. If we get separated in here, we'll never find each other again."

I think back in horror to the hours when Freja and Emilie were lost in the snowstorm. I never thought I'd see them alive again.

When no one responds, I stop and turn to face my family until we're once again gathered in a small group. "Do you understand what I'm saying?" I ask, staring seriously at each of them in turn. "It's important that you understand. Under no circumstances can we get separated in here."

Emilie looks up at her mother with wide, fearful eyes. "We'll never get lost again, will we, Mum?"

Freja takes her face in between her hands and bends down to kiss her on the forehead. "Never again!" she promises. "We've made that vow to each other."

"What about you, Kristian? Did you understand? No one turns onto another walkway unless we all go together. We keep going straight until I say otherwise."

Kristian, still mourning the loss of both Mali and Fatima on the same day, looks away, but he nods. He holds me responsible and would prefer to go his own way, but he's still young, and we're in an unfamiliar environment. Reluctantly, he leaves the decision-making to me, even though it burns inside him to take control.

I keep staring at him until he finally turns his head, and we make eye contact.

"What?" he asks irritably, throwing his arms out in frustration.

The movement knocks into an older man, who loses his balance and steps into the ankle-deep mud beside the walkway. He looks up, confused, with a vacant expression in his eyes. It's probably not the first time it's happened, and it likely won't be the last. I reach out to help him up. He briefly looks at my strong hand before grasping it. His hand is so frail that I can feel the bones scraping together as I close my fingers around it and pull him up onto the walkway. I'm surprised by how light he is.

"Sorry!" I say in English as he stands once again on the rain-soaked wooden planks of the walkway. "It was an accident."

He stares at me blankly for a moment before disappearing back into the crowd as if nothing had happened.

Maybe he didn't understand English, I wonder vaguely.

I can't shake the disillusioned, empty look in his eyes. It's as if he's mentally left all the misery of the camp behind and now exists in some parallel universe, accessible only to him, in his own imagination.

A chill runs down my spine because it's the same empty look I see wherever I glance.

"How are we supposed to live here?" Freja asks anxiously, as if she's read my thoughts. "Most of these people are just shadows of themselves. Will we become like that too, after a couple of years here?"

A couple of years, I think sadly. It's almost too overwhelming to imagine that we'll still be here in a few years. But what other options are there?

"First, we need to find a place to stay out of the rain and the night. Then we can worry about how to avoid losing our minds."

Emilie looks up at me, alarmed. "Do people go mad from being here?" she asks.

"Don't worry," Kristian replies sarcastically before I even have the chance to speak. "You can't lose something you never had. Between the two of us, I'm the only one with anything to worry about."

She reacts immediately, kicking him on the shin.

"You're an idiot, Kristian! You've been that way ever since you fell in love with Fatima."

"Enough!" Freja cuts in. "We need to stick together, not argue. Let's just try to find this 'Gaza Strip,' wherever it is..."

A woman wearing a drenched, torn-down puffer jacket stops and looks at us. The jacket was once a shiny red, but now it's so dirty that the colour barely shows through.

"'Gaza Strip?'" she says in Swedish. "It's down by the toilets at the western end." She points towards the farthest end, the direction we're already heading. "Right by the fence.

Her long, mousy brown hair hangs wet over her shoulders, clinging to her cheeks like withered cobwebs. Unlike most people outside on the walkways, there's still a spark of life in her green eyes, which now study our sealskin jackets closely. She notices the sealskin blankets in Freja's arms and reaches out to touch them. I see that her nails are unusually long— longer than seems practical in a place like this.

"They're soft," she says. "I bet they're warm too?"

"They certainly are," I reply.

She turns her attention to me at the sound of my voice.

"What a handsome man," she remarks, looking at me more closely. "So masculine and muscular."

She reaches out toward my face, but I quickly take a step back to avoid her touch. She seems unpredictable.

Before I can fully regain my balance, she spins around, grabs one of the sealskins out of Freja's arms, and takes off at full speed through the mud. Within moments, she disappears among the tents.

Kristian is about to chase after her, but I grab his shoulder just in time, stopping him from jumping into the mud in a bid to retrieve our blanket.

"Let her go. You won't stand a chance of finding her in this chaos. She could already be inside one of the tents or heading to the other end of the camp. If you try to catch her, you'll just get lost, and then we'll have even bigger problems than losing a blanket."

"But we need that blanket," he protests. "It's already freezing, and it's only the end of September. You don't know how cold it gets here in winter."

"We'll manage. Let's just move on before something worse happens. And hold on tight to your belongings—we can't afford to lose anything else."

"I-I'm sorry," Freja stammers, tears already streaming down her cheeks. "It happened so fast. I didn't even realise what was happening until she was gone."

"It wasn't your fault," I say. "She caught us all off guard. We just need to be more careful. She won't be the only one trying to take things from us. It's every person for themselves in here."

As we move closer to the western end, the ever-present stench grows stronger—a foul odour caused by the sheer number of people crammed into this place with poor sanitation. It's hard to imagine that there are enough toilets for all these people, let alone any bathing facilities.

By the time we finally reach the far end of the camp, dusk is setting in. The stench from the toilets is so overwhelming it burns our lungs as we breathe, and it takes real effort not to retch. The toilet and sanitation buildings line this part of the camp's fence, stretching almost from the northern side of the camp to the south. Outside the buildings, there's a constant stream of people coming and going. Later, we'll learn that this flow never stops. Day and night, people queue to relieve themselves or take the rare chance to use the sparse showers.

This part of the camp never sleeps.

The 'Gaza Strip' turns out to be a roughly 100-metre stretch at the southern end, directly next to the toilet buildings. A row of tents stands there, often with available beds due to the unbearable smell and the constant noise from the nearby toilets throughout the night.

Separated by a 20-metre-wide strip directly adjoining *Shangri-La*, we notice an almost identical camp on the other side. Between the camps, sanitation workers labour around the clock with large, noisy vacuum trucks to empty the toilets on both sides.

I stare at the fence on the other side, shocked to discover that there's another camp so close to ours. So many people, forced to flee their homes due to climate change, now crammed into camps designed to hold far fewer than the numbers they now shelter. It's horrifying.

A young man, probably in his mid-thirties, steps up beside me.

"Bloody Arabs!" he mutters angrily, speaking in English with a thick German accent. He unzips his trousers and starts urinating through the fence, sending a powerful yellow stream into the mud. All the while, he watches me closely.

"New?" he asks as he finishes.

He lets the last few drops fall before zipping up again.

"Sorry?" I ask, confused. "What do you mean?"

"Are you new here?" he elaborates, pointing at our sealskin blankets.

"Yes," I reply curtly, gripping the blankets tighter.

He doesn't miss my defensive gesture and bursts out laughing—a loud, pig-like sound, as if a pig were being dragged across railway tracks.

"Don't worry," he says, suddenly cutting off his laughter. "I'm not looking for trouble. You look like the kind of man who could break someone in half with his bare hands. Where are you from? It's been a while since I've seen anyone in such good physical shape."

"We need a place to sleep," I say, ignoring his question. "Me and my family. There are four of us."

I gesture to Freja, Emilie, and Kristian, who stand beside me. The man looks past me and spots Freja.

"A Valkyrie!" he exclaims, his eyes lighting up when he sees her wet, reddish hair and broad shoulders. "Are you from Scandinavia?"

"Denmark," I reply.

"She's beautiful," he says, taking a step past me to get a closer look at her.

Freja turns her face away, embarrassed.

This man makes me uneasy. Everything in this place makes me uneasy.

I reach for Freja's hand.

"Let's go," I say. "We need to find somewhere to stay before it gets dark."

The man turns back to me. "There are two free beds in my tent. You can sleep there if you don't mind the noise from the Arabs..."

I study the man carefully. He has curly blonde hair that

hangs wet over his forehead, which he occasionally brushes aside with a hand missing its little finger. His stubble suggests he owns a sharp razor, despite us being searched for any kind of weapons before entering the camp. He wears a black ski jacket and black jogging trousers with a hole in one knee. A large bulge is visible through the soft fabric of his trousers. He bursts into his pig-like laugh again when he catches me staring at the bulge.

"What can I say? You've got a fine-looking wife. So, do you want the beds or not? If not, I'll leave you to it and head back to the dry."

I exchange a brief glance with Freja. We have a quick, silent conversation, developed over many years of marriage and during long, cold winters when we've needed to share our thoughts without the children overhearing.

Can we trust this man? Will I be able to protect my family if he tries to attack us?

Freja shrugs, defeated.

Can we really trust anyone but ourselves?

She looks up at the sky, where night is quickly closing in.

We need somewhere to sleep.

Finally, she gives a barely noticeable nod. We have to accept the offer. There's no other choice.

"We'll take it," I say.

"Great," he replies casually. "Let's go then. It's in the corner, as close to those bloody Arabs as it gets. My name's Hans, by the way. And you lot?"

"I'm Magnus. The Valkyrie is my wife, Freja. And these are our kids, Kristian and Emilie."

"What do you mean by 'as close to the Arabs as it gets?'" Kristian interrupts with the little English he's managed to learn.

We'd started teaching him English during our last winter's confinement.

"I thought Arabs and whites weren't placed in the same camp?"

"They aren't," Hans confirms. "But the camp over there, on the other side of the fence, is full of them. That's why this area is called the Gaza Strip. Really, it should be the name of their camp, since they've taken over the entire area with their infernal noise, but here, people refer to this section that borders them as the Gaza Strip.

Apart from the noise from the Arabs, who call to prayer five times a day, the stench from the toilets, the constant buzz of people all night, the roar of the sewage trucks working around the clock, and the wind hitting the tent all winter, it's actually not the worst spot to be in. Tucked away in a corner of the camp. Our tent isn't along one of the main pathways, you see, so there's not as much foot traffic. And the criminal gangs, who think this area is beneath their standards, mostly operate closer to the middle of the camp, where the smell from the toilets isn't as bad."

"Criminals?" Freja asks nervously.

"Yeah, you can't really avoid them in a place like this. But it's not as bad as it sounds. It's mostly protection rackets—they take food rations from the people in the nearby tents in exchange for 'protecting' them. In return, no one else dares to steal their belongings because they'd be held accountable.

We're spared from that here, but we do have the occasional intruder sneaking into the tent, looking to steal something. So, guard your belongings, never leave anything unattended. Especially since your beds are right by the entrance."

Hans turns out to be a rather straightforward man, with no immediate signs of hidden motives for offering us a couple of beds for the night. His tent is located in the farthest southwestern corner. Inside, 30 camp beds are arranged in three rows stretching from the back of the tent to the front. At the very front, just inside the double layers of canvas covering the entrance and blocking the draught, are the two beds that will be ours for the foreseeable future.

Two green camp beds, right at the front and in the middle row, where we'll be constantly disturbed by everyone coming and going at all hours of the day and night.

But we can't be picky. Not now.

We have a place to sleep, and that's what matters. We can always try to find a better spot later.

The tent is rectangular with a peaked roof angled at 40 degrees to help the rainwater run off. Even so, puddles form on the top, causing the stained canvas to sag lower and lower until one of the residents gets up to push the water off from underneath.

Long clotheslines run across each row of beds, loaded with damp clothes hung out to dry after their owners ventured outside.

We quickly realise that clothes rarely dry fully in these damp autumn days, and if you get properly soaked, the clothes drip from the lines directly onto the beds below.

The floor of the tent is made of planks laid across the ground, with half-centimetre gaps between them. Just like the walkways outside, they are fixed with screws, allowing the wood to expand and contract with the humidity. Beneath them is a hollow space where I can hear rats fighting for food at night.

Hans introduces us to his girlfriend, Nadja, as soon as we

step inside. The two of them have been here the longest, which has earned them a sort of leadership status and the privilege of beds at the center of the tent. From there, they don't have to worry as much about thieves sneaking in from outside or the cold drafts that constantly whip through the back of the tent. Unlike most others, neither Nadja nor Hans seems eager to move to a tent further inside the camp, away from the stench and noise.

"What are we supposed to do with these red tokens?" I ask Hans, holding out four red plastic discs. "They gave them to us along with our blankets before we were let into the camp."

"You show them when you collect your food rations," Nadja replies. "One day a week, everyone with red tokens gets their weekly ration. The day after, it's the turn of those with green tokens. Then the yellow ones, until it's the red's turn again after a week."

She reaches into her pocket and pulls out a green token.

"We've got green ones. Every fourth week, along with your weekly ration, you'll also get a silver token. That gives you access to a two-minute shower anytime during the next four weeks."

"One shower every four weeks?" Freja asks, astonished.

We've gotten used to conserving water in the winter, but we've always been able to wash with a wet cloth. One shower every four weeks seems cruel and completely unsanitary, especially in a place like this, with so many people in such close quarters.

"What happens if we lose a token?" I ask.

"Then you don't get your weekly ration," Hans answers bluntly. "So, look after it. You won't get a replacement. It's one token per person. People have starved to death for losing their token. Sometimes family members share their rations if one of them loses theirs, but the rations are carefully calculated based on how much energy a man, woman, or child needs. When you share, everyone gets too little. If the man's token is lost, it doesn't take long before the whole family suffers badly because his energy needs are greater than the others'."

"Do they just let people starve?" Freja asks, shocked. "Surely that's against human rights?"

Nadja gives her a wide-eyed look and bursts into her distinctive cackling laughter, revealing a large gap between her front teeth. Despite the grim conditions in the camp, Nadja has an easy laugh.

"Human rights? Do you really think you have rights as a climate refugee? You're considered an immigrant at best, tolerated at worst. The fact that we all once belonged to the same European Union means absolutely nothing now. Human rights are on hold. They only apply as long as the Western lifestyle isn't under threat."

"When is it our turn to collect our ration?" I ask. "We haven't eaten in two days now, and we're starting to feel it."

"Good question," Nadja remarks and shouts loudly into the tent, "Do we have any red tokens in here?"

A man in his late forties responds from the back of the tent, confirming they do.

"When are you due for your next ration?"

"In two days."

"In two days?" Freja exclaims in shock. "We can't wait that long."

Nadja looks at her sympathetically. "You'll get used to the hunger," she says dryly.

"Most people move to another tent after a couple of

months," Hans explains, deftly changing the subject. "There are always a few spaces that free up here and there, when people succumb to illness, or if they get kicked out of their tents for one reason or another. Maybe that's the real reason we choose to stay in this stinking rat hole." Hans laughs knowingly and winks suggestively at Nadja. "People would just kick us out after a few nights."

Nadja bursts into another fit of cackling laughter, leaving us confused about what's apparently an ongoing joke among the other tent residents. What we later come to find out is that Hans and Nadja have loud sex every night in their squeaky camp bed in the middle of the tent, with all 48 residents able to listen as Nadja reaches her climax. Which she does on most nights. The longer-term residents have given up making objections. Instead, they've chosen to accept it as part of the background noise that comes with living in the so-called Gaza Strip area of the camp. Sometimes, when Nadja hits a particularly obvious peak in her orgasm, there's a spontaneous round of applause and cheering from the regulars.

"It's the only pleasure no one can take from us," Nadja laughs, after which everyone settles down to sleep.

Their escapades quickly become part of the nightly ritual, something I would much rather spare Emilie and Kristian from witnessing. On the other hand, it's probably the least of all the potential traumas they are being exposed to in these years. So I shrug it off, and before long, I even start joining in with the cheering.

Freja and I share a camp bed. Sometimes, it's inevitable that we ourselves get a bit worked up lying so close together and listening to Hans and Nadja, and although we kiss and caress each other like a pair of love-struck teenagers, there's still a line we don't cross. It feels as though, if we went all the way, it would be a silent acceptance of our miserable situation—a recognition that we've resigned ourselves to the fact that we'll spend the rest of our lives in this camp. And we're not ready for that yet.

16 Freja

I wake to the sound of the Arabic alarm clock — the call to morning prayer from the neighbouring camp. I stay lying down in bed with my eyes closed, listening to the imam's piercing singing voice, its pitch rising and falling rhythmically in the traditional Arabic style. For a brief moment, it drowns the constant hum of people moving to and from the toilets, which has kept me awake for most of the night.

I let myself be carried away by the imam's voice, which lifts me up and out of the wretched, stinking camp that has become our new home.

Away from all the snoring. Away from the rain. Away from strangers you constantly have to be on guard against, because they either want to steal your belongings or your food ration. Away from the creaky camp beds that groan during the night as people turn in their sleep. Away from the stench that scratches at your airways and burns your eyes, making tears run down your face. Away from Hans and Nadja, who celebrate every midnight hour as if it were their last. Away from the gnawing hunger, and back to memories of life in Denmark, which suddenly doesn't seem so bad after all.

I know it's an illusion — that the memories of the tough life back home are softened by the fact that we haven't yet adjusted to life in the camp. Every day is a new struggle to reconcile ourselves with living so close to others after having been isolated for so long, used to fending for ourselves. Now, we are completely dependent on the help and charity of others, a feeling I find incredibly difficult to come to terms with.

I catch myself longing for home, even though deep down, I'm not at all in doubt that the coming winter up north will be brutal and long.

Two more imams join the chorus from indeterminate locations deep inside the neighbouring camp. They break the purity of the first imam's song, which suddenly no longer sounds like a virtuoso to my ears but rather like a hoarse goose caught in a barbed wire fence.

My escape from reality is abruptly cut short by the scent of Farhana's hair lingering in my nostrils. Where might she be now? Is she in relative safety like us? Have they also found somewhere to shelter for the night?

A tear escapes from the corner of my eye and rolls down my cheek. Emilie sees it. Apparently, she's awake too. Who wouldn't be in this racket?

"Why are you crying?" she asks, wiping the tear away with her small fingers.

I open my eyes and stare straight into her large blue eyes, which gaze back expectantly. She's lying in the camp bed next to mine, which she shares with Kristian. They sleep head to toe —it gives them more room in the narrow bed.

"I just miss Farhana," I reply. "I hope they're safe."

"I miss Fatima too," she says seriously. "Even though she got boring after she and Kristian became boyfriend and girlfriend. But I miss Mali even more. She was my very best friend ever."

I smile sympathetically. I'm so sorry for the childhood they are growing up with—so full of pain and suffering. I would give both my kidneys and my heart if it meant they could grow up feeling free, able to do almost anything they wanted.

But that seems a long way off, and perhaps it's even that very same life philosophy—doing whatever we want just because we can—that has driven the world so far off track.

I often thought that humans are far too complex to be the rulers of the world. The combination of our pleasure-seeking nature and curiosity makes us unsuitable to sit at the top of the food chain, from a scientific perspective. We are the species that has lived the shortest time on earth, and we are already well on our way to wiping ourselves out without even looking back.

If intelligence is defined by the ability to act purposefully, think rationally, and handle one's environment effectively, then we have certainly failed as a species. We can't even manage to participate in nature's ordinary agenda without destroying it. Intelligence is about being able to fit naturally into the environment where you belong, so you can live there safely and securely tomorrow as well.

Suddenly, the three imams stop, all at once. Immediately, the hum of the camp returns—the noise of thousands of people bustling in and out amongst each other, talking across multiple languages and dialects, most of which are completely incomprehensible to me.

"We must go and collect our weekly ration," Magnus mumbles sleepily into my ear. He lies behind me, his arm draped around my waist. The camp bed we sleep in is only 80 centimetres wide, so no matter how much we turn and shift, we always end up in the same sleeping position—with my back to Magnus, nestled into his warm body.

This is the third time we are going to collect our weekly ration, which is so meagre that it is a struggle to make it stretch.

We went four days without food after we first arrived in

France until we finally received our first weekly ration at the *Shangri-La* in Spain. Fourteen kilos of freeze-dried rice, chickpeas, and lentils. Four kilos for Magnus, 3.5 kilos for Kristian and me each, and three kilos for Emilie. When the bags were handed over after we showed our red tokens, we were shocked by how little it was. Halfway through the first week, we realised that the food we'd been given would barely last us five days.

Since then, hunger has been a constant companion, which every morning, when I swing my legs out of bed, sends cramps deep into my stomach.

Nadja says you get used to it—to being hungry. She says the cramps will eventually subside, and until then, I should drink plenty of water to trick my stomach into thinking it's full.

We fetch water in the five-litre plastic jugs they gave us, which we fill up at the taps in the shower buildings. The first time Emilie and I stepped into the women's building, I involuntarily vomited all over the floor. The smell was so nauseating, so intense, so sharp, that my body's natural reaction was to empty my stomach of everything it contained, which at that point was little more than sour bile.

The air scratched unpleasantly at my lungs with every breath I took. Most of us breathe in short, shallow bursts while inside, but as a result, several people faint daily from lack of oxygen to the brain. The air is so thick and waterlogged that you could cut bricks from it. The oxygen seems severely reduced, so even if you force yourself to gulp down large amounts of the latrine-scented air, you constantly feel like you're on the verge of passing out.

I forced myself to endure long enough to fill my water jug completely, though I recoiled at the thought of drinking water drawn under such unhygienic conditions.

Emilie pinched her nose with her fingers, refusing to breathe, which only meant that when she could hold her breath no longer, she was forced to take an extra-deep inhalation of the foul air. It scratched her throat, triggering a long coughing fit.

With one hand on the water jug and the other on Emilie, I led her outside, where the air was slightly better. For days afterwards, she refused to return to the building, no matter how much she needed to pee. Instead, she held it in so long that Kristian woke up the second night in a soaked camp bed. Both he and the bed were drenched in the urine of a traumatised girl whose bladder couldn't hold any more without bursting.

I don't think we'll ever fully get used to the nauseating stench of human waste that frames the area. However, after just a week in the Gaza Strip section, it bothers us a bit less.

The fact that we breathe the air day and night, sleep in it, and eat in it certainly plays a major role in the adjustment process.

"Let's get going," I say, swinging my legs over the side of the bed. I already have my shoes on, as I sleep in them out of fear they'll be stolen during the night if I leave them by the bedside.

I leave the sealskin blankets with Hans and Nadja, who promise to look after them while we're away. The two of them have been an invaluable help in getting us somewhat settled into the camp's daily routines. Without them, we'd have been lost, and if you can even talk about forming friendships in a place like this, where everyone is their own master, they're probably the closest we'll get to it.

Nadja is still lying in bed as I approach. She reaches out for her thick-lensed glasses, which make her eyes look larger when she is wearing them. "Without them, I can't even see my own breasts," she says with a big smile, looking up at me.

I hand her the blankets, which she immediately tucks under her head like a makeshift pillow.

"We're off to get our rations," I announce a bit awkwardly. "Thank you for keeping an eye on our things while we're gone."

I'm still a bit nervous about leaving the valuable sealskin blankets with someone I've barely known for long, but it's too risky to carry them all the way through camp and back again. Losing the blanket to the Swedish woman on the first day still haunts me, and I don't want to risk losing any more, so I feel I have no choice but to trust Hans and Nadja's honesty.

"Don't worry," she reassures me, as if reading my mind. "The blankets will still be here when you return this evening." She rubs her face against the soft sealskin. "Perhaps a little more worn," she adds with a mischievous glint in her eyes.

She and Hans already seem to take great pleasure in snuggling under the soft skins when we're off collecting rations.

"Say what you will about us. But thieves, we are not. Perverts, yes. But not thieves."

She bursts into a brief, cackling laugh.

I find it hard to come to terms with the thought of what the two of them might get up to, wrapped in our blankets, but I don't have anyone else I feel safe trusting. Fetching rations is an all-day affair. The pressure on the distribution point is immense when 40-50,000 people need to be served on the same day. Anything could happen in that time. Moving to a different tent and disappearing into the crowd with our blankets would be the easiest thing in the world.

We haven't seen a trace of the Swedish woman since our arrival, though I'm not sure I'd even recognise her if we did. Unless, of course, she's still carrying around our blanket.

As with so much else in the camp, I have to swallow my pride and reluctantly accept things as they are, no matter how much they offend my sense of trust. So, I return Nadja's laughter with a forced smile, hoping she doesn't see through me too easily.

"Thanks, Nadja. We'll try to be quick."

● ● ●

The camp hums with activity. For the first time since we arrived, the rain has eased, and the sun occasionally peeks through small gaps in the clouds. It's wonderful to see the light again, even if only for brief moments. I'd much prefer the temperature to drop just below freezing, when the sun shines more frequently from a clear sky, than endure this draining, relentless rain.

Even the rats have left their hiding places under the sturdy tent floors, where they live in an extensive network of tunnels likely stretching beneath much of the camp. I sometimes spot them emerging suddenly and scurrying across the slick walkways.

One particularly large one — the size of my forearm — suddenly appears in front of me as we turn down a walkway leading further towards the camp's centre. By accident, I kick it, sending it half a metre across the boards, narrowly avoiding being stepped on by a middle-aged man. Like us, he's trying to squeeze through the throng of people moving in every direction. The rat frantically leaps into the muddy gap between the walkways, swiftly swimming across to the other side and disappearing under a tent.

I shudder at the thought of such large creatures crawling among us. Although we owe our survival to their Nordic relatives, I can't shake the idea that the rats here in the camp grow fat on human waste, potentially carrying all sorts of diseases.

The camp's hygiene is abysmal, sanitation is downright unsanitary, and access to medicine and wound care is clearly non-existent. The camps are also overcrowded, and it's only a matter of time before an epidemic breaks out, sweeping through the camp like the Spanish flu at the end of World War I. If that happens, we wouldn't stand a chance. The conditions here are perfect for the rapid spread of disease, and once it takes hold, it could easily wipe out the camp within weeks. As I look around, I see people who are both mentally and physically broken down, their immune systems likely severely weakened.

I hold tightly to Emilie's hand, making sure she doesn't get separated from me, and I notice her scratching her scalp intensely at regular intervals. We've yet to take the plunge and use the small shower cabins near the toilets. The silver tokens lie safely in my pocket alongside the red ones, which we'll soon have to present to collect our weekly ration. Perhaps it's time we use them?

The thought of standing naked and vulnerable with Emilie among so many other women, all just waiting their turn, fills me with dread, but we have no other choice. I decide we'll go in the late evening, after we've returned and eaten our food, when the crowd of other refugees has thinned out a bit.

I feel as though all my dignity as a woman and a human being is being stripped away from me as I gradually become more and more integrated into the camp's soul-crushing rhythm. It seems designed solely to keep us physically alive while breaking us mentally, ensuring no one gets any ideas of rebellion.

Magnus stops in front of me.

"Let's try that way," he says once we've all gathered around him. He points down a walkway on the left, which looks a bit less crowded.

"Maybe we'll get through quicker that way."

We don't get far before we realise why it's less busy than the other paths. The wet boards are as slippery as brown soap. Emilie's feet suddenly slip out from under her. In trying to stop herself from falling, she tightens her grip on my hand, causing us both to lose balance. Before I can react, we're tumbling on the greasy boards. I land hard on one hip and lie there in pain, watching Kristian and Magnus disappear into the crowd further down the walkway. They haven't seen us fall. I bite the pain and quickly help Emilie on her feet. We need to catch up to them as soon as possible. Even though we've agreed never to take a new path without regrouping first, I feel safer when we all stay together.

"Are you alright?" I ask.

She nods and points desperately in the direction where Magnus and Kristian have vanished.

"Come on, Mum. We need to hurry!" She doesn't want to be left behind again either.

We stand for a moment to regain our balance, then carefully continue down the slippery walkway. I notice a man stomping his feet hard into the boards with each step before shifting his weight onto his leading foot. I realise he's kicking through the slimy surface to find firmer footing beneath. It takes some practice, but once we get the technique down, we move much quicker.

We catch up with Magnus and Kristian about 100 metres ahead. They're waiting for us on the other side of a wide belt of mud that has flooded the walkway, where it slopes down on one side.

A young couple has just slipped off the boards trying to cross and is now floundering together in a 30-centimetre-deep mud-hole. They're soaked through. I feel for them, knowing there's nowhere they can dry their clothes. For once, the wind has died down along with the rain, which is lucky for them, as at least the cold won't sap their body heat. Still, they should try to find some warm blankets as soon as possible.

I want to help them up, but the chances of ending up in the mudhole with them are too high. It's a risk I can't take, so I pretend not to have seen them. I can hardly believe I've reached a point where I can turn a blind eye to others' misfortunes, but the circumstances force me to. I can't afford to risk my own health to save theirs. I'm forced to think of myself and my family if we are to survive, a truth that pains me, as it goes against my natural instinct to help those in need.

"Careful!" Magnus warns as we approach. He points to the edge of the walkway, opposite the young couple. "Use that edge to stop yourself from ending up in the mud as well."

I stare at the edge he's pointing to. It's just as coated in mud as the rest of the boards. I don't understand what he means.

"Like this," says Kristian, as he effortlessly crosses over to us, balancing along the edge with his boots.

The edge digs into the soles of his feet, providing traction and preventing him from slipping, much like how we used crampons on ice back in Denmark.

As Kristian reaches us, a woman suddenly and without warning pushes past. She heads straight on, skating her feet forward effectively without losing contact with the ground. Halfway across, where the walkway slopes the most, she starts to slide sideways. Panicking at the thought of landing in the mud with the young couple, she forgets her technique and tries to leap to safety on the other side. The moment she lifts one leg and prepares to push off with the other, her foot slips out from under her. She lands with a splash in the middle of the walkway, sliding sideways into the mudhole, knocking the young woman over once again.

Kristian hurries back to Magnus. Once he's safely on the other side, I encourage Emilie to follow. She steps cautiously into the mud, feels for the edge with her foot, and once she finds it, she carefully shifts her weight from her back foot to her front. She quickly gets the hang of it, and soon she's safely on the other side.

Once I find my balance, it's relatively easy to cross the mud belt. I can feel the edge under the arch of my boots and balance like a tightrope walker to the other side, where I find firm footing on the slippery boards.

The closer we get, the more packed the crowd becomes with people either heading towards the distribution point or already returning with their rations. Most of those carrying their rations hold the bags of food protectively in their arms, hugging them to their chests.

Despite the fact that we all feel our muscles wasting away since arriving at the camp, Magnus, Kristian, and I are still larger and stronger than most around us. So we push on, forging our way through the otherwise impenetrable crowd, until we finally reach the distribution point.

Safe behind the four-meter-high wire fence that surrounds the entire camp, a long row of tables is set up, where up to 50 aid workers distribute rations. They have exactly eight hours to serve the thousands of people, so time for each distribution is tight if everyone is to be served.

The noise is deafening. People shout over each other, loudly trying to push forward to the counters. A Dutch woman with a small child on her hip desperately tries to get one of the aid workers to call for help for her little boy, who seems seriously ill. He sits apathetically, his head resting on his mother's shoulder, staring at me with feverish eyes. The aid worker says something in Spanish and dismissively waves her away. She quickly turns to Magnus, gesturing impatiently for him to show her his red token.

The woman with the child lingers, watching as the aid worker inspects Magnus's token with the number one clearly imprinted in the plastic—proof that he is entitled to an adult male's ration. Both my and Kristian's tokens bear a clear number two, while Emilie's token has a three.

The woman on the other side of the fence hands the token back to Magnus and passes his ration through a small opening, just large enough for the blue canvas sack to slide through. When Kristian steps forward and hands over his red token, the Dutch woman speaks up again. She's crying and pleading in English, asking if no one will help her poor boy. The aid worker continues to ignore her. She turns to pick up a ration pack from a pallet of green canvas sacks. She's in a hurry; she has to hand out 1,000 sacks before the distribution point closes and she can go back to her safe home to make dinner for her own family. The 10 or 20 minutes it would take to find someone to help the little boy would mean that 20 to 40 people won't receive their ration this week. If they help one person, others will quickly follow, asking for help for themselves or a sick relative. And then suddenly, there are hundreds or thousands who won't receive their ration. It's all about efficiency. There's no room for showing compassion or charity. It's not her job.

I take my green sack, then Emilie receives a smaller one—the red one, meant for children. I feel nauseous. I can't understand how anyone can just stand by and not help someone in need. Sick children? I understand they have to be efficient, and that this may not be the right time and place for help. The problem is, there's nowhere else to turn to. Where should a desperate mother go to get medicine for her sick child? There's no medical facility because there are far too many of us for the doctors and nurses in Spain to help even a fraction of us.

Of course, there are doctors and nurses among the many refugees in the camp, but without medicine, they're often powerless. Nadja says medicine has become a major shortage. The world's largest pharmaceutical manufacturers were located in northern countries like the USA, England, France, Germany, Switzerland, and Denmark, but when the frost really set in, most had to move production south, as much as possible, before the factories were forced to shut down. As a result, total production is now only a third of what it used to be, while the need is four times greater. Everything that is produced goes to those on the right side of the fence. Those outside the camps. The ones whose economies are burdened by having to help the many needy people from Northern Europe—the immigrants.

No one asked for this heavy burden to be placed on their shoulders, and most people, quite naturally, feel they have more right to the medicine than we do. They're the ones keeping us alive, not the other way around. Without them, we're doomed, and with that reasoning, the distribution of medicine makes sense. It's not up for debate. Those with money get the priority.

Magnus quickly takes Emilie's sack from her so we don't risk someone trying to snatch it on the way back. He signals for us to follow him. With his shoulder and elbow, he cuts a path through the crowd like a rugby player breaking through one defense line after another. Like a four-part caterpillar, we follow each other so closely that we nearly trip over one another's feet. Kristian and Emilie follow Magnus closely, with me bringing up the rear. Falling to the ground here would mean being trampled to death, but the crowd is so tightly packed that as long as we stick together, it's nearly impossible to fall.

I hold my canvas sack tightly to my body, my arms locked around it. When someone's foot accidentally juts out in front of me, I have to shove off a random person with my shoulder to avoid tripping. Someone grabs my sack and tries to pull it out of my hands, but I'm stronger than most, and I have no trouble holding on to it.

It's so crowded and claustrophobic that I'm more worried about whether Emilie is getting enough air due to her shorter height. Unlike Kristian, who has grown taller than me, she has to make do with the sparse air that filters down between the warm bodies.

We haven't drunk anything since we left this morning, as it's hard to carry a five-liter water jug while also protecting your food ration from theft. So we left the jugs behind in the tent. My mouth is dry, and I can only imagine how Emilie must be feeling. She's holding on tightly to Kristian's jacket in front of her, but I can sense her grip weakening, and she staggers from time to time. I keep a close eye on her as we push forward.

"We're almost through," I shout to her.

I begin to glimpse the edge of the crowd over the thousands of heads, where the mass of people starts to thin.

"Hold on, sweetheart. Just 50 more meters, and we can rest again."

It feels like an eternity before we finally break through the last row of tightly packed bodies, and we can break formation.

Emilie immediately collapses onto the footbridge.

"I'm dizzy," she complains, bending her head between her knees.

She breathes in short, rapid gasps, as if she had just sprinted 100 meters. I sit beside her. She's paler than usual.

"Breathe slowly and deeply, all the way into your lungs, so the oxygen has time to absorb into your blood," I say.

I place my hand on her back to monitor her breathing, making sure she takes deep breaths and holds the air in for a few seconds before slowly exhaling again. Magnus sits down on the other side of her.

"Is she okay?" he asks, concerned.

"It's not good for her to come along to fetch rations," I reply. "The rest of us have our heads in the fresh air, but she doesn't. One of these days, she's going to faint in there."

"But what else can we do? If she's not there to show her token, she won't get any food."

"It's completely absurd," I rage. "If the child gets too sick to collect rations, she has to go without? But if she doesn't get food, her immune system will get no nourishment, and she'll never recover. What kind of logic is that? We should be able to leave her with Hans and Nadja and still collect her ration on her behalf."

Emilie looks up, startled.

"You can't leave me," she pleads urgently. "You promised we'd never be separated again, Mum."

"We won't leave you," Magnus reassures her. "That's not going to happen. You can relax. No one can collect a ration that doesn't match their age or gender, so you have to show up. I think it's to prevent tokens from being stolen."

"They can still be stolen," Kristian counters. "I could, in theory, steal Nadja's token and get her ration. We have the same number on it, and it's on a different day than mine, so no one would ever know."

"That's true. But you can't steal a child's token and get a child's portion. So there's some security in making sure the kids get their ration—unless, of course, they steal from each other."

"Still, they're forced to go through that hell, risking their lives week after week," I interrupt. "The whole system makes no sense at all, if you ask me."

Emilie leans on my shoulder and stands up. "Let's go back to the tent. I need to lie down."

She sounds tired, although her breathing seems normal again.

"Okay, sweetheart. I think we all need a break now."

We've barely started the walk back when the rain returns. Like a loyal companion, it follows us wherever we go as we hurry back towards the tent.

All around us, people rush with their canvas bags in different colours. Most want to get under shelter before their bags get damp. If that happens, it won't be long before the contents begin to mould and become inedible. Normally, though, the dried rations can last for years, as long as they stay dry.

Emilie breathes heavily. We have to adjust our pace for her, so we're constantly bumped into from all sides as people, moving faster than us, push past without restraint. I hold her hand while clutching my sack tightly to my body with the other arm, hunched over to protect it as best as I can from the relentless rain streaming down my back.

I can feel it every time someone bumps into her, as it jerks my arm. At one point, she's shoved so hard she lets go of my hand and falls to her knees in the middle of the path. At that same moment, a large man, carrying one of the blue sacks, comes puffing by. It swings side to side in his arms as he waddles along as fast as his massive belly will allow. It's been many years since I've seen a stomach that size—except maybe on the largest grey seals Magnus used to bring home in late summer. How he's managed to stay so well-fed here in the refugee camp, with the meagre rations we survive on, is beyond me.

The man doesn't see the girl fall in front of him. Moving at full speed, he stumbles straight into her frail body and trips, crashing with his full weight onto the wet planks of the pathway. There's a loud thud, and the entire bridge shudders under his bulk. For a moment, I fear it will collapse.

Suddenly, everything goes silent. People stop and stare in awe at the man, who slowly gets to his feet, frantically looking around for the canvas bag he had been clutching moments earlier.

"It's Thomas," I hear someone whisper in English.

Emilie starts crying loudly. She's obviously hurt from the man, Thomas, tumbling over her.

When Thomas see his blue sack lying in the mud beside the

path, he explodes in a fit of rage. He turns furiously, scanning the crowd for the culprit. His eyes land on Emilie, sitting alone on the pathway, crying. Magnus rushes to her and helps her to her feet. He steps in front of her to shield her from the angry man when he notices the piercing look of malice in his eyes.

Thomas spits something unintelligible between his clenched teeth and takes a few heavy steps forward. He pushes Magnus aside and reaches for Emilie, but Magnus is strong and holds his ground. Instead, Magnus shoves him back, and Thomas stumbles two steps backward in surprise. The man stares at Magnus, clearly shocked that someone had the strength to push him. It's likely been a long time since anyone dared challenge him physically.

"Stay away from my daughter!" Magnus yells in English. "It wasn't her fault you weren't looking where you were going."

There's an audible gasp from the onlookers.

I have no idea who Thomas is, but judging by everyone's reaction, he's clearly someone they either respect or fear.

Thomas's nostrils flare. His face, where visible under a patchy beard, turns a purplish-blue as he shouts something in German: "Gib mir deinen Sack, Schweinhund!"

I don't understand German, but the way he reaches for Magnus's blue sack makes it clear what he wants. Thomas's own ration has been ruined in the mud, and now he wants it replaced.

Magnus fights back with all his strength. For a moment, they wrestle until Magnus shoves Thomas off the edge of the path, causing him to step into the 10-centimetre deep mud with one foot. Thomas, startled by the slippery ground, lets go of the sack, afraid of falling backwards into the muck. But he quickly regains his balance and pulls his foot free from the mud again.

"Run!" Magnus shouts.

As if on cue, the four of us turn and sprint. I instinctively grab Emilie's hand, and together we zigzag through the crowd. I can hear Thomas roaring behind us, giving chase like an enraged rhino.

When we reach the junction leading to the slippery path with the sunken section, Kristian shouts, "This way!" and turns without waiting for a response.

On the slick section, he instantly adjusts his running style, kicking down with the ball of his foot to gain better traction.

As Emilie and I turn onto the path, I immediately feel the slippery surface underfoot. For a moment, I panic as I feel my shoes slide, but then I remember the technique and instinctively copy Kristian's altered running style.

Magnus is close behind us, clutching both canvas bags tightly to his body. Twenty metres further back, Thomas also turns onto the path. He immediately slows down as he feels the slippery ground but, eager to reclaim his rations, presses on anyway.

At the mud stretch, we come to a halt. We have to cross it with extreme caution. If anyone loses their footing and slips into the mud, there's no other choice but to face the rhino behind us. Kristian carefully makes his way across first, followed closely by Emilie.

Thomas is closing in fast, despite the slippery surface causing him obvious difficulty.

When I step onto the edge, I take a moment to find my footing, but once I feel the edge under my arch, I quickly make it across to the other side. Now it's Magnus's turn. He gingerly steps onto the edge, one foot at a time. With no arms free to balance himself, he wobbles dangerously as he inches further out. Halfway across, he loses his balance and is about to fall face-first, but with an acrobatic leap, he manages to jump the rest of the way and lands safely on the other side. He immediately loses his footing on the planks and falls backward onto his back, still clutching the two bags tightly to his chest.

When Thomas sees Magnus just a few metres ahead, within reach, he picks up his pace. He's panting heavily from the short sprint. Ignorant of the mud's especially slippery nature, he recklessly charges into it and immediately loses his footing. Like an oversized Bambi on ice, his legs shoot out from under him. I watch his trajectory through the air like a bumblebee unaware it shouldn't be able to fly until he crashes headfirst into the deep puddle with a massive splash.

Without waiting to see if he's alright, we quickly turn and vanish into the crowd.

For the first time, I'm grateful that the camp is packed to the brim. Despite the camp's area being no more than ten square kilometres, it's relatively easy to remain somewhat anonymous inside the perimeter. At least it should be possible to avoid running into Thomas again. His sheer size makes him hard to miss, surrounded as he is by nothing but skinny figures.

It reassures me somewhat, but I'm still shaken by how some people can take out their frustrations on a child, even though the child is in no way to blame for the accident. Sure, she was in the middle of the walkway, but she had been knocked over by someone else. It's not her fault.

Once we're safely back in the tent, I take off Emilie's shirt and check her entire upper body. Aside from what will probably be a bruise across her back, she seems to have escaped the collision relatively unharmed. She moves as freely as ever, and though she'll likely be sore for a few days, we can breathe a sigh of relief.

"Just imagine if you'd had to fight Thomas," Kristian says, addressing Magnus.

They sit across from each other on their beds, carefully observing the examination of Emilie. Kristian's trust in Magnus is slowly being restored, although neither Mali nor Fatima can be mentioned for more than a few moments before Kristian slips back into a mix of self-pity and fatherly accusations. As the days pass, the wounds will likely heal, but for now, he needs time to place the pieces together and mend his broken heart. While he does that, all we can do is open our arms whenever he reaches out.

"Do you think you would have won?" he asks.

"I really don't know," Magnus laughs, scratching his thick beard under his chin. "He was huge."

"He was fat!" Emilie chimes in, pressing her hands to her cheeks in shock. "I've never seen anyone so fat before."

"He actually looked a lot like that big seal I brought home the summer before last. Do you remember it? The one with nostrils so big Emilie could fit her whole hand into one? And a belly so massive that your mum and I couldn't even reach around it, even when we held each other's hands."

"Magnus!" I interrupt, feigning shock, while conveniently leaving out the fact that the same thought had crossed my mind earlier in the day. "Hasn't your mother taught you that it's not okay to make fun of others?"

"I'm not," Magnus responds, matching my mock outrage with a hefty dose of Danish sarcasm. "I'm making fun of the poor seal. And it doesn't really deserve that. It had a much nicer beard than Thomas, and moved far more gracefully — even when it charged across the ice."

"Charged?" I ask, surprised. "What do you mean by that? You never mentioned it before."

"There wasn't much to tell. It was just protecting its group, so it launched a small attack, but I took it down long before it got anywhere near me."

"I don't think you'd have won, Dad," Kristian continues. "Did you see his hands? They were nearly twice the size of yours."

"Well now, that really hurts my pride, lad," Magnus laughs, reaching out to ruffle Kristian's hair.

Kristian nimbly ducks to avoid the playful attack.

"Better to be small and quick than big and slow," he grins. "Just look at Emilie—she had no trouble taking him down. Emilie and Thomas, today's David and Goliath!"

"What's so funny?" Nadja suddenly asks in English, ducking under the tent flap. She's just come in after being outside on an errand.

"Emilie took down Goliath!" Kristian explains, seamlessly switching to English. Just a few weeks after arriving, he's able to hold full conversations with both Hans and Nadja.

I've long known about Kristian's remarkable ability to absorb new knowledge and apply it in different contexts, but his quick grasp of languages still surprises me. He didn't grow up, like Magnus and I, surrounded by English texts, TV shows, movies, or video games. English wasn't really a part of his life before coming to the camp. There's no doubt that Kristian is exceptionally gifted. What couldn't he achieve in a functioning society if given the chance? Watching his life waste away here in the camp breaks my heart, and I have to force myself not to let my thoughts spiral.

"Not understood?" Nadja replies, looking confused. She

glances at me for help.

"We had a bit of an incident on the way back," I explain. "Emilie tripped, and this guy named Thomas fell over her and dropped his ration into the mud. A huge guy, I'm telling you. He got so angry that he chased us down the walkway until he slipped and fell into a big puddle of mud with his entire body."

As I recount the story, Nadja's face gradually loses its colour. "Oh no," she exclaims, worried.

Her heavy glasses have slipped down her nose, pinching the tip and giving her voice a more nasal tone.

"Not Thomas. Anyone but Thomas."

"Who is this Thomas, then?" Magnus asks.

"He's the worst of them all," Nadja answers bluntly.

With a familiar motion, she mechanically pushes her glasses back up to the top of her nose.

"He hangs around somewhere in the middle of the camp. I'm not sure exactly where, because I try to stay as far away from him and his gang as possible. Why do you think he's the only one here who's managed to stay so well-fed?"

She suddenly stops when she notices Hans approaching the exit. She waves him over.

"Hans, tell them who Thomas is!" she orders as soon as he's within earshot.

"Can I at least take a piss first?"

"Hurry up," she replies, waving him off with an irritated hand. "They've crossed paths with Thomas, and they need to understand who he is. Not that I think it will help much now. Once you're in his sights, he never lets you go."

"For fuck's sake," Hans exclaims, shocked. "I'll be back in a minute. I'll just go behind the tent and piss through the fence."

"Be careful the guards don't see you with your cock hanging through the holes, or they'll just cut it off, and then I won't have any good use for you."

"Good God, woman! The way you talk! If it weren't for your big tits, I'd have left you long ago." He spins around and heads toward the exit, giggling loudly.

"That's your best feature!" Nadja yells after him.

Kristian suddenly jumps up from the bed and runs after Hans. "Wait, I'm coming with you!"

Before we even realise, both he and Hans have disappeared out of the tent.

Nadja must have seen the panic in our faces because she immediately places a reassuring hand on each of our knees. "Don't worry. No one ever goes behind the tent. The endless autumn wind blows the rain straight into your face back there, so no one likes to stay there for long. How he manages to piss through the fence in that headwind is beyond me. Anyway, that's his problem. Stay here, and I'll tell you who Thomas is."

I exchange a worried glance with Magnus. Although I'm slightly unsettled by Nadja's reaction to our run-in with Thomas, it's nothing compared to the panic I feel when I lose sight of one of my children.

Shouldn't Magnus follow him, to make sure he doesn't get lost in the crowd? Then again, he's just going behind the tent. Surely he can't get lost there?

Back in Denmark, we used to let him go to the library on his own to fetch books, though always with Mali by his side. That sense of security is gone now, but we silently agree to give him the freedom to be himself, as long as he's just going behind the tent.

"Thomas is the leader of a vile gang that, as I mentioned,

hangs around somewhere in the middle of the camp," Nadja begins dramatically, interrupting my and Magnus's half-telepathic conversation.

"He extorts protection money in the form of food rations from all the poor souls living in the tents around him. Imagine, his territory includes at least 20 tents, each housing 50 people, all paying him a weekly cup of food from their own rations. Thomas is never going to go hungry as long as he's living here."

"That's about 150-200 kilos every week," I exclaim, shocked. "How many of them are there to share all that extra food?"

"I don't know for sure," she replies, "but I've heard the gang has an entire tent to themselves. I doubt any of them share beds, so I'd guess there are about 25-30 members?"

"In that case, that's only half a ration extra per gang member each week, but surely that's not enough to get so fat."

"Maybe not," Nadja replies. "But I don't know how many tents they're collecting rations from. Their territory could be twice as big, or even larger. Who knows..."

"Why doesn't anyone revolt?" Magnus asks. "They're outnumbered, at least ten to one."

"I think people see it as a reasonable price to pay to protect themselves from random theft by others. After all, it's better to give up a cupful of your ration to Thomas than to lose your whole ration to some common thief who doesn't fear the consequences. With Thomas as their protector, no one dares to steal from anyone under his protection."

"Why not?" Magnus asks. "Surely it's not that hard to hide among the hundreds of thousands of people swarming around in here?"

"You'd think so, but Thomas doesn't just rely on his gang

members to keep watch. He gets everyone who's paying him protection money to help track people down, and suddenly you've got thousands of eyes looking for the thief. How hard do you think it is for him to find a family wearing sealskin coats that already make them stand out from the crowd?" She points at our thick coats. As long as we're wearing them, no one even needs to remember our faces.

"We should be able to talk to him, surely?" I say, though even I can hear the naivety in my voice. "Emilie's just a child, and it wasn't even her fault that she fell. Another man pushed her over."

Nadja looks at me intently. Her glasses have once again slipped down to the tip of her nose. I can see she's wrestling with herself. Finally, she takes a deep breath and decides to continue: "The rumour is that Thomas controlled the entire cocaine market in Berlin before the world fell apart. So, he's not just some random guy. You don't get to the top of that business without being willing to go all the way.

Hans and I are both from Berlin, and Hans was addicted to cocaine for a while. He owed his dealer a couple of hundred euros. Not much, really. Just a few hundred euros. But that was enough for them to beat him black and blue and threaten to cut off his fingers, one a day, until he'd paid back his entire debt plus the interest that kept piling up every day. And that was just the dealer and his closest cronies. According to what I've heard, Thomas was the top guy, the one who imported the stuff into the city. So just imagine what he could do to those who owe him something now?"

I'm shaken. I don't know what to say or what to think.

What might he do to us if he finds us?

I think of Hans, who's missing a little finger, and shudder involuntarily. Is Magnus next?

I see Thomas in my mind's eye, storming down the walkway, trying to push Magnus aside, intent on getting hold of Emilie. I don't get much further in my thoughts because at that very moment, Kristian comes bursting in.

"Zaid is in the camp across from us!" he shouts excitedly. "I saw him when I was peeing. I called out to him, and he waved briefly, but then he quickly disappeared into a tent again. It's him! I recognised the sealskin jacket straight away. I think he, Farhana, and Fatima are living in the tent right across from ours!"

• • •

At night, I lie awake long after Hans and Nadja have sung their usual lullaby. Nadja clearly wasn't in the mood this evening, as the hymn was short and met with no applause, though for a brief moment she sounded exactly like the imam who wakes us every morning with the call to prayer. Perhaps the situation with Thomas is affecting her as well, even though it's us who will suffer if he finds us.

Magnus lies with his arm wrapped closely around me. Every so often, he lifts his hand to his face and scratches his beard vigorously.

"I think I've got lice," he whispers, then promptly begins snoring right in my ear, carefree.

It's an ability I envy—the ability to fall asleep even when everything around us is falling apart. I don't have that ability. Instead, I lie awake, worrying about all the things that may or may not happen.

My hip, on the side I'm lying on, starts to ache, so I try to find a more comfortable position. But the space is so tight that all I manage to do is elbow Magnus in the stomach, causing him to wake with a startle.

"Can't you sleep?" he asks groggily, pulling me closer to him.

"I'm thinking about Thomas," I reply, concerned. "Do you think he's already looking for us? How can we stay hidden if he can mobilise so many people to watch for us?"

"I don't know. We'll have to try and figure something out tomorrow."

He scratches his beard fiercely.

"Bloody lice."

"Do you really think it was Zaid that Kristian saw?" I ask then.

"I don't know. I hope so."

"Who else would be wearing a sealskin jacket?"

Magnus remains silent for so long that I start to think he's fallen asleep. Then, suddenly, he speaks again. "I hope it's Zaid. And I hope that he, Farhana, and Fatima are all doing well under the circumstances. But there's also a chance that someone has taken the jacket from him. Like the woman who stole our blanket when we first arrived."

"But whether it was Zaid or not, they must still be somewhere in that camp across from ours. Isn't that right?" I ask, hopefully. Just the thought that I might see my friend again fills me with joy and a sense of optimism that everything will be okay, something I desperately need right now. Even if I can only see her from a distance, just knowing she's nearby and safe makes me unconsciously smile to myself in the dark.

"Kristian seems pretty convinced," Magnus replies sleepily.

Soon after, his breathing becomes heavy. He's fallen asleep again.

I lie there for a long time, thinking about Farhana, Fatima, and Zaid. What's their camp like? Is it like ours? Have they settled into a tent similar to ours, and have they made new friends who can help them through the worst days?

As my thoughts drift, I slide in and out of dreams where Farhana and I are back in Denmark, helping each other fell a massive oak tree, enough firewood for an entire winter. In my waking moments, tears stream freely down my cheeks. I ask myself how we're supposed to survive in this camp, where hunger, cold, disease, and gangs are just part of the daily struggles.

Later in the night, when I must have drifted off again, I wake suddenly as I feel Magnus's foot slowly slide up my leg, outside the blanket. Starting from the foot of the bed, it creeps higher and higher until it finally rests heavily on my hip.

I don't give much thought to how he's managed to get his foot all the way up there, considering how closely we're lying together. Not until the foot suddenly makes a couple of quick circular movements do I realise that it can't possibly be his foot.

"Magnus, is that you?" I whisper.

There's no response.

I assume he must have caressed me in his sleep and think nothing more of it until it strikes me that his arms aren't long enough to reach my leg all the way from the foot of the bed. I try to turn my head to catch a glimpse of the hand I imagine resting on my hip, but Magnus's arm is draped heavily across my chest, blocking my view.

It's pitch dark inside the tent, so I wouldn't be able to see anything anyway. I free my arm from Magnus's grip and reach out past the blanket to find his hand. As I place my hand on his, the hand hisses loudly and gives a powerful push-off, landing on the floor beside the bed with a loud thud. The nails scrape across the wooden planks as it swiftly scurries away, disappearing into the far end of the tent.

I lie there, completely still, listening as the sound fades into the distance, unable to make any sense of it. How can Magnus's hand leave his arm, jump to the floor, and run away? Am I still dreaming?

Suddenly, it hits me with disgust—it must have been one of the huge rats, one of those that live under the floorboards, that had been resting on top of me. Once I manage to connect the movements and sounds in my head, panic surges uncontrollably through my body, rising up to my throat, where it gathers strength before bursting out through my lips, manifesting in a series of hysterical screams that tear through the darkness around us.

17 Magnus

When you stand in the farthest corner of the Gaza Strip, just behind our tent, you have a magnificent view over the Spanish plateau. The heavy rain has transformed the usually dry plain into a lush green carpet that stretches as far as the eye can see. On rare occasions when there's a break in the rain, and the sun pierces through the clouds, you can just about make out the Montes de Toledo mountain range, which divides the Meseta plateau to the east. Covered in large oak forests, the mountain range looks like an ordinary hilly landscape from a distance. However, when you compare the mountains to the thousands of electricity-generating wind turbines scattered across the plateau, it becomes clear that the highest peaks actually rise about a kilometre and a half into the sky. Wherever you look, the turbines patiently turn, serving as undeniable proof of the industrial world's constant thirst for electricity.

In an effort to slow down the advance of climate change, the demand for renewable energy sources rose dramatically. Wind turbines ultimately proved to be one of the most productive and cost-effective solutions. A single land-based wind turbine can provide electricity for up to 1,000 households, so a windswept plain like Meseta has no trouble powering the majority of the Spanish population as long as there are enough turbines.

Of course, there was initially significant opposition to the wind turbines, both from conservation groups and the general population. The arguments against them were many. Most people opposed them because they believed the turbines disrupted open landscapes, posed a threat to birdlife, made noise, and rendered outdoor life impossible for those living nearby.

Even stronger opposition emerged after a global resistance movement against the installation of more wind turbines in natural areas successfully convinced large segments of society that wind turbine electricity was costly for the economy and, therefore, for the standard of living that people had built and wanted to maintain. These were often the same groups that refused to face the reality of climate change, even when the rain began to pour more consistently over the vast desert areas of North Africa. These regions, which had received no more than ten centimetres of rain per year for centuries, now got so much that the land had become farmable.

As has happened many times before, humanity demonstrated a shocking short-sightedness, resulting in a marked slowdown in wind turbine production until long after the effects of climate change could no longer be ignored.

In the meantime, Europe went through a period of reliance on natural gas, of which Russia was a major supplier from the Siberian tundra. Europe soon found itself in a situation where Russia controlled half of its energy production. At the same time, traditional electricity production was drastically reduced, sacrificing coal, oil, and nuclear power. Year by year, the situation escalated until Europe no longer controlled its own energy production. In other words, Russia could shut down large parts of Europe's power grid simply by turning off the supply. Defence systems, healthcare, the economy as a whole – all had been placed in the hands of the sleeping bear.

Finally, Europe realised the unsustainability of being so heavily dependent on Russian influence. An emergency plan was implemented, consisting of various political measures designed to return energy production back to European hands. The production and installation of thousands of new wind turbines across much of Europe became a central part of this plan, and many of the wind turbines on the Meseta plateau are a result of it.

Row after row, they stand like stiff, grey steel trees with their leafless, three-bladed fibreglass crowns, tirelessly producing the much-valued electricity for as long as the wind blows.

I can't help but smile at the thought of how deeply dependent we all were, and many still are, on this precious electricity before the frost set in. How much stronger has the bond within our own little family become since electricity was no longer available to us?

Electricity is a luxury, no doubt about that. But when you think about it, the invention of electricity was also the accelerator for the drastic climate changes our planet has been thrown into. Without electricity, we would never have been able to transport ourselves by planes, cars, or large container ships. The industrial era would never have taken place, and the need for large-scale oil extraction and coal burning would not have arisen. But at the same time fetching clean water from underground would have been far more complicated. Central heating systems wouldn't have existed. Healthcare would have been severely crippled, meaning far fewer people would have survived childbirth and diseases. Without electricity, the earth's population simply wouldn't have exploded to the level we see today, where there is no longer enough space for everyone.

Since Kristian came running in last week and loudly proclaimed that Zaid is in the camp opposite, I now spend much of my time in the cold and wind behind the tent, hoping to catch a glimpse of either him or Farhana. So far, however, I haven't seen a trace of my Syrian friend, his beautiful wife, their daughter, or their grey-spotted seal-skin jackets.

The camp seems to be at least as overcrowded as ours, but five times a day, a quarter of an hour after the call to prayer, the camp is swept clean of people. If you happened to pass by at that time, you could easily get the impression that the camp was empty, if it weren't for the unified hum of the many praying people. The only movement outside the fence that surrounds our own camp then comes from the armed guards patrolling between the camps and from the sewage trucks, which use their large hoses to empty the toilet cabins several times a day.

First, they attach a large suction hose to a snap coupling, about the size of a man's waist, located at the bottom of the tanks near the ground. Then they suck the tanks empty, after which they connect a pressure hose to a connection stub further up and flush out the remaining contents. The entire process takes no more than ten minutes, usually less than the duration of the prayers in the neighbouring camp. When the prayers are over, the camp once again buzzes with life, and you wonder where all the people suddenly come from, along with the noise they bring with them.

Kristian keeps me company, eager to see Fatima again. I'm glad for his company. It gives us a chance to repair our strained relationship, which seems to have improved significantly now that he's convinced Fatima is within reach again. Even if she is separated from us by two rows of barbed wire fences. Besides, Kristian's eyesight is much sharper than mine, making it easier for him to distinguish faces across the 20 metres of land that divide our two camps.

The guards are approaching again. One of them, a heavily built man with a large, well-trimmed beard, glares at me maliciously as they pass by. He barks something in Spanish, which I don't understand. When I don't respond, he comes right up to the fence and threateningly points his rifle at me, slowly repeating his question, still in Spanish.

I have no idea what he's asking, so I just shrug and lower my gaze to indicate that I don't understand the question and that I'm not looking for trouble.

He stands there for about a minute, regarding me with a superior expression, while his colleagues continue their patrol on the opposite side of the alleyway.

Although it requires swallowing all my pride, I keep my gaze firmly fixed on the ground around the guard's feet to avoid provoking him. I notice a transparent plastic bottle lying against the fence, right next to the soldier's boots. The bottle is half-filled with gravel and what looks like a rolled-up piece of paper. Curious to see what's inside, I wait patiently until the soldier, with a sneering grin, finally turns to follow his colleagues. They've already moved some distance down the length of the Arab camp. With long strides, he crosses the alley between the two camps until he catches up with them again.

I wait until they're nearly out of sight before bending down and pulling the bottle through the gaps in the fence.

"What is it?" Kristian asks, curious.

He barely acknowledges the soldier's provocative behaviour. Despite his young age, he has quickly realised it's pointless to insist on fair treatment when, deep down, we're unwanted by everyone.

"I don't know," I reply as I unscrew the cap and pull the

rolled-up piece of paper from the bottle. The paper is wrapped around a pencil with an eraser on the end. As I unroll it, a short Danish message written in faint pencil lines appears.

K. – is everyone okay?
We're registered and have a place to sleep. We're all fine. The only question is, for how long…? Food is scarce, and the conditions are extremely unsanitary. Every day they carry out dead bodies. They say it'll get worse when winter comes.
Write back. Don't use any names – you're infidels!
-Z-

"It's from Zaid," I exclaim excitedly. "They're okay."
I hand the letter to Kristian so he can read it himself.
It only takes him a few moments to read the brief message, after which he quickly reaches for the pencil in my hand and begins to write a reply on the back of the paper. But he hesitates before writing the first letter.
"What does he mean by 'Don't use any names – you're infidels'?"
I grab the letter and study the last sentence again. It doesn't make much sense at first, but knowing Zaid, he wouldn't have written it unless it was important. I hand the letter back to Kristian.
"I don't know. But we'd better respect his wish. No names."
Kristian thinks for a moment, then starts writing.

Everyone is okay! We lost a blanket, but we're managing. We have a tent and two beds. Loads of rats. Toilets are disgusting.

319

How is your daughter doing?
What do you mean by saying we're infidels?
-K- & -M-

He quickly shows me the letter before rolling it back up and putting it into the plastic bottle, not waiting for any further input or suggestions from me.

"So, the only question now is, how do we throw it all the way over there so it lands close enough to the fence for him to reach it? We've only got one shot, so we need to get it right the first time."

"What do you mean?" Kristian asks, sounding slightly irritated. "It's only 20 metres away."

"What I mean is, you won't get much momentum if you try to throw it with your arm sticking through the wire fence. The bottle probably won't even make it halfway. The alternative is to throw it over the fence, but it's four metres high, and it will take a pretty strong and accurate throw to get it to land close enough to the fence."

Kristian nods thoughtfully. "And at the same time, the throw can't be so strong that the bottle ends up too far inside the camp," he says.

"I don't think we'll need to worry about that," I reply. "We probably won't be able to throw it that high or that far with just our arm strength."

Between the southern end of the wire fence and the row of tents is a strip about a metre wide along the inside of the fence, where the guy ropes holding the tents securely to the ground criss-cross like a web of sturdy nylon straps.

"Let's test the weight of the bottle and see how far we can throw it," I say, pointing behind us. "Back here behind the tents, so at least we have some idea of what we're dealing with."

I crawl over the tangled ropes until I'm about 25 metres away from Kristian.

"Careful to not throw it over the fence," he says.

The first cautious throw lands five metres in front of me, and then the bottle bounces another two metres forward, ending up far too far away for me to reach through a wire fence.

I pick up the bottle and return to where I was standing, grateful we didn't just dive into it without a few practice throws first.

I stand for a moment, weighing the bottle in my hand before throwing it back. I try to give it enough height that it would, in theory, pass over the wire fence, but this results in the bottle losing forward momentum. It lands halfway between us.

"Try putting all your strength into the next throw," I say as Kristian picks up the bottle. "And also try to get some height on it."

The next throw lands right at my feet.

"Perfect," I cheer, throwing the bottle back as hard as I can.

The bottle flies in a high arc through the air before dipping down and landing with a thud in the wet earth a few metres in front of Kristian.

"You throw like Ron Weasley," Kristian laughs, referencing Harry Potter's slightly clumsy best friend, a character we've often laughed at during the long winter days back home.

"Oh, ha ha," I reply, feigning offence. "Let's see if you can repeat that last throw. Then maybe you'll have something to back up your arrogance."

Seconds later, the bottle is once again flying through the air in a steep curve, landing right at my feet.

"Okay, I surrender, Miss Hermione," I laugh, firing back a reference to Harry Potter's perfectionist friend. "Do that ten more times, and we'll give it a proper go."

We continue tossing the bottle back and forth for the next 20 minutes. Kristian quickly finds a rhythm that ensures the throw lands within arm's reach of my feet every single time. As for me, I can't seem to get it any closer to him than two metres, no matter how hard I throw it. It soon becomes clear that Kristian will have to bear the heavy responsibility of being the official bottle-thrower from our side between the two camps.

At some point, a few scruffy, curious souls appear from behind the tents. Children and adults drawn by the laughter, coming to see what we're doing. They seem to think we're playing a game, as they tirelessly linger and cheer loudly each time Kristian manages to place the bottle right at my feet. Not wanting to attract too much attention to the fact that we're communicating with someone in the other camp, we continue throwing the bottle until they finally tire of the game and the cold and wander off again.

Even though we're now alone, we decide to wait until dusk when the long shadows fall over the Meseta and the imams call for the final prayer of the day. By then, most people will be settled inside their tents, and we can carry on with our plan relatively undisturbed.

Kristian steps about five metres back from the fence and prepares for a powerful throw, just like the ones we've practised all afternoon. With one arm stretched out in front of him, he bends gracefully backwards before slinging his right arm forward like an Olympic javelin thrower. His fingers release the bottle at exactly the right moment. We watch its flight over the tall barbed-wire fence and into no man's land between the two camps until it disappears into the growing darkness. I listen for the sound of it hitting the fence or the ground on the other side, but the noise from both camps drowns out all other sounds.

"Can you see it?" Kristian asks nervously.

"No. What's your gut feeling?"

"I think it's close to the fence. It was a good throw."

"Then let's trust that," I say, ruffling his hair affectionately. "We'll have to wait until tomorrow to find out. Until then, there's not much more we can do but head to bed and hope Zaid replies soon."

The next morning, we jump out of bed as soon as the light filters into our tent, accompanied by the imams' early morning calls to prayer. Eager to confirm whether the bottle made it, we quickly head behind the tent and strain our eyes to spot the bottle's shiny surface along the fence near Zaid's camp.

Five minutes later, we have to acknowledge the bottle is gone.

• • •

During the morning, another low-pressure system passes over the camp. Wind and rain replace the few preceding days of sunshine, immediately plunging the camp's mood back into the gloomy state that typically dominates much of its vast area. The temperature drops sharply to just above freezing, signalling the imminent arrival of winter.

I dread to think what winter in Spain might bring. The tents don't seem suited to offer the necessary protection against the cold, but Hans and Nadja reassure me that although it's unpleasant and cold, most people manage to survive.

"But don't be fooled," Hans warns. "Diseases spread rapidly throughout the camp during the long winter months. You can already sense it when walking around now. Many people have caught the season's first bout of flu, and that number is going to skyrocket. Few will escape without being bedridden at some point. How long you're sick depends entirely on your health. The four of you should be fine, but many others are visibly weakened and already have compromised immune systems. Most of them won't make it through the winter if they get the flu."

I take a moment to look at the grey-black stains on the roof of the tent. Heavy water droplets cling to the underside, threatening to fall at any moment. The humidity inside the tent is not much lower than outside.

In the month we've been here, there has already been such a turnover in our tent that we've moved five rows closer to the middle, where it's less draughty. The stench from the toilets becomes unbearable for most, and those who don't move for that reason alone eventually do so when the imams' loud voices penetrate the deepest parts of their inner ear one too many times, setting the hammer, anvil, and stirrup in motion. Some people have a higher tolerance than others. Some complain of ear pain within a week, while others seem almost unaffected by the noise. As for us, we're somewhere in the middle.

Even though we were used to the peace of being alone during many winters back home, the constant howling of the winter storms outside was often so irritatingly loud that we learned to block out the noise to avoid going mad.

I observe one of the new arrivals, who has taken over the camp bed that Freja and I had near the entrance. He's a thin-looking man who, due to overcrowding in the camps in France, was recently transferred here along with thousands of others. Yellow pus drips continuously from one of his ears, and he's constantly pressing his fingers into his ear canal as if to alleviate the pain from the middle ear infection. He reads tirelessly from a battered book with a tattered red cover that he brought with him into the camp. It's one of five books he zealously guards, never letting them out of his sight for even a moment, although he's likely already read each of the five books many times during his years in the French camp.

Kristian, instantly recognising a kindred spirit, has been eagerly trying to borrow just one of the books, but so far without much success. He craves new knowledge to feed his young mind, and these are the first books he's seen since we left Denmark. All the books that might have existed in the houses we sought refuge in during our journey from Denmark had long been consumed by fire.

"This is terrible!" Freja exclaims. "How can they just let people die like this?"

"A common flu has always claimed the lives of the weakest in society," I respond. "There's nothing new in that."

Nadja, who had been standing behind Hans, massaging his shoulders, sits down on the camp bed beside him. "But unlike in a well-functioning society, where there's plenty of food, heated homes, and free healthcare, the number of people here too weak to survive even a common flu is much higher than we're used to."

"Last winter alone, more than 3,000 people died in our camp," Hans interjects. "That's far more than in all of Berlin during an average winter when the world was still normal, even though the city had over three million residents back then."

"That's an alarming number," I say, shocked. "How many camps like ours do you think there are in this area?"

Hans leans forward conspiratorially. He enjoys being the centre of attention and the source of all knowledge, no matter how grim. "Well, I've never been outside the barbed wire myself, but I once spoke to someone who had tried to escape. He was quickly spotted by the guards, who patrol everywhere, and was sent back to *Shangri-La*, but he told me he'd managed to count at least 15 other camps. Fifteen! Just in this area! That's between four and five million people."

"I can't even begin to comprehend that," Freja gasps, horrified. "That means they let around 45,000 people die each winter ... that's the entire population of a mid-sized Danish town!"

Emilie looks up at her mother in alarm. "Are we going to die too?" she asks anxiously.

"Absolutely not!" I reply quickly. "You heard what Hans said earlier. Our family is strong. A measly flu epidemic can't get us. Don't worry." I wink at her conspiratorially. "As long as we make sure to eat our food and keep up good hygiene, everything will be fine."

I try to sound brave, but the truth is, I'm nervous about the coming winter. We're not getting nearly enough food to maintain a healthy immune system, and it's practically impossible to follow proper hygiene in a camp this overcrowded.

Emilie nods seriously, not entirely convinced.

"Which reminds me, I'm hungry," I say, standing up. "It's time to go collect our weekly food rations if we want to get it before the day's over."

I try to distract her from all the talk of sickness and death.

"I don't want to," she says, though she must be hungry too. "Can't we do it tomorrow?"

"You know we can't."

"What if we run into Thomas again?"

"We won't. We'll find another way there. Besides, he's probably forgotten all about us by now. Do you need help buttoning your coat?"

"Why? I can do it myself." She begins buttoning her warm sealskin coat, which she's had on all morning.

The sudden drop in temperature has settled like a chilly blanket over our mattresses, so we all woke up cold and shivering. It's nothing compared to the extreme temperatures we know from Denmark, but still enough that her lips were slightly blue when we got up.

Once again, we leave the blankets with Hans and Nadja, who promise to take good care of them, then promptly drag them down to their sleeping area. I try not to think too much about what they'll be used for while we're away.

Outside, the rain has turned to sleet, which stings and pricks our skin. People without any reason to be outside retreat to their camp beds, leaving the walkways less crowded than usual. However, as we approach the distribution point, the crowd becomes so dense that it's almost impossible to move through.

Along the way, I can't help but notice that many seem to be severely afflicted by the fever Hans had mentioned. Glazed eyes and deep, phlegmy coughs speak for themselves, yet despite their illness, the affected are still forced to show up if they want to collect their ration.

The risk of infection is unavoidable, and it's only a matter of days before the fever spreads like wildfire through the camp. I pull the neckline of my thermal undershirt up over my nose and mouth to reduce the risk of inhaling any airborne viruses, and I urge Freja, Kristian, and Emilie to do the same.

The shirt has a strong smell of sweat, reminding me that Kristian and I can't put off visiting the filthy bathing facilities much longer.

On the way back, after receiving our rations, I spot a large sign along the northern side of the fence that I hadn't noticed before. My limited high school Spanish comes in handy as I translate the text.

Obitorio. Morgue.

"Has that sign always been there?" I ask Freja.

"I don't think so. I haven't seen it before."

"They're preparing for this season's flu epidemic," I say grimly. "Over the next five months, we're going to see a lot of bodies carried in there."

"Twenty a day on average. At least. It's disgusting to place it so close to where they distribute food rations too."

She's outraged, and rightly so, I think.

I don't understand how anyone can treat other people with such little empathy or compassion, but Zaid and Farhana were right all along. We're unwanted. It's as simple as that. Distributing food rations and disposing of bodies are logistical problems to be solved as cheaply and efficiently as possible. Nothing more. Decency no longer matters. More than half a million food rations must be distributed daily across the 15 camps. 300 bodies have to be disposed of.

Logistics.

"It's inhumane," rages Freja as we pass the sign.

Our entire attention is focused on this so-called 'death gate', so we don't see the danger until it's too late. Only when Kristian suddenly yanks me to a stop by pulling hard on my arm do I realise something is wrong. I look up and see ten grown men quietly forming a circle around us. Unconsciously, I tighten my grip on the sack in my arms.

"Who are they?" Freja whispers in fright.

"Emilie, Kristian. Get behind me, quickly," I urge.

I grab Emilie and push her behind my back. Kristian stays visible but still takes a step backwards.

I glance around at the men, who are slowly closing in and tightening the circle around us. It's too late to try and escape.

We're trapped.

"What do you want?" I ask nervously in English, while keeping an eye out for potential ways to get out.

"You're wanted," says one of the men in front of me, with a thick British accent. He has sunken cheeks and a long, scraggly beard that hasn't been trimmed in years. Under his nose, there's a yellowish, oozing cold sore, which he occasionally wipes with the back of his hand. Snow has settled in wet patches on his shoulders and the black Adidas beanie pulled low over his ears.

He grins maliciously, his gaze lingering on Freja as he speaks.

"Thomas wants to talk to you. He's been looking for you all week."

Thomas!

"Why?" I ask, trying to sound surprised.

"You'll have to ask him yourself," he replies. "We were just sent to find you. But I'm pretty sure it's about the incident last week."

"What incident?" I naively try to sow a seed of doubt, hoping he'll believe he's got the wrong family, but the man isn't fooled.

"You can play dumb if you like. But believe it or not, there aren't many others walking around in such fine fur coats. Yet it's only now we've managed to track you down, even with a reward on your heads."

I keep up the act. "But we only traded for these coats this week. A family was desperate to get rid of them. Now we know why. You've got the wrong people."

The man stares into my eyes for a long time before speaking again.

"You must really think I'm an idiot. If it wasn't for the fact that Thomas himself put out the alert for you, I would've taken those warm coats and your rations right now. Left you out here in the cold. But you're lucky. I'll just have to settle for the reward Thomas has promised. Enough talk! You'll come quietly, or we'll take turns with your lady friend there." He nods towards Freja. "The order is to bring you back to Thomas alive, but no one said we couldn't have a bit of fun with her before handing you over. God knows, there's not much else to do in this godforsaken camp."

I give in the moment the threat is made. I would never endanger my family, so we follow them dejectedly until we reach Thomas' tent in the centre of the camp.

I fear the meeting with him. Given that he's gone as far as to offer a reward for our capture, I can only expect the worst. If it were just Thomas I had to defend my family from, I wouldn't be so worried—slow and fat as he is. But his power seems far-reaching, and people are willing to follow his every command.

Who knows what they'll do to please the former cocaine king-pin from Berlin?

The man with the Adidas beanie steps inside the tent humbly. It's clear he doesn't live there and isn't part of Thomas' inner circle.

We wait outside, held back by the remaining nine men.

Most of the camp's other residents are still huddled inside their tents. They only come out reluctantly, as freezing rain and sleet continue to fall.

Shortly after, the man reappears, motioning with a wave of his hand for us to follow him inside. As we step in, the first thing I notice is the temperature difference. It's significantly warmer inside Thomas' tent than in ours, where the temperature barely rises above a few degrees outside.

In the centre of the tent stands a gas heater, pumping out warmth in all directions. I briefly wonder where they get the gas to keep it running, but Thomas, reclining in a worn-out armchair next to the heater, interrupts my thoughts. The chair he sits in is the old-fashioned kind with wings on the backrest, where the padding pokes out through open tears.

But it's neither the heater nor the chair that grabs most of my attention. It's the blanket wrapped around his fat body. The beautiful grey-spotted fur contrasts sharply with the tattered upholstery, making the man look even larger than he is. The blanket that was stolen from us on the very first day is now in Thomas' possession.

Thomas smiles warmly as we're ushered in. The floor has been cleared in a space about three-by-three metres in front of him. He gestures for us to sit down. I sense the invitation isn't as optional as it appears, so I urge my family to follow his lead and sit on the bare floorboards.

"I see you've just been to collect your rations," he says jovially, nodding towards the coloured sacks now lying at our feet. "That's good. It's important to eat and stay fit."

The difference between the Thomas sitting in front of us now, wrapped in our sealskin blanket, and the Thomas who tripped over Emilie last week and dropped his ration into the mud is striking. If you hadn't met him before or heard the stories, you might easily mistake him for a kind man, simply looking out for our well-being.

"I also see we share the same good taste in fur."

I'm tempted to point out that his blanket was stolen from us, but I'm sure he's well aware of that, so I stay silent and wait.

Around us, the beds are filled with men lazily watching what's happening in the centre of the tent. From the corner of my eye, I notice they're in better physical shape than anyone else I've seen in the camp. They clearly benefit from getting more to eat than the others, and several of them are now shovelling food into their mouths while enjoying the spectacle.

"All of that's good," he says, closing his eyes long enough for me to think he's fallen asleep. Suddenly, he opens them again. "Unfortunately, we have a bit of an unpleasant issue," he says. "The girl over there was, as you know, the reason I lost my entire week's ration last week."

He nods towards Emilie, who sits huddled close to Freja, trying to hide her face in her coat.

"Luckily for you, I can handle it," he laughs, patting his stomach. "But that's only because I'm sure I'll get enough to eat every day. And I only do because people respect who I am. Do you understand that? If people in this camp lose respect for me, I'll lose the right to keep this body well-fed."

"It was an accident," Freja suddenly interrupts. "She's just a little girl who got knocked over by some random person."

Thomas directs his attention towards Freja. He stares at her intensely for a while, until the man lying in the bed closest to Thomas gets up and kneels on the floor beside her. He begins to stroke her cheek with his hand while studying her face intently.

"So beautiful," he whispers.

Freja tries to pull her face away from his touch, but he doesn't give up and instead lets his hand slide to the back of her neck.

I'm about to jump up and pull the man away when Thomas firmly intervenes. "Lars, not now!"

The man, apparently named Lars, immediately withdraws back to his bed.

"As you can see, I am well respected here in the camp."

The fire in the gas heater suddenly sputters and goes out. It leaves a void that the cold quickly fills. Another of Thomas' companions immediately leaps up with a new gas cylinder, which he swaps with the empty one in no time. Shortly after, the warmth radiates from the heater again.

"You're probably wondering where I get the gas from?" Thomas says with a welcoming smile. "The fact is, even the guards outside, who are here to ensure the camp doesn't explode into anarchy, need an ally inside to maintain peace and order. I have a deal where they provide gas for my heater, and in return, I make sure people inside the camp stay calm. It's a good arrangement for both sides. Just imagine what would happen if people here suddenly one day decided that they didn't want to stay anymore. That they wanted out? It could end terribly. Guards forced to shoot rioters on one side, and rioters tearing guards apart on the other. It can only go in one direction; a massacre."

We sit for a long time, listening to Thomas give his monologue. I still don't understand what he's getting at, but eventually, he finally reaches his conclusion. He wants Emilie's ration, he says!

"But then we won't have enough to survive on," I exclaim. "There's barely enough for all of us as it is."

The smile that had so far been plastered on Thomas' fat face hardens into a grimace that instantly sends shivers down my spine. "You made a fool of me last week," he insists. "The girl must pay a price for that. Otherwise, everyone in the camp will think they can get away with mocking the great Thomas without consequences. But that won't do, will it?"

"Surely there's another solution?" I say desperately. "It was just an accident! Everyone can understand that. What about that blanket there?" I point to the sealskin blanket draped around his fat belly. "It was stolen from us on the very first day we were here. No one could mistake where that blanket came from when they see us with our sealskin jackets. Can't we let people know that the blanket is the price for her mistake? That way, you've already received your payment, and we can all walk away with our heads held high?"

"This blanket was given to me as payment for someone else's wrongdoing," he rejects curtly. "It's the girl's ration. Full stop!"

He signals to Lars, who immediately jumps up and strides over to Emilie to snatch the red sack from her arms. I leap up furiously, ready to fight for her food, but I'm instantly restrained by strong arms from behind.

Thomas heaves himself up and waddles over to Freja, who has also gotten to her feet in the meantime. He grabs her by the hair at the back of her head with his fat fingers and pulls her head close to his own. "Some people have a hard time accepting my decisions at first," he says menacingly.

I don't even have time to respond before he suddenly forces his lips hard against Freja's in a long, obscene kiss that sends waves of suppressed fury through my body. Freja tries to push him away with both her arms, but Thomas holds her firmly. Kristian springs into action and manages to land a powerful blow to the side of Thomas' large belly before two men grab him and pull him away.

Thomas lets go of Freja, who instinctively jumps back two steps. She has blood on her lip. Thomas turns towards me and flashes me a sly grin.

"Okay," I plead desperately. "You win. Take the girl's ration. We'll manage one week without her share."

"I'm sure you will," Thomas replies sternly. "But I think you've misunderstood me. I'm not just talking about a single week's ration." The smile vanishes in an instant.

He nods to Lars, who immediately gets up again and grabs Freja.

"Every week, when you go up to collect your rations, you'll pass by this tent and deliver the girl's ration to me personally."

"Every week?" I exclaim, shocked. "How are we supposed to survive without her ration? You can't demand that from us!"

Thomas takes two heavy steps forward until he's standing so close to me that I can smell his breath. It reeks nauseatingly of rotten eggs. "Every week!" he insists. "And just to make sure you understand the message, here's a little warning in case you're thinking of trying to avoid me and hide in the crowd."

He sits down in his armchair and gestures to Lars, who immediately forces Freja to her knees in front of the nearest camp bed. With one hand gripping her neck firmly, he pushes her upper body down onto the mattress. Two men step in and hold her arms so she can't escape. With his other hand, Lars pulls down her trousers, exposing her white buttocks. He spits into his hand, which he then slips between her legs, rubbing it back and forth to moisten her vagina. Then he pulls down the front of his own trousers. His stiff penis appears, large and threatening, swaying over her bare buttocks like a pale viper.

Lars briefly turns his head to see if he has my attention. Then he winks conspiratorially at me with one eye before brutally thrusting his long shaft into Freja's vaginal opening, pushing as deep as he can.

She screams in pain as he penetrates her.

Everything happens so fast before my eyes, and yet I feel like it's happening in slow motion. My entire body is screaming to rush to her aid, but my brain is too slow to fully comprehend what's happening.

In the distance, I hear Emilie crying. Kristian's voice mixes with Freja's screams, which pierce through the ice-cold haze that clouds my brain like an ice pick. I finally try to go to her rescue, but my arms are pinned. I kick backward, trying to hit one of the men holding me, but I hit nothing but empty air. My heart pounds so violently in my chest that for a moment, my vision goes black.

I force myself to watch the rape of my beloved wife, who is helplessly fighting to free herself.

Lars thrusts into her again and again, for what feels like an eternity. The sound of his thighs slapping against her buttocks mixes with the screams and threatens to etch itself into my memory forever.

I don't understand how we ended up here or how it's possible that I can't even protect my own family from all the evil around us. I'm paralysed. All I can do is helplessly watch as she is violated in front of me and our children.

A series of quick, uncontrolled thrusts finally ends the rape as Lars lets out a guttural roar and ejaculates deep into her tormented body.

● ● ●

Finally! I've been waiting for a response all week. Two hens in a cage, just staring, will find no grain.
Daughter and mother are doing well – for now! Disease is spreading rapidly!
Fanaticism is rampant in the camp. Shia Muslims, originally fleeing from the Sunnis who have successfully established an Islamic caliphate in the Middle East. But there are also many Yazidi Kurds. Tensions between the two groups are high in our camp. I fear a bloody conflict will soon break out. Only the influenza is preventing it for now. These are the same conflicts we fled from back then. Sharia law rules here. It's dangerous to be seen communicating with infidels from the West. Keep contact only at night. Infidels are being blamed for climate change!

18 Freja

My stomach rumbles.

I've just poured cold water over the mixture of freeze-dried lentils, beans, and chickpeas in my cup. Now it'll take about 20 minutes for the mixture to soak up enough water for me to eat. The spoon in my hand stirs the cup lazily, in a slow, monotonous motion, while my thoughts drift away. Far away to a land where you don't risk dying from cold, hunger, or a simple flu. Where law and order still prevail, and where rape isn't an accepted punishment by the authorities.

Does such a place even exist anymore, now that most of the world's population has been displaced by the frost in the north, wars in the Middle East, floods along rivers and coasts, or the drought and wildfires?

I dream of a Mali where lush fruits hang heavy on low branches, threatening to snap under the weight. Where the fields are green, and the corn stands tall, bright against the red soil.

I dream of lying in a meadow full of sweet, woolly lambs, leaping carefree around me.

I dream of a Utopia, one I fear no longer exists. Maybe it never did.

I sit restlessly. Even though the weeks fly by, the skin on my buttocks still burns. Lars's massive member still penetrates my insides like a pneumatic drill, bent on destroying the last remnants of self-respect I might have.

I can still feel the pain when the head of his penis hits the innermost part of my vaginal wall, where it can go no further. It burns, throbs, and stings when I pee, and I fear I have a pelvic infection. I don't know how to heal myself, other than by drinking lots of water, but that just makes me pee more, without helping the stinging at all. I can't stop wondering if Lars has damaged me inside. Has he torn me apart, ripped me to shreds, though I'm not bleeding? At least not physically. Mentally, I bleed burning streaks of guilt and shame that pour out like lava, a steady stream of self-blame.

I've been humiliated in front of my family, who I now struggle to look in the eye, as if it was they who did the unforgivable.

Emilie refuses to leave my side. She feels guilty about my fate and wrestles with her conscience, even though Magnus tries to convince her otherwise. In reality, none of us are to blame for anything. That's the plain truth. Yet, we all battle inner demons.

Magnus feels ashamed that he couldn't protect me when I needed it most. Kristian is angry because we've forced him away from Denmark to an unsafe place, where Mali has been shot, friends have been separated, and the family humiliated and starved. Is he right that we should have stayed in Denmark? If we had known everything we know now, would we have chosen not to leave? For days, that question has tormented me, day and night, and each time, I come to the same conclusion. Had we stayed in Denmark, we would certainly have died soon, and that knowledge makes me feel stronger.

Life in the camp is monotonous. It's easy to get swept away by the destructive whirlpool of self-pity when there's nothing else to occupy you, but there's no room for self-pity. There wasn't in Denmark either, at least not in summer, when our survival depended on building up stores large enough to get us through the winter. But even in winter, self-pity was your worst enemy, ready to destroy your mental health as easily as dandelion spores blown by the wind.

I force myself to be strong, even though it's hard. But day by day, I manage to dull the embers, until one day, at long last, I'll be able to bury the memory of the rape. That day will come when I once again stand strong, as robust as the Vikings I am a distant descendant of.

The legumes in my cup have soaked up the water. They're ready to eat. I take a spoonful of the mixture and chew slowly, like a cow chewing cud. The texture is grainy, and the taste is bland. It needs salt. I find myself missing the iron-rich, bitter taste of seal meat, if only for the sake of having some flavour to what I'm chewing.

When I've eaten everything, I'm still hungry.

The loss of Emilie's ration is taking its toll. Magnus and I pretend we've all had our rations reduced, but in reality, we've cut back the most on ourselves, so the children have something to grow on. Their brains, bones, muscles, and tendons aren't fully developed yet. They need nourishment if they're ever to grow up healthy and experience the world's wonders, the ones only Magnus and I know, once the frost retreats and the world returns to normal.

But the reality is that both Magnus and I are losing weight quickly, leaving us with little strength to fight off the flu that's threatening to knock down the entire camp. It's clear that this situation can't last. If Magnus and I die, Emilie and Kristian will be left orphaned. Alone in a camp where adults have no problem stealing from children just to buy themselves a few more weeks.

We simply must find another solution as soon as possible.

"Are you done?" Magnus asks kindly.

He gently takes my empty cup from my fingers and goes out to rinse it along with his own and the children's.

If it weren't for Magnus, I'm not sure I could stay strong in the belief that we'll survive. He's my rock, my soulmate. We're going through this terrible time together, and together, we continue to handle all the ups and downs. I'm convinced of that.

"I think he's dead," Kristian suddenly says, pulling me from my thoughts.

"Who's dead?" I ask, confused.

For a moment, I'm distracted by an elderly man at the back of the tent, who bursts into a long coughing fit. I can clearly hear the phlegm in his lungs as he coughs.

"The man with the books," Kristian replies, craning his neck to check for movement.

The man lies completely still. Even from here, you can see the thick, glossy scabs from the infection seeping from his ear. The man has hardly spoken to anyone the entire time he's been here, only leaving his bed to collect rations or go to the toilet, always carrying his books in a backpack strapped to his front so no one can steal anything from it.

"He's not moving."

"Maybe he's just asleep?" I ask, hopefully.

Even though the man was the first to bring the flu into our tent, and for more than a week has been coughing violently and rasping for breath at night, I can't reconcile with the thought that he might be dead.

"No, he's definitely dead. He's not breathing."

At that moment, Magnus steps through the tent flap, followed by several others, all of whom pass the man without giving him a second glance. "What are you staring at?" he asks as he approaches.

"The man with the books is dead," Kristian replies. "Take a look for yourself. He's not breathing."

Magnus turns around and looks at the man five rows back.

"Are you sure? I just passed him along with several others. None of us noticed anything."

"Why would you?" Kristian replies cynically. "The man never talks to anyone. He just lies there reading his books all day, when he's not sleeping. But now he's dead. Just look for yourself…"

Magnus walks over to the man, with Kristian close behind. After a moment, I see him shake the man's shoulder before checking for a pulse on his neck. He shakes his head, evidently finding none.

"He's ice cold," Magnus says as they return. "He must have died last night, after we went to sleep."

"What do we do now?" I ask. "We can't just leave him lying there."

"We'll have to take him to the morgue," Magnus replies, shrugging as he scratches his beard vigorously.

Even though we often hear about people dying around the camp, this is the first death we've experienced inside our own tent. Judging by the number of sick people and the sound of all those struggling to breathe, it probably won't be the last.

"We'll have to ask Hans and Nadja to help us carry him there," I say. "We can't do it alone."

Wrapped in his own blanket, we soon find ourselves panting and groaning as we drag the dead man's body through camp. I feel guilty that I don't even know his name, but that's the case with most of the people who live in our tent. Most of those with family stick to themselves within the close confines of their own inner circle, while those alone gather in small groups. Very few stand out enough that everyone knows their names. Hans and Nadja, of course, are exceptions.

I think it's because everyone is fighting their own battle for survival, and there's little energy left for socialising.

The closer we get to the morgue, the more people we come across, like us, on their way with dead relatives, friends, or strangers without any close connections. Some openly cry, others have a bitter look in their eyes. Still others, like us, are simply transporting someone no one knew.

Even though the man is thin, he's still heavy. The strength we built up in Denmark is quickly fading, partly due to in-activity and partly from the lack of food. We quickly tire, both in body and breath, and have to lay the man down on the boards while large snowflakes lazily cover the ground around us, muffling all sounds with a sombre white blanket.

At the morgue, we have to queue for a long time to dispose of the body.

"I think it's going to be a hard winter," Hans says, shivering in the cold.

"Because of the temperature?" Magnus asks.

"Because of the number of dead," he replies.

Immediately after, he holds one nostril shut and blows a snot rocket into the snow at our feet.

• • •

Back in the tent, we find Kristian deeply absorbed in one of the man's books: *1984* by George Orwell. It's in English, which doesn't seem to be a problem for him.

Emilie jumps up as soon as she sees us.

"Finally. Why did it take so long? Did something happen?"

She doesn't like me being out of sight, afraid of losing me, but it wouldn't have been appropriate to take her to the morgue. I give her a big hug.

"There were many others there, delivering one of their dead."

"I thought Thomas had taken you again," she sobs, letting her tears flow freely.

"You don't need to worry about that, my love. As long as we hold up our end of the deal, he'll leave us alone."

I run my hands up and down her back. She's thin, but I don't think she's lost any significant weight. It's hard to tell under the thick sealskin coat. I decide to take her for a bath this evening. It's easier to assess her physical condition when she's naked in the shower. We don't bathe as often as we should, and I haven't bathed since the rape. Partly because the stench in the rooms is so revolting it's hard not to throw up, and partly because I feel humiliated and vulnerable getting naked in front of all the women constantly moving in and out of the facilities. I fear that just by looking at my body, they'll know what happened to me in Thomas' tent. That they'll judge me, as if I'm to blame for what happened.

I know it's just in my head, that no one really cares about me or my body while I'm bathing, but I can't shake the thought.

"Is it good?" I ask Kristian, referring to the book.

He nods absentmindedly.

"He's been like that since you left," Emilie says. "As soon you took the man's body out of the tent, Kristian went over and rummaged through his things until he found the books in his bag."

"It's fine," I reply. "He's missed reading. Kristian needs to keep his mind active to avoid going mad. It's good if the books get passed on to him — they'll be of the most use there."

I release Emilie and sit on the bed next to Kristian. His brown hair is getting long, fanning out across his shoulder blades and falling loosely into his eyes.

It suits him, I think.

Unconsciously, he brushes the hair away from his forehead, tucking it behind his ears, but it soon falls back down again. Suddenly, he scratches his scalp so furiously I'm worried he'll draw blood.

"What other books did he have?" I ask, inspecting Kristian's head.

He stops reading and reaches under the bed, pulling out the bag of books. "*Roots* by Alex Haley," he says, pulling out a thick book. He caresses it with his fingers before placing it on the bed and retrieving the next one. "*The Diary of Anne Frank.*"

"Classics," I mumble, still rummaging through his hair. "Seems the man had a taste for good literature. Maybe he was a teacher..."

"*The Kite Runner* by Khaled Hosseini."

The last book he pulls out is much thicker than the others: *Shantaram* by Gregory David Roberts.

"You're in for some really great reads," I say. "They're all gripping stories of survival and finding joy in life despite all odds. All of them have gained international recognition."

I let the last strands of his greasy hair slip through my fingers. My inspection is done.

"You've got lice, unfortunately. Same as Magnus and Emilie."

And probably me too, I think.

"Maybe the man found strength in reading about how others survived the fates they were dealt," Kristian says, ignoring my last comment. "We must never give up!"

"You're absolutely right," I say, standing up to go over to Hans.

I want to borrow the scissors I've seen him use to trim his beard. He's not keen on lending them out, but when I remind him of what he and Nadja get up to under our blankets every time we collect rations, he bursts into one of his famous pig-like snorts and hands me the scissors anyway.

We must never give up.

I can't get the sentence out of my head. It refuses to leave my thoughts, like an angel perched on my shoulder, whispering it into my ear as I cut lock after lock of Kristian's hair, letting it fall to the ground.

I must never give up. *We* must never give up. We owe it to ourselves and each other. If we give up now, the entire journey from Denmark will have been for nothing—all the hardships. We might as well have laid down and died at home. We need to get creative and find a way to get all the food we need, even if we have to give up Emilie's share to Thomas.

"There. You're done," I say to Kristian, as the last clump of hair falls to the ground. I've cut it all off, leaving only half a centimetre in hopes of giving the lice no place to stay. I feel a little sad seeing him without his beautiful hair, but I push the feeling away, thinking it's better to deal with the lice. The hair will grow back anyway.

"What happened to the man's ration?" I ask thoughtfully as I move on to trimming Magnus' coarse locks.

"I don't actually know," he replies. "Why do you ask?"

"We need more food."

"He was sick, wasn't he? Maybe he wasn't able to collect his last ration."

"What about his token?"

"It was in his pocket. Hans handed it in at the morgue when we dropped off the body. He said that if we didn't hand it in, they wouldn't take the body. We'd have had to keep him here in the tent."

I grab Magnus' head with both hands, pulling it forward to make it easier to trim the hair on top. The lice have left large red patches on his scalp where they've greedily sucked blood. In several places, there are scratch marks from where he's gone a bit too hard in trying to relieve the constant itch. I take a lock of hair and hold it close to my eyes. Eggs cling to the lower part of the strands in thick, whitish-yellow clusters.

Magnus shrugs. "At some point, they'll have to accept them. Otherwise, the dead would just pile up in here as they rot among us. It's inevitable people will steal the tokens."

I glance over at Hans and Nadja's bed. When I catch their eyes, I wave them over. "What would have happened to the man we took to the morgue if we hadn't found his token?" I ask as soon as they arrive.

"They wouldn't have accepted him," Hans replies.

"At some point, they'd have to," I insist, looking him directly in the eye.

"Well, yes... People just leave them by the fence next to the morgue. But it doesn't happen as often as you'd think, and that's all thanks to Thomas."

"Thomas?" I exclaim in surprise. "What on earth does he have to do with it?" It can't be that awful man is standing in the way of all our chances of survival.

Hans smiles nervously and begins to explain: "His hench-men keep a close watch on everyone delivering the dead. If anyone leaves a body by the fence because they don't have the deceased's token to hand over, they are immediately taken to Thomas, who deals with it using the same method of punish-ment that you yourselves have experienced. People lose part of their already meagre ration, and since we all get too little as it is, no one dares take that risk. In a way, you could say that Thomas is indispensable here. Otherwise, the bodies would just pile up everywhere because people steal the tokens. Murder would become routine, but because there are so many of us, it's difficult to get away with it without being discovered and brought to Thomas for punishment."

"What's the punishment for murder?" I ask bitterly. Once again, I reflect that our punishment—my punishment—doesn't match the crime.

Hans notices the change in my expression, his face softening as he places a comforting hand on my arm—the hand that's missing a finger. "I know your experience with Thomas hasn't been... uplifting," he says sympathetically.

The news of my rape spread through the camp like wildfire, reaching Hans and Nadja the very next day. This is how Thomas maintains order—by spreading word of such events, fostering fear so that others will think twice before breaking his rules.

"If it weren't for Thomas, this place would fall into total an-archy," Hans continues. "I'm absolutely convinced of that. Like him or not, his methods, as brutal and over the line as they are, work. I know that all too well from bitter experience."

He raises his hand, wiggling the stump where his little finger used to be.

Later, after Hans and Nadja have left, I become lost in my own thoughts again. We need to find a way to get more food. The hunger gnaws at my insides, devouring me from within. I can feel my strength draining away far faster than before. Even just cutting Magnus and Kristian's hair has left me lying exhausted on our bed, while Magnus is left to finish trimming Emilie's locks. Before that, he shaved off his own beard, revealing his hollowed cheeks as another grim reminder that we can't let the food situation continue like this much longer.

As I lie there, I can hear the man at the back of the tent coughing constantly. Sometimes it's so violent that he gasps for breath, which triggers yet another coughing fit.

His wife is doing her best to help, but she's also on the verge of collapse from fever. Maybe we should keep an eye on them, I think cynically. Be ready to grab their rations when death comes. *If* it comes.

But I quickly push the thought away. No matter what happens, I can't bring myself to scavenge among the sick, hoping to claim the food they might leave behind if they don't survive.

"Now it's just Mum left."

Emilie's voice cuts through my thoughts. I turn my head to see my family, sitting close together on the children's bed, smiling conspiratorially. A giggle escapes me when I see them, looking like freshly shorn sheep with round, speckled heads. The sight is so grotesque that I can't help but laugh. Even though I try, I simply can't hold it in.

Emilie grins broadly. "Your turn now, Mum. You need a haircut too."

Magnus makes a dramatic snipping motion in the air in front

of me, then grabs one of my hands. Twenty minutes later, my head is just as round and closely cropped as the others. It feels strangely cold on my scalp, no longer protected by my once-thick hair. Emilie and Kristian burst out laughing and collapse onto the bed when they see the finished result.

"You look like a seal!" Emilie gasps, rolling onto her stomach as she laughs uncontrollably.

"She's right," Magnus agrees. "You really do look like a seal, especially in that grey, spotted seal-skin coat with your short, round head."

"What do you think you look like, then?" I laugh, jumping onto their bed to give them both a playful shake. "A pair of baby seals and one big, grumpy bull seal."

Kristian sits up straight. "May I introduce the Seal Family of Denmark?" he announces solemnly.

For the next five minutes, we laugh uncontrollably, a stark contrast to the hunger, sickness, cold, filth, and rats that surround us every second of every day, whether awake or asleep.

But all the laughter comes to an abrupt halt when the wife of the sick man at the back of the tent breaks into hysterical sobs. Her husband has stopped breathing. Their nearest neighbours rush to help despite their own flu symptoms, but all efforts to revive him fail. He remains dead.

The mood in the tent plummets as everyone realises another death has occurred—two within the same day. The silence is deafening, despite the noise from outside and the woman's inconsolable crying.

I can hear the rats scratching beneath the floorboards. Disease carriers, just like during the Black Death in the Middle Ages, when they brought fleas and lice that spread the plague to people across all social classes, from peasants to nobility.

Influenza isn't spread by rats, but by humans to other humans. And there are plenty of humans, both within the cramped confines of the tent and beyond the barbed wire fence surrounding the camp—especially out on the Meseta, the flatlands that host so many other refugee camps.

A person with the flu normally infects only one other person on average, via droplets in the air from sneezing or coughing, or through direct contact. This means that if you keep your distance, the flu should die out relatively quickly. But keeping distance is not an option in a camp where 300,000 people live in close quarters on just a few square kilometres. Any hope that we might avoid getting sick ourselves is an illusion. All we can do is wait for our turn. The only small comfort is that influenza isn't usually deadly in healthy people. But two have already died in our small tent of barely fifty people within the same day. Healthy is not a common condition among those living in the same square kilometres as us. It's simply not possible—to live a healthy life or to maintain a strong and resilient body in here.

"We have to get out of here," I whisper, trying to catch Magnus's eye. I can no longer bear the thought of life in this camp. The claustrophobia tightens around my throat, making me feel like I'm suffocating.

Magnus doesn't seem to hear me, so I reach for his hand. When he looks up, I repeat myself over and over. "We have to get out of here. We have to get out of here. We have to get out of here."

The fear must be clear in my exhausted eyes, because he pulls me close, worried. Together we lie down on the bed. I fall asleep to the sound of a flu epidemic spreading, for once not noticing the spiritual duet of the imams at sunset, nor Hans and Nadja's obscene duet at bedtime.

● ● ●

The stench of excrement nearly knocks me off my feet as Emilie and I step inside the building that houses the women's shower facilities.

The showers are located at the northern end of the long building, opposite the toilets in the southern end. The ventilation is clearly insufficient, and with the constant use of the many showerheads by bathing women, droplets hang thickly on every surface. The floor is dangerously slippery, covered in slush from the endless stream of shoes passing through every minute, 24 hours a day.

During the night, when the frost sets in and the temperature drops to minus ten degrees, the air becomes crisper, and the droplets freeze into tiny icicles that hang from the ceiling everywhere. When they melt by midday, it rains indoors with an icy drizzle that's impossible to avoid dripping onto your bare skin. When you're in the shower, though, it hardly matters, as the water is always so cold that I suspect it would freeze if it weren't for the constant flow through the pipes.

All the shower stalls are occupied, so we queue up and wait for our turn. I try to avoid looking at the women bathing, but there aren't many places to rest my gaze without turning my back completely. And if we do that, we'll just lose our place in line. So, I stare down at the floor, while discreetly keeping an eye on the showers.

A mother and her two daughters are finishing up. The girls, who can't be much older than five and seven, are both so thin that their bones jut out sharply beneath their skin. They're shivering with cold, struggling to stand still while their mother tries to make the most of her own two minutes, granted by the shower tokens. She's cleaning a deep pressure sore on her left hip, about the size of a coin. The wound is oozing and clearly painful, as she touches it gingerly. Like her daughters, she is emaciated. The sore has developed right over the protruding hip bone, where the bone lies closest to the skin. I imagine it must have formed due to the few and cramped sleeping spaces, making it difficult to turn often enough to relieve pressure on different parts of the body.

I've felt the pain myself, waking up in the morning after having lain on one side the entire night. Automatically, I reach for my own hip and rub the sore skin. Spurred by the sight of the woman's wound, I pull down the waistband of my trousers and inspect my own skin where it feels tender. There's no open wound, but I notice a red patch, smaller than the woman's but concerning nonetheless. Disturbed, I check my other side, but thankfully, it shows no signs of damage.

I resolve that from now on, Magnus and I must make a point of changing positions more frequently during the night to prevent pressure sores from forming. An untreated sore can quickly become infected, growing larger and more painful. Like a black hole, it consumes the surrounding tissue, muscles, tendons, and bones, until the bones are fully exposed. That cannot happen to any of us, I think, but I'm unsure how we'll manage. Exhausted as we are, we both normally sleep soundly throughout the night.

The two little girls want to get dressed, but something seems to be keeping them from crossing the few metres to the bench in the middle of the room where their clothes are piled, along with the clothing of the other bathers. The older girl crouches down and peers under the benches, apparently spotting something that frightens her. She jumps up in alarm, waving her arms wildly and urging her mother to hurry up and finish her shower.

I try to see what the girls have seen, but it's only when the mother finishes her shower and walks over to lift their clothes that I spot the two large rats. They're feasting on one of their own kind right beneath the bench where the girls' clothes are.

I shudder at the sight of the grisly scene. Though it's not the first time I've seen rats here, it's the first time I've witnessed their cannibalistic tendencies. Emilie lets out a startled yelp when she sees them too.

The dead rat's belly is wide open, and both rats have their heads buried deep in its abdomen, feasting on its entrails. They seem entirely unfazed by the presence of so many people around them.

I loathe these vile creatures, which are everywhere in the camp. Often, you can even hear them scurrying around at the bottom of the latrines after they've been emptied and before the pit is covered again by human waste. I'm disgusted by the memory of how we once survived by eating the rats that sought refuge in our house during the frost outside. I try to convince myself that those rats weren't as unhygienic as their Spanish cousins, who so gladly bathe in filth and eat their own kind. But deep down, I know that a rat is a rat, no matter where in the world it lives.

I dread the thought that we may one day be forced to eat these creatures again if we don't soon find a lasting solution to our food problem.

"Why are they eating each other?" Emilie asks.

She tries to pull away from my rough scrubbing, as I work to remove the thick layers of grime around her ankles, toes, and neck. I notice that her muscle mass has diminished significantly, though she's not yet as skinny as the two girls.

"I don't know," I answer absently. "Stand still so we can get rid of this rust. Otherwise, you'll get eczema."

"But it hurts," she protests.

"It's stuck on pretty tightly."

I use a piece of cloth from the burlap sacks we receive our rations in to scrub her body clean. She gets pink patches where I scrub harder, but at least the grime loosens from her skin and is washed away with the dirty bathwater.

"That's disgusting."

"What is?"

"That they eat each other."

"Yes, it is disgusting," I agree.

Suddenly, I recall the taste of them—less intense than seal meat, but still with a strong gamey flavour, mixed with dirt, which I can only imagine came directly from the sewer. My stomach churns with a series of nauseating spasms, as if trying to expel the rat meat I force-fed it all those years ago.

I glance at the two rats. One has now crawled out of the abdomen and is sitting there, cleaning its bloody whiskers with its paws.

"Hunger can drive you to anything," I say, but I don't elaborate further. As I've mentioned, I'd rather not think about rat meat becoming a potential food source again, even in a worst-case scenario. Not after seeing firsthand the monstrous behaviour of these large creatures here in the camp, where I've witnessed their revolting habits and lifestyle that seem poised to spread new deadly diseases.

The water from the shower suddenly stops. Emilie's two minutes are up. I believe I've managed to scrub most of the dirt off, so I send her back to the bench—partly to get dressed before she gets too cold and partly to guard our clothes so no one steals them.

Her skin has a rosy glow where the blood is circulating close to the surface. In addition to being effective against grime, the burlap cloth also helps to get the blood flowing faster under the skin, generating extra warmth for the rest of the body.

I grab my own token from the top of the coin box, where I'd left it, with stiff, cold fingers, and insert it into the slot. Water starts streaming out of the showerhead again. I step under the spray and gasp loudly as the cold water envelops my body, squeezing the air out of my lungs. The breath I then inhale in large, greedy gulps burns my throat and lungs, triggering a violent coughing fit that lasts for most of my precious shower time. By the time I recover, I can already feel the first signs in my throat that the flu has found its way into my body.

19 Magnus

Mum has fallen ill with the flu. She's in a very bad way, struggling to breathe and unable to collect her ration herself. Daughter and father have mild symptoms. Worsening expected soon. Many have already died. Three in a single week, just in our tent alone. The camp is in chaos.

Kristian looks at the note before placing it in the bottle. The faded lines from previous letters can faintly be seen behind the text, but the words in the newest letter are still legible. He takes a few steps back and then throws the bottle into the darkness.

"I hope they make it through the epidemic safely," I say, swallowing with difficulty.

My throat feels thick and burns deep down into my gullet. The fever is starting to take over. I alternate between shivering with cold and feeling like I'm burning up, barely able to stay upright. Beads of sweat drip from my forehead, even though a freezing wind blows in from the west.

The illness is sweeping through the camp, leaving hardly anyone untouched. Even big Thomas had feverish eyes when Kristian, Emilie, and I passed his tent earlier in the day to drop off Emilie's ration.

I tried once again to appeal to his conscience, arguing how unfair it was to hand in her ration when Freja was too ill to collect her own. But he wouldn't budge.

"The decision is final," he said.

According to his logic, we must have grown used to the smaller rations by now, so losing Freja's share this one week should only be seen as a minor setback.

"You'll manage just fine. I bet she isn't eating anything anyway when she's sick," he insisted.

As much as I hate to admit the vile man is right, it's still the truth. Freja has hardly taken any food lately, with the illness ravaging her body. She's unmistakably weakened, lying in bed all day, unable to get up on her own. Her breathing is laboured, and she gasps for air with the slightest effort.

I'm very worried about her. Even though those who have succumbed to the flu so far were more weakened than she was when the illness struck, there have been very few who have come out the other side fully recovered yet.

Freja has been bedridden for two weeks now, and she's only gotten worse with each passing day. Nadja has also fallen ill. For the first time since we've been here, we don't fall asleep to the sounds of pleasure but to the rasping breaths of sick people fighting a lonely battle to overcome the flu that has taken control of their bodies.

Over in Zaid's camp, one of the imams has been replaced by a darker, deeper voice, which is not as piercing when calling for prayer. I'm worried for my friend, as the flu is surely wreaking havoc in their camp too.

To tell the truth, I fear for Freja's life. For some inexplicable reason, the flu seems to hit adults the hardest, while sparing the children, who often only suffer from a sore throat and a runny nose.

Back inside the tent, I lie down beside Freja under the warm sealskin blankets. She's shivering so violently from the cold that I can feel the vibrations from her body all the way down to my toes. She breathes in small, laboured gasps. I adjust the blankets around her, making sure nothing blocks her nose or mouth.

Yellow mucus runs from one of her nostrils, but she's too exhausted to wipe it away herself, so I find a rag made from torn canvas sacks and gently wipe her nose with it.

"How are you feeling?" I ask helplessly.

"Terrible," she whispers with her eyes closed.

Emilie sits on the bed and gently strokes her mother's cheek, as if she were made of fragile glass.

"When will you get better again?" she asks, with a child's optimistic belief that their parents will always be there to take care of them.

Freja smiles weakly. "Soon, my love. Soon." Her voice is a whisper, barely audible over the other sounds of the camp.

Emilie looks at me anxiously. "She'll get better, won't she?"

"Yes, of course she will," I reassure her.

I dearly hope I'm right.

Without warning, Freja suddenly breaks into a rasping coughing fit, sending small sprays of saliva directly into Emilie's eyes, who had been sitting on the floor with her chin resting on the bedframe just inches from Freja's face.

I jump up in alarm and manage to get her into a sitting position, where she continues to cough up small spurts of yellowish mucus from her lungs until, finally, she spits out a glob of phlegm the size of a coin onto the floor. Afterward, she gasps desperately for breath, trying to take in deep, wheezing breaths.

I look at Emilie with concern as I gently wipe away a glob of yellow mucus from Freja's mouth. I can't help but think of the elderly man who died earlier this week. He had sounded exactly like Freja does now. I feel powerless, frantically wracking my brain for ways to help her condition.

Freja used to prop up pillows and blankets behind Kristian and Emilie when they were sick, to keep their airways as open as possible. I remember that much. I decide to do the same for her.

Lying on her back, with her upper body slightly elevated, Freja's breathing soon becomes calmer. Shortly after, I can hear that she's fallen asleep again.

"How's your throat?" I ask Emilie. "Is it getting worse, or is it still the same?"

"The same," she says. "It's not too bad yet. Will I get as sick as Mum?" Her blue eyes have taken on a glossy sheen, as if she's developed a fever.

I reach out and feel her forehead. It's warm. Maybe too warm, but nothing alarming. "I don't think it will be as bad for you," I say. "It seems that children handle the illness better, much better than the adults."

"Why is that?" she asks, relieved, as if a weight has been lifted off her chest.

"I don't really know. That's just how it is sometimes. Some illnesses hit adults harder, others affect children more, and some don't discriminate. This flu seems to target the adults."

I lie down wearily on the bed next to Freja. There's hardly any room for me now that I've propped her up on her back, so I'm lying with my hip on the hard bedframe, but I barely notice it. The pain in my throat and gullet easily overshadows the pain in my hip.

"I need to close my eyes for a moment," I say, letting my eyes fall shut. It feels like I have sand under my eyelids, but the sensation doesn't go away, no matter how much I blink or rub them.

Emilie starts to say something, but I don't hear the end of her sentence before I fall asleep myself.

The fever is tightening its grip on me, stoking the fires deep within the darkest recesses of my body, where the immune cells never quite reach.

I sleep heavily, a dreamless sleep, only waking when the camp comes to life the next morning. My throat feels rough like sandpaper. It's as if I'm swallowing barbed wire every time I gulp down my saliva. The cold water I drink gives brief relief, but the pain quickly returns.

Freja is still asleep. She hasn't moved all night. Her chest rises and falls gently beneath the blanket, in rhythm with her breathing. I can no longer hear any rattling in her airways, but I don't know if that's good or bad, as her breathing seems to have grown weaker overnight.

Suddenly, my hip sends waves of intense pain to my brain, which immediately focuses all its attention on the area that hurts the most. The pain is so strong that, for a moment, I forget all about my throat. I struggle to get out of bed, but I'm too weak to stand, so I fall to my knees beside it. There, I remain.

The metal frame of the bed has, during the night, pressed so deeply into the flesh around my hip that it's left a fiery red indentation. If I had the energy, I'd be sick with worry, but I'm far too drained to care.

The illness has taken over my body, and there is nothing I can do but surrender to its demands for rest. But first, I need to make sure Freja is improving, and that she hasn't slipped into a new and more severe phase of the illness's insidious cycle.

It's becoming quite clear that the flu epidemic ravaging the camp is one of the more serious kinds.

Freja only stirs slowly when I shake her arm. I try to speak to her, but my voice has disappeared during the night, and only a barely audible whisper escapes my lips. I gesture to Kristian, who is still lying in his bed. His eyes are open, so he's awake, even though he hasn't gotten up yet. He needs to help her get some water. Kristian immediately jumps out of bed and holds a cup of water to her lips. However, she chokes on the first sip and ends up spitting it all over the sealskin blanket. Afterwards, she coughs ominously. When she regains her senses, she looks at me with tear-filled eyes.

"I need to pee," she whispers. She, too, has lost her voice.

She tries to swing her legs over the side of the bed and stand up, but she has no balance and falls back into the bed like a doll made of soft rubber.

I quickly realise that trying to help her to the toilet is pointless, as neither of us has the strength to stay upright all the way there. Instead, I help her pee in my drinking cup while she squats beside the bed. Her urine is a deep yellow and smells strongly of ammonia—a sure sign that she's not drinking enough, while the fever drains her body of fluids.

I hand the half-filled cup to Kristian when she's done. He takes it with a wrinkled nose and quickly rushes behind the tent to pour it out on the other side of the fence. When he returns just moments later, he's holding Zaid's message in a bottle.

"Did you rinse the cup?" I whisper weakly, exhausted as I take it from him.

He shakes his head slightly while unscrewing the bottle's cap and fishing out the letter with his index finger.

"Here, give it to me. I'll go rinse it properly," says Emilie, springing out of bed and reaching for the cup. She doesn't look sick at all, though I can hear she's a bit congested. "He's got nothing but Fatima and his dumb books on his mind," she says indignantly, turning away to head towards the exit.

Kristian finishes reading the letter and hands it to me. "They want to escape the camp," he exclaims, stunned.

Sitting on the floor beside Freja, her head resting limply against my shoulder, I read Zaid's letter.

I'm sorry to hear about your wife/mother, but she's strong, so I'm sure she'll pull through. Have faith in her inner strength. I'll pray for her swift recovery.

We're still healthy here, but we need to get away from this place. It's not safe to stay. The disease is claiming more and more lives, and as if that wasn't enough, the conflict between the Shia Muslims and the Yazidi Kurds is intensifying. Soon, as many will die in Allah's name as from the flu. All women wear burkas, which were issued when we arrived. We live in the Shia part of the camp, but I can't keep up the pretence much longer. I'm not a radical Muslim, you know that, my friend. I'm not fanatical. I can neither raise my daughter with violence nor control my wife with fear. I believe in Allah and the Prophet Muhammad, but what I see here is not the Islam I know. This is masculine dominance, nothing more. Lust for power and the oppression of women, children, and alternative faiths, legitimised by a few select passages from the Quran. If I'm discovered to be lenient towards my wife and daughter, I risk being cast out and ending up in no man's land, where my life will depend on

*the mercy of others. I have no illusions that I'll be allowed
to live for long in that case. What will happen to my family then? They'll be separated, married off, and likely
never see each other again. I see no other way out—we
must leave.*

I'm shaken, stunned to hear about the tightrope my friend is forced to walk. Shaken to learn that, apparently, we humans have learned nothing at all. The persistent belief that God or Allah, or whoever one dedicates themselves to, will save you and grant you eternal life in paradise as long as you're willing to kill in His name, remains a mystery to me. There's not much historical evidence to suggest that acting according to reli- gious doctrine has created a better world. Whether it's those who follow the many commandments of the Bible or the Quran, whether they do so as radical fanatics or more moder- ate believers. It's not surprising, though not particularly clever, that radical Muslims, who reject the well-documented conclusions of science, blame the Western world for the planet's destruction. The oil they've helped extract and sell worldwide has been one of the planet's biggest climate cul- prits for decades. But if you're unwilling to deviate from the text of one book and adopt a broader worldview or under- stand how the world scientifically functions from north to south and east to west, then there's naturally little hope for progress.

On the other hand, the same can be said of science. Science has contributed to humanity's exploitation of the Earth's re- sources to the point where it's no longer sustainable. Many in the Western world have referred to science as the religion of the enlightened world, but the truth is, science is nothing more than the engine driving capitalism. Capitalism, on the other hand, has been the dominant doctrine of the Western world since the industrial age began. Any measures aimed at limiting our freedom to consume were regarded as both restrictive and reactionary. In that respect, our ability, or willingness, if you will, to live in peaceful coexistence with all the world's other populations was neither more tolerant nor pragmatic. It's undeniable that our consumption patterns in the Western world have indirectly contributed to the deaths of millions of people worldwide and ultimately driven millions of others, including ourselves, into exile.

These are two vastly different worldviews.

The question is, when all is said and done, can one really point to either and claim it's more right than the other?

Naturally, we don't accept the radicalised Muslim world's view of women or their holy war against us, the infidels. It goes against all common sense and the human rights we cherish so much. But at the same time, we reserved the right to consume in a way that impacted the weaker populations of the world—those who didn't have the means to partake in consumption but were forced to accept the consequences.

Kristian takes the letter from me when I've finished reading.

"They can't escape," he insists anxiously. "The guards will just shoot them if they try. There are guards everywhere. They'll never make it out alive."

Emilie returns with my rinsed cup. "There are hardly any people outside," she says, cutting off Kristian. "Not like usual."

"Everyone's sick," I explain, drained. "No one has the energy to leave their bed, let alone the tent."

Even speaking is an enormous strain on me. It's such a small thing, but it costs me an absurd amount of energy. I want to get back into bed, but my muscles won't obey. I ask Kristian to help his mother drink some water and then help her back to bed. Once she's comfortably settled, I take his outstretched hand and, with his help, struggle to the opposite end of the bed.

So that we can both lie slightly elevated with a blanket at our backs, preventing our breathing from being unnecessarily blocked, I lie opposite Freja, our legs intertwined in the middle of the bed. She's already asleep by the time I tuck my legs under hers. She was asleep while sitting on the floor with her head on my shoulder, and now she snores softly, her mouth hanging open.

Emilie carefully wraps us in the warm blankets.

I briefly recall a time many years ago when we'd lie like this, each with a book and a cup of hot tea, and spend an entire afternoon simply enjoying each other's company in silence. We found it romantic that we could share time together in bed without it necessarily leading to lovemaking. Just being together, feeling each other, while being immersed in our own worlds. It was life-affirming. But there's nothing romantic or life-affirming about the scene in the tent right now. All around us, people are coughing up phlegm and groaning in pain. People are battling a vicious illness that could very well take your life, just as it took the lives of others before you.

"What should I write to Zaid?" Kristian asks, his mouth full of legumes.

He must have set them to soak as soon as he opened his eyes.

I have no appetite myself, and though I know my body needs nourishment to fight the illness, I simply won't be able to force anything down. Not even if it were a tenderloin stew with crispy pearl onions, fresh mushrooms, and juicy cocktail sausages—my favourite dish from when I was young, and the world hadn't changed yet. That was before Kristian and Emilie were born.

"I don't know," I mumble sluggishly. "Let's look at it tomorrow."

Kristian lies back in his own bed.

"We have to warn them not to leave," he says thoughtfully.

"Tomorrow," I whisper again, barely audible, and close my eyes.

Never before have I experienced a fever burning so intensely in every single muscle fibre. And as if that weren't enough, my skin also burns and stings where the metal frame of the bed has left a mark. I don't have the energy to check, but I fear that what I'm feeling is the beginning of a pressure sore, which it's already too late to treat. I've been lying with my hip pressed against the metal frame for far too long, and there's a strong chance I've cut off the oxygen supply to all the cells in the area, leaving them to fight a losing battle, much like the people around me.

● ● ●

I'm startled when Kristian wakes me again, telling me it's time to collect our rations. Has a whole week really passed since we last picked them up?

I can't remember the last time I ate. I'm hungry, but I also feel nauseous. I don't think I'd be able to keep any food down, even if I tried.

I look up and meet the eyes of both Kristian and Emilie, who are staring at me with concern. I can see their noses are red, but otherwise, they seem fine. The illness appears to have passed through them far more gently.

Kristian hands me a cup of cold water, which I gratefully accept. It feels heavy in my hand. I drink and enjoy the sensation of the cool water running down my throat. When I finish the cup, he refills it. My body is screaming for fluids, and even after downing three cups in quick succession, I'm still thirsty.

"Do you think you can manage to get the rations today?" Kristian asks after a while. "Mum's still too weak to collect hers."

I shake my head slightly. I have a pounding headache and neck pain. Any movement seems overwhelming, and I can't imagine making my way across the entire camp to get rations. It's not just the nearly four-kilometre journey each way, but the time it takes as well.

"How's Mum doing?" I ask, giving Freja's foot a gentle squeeze.

My voice has partially returned, but it sounds rough to my ears, and my throat still feels as though I've swallowed shards of glass with the water.

"I'm awake," Freja replies, eyes still closed. "Tired, but awake."

"How do you feel?"

"Like I've been run over by a lorry. But I think I can feel some progress. My throat doesn't hurt anymore, and the headache's gone. I can breathe a bit easier again."

"When did you last eat?" I ask, just as a lump of phlegm gets caught in my throat. I break into a long, painful coughing fit.

"I don't know. I'm not hungry," she says once I finally stop coughing, gasping for breath.

She still sounds weak. I doubt she's eaten much in the two weeks she's been bedridden. I'm sure about the first week, but I can't be certain about the second, as I've been bedridden myself with a high fever. I can barely tell one day from the next, but as far as I know, I haven't eaten either since falling ill.

I feel dazed, but somehow I conclude that last week's rations must still be mostly intact. There should be enough for Kristian and Emilie to eat for the entire week. The chances of Freja's or my own appetite returning this week are slim to none.

I have no doubt that we'll both be severely malnourished when the fever finally burns itself out, but we'll deal with that when the time comes. Right now, the most important thing is that the children have food and can get through the week without having to cross the camp to fetch rations on their own. Two defenceless children would be an easy target for someone desperate, who, like us, has had to skip one or more rations due to illness.

Satisfied that the food situation seems under control for now, I lie back in bed and close my eyes. Even though I've only been awake a short while, I'm utterly exhausted. I focus on my breathing, which feels laboured and heavy, as if my lungs are coated in a thick layer of material that's preventing the oxygen from being properly absorbed into my blood to fuel my body's cells. Moments later, I let myself be drawn back into the healing world of dreams, where I no longer feel the pain in my hip or the lack of oxygen.

The following week, I drift in and out of varying degrees of consciousness. On the tenth day since the illness took hold of me, I experience a life-threatening crisis, which appears to be a defining moment in the illness's diabolical life cycle. Later, when the illness finally loosens its grip on the camp, we understand that it's precisely at this critical stage that those who died had given up the fight. Like an invading enemy, the illness had seized control of their bodies, claiming new territory and overcoming their defences until there was nothing left alive.

I wake from a nightmare in a state of panic, suddenly feeling like I can no longer draw enough air into my lungs. No matter how hard I gasp for breath, it makes no difference. The oxygen simply refuses to pass through the lung tissue to the alveoli and into the bloodstream, which means my body isn't receiving the life-sustaining oxygen it needs. Instinctively, I feel as though I'm hovering between life and death.

I reach out frantically for Freja but don't find her beside me in the bed anymore. Where is she? I think in terror. She couldn't have died while I was lost in a fevered haze, could she?

I struggle to sit up, desperately trying to draw air from the cold, stinking air around me. But my body refuses to cooperate, and all I achieve is a sensation of being suffocated, as if there's a bag over my head.

I look around in a state of shock and see Kristian getting out of bed to come to my aid. Before I know it, he's pulled me up into a sitting position with a strength most grown men would envy.

As soon as I sit up, I feel the phlegm loosening slightly from my lungs—just enough to gulp a few precious mouthfuls of that glorious, life-giving oxygen. Then I break into the worst coughing fit I can ever remember experiencing. Afterwards, the phlegm in my lungs has loosened enough for me to breathe more freely, though still with considerable difficulty.

"Where's Freja?" I ask, breathless.

"She's gone for a short walk with Emilie to get some movement back into her muscles," Kristian replies, trying to calm me. "She says she's almost feeling well again." He smiles in relief as he speaks. "She's been drinking plenty of water and even ate a cup of our rations, but she's still very weak. Emilie doesn't leave her side when she goes out for some fresh air."

A weight lifts from my heart when I hear his words. *Getting some fresh air in the midst of all this stench*, I think with amusement.

I can't help but smile.

Freja has survived the illness, and so will I, I think triumphantly.

I haven't come this far just to die from a wretched virus infection.

20 Freja

"Why didn't you drop off the girl's ration last week, as we agreed?" It's Lars who greets us today, staring at me with a lustful glint in his eyes that sends a chill down my spine.

Thomas is apparently still sick. As I glance around, I spot his enormous body, half-lying, half-sitting in a bed near the warmth of the gas stove in the centre of the tent. He watches us from a distance. Even though he's delegated responsibility to his second-in-command, he still keeps a sharp eye on everything around him.

I can see he's struggling to breathe more than usual. Why can't he just die already? I think coldly.

I catch myself wishing that the illness would claim Thomas as one of its many victims. Even though nearly five percent of the adult population in the camp has succumbed to the illness, it seems Thomas is going to make it out on the other side.

"Neither Magnus nor I had the strength to collect the rations last week," I respond, preparing myself for a confrontation. "We've both been ill. Magnus is still sick, which is why he's not with us today."

"That's no excuse. The girl should've come on her own," Lars says. "You're not the only ones, you know. We've got people here who are too sick to collect their rations as well, people we care for. When deliveries are missed, we have a situation that shouldn't happen. We're starving. And do you know what, sweetheart? None of us like to starve."

"But neither she nor her brother could make it."

I try to sound in control, but in truth, I'm trembling with fear, terrified of a repeat of the rape as punishment for what they see as our debt. But what can I do but try to stand strong and intimidating? The problem is, I don't feel strong at all. I feel weak after three weeks of illness, barely eating anything, and when I speak, I can hear the anxiety in my own voice.

"But we're here now, and here's her ration, as agreed." I place the sack down on the floor between us in a show of defiance.

Lars, who doesn't seem entirely comfortable in his role as substitute, keeps glancing nervously over at Thomas. From the corner of my eye, I see Thomas motioning for Lars to come closer. Lars spins around and scurries over like a whip cracked at his heels. Shortly after, he returns.

"Thomas wants your ration instead of the girl's as compensation for last week's missed delivery," he says with far more confidence.

I stare at him, shocked.

"He can't be serious," I exclaim, distressed. "How are the four of us supposed to survive on just two rations, one of which is a child's? Let alone regain our strength after being bedridden for so long?"

Lars shrugs indifferently. "That's what Thomas wants."

"There must be another solution," I say, letting the tears flow freely against my will. I hate showing my vulnerability like this, but it all feels so unfair that I'm slowly falling apart. "It doesn't make any sense. If we don't get enough food, we won't survive much longer, and then Thomas will get nothing."

Thomas waves Lars over to him again. I can't hear their conversation, but even if I could, it's in German, so I wouldn't understand. I watch as Thomas points to the men lying around the tent. Some are sick, coughing or groaning in their sleep. Two beds are empty, and I conclude that they must have lost people to the flu in here as well.

Lars returns. He lets his gaze wander slowly up and down my body before relaying Thomas's message once more: "I was lucky enough to have the pleasure of a test ride the first time we met, so to speak." He suddenly reaches for my breast, but I manage to react in time and jump back, startled.

Kristian quickly steps in front of me. I'm grateful for the small protection he's trying to provide, although I doubt there's much he can do if they decide to assault me again.

I loathe having to stand face to face with my attacker, having this conversation and pretending as if nothing happened, but I feel like I have no other choice. The consequences of staying away are too frightening, so I grit my teeth and force myself to listen. At the same time, I feel lightheaded, a reminder that I should eat more.

Lars looks momentarily surprised by my reaction, but only briefly. A wide smile suddenly spreads across his thin face. A boyish, charming smile that I'm sure has seduced many unfortunate women over the years.

"As I said, I had the pleasure of the first turn," he begins, pausing for dramatic effect before continuing. "My friends, on the other hand, they've been pestering me ever since, wanting to know all the juicy details, you know... How tight were you? What was it like to fuck you from behind, smelling all your horny juices? How soft is your ass? That kind of intimate stuff, you know... If you ask me, I think it's a bit vulgar, but you have to understand, around here, there's not much new pussy to go around. New pussy is in high demand, and everyone wants to try it out. But when people have been here for more than half a year, they start getting lazy with hygiene. The muscles waste away, and all that's left are bones. Do you know what it feels like to fuck bones? Honestly, it's no fun at all. It hurts every time you thrust hard."

I stare at him, wide-eyed. My fear must be clearly etched on my face because he hurries to continue.

"Don't worry, no one's going to take you by force. That was a one-time thing. We had to make an example of you, you understand. No, this is an offer, and it's entirely up to you. You can choose to keep handing over the girl's rations as agreed, or you can choose to entertain the boys, one after the other. It's your choice. No pressure. It's all voluntary."

I hear what he's saying, but I'm not sure I fully grasp the message. Is he asking me to prostitute myself in exchange for keeping Emilie's rations in the future? I can't think clearly. I haven't eaten much since recovering, and my brain feels empty.

The heat in the tent is making me nauseous, and I feel like I'm about to pass out. I feel Kristian pushing me backwards, out of the tent. I follow mechanically, unable to make a decision or form a coherent thought.

The last thing I hear before we step outside is Lars's voice: "Don't take too long to decide, sweetheart. You're starting to deteriorate too, and your value is dropping. It won't be long before the offer expires. We can find bones anywhere."

Later, after I've forced down half a cup of soaked beans and lentils into my shrunken stomach, I can finally think clearly again. The offer, or whatever you'd call it, seems so grotesque that I dismiss it as Thomas's peculiar way of emphasising that the demand for Emilie's ration is non-negotiable. Whether we starve is not his problem.

Kristian is furious, talking endlessly about taking on Thomas himself, maybe even killing him.

"That would solve the problem," he claims.

"And what do you think will happen if Thomas dies?" Magnus asks, overhearing Kristian's rant for the 20th time.

Magnus is over the worst of it, and thankfully it's only a matter of days before he's well enough to leave the bed.

I haven't told him about the obscene offer, and I've instructed Kristian and Emilie to keep it to themselves. There's no point in worrying him unnecessarily while he's still recovering.

Kristian doesn't answer, so Magnus continues patiently: "Then the next in line just steps up and takes Thomas's place. These kinds of gangs always have a second-in-command. The only thing you'd achieve is putting a target on your own back. Maybe even on your whole family's."

"Kunta Kinte refused to be broken, and so should we," Kristian says, referring to the Gambian-born slave from the book *Roots*, which he's already halfway through.

"That's true," Magnus agrees calmly, as I help him pull his trousers a bit down.

I will inspect the wound on his hip, and I draw a sharp breath through my teeth when I see it. Even though I clean it as best I can with water, it won't heal. There's tissue damage all the way down to the underlying flesh, but luckily, it doesn't smell too bad. I still have hope that it will heal once Magnus's immune system has finished fighting off the flu. The combination of pressure and the illness's terrible ability to block oxygen supply to the body's cells has definitely made the problem worse than it should have been. The cells have simply collapsed from lack of oxygen and insufficient fluids or nutrients to repair themselves.

"If I remember the story correctly, Kunta Kinte was punished with whipping for being defiant," Magnus says. "So much so that he almost died from it, isn't that right?"

"They cut off one of his feet so he couldn't run away anymore," I confirm, joining the conversation.

I remember the book vividly, one I read in secondary school. To this day, it remains one of the best reading experiences of my life. One of those stories that must never be forgotten. One that should be kept alive at all costs to remind us all of the atrocities humans can commit for their own gain.

"Kunta Kinte was too valuable for the plantation owner to get rid of, and killing him wouldn't have benefited the owner either, so instead they cut off his foot, rendering him incapable of escaping. And it worked. Kunta Kinte settled down. He even got married and had children."

"So, you think it's fine to keep handing over Emilie's ration every week, even though we can't spare it? Don't you think I've noticed that you and Dad give Emilie and me more than you take for yourselves? You've both lost so much weight because you haven't eaten anything for three weeks! This can't go on."

Anger is simmering just below the surface. If I know him well, it's masking a deeper uncertainty that he doesn't know how to express.

"No," I say, holding Kristian's gaze.

He's clearly worried about us, but we must do everything we can to prevent him from taking rash action on his own. It will only create problems for him or for all of us.

"You can compare Thomas to the plantation owner in your book. If we don't fall in line, he'll just keep punishing us more and more until we stop resisting. In here, food is worth as much as gold. Actually, it's worth more because gold can't nourish you, and you have no use for it in here. If you resist, he'll just punish us by taking your ration too, and it'll go on like that until we no longer have the energy to rebel.

Kunta Kinte tried to escape. He didn't succeed. In the same way, we can't escape Thomas as long as we're locked up together behind a four-metre-high barbed wire fence. We have no choice but to comply and avoid drawing any more attention to ourselves than necessary."

Kristian is about to defend his point, but he's interrupted by a loud, tearful scream that makes the hairs on my arms stand up.

It's Hans, standing and staring helplessly at the bed where Nadja has been lying ill for the past few weeks, while he has miraculously avoided infection himself. Instead, he's been caring for her as best he knows how.

"She's dead," he screams in despair, clutching his head with both hands. "My darling is dead! Please, somebody help me! Help her! I'm begging you!"

His grief is so palpable that a chill runs through the tent. Everyone stops whatever they were doing, and all conversation ceases, leaving only the sound of Hans's desperate cries echoing at full volume.

"Oh no," I say, rushing to his aid.

I have no idea if there's anything I can do for Nadja, or if it's already too late, but the first thing I do when I reach her is check for a pulse. Finding none, I place my ear close to her mouth. Not even the faintest breath escapes her blue lips.

Meanwhile, Hans is running frantically around, pulling at his hair, desperately trying to get someone to help me bring his beloved wife back to life. No one rises. Either they're too ill to help, too exhausted, or grieving themselves over the loss of someone they love. Everyone seems to be in a collective state of shock, paralysed by the fact that the most vibrant resident of the tent is no longer among us. And there's nothing I or anyone else can do to change that.

Nadja's death sends shockwaves through the tent. Though she's far from the first to leave us, she was such a tenacious spirit that she greatly contributed to keeping most people's spirits up, even when life dealt us its harshest blows.

It feels so pointless and undignified that we're forced to leave her by the fence near the mortuary because there aren't enough aid workers to receive her when we arrive. There she lies now, all alone, alongside hundreds of other lost souls.

I feel so helpless, so lost, as I see her lying there on the ground, side by side with so many others. Now, more than ever, I feel unwanted. Our European neighbours want nothing to do with us, that much has long been clear to everyone. They'd rather see us dead and gone, buried in our homeland, so they don't have to deal with us.

In the weeks that follow, the epidemic slowly loses its grip. Perhaps it's because the temperature has dropped another notch well below freezing, even during the day. Maybe the virus doesn't thrive in colder temperatures, or maybe there are simply no more people left to infect. Whatever the reason, the flu is retreating, and now more people are dying from the cold than from illness.

Hans grieves endlessly for Nadja. We try to be there for him as much as we can, but we're fighting our own battles too.

Despite our warm sealskin clothes, it's hard to fend off the frost when we have no way of lighting a fire, such as in a stove.

The canvas tent provides only minimal protection, and the only source of heat comes from our own bodies. In this respect, it actually proves helpful that we're crammed together with too many people inside each tent. The combined body heat we emit is just enough to keep the cold at bay most of the time.

The lack of food, however, does nothing to improve the situation. Magnus and I are recovering only slowly from our illness, and I constantly shiver from the cold, day and night.

Even the rats suffer in the cold. More and more often, they seek shelter inside, looking for suitable places to nest. And as if it weren't enough that we're forced to share our rations with Thomas and his gang, we wake up several times to find that the rats have gnawed holes in the canvas sacks and helped themselves to the contents. Kristian and a few other boys try to stomp as many rats to death under their heels as they can, but the rats are too fast, and there are too many of them. For every rat they kill, at least five more seem to appear.

Kristian and Magnus have resumed communication with Zaid, who eventually also fell ill, though his letters suggest that neither he, Farhana, nor Fatima were severely affected. He says he's working on an escape plan to get them all to safety far from Europe.

I find it hard to imagine where such a place could be or how it's possible to escape unscathed. The entire camp is patrolled 24/7 by aggressive guards with machine guns. Guards who don't hesitate to smash the butt of their guns into your face if you stand too close to the fence or stare at them for too long.

I'm filled with anxiety for my friends' safety because, even though Zaid says their situation is unbearable, even dangerous, at least they're alive. On the other hand, I understand their dilemma, which in many ways mirrors our own. Both they and we live at the mercy of others, and if we want any chance of survival, we have to play along with a tune that doesn't harmonise with our own.

In the same way, I fear that I may end up being forced to sell my body to ensure my family has enough food to survive the winter. I think of Farhana and the story she told me, and what she had to do so that she and Zaid could survive. If it comes to that, I wouldn't be the only one in the world forced to sacrifice myself for my family's sake, and I certainly won't be the last, should I end up accepting the offer.

I can't shake the thought, as my stomach screams with hunger, and I can hear Magnus's doing the same. We need to rebuild our reserves if we're not to be among those who succumb to the next epidemic that sweeps through the camp.

In the end, unless some groundbreaking change comes to our lives soon, we'll have to face the unfortunate truth that the only purpose left for us now is to wait for death. Every day we wake up is just another day we must endure until death finally taps us on the shoulder and releases us from our misery.

Death.

Why do we resist it, really? For what purpose do we cling so desperately to life when all it offers us is pain, hunger, and a lack of compassion? What is our future, truly? Here, as it was back home, our future seems the same, and it is not life that stands with open arms, welcoming us. Mother Earth, on the contrary, seems eager to be rid of us.

But back home, we fought bravely to survive. Why shouldn't we do the same here? Maybe, if we're lucky, we'll eventually experience the miracle we're all waiting for. Maybe, if we survive just one more year, things will return to normal again?

21 Magnus

The messages in bottles fly back and forth through the darkness between the two camps. All this time, I haven't seen Zaid even once, and now it seems I probably never will again.

We've found an escape route. I believe that within two weeks, everything will be ready for us to leave this hated camp and all its mad inhabitants behind. I honestly don't know who is worse anymore. It seems as if they're competing to see who can enforce the strictest form of Sharia. As if they believe their chances of being saved by the Prophet Muhammad and welcomed into Paradise increase the more they punish their women. All reason has vanished, giving way to a contagious madness that even some of the harshly beaten women are starting to believe in. They think that if they just endure all the violence with their heads held high, a better world awaits them on the other side. I feel so sorry for those fools, but there's nothing I can do except ensure that neither my wife nor my daughter live in this madness any longer than absolutely necessary. It's the same thing we fled from in Syria.

"What are you doing?" Hans asks, suddenly appearing and startling us both.

Since Nadja's death, he's been clinging to us like a shadow. He's afraid of being alone with his grief, but I had thought we'd have enough time to exchange letters with Zaid since Hans had loudly declared he was going to wash all the illness and dirt off his skin.

"Are you back already?" I ask, carefully avoiding his question.

It's best that as few people as possible know we're communicating with someone in the other camp. So far, we've miraculously managed to keep it a secret.

"I was lucky to find a free shower straight away. I've never had that happen before." He stares at the bottle message in Kristian's hand. "What's that?"

"How did you know you could find us back here?"

"You weren't inside, so I tried back here first. I've seen you both come here so many times in the evenings. What are you doing?"

He's far too curious, and I'd rather not involve him for fear he might accidentally let something slip to the wrong person and ruin Zaid's escape plans.

"We just like to come back here to get a bit of peace," I say. I hope he picks up on the not-so-subtle hint. "In Denmark, we were never really in large groups. We miss the quiet. So, we come here to get away from it all before going to sleep. That's all."

My breath forms small clouds as I speak.

Hans studies my face for a while, as if trying to read the small signs that might reveal whether I'm telling the whole truth or hiding something from him.

"You can trust me, you know that, right?" he says, quickly turning his head to the side and, with two fingers, holding one nostril closed as he blows a large glob of snot into the snow.

"I know, Hans. You're a good friend."

"Then why won't you tell me what's in the bottle that Kristian is hiding behind his back? Why is it so secret?"

The full moon has long since risen in the frost-clear night sky. The light reflects off the snow beneath our feet, making it hard to hide anything in the darkness.

Hans must have seen us reading the letter from a distance when he arrived. And the fact that Kristian is now hiding it behind his back, pretending it's nothing, is an obvious insult to Hans's intelligence—not to mention a rejection of his friendship.

I look at Kristian, who stares back at me, unsure of what to do. After a moment, he shrugs in defeat.

"If it weren't for Hans and Nadja, we probably wouldn't have our precious sealskin blankets anymore," he says. "I think we can trust him not to betray us or Zaid with this."

I nod thoughtfully. He's right.

Hans has never shown us anything but loyalty. We should be able to trust him and show him the respect he deserves. I turn towards him and place a hand on his shoulder.

"Do you promise to keep what I'm about to tell you a secret?"

"Of course. Scout's honour. Your secret is as safe with me as it is with you."

"I hope so because it's our friends' lives at stake if you talk."

Hans nods seriously.

"Trust me. Which friends? I thought you only spoke with Nadja and me?"

In truth, there's not much we *can* tell him. We don't know the details of the escape plan, and the fact that we have friends in the Arab camp shouldn't matter to anyone but us.

Still, I feel like I'm betraying Zaid by revealing what little I do know.

Unfortunately, the general prejudices against anyone outside our immediate neighbours have grown so strong that few people trust those with different religions, philosophies, or even everyday viewpoints anymore. I worry that loyalty to our Syrian friends wouldn't weigh much if that knowledge suddenly became valuable in a deal with the guards—or with Thomas and his cronies, for that matter.

When I finish explaining, Hans smiles dismissively.

"Well, it wasn't as interesting as I thought it would be," he says. "What goes on in the Arab camp isn't any concern of ours. And with the racket they make over there, day and night, I don't blame him for not wanting to stay."

"Just keep quiet about what I told you, okay? It really isn't anyone else's business."

I nod to Kristian to continue what we were doing before Hans interrupted. He pulls the pencil from the bottle, flips the letter over, and begins writing a message on the back. The paper is now rather grubby after so many erasures of old text.

We wish we could go with you. There's no future for us here. But where could we go? Where would we be welcomed, even if it were possible to join you? Is there anywhere left in this decaying world where refugees like us are still welcome? We once talked about eating oranges and dates together. There are none of those here. Do you think there are where you'll end up? We miss you. Will we ever see you again? We're curious about how you plan to escape, but we understand it's too risky to reveal your plan. Please send my regards to your daughter. I cry knowing I won't see her again, but her face is still so clear in my memory. The most important thing is that she is safe, and you say she isn't now. I will never forget her. Please tell her that.

Kristian cries as he places the rolled-up letter back into the bottle and throws it over the fence. Heavy tears for a lost love, cruelly ripped from his arms before he even had the chance to fully embrace it. I feel for him. His first great love is just a few metres away, yet so far out of reach. And now he learns that she's on her way again, with no one able to tell him where to.

I pull him close and give him a solid hug. His whole body is shaking, he's so broken.

Suddenly, Hans steps forward. He, too, has lost someone. He, too, needs to know that there are still people who care for him. With a soft sigh, I open my arms and let him join the embrace. So many family members and friends are gone that we must learn to value all the more those who still wish us well.

Somehow, we'll get through this. I'm sure of it. We managed to adapt to the changing climate in Denmark, so why not here as well?

I try to stay positive, but it's difficult. In Denmark, we were lucky, I think grimly. Here, we are no longer the masters of our own fate. Here, we are bound by Thomas' rules, and Thomas' rules are designed solely to ensure that Thomas survives—not us.

● ● ●

It's a strange feeling, always being hungry, getting far too little to eat, yet still feeling the need to relieve myself. I've pulled my scarf up over my nose, trying to shield my sense of smell and protect my lungs from the stinging sensation that fills every breath I take while in the latrines.

Outside the building, there's a bright blue sign with an illustration of a modern flush toilet. In reality, though, it's just a row of holes over large, oval fibreglass tanks, with a toilet seat mounted above each hole. The tanks are emptied twice daily by the vacuum trucks that constantly shuttle back and forth between our camp and the neighbouring Arab camp. Learning their schedule has turned out to be one of the more important rhythms of the camp because if you've settled in with your backside firmly planted over the hole when the tanks are being emptied, the vacuum created is so strong that it's nearly impossible to free yourself. If you don't manage to escape before they start rinsing the tanks, you'll also get an involuntary, but very thorough, colon cleanse. The suction is so powerful you feel like you can taste what you ate a month ago—salted seal meat in my case, when I first experienced this free spa treatment.

Once you get the rhythm down, though, it's much better to be first in line. The tanks are surprisingly clean, and the smell is far more bearable. We who live in the Gaza Strip have an advantage in that respect, as a considerable part of the day is spent watching what's happening on the other side of the fence. In doing so, we automatically learn the daily routine of the vacuum trucks—a useful distraction that helps another day pass in boredom without going mad.

My stomach feels bloated. Most of what I pass is nothing but gas and liquid, a clear sign that my body is absorbing all the sparse nutrients it's fed, letting very little through. But even that isn't enough.

I stare lazily at my exposed thigh muscles, waiting patiently for the last hard lump to leave my system. Once, my legs were swollen with raw strength from hauling heavy sledges across long distances, but now they've wasted away to almost nothing.

How long have we been here? I wonder. Half a year, maybe. Maybe a little longer. It's hard to tell one day from the next, but spring must be just around the corner. One or two more months before the snow really begins to melt? The snow that falls in the camp never stays for long, trampled into slush by thousands of feet. But fresh snow falls regularly enough that it's never fully gone until the sun's rays finally manage to banish the winter frost in spring, Hans has told me.

"Are you planning to sit there all day?"

I look up in surprise. A thin woman stands in front of me in the open stall, staring at me with tired, bloodshot eyes. How long has she been standing there? I wonder.

There's always a crowd waiting to use the toilets, so it's not surprising that she's standing there, but it's the first time anyone has addressed me directly while I'm sitting here. Modesty is the first thing you have to give up when you arrive at the camp, where men and women relieve themselves in open stalls and bathe in large communal areas, though men and women are separated for the latter. One unspoken rule to maintain a shred of dignity, however, is that you don't look directly at the person occupying the toilet before you. Speaking to them is downright rude.

I don't have the energy for a confrontation. I feel just as exhausted as she looks, so I simply reach for the water hose I share with my neighbour to the right. We maintain eye contact as I clean myself, then, without a word, I leave the stall—still feeling as though something remains inside me that I ought to be able to push out.

Maybe next time, I think wearily.

Back in the tent, I find Kristian and Emilie lying on the bed. Emilie snores softly, while Kristian stares blankly up at the mouldy canvas above him. Since Zaid's last letter, he's been unreachable, trapped in his own grief. The mere knowledge that Fatima was somewhere nearby was enough to keep his spirits up all this time, but now it seems that even that lifeline is slipping away like dew in the morning sun.

"He's suffering," says Freja, looking sadly at Kristian. "He hasn't gotten out of bed all day."

"I know. But I don't know what I can do for him... Zaid's family is trying to escape, but there's no guarantee they'll succeed. Hans says he's seen many others try, but very few make it. Spain seems determined not to let us out to mix with the locals. You've heard the gunshots too. Hans claims they're shooting at people trying to escape."

"I still wish we could go with them," she says, looking at me seriously. "We won't survive in here. No one survives in here. We'll die of hunger within a year, if another epidemic doesn't kill us first."

"Even if we had the chance, do you really think Emilie could handle another escape into the unknown? There's no guarantee things would be any better wherever we end up, if we even make it that far. I wish them all the best, but I don't think I can face that uncertainty again."

Freja shrugs resignedly. "I know you're right. Where would we go, anyway? Didn't Zaid also write that the Islamists have succeeded in establishing a caliphate in the Middle East?"

"He did," I confirm.

"Did he say how far it stretches?"

"No, he didn't."

She thoughtfully runs a hand through her short-cropped hair. Cutting it short worked quickly against the lice, which we're almost rid of now, so we borrow Hans' scissors from time to time to keep it trimmed.

"Europe has probably given up the war against the jihadists. They've got enough problems with the many refugees from Northern Europe. That's clear. The situation with the climate is probably the same in the U.S. and Russia, so the jihadists have been free to establish themselves in the region. There's no telling how far a self-proclaimed caliphate like that stretches."

"You're probably right, but as I recall, very few of the Islamist groups manage to agree on much. At best, the area is likely fragmented into several small, unconnected caliphates."

"That's possibly true," says Freja. "In any case, it could mean there's a long way to the nearest safe haven. I doubt the jihadists would welcome anyone who doesn't adhere to the strictest version of Islam, no matter who rules in a given caliphate." She sighs deeply. "There's nothing for us up north. France is no better than here, and the same likely goes for the few European countries that still function. Our only option is to go south, through the caliphates."

"I imagine they'll try to cross the Strait of Gibraltar to Morocco," I say, agreeing with her. "But who knows whether the groups that were operating in Algeria have taken control of Morocco, moved into Libya, or just taken power in Algeria. If they've even succeeded in establishing a caliphate there."

We know nothing, and very little information from the outside world filters in to us. Maybe there's safe passage in Morocco. Maybe the caliphate Zaid talks about is limited to Syria and Iraq. If that's the case, it's far from here and won't affect their journey through the North African countries."

"I'm tired of not knowing anything," she sighs.

"It's a dangerous journey, for sure. It won't be much easier than the journey from Denmark."

I bend down to grab my water bottle from under the bed. My stomach aches from hunger, so I'll try to satisfy it with half a litre of water. I don't even know anymore what hurts more—the hunger pains or the pressure sore that refuses to heal. Both are constant reminders that we need to find a source of more food, even if it means stealing. I don't like the idea of surviving at someone else's expense, so I'm putting off the decision for as long as I can. Sooner or later, though, we won't have a choice.

"It's a dangerous journey. But it's also dangerous to stay here, Magnus. There's nowhere left where we can feel safe. What will become of us?"

Freja starts crying, first softly, then soon the tears pour down like autumn rain from a thundercloud. I comfort her as best I can, but as so often before, there's nothing I can say to make the uncertainty, despair, or hopelessness go away.

"I'm going to check if Zaid has sent the bottle back," I say, once her tears have subsided.

She nods dejectedly and collapses back onto the bed. We spend far too many hours in those beds—partly to save energy, and partly because there's simply nothing else to do.

The bottle stands upright against the fence when I arrive. I look around nervously, terrified someone has discovered our communication line. I can't see anyone nearby who might be watching me though. It's quiet on the other side of the fence too. I lean discreetly against it, scanning the area carefully until I'm sure no one is paying attention to me.

I wonder if Hans could have beaten me to it and read the letter? But why would he? He can't understand Danish anyway.

I stand for a long time, racking my brain, but I just can't think of any logical explanation for why the bottle is standing upright like that. In the end, I conclude it must be a coincidence, so I slowly crouch down, still with my back to the fence. Discreetly, I reach behind me and pull the bottle through the gaps in the wire mesh. The wind gusts fiercely from the west, nearly tearing the letter from my fingers as I pull the crumpled paper out of the bottle and unroll it to read the contents. The letter is short.

> *Come with us. It's still possible, but we can't wait much longer. However, I don't know if you'd be better off fleeing again. We have no choice. That becomes clearer with each passing day. You must do what's best for yourselves, but know this, my friends: if I can, I will do everything in my power to help you move forward.*

I read the letter three times before rolling it up and placing it back into the bottle. Freja is right—if we don't find a solution soon, especially to the food problem and Thomas, we won't survive much longer here. But I'm convinced our chances aren't any better on the other side of the wire fence. Quite the opposite.

I have to write back and tell him that we can't flee with them, but I can't throw the bottle far enough myself. I need Kristian's help, and unfortunately, that means I'll have to tell him about Zaid's offer. But I'm afraid to show him the letter. Afraid he'll insist on going, just to be with Fatima. If that happens, I'll lose him forever—whether I allow him to go on his own or force him to stay with us. He'll hate me for stopping him from trying to find a better life with the girl he loves. And it makes no difference that they've only just entered their early teenage years. First love runs deep. I don't doubt Kristian is convinced that he and Fatima are meant to be together forever. The thought that I could be the reason it doesn't happen, no matter how unreasonable that seems to an adult mind, is almost unbearable. I'd rather avoid him finding out about the offer at all, if I can.

Dejected, I make my way back to the tent, where I find Hans and Kristian deep in conversation about whether *Shantaram* is truly a memoir or pure fiction. Hans, who often boasts about not having read a book since he left school, has, of course, never read the story of the Australian criminal who fled to India and lived in the slums. Yet he has no problem offering his opinion on whether it's even possible to live such an adventurous life while on the run from the law.

"Take it from someone who's had experience hiding from the police," he says. "All you think about is staying out of sight. Being invisible. What your protagonist describes is anything but staying invisible. It's just not possible."

I don't catch Kristian's reply, though I'm sure he's giving Hans a run for his money. Instead, I focus on composing the letter I'll have Kristian send back to Zaid.

Thank you so much for your generous offer. We all long to be far away from this flea-infested mud pit, but I'm afraid we have to decline. Our courage falters when we think about where we'd go. Is there anywhere left in the world that would open its arms and give us a new chance at life? We hope we're wrong and wish you all the best. You don't have a choice—you can't stay. We understand that. I hope you find a new path, because you deserve it more than anyone. Will we ever see you again? I don't think so, but you'll live on in our hearts. Take care of yourselves.

"Kristian," I say, interrupting their conversation. "I need your help to throw the bottle back to Zaid. They're leaving soon."

22 Freja

For the first time since we arrived, I walk through the camp completely alone. I feel vulnerable without Magnus to protect me or my children to hide behind. Of course, I'd never physically hide behind them, but mentally, I feel stronger and braver when they're under my care. Like a lioness defending her cubs against intruding males. But without them, I feel fragile—like a mouse in a courtyard full of alley cats. I try to avoid making direct eye contact with the people I pass, so as not to attract unnecessary attention. In truth, I doubt anyone takes any notice of me. I'm just another woman rushing through the camp in isolation.

The flu's devastation has left a wide trail of widows, widowers, and orphaned children, whom no one has the energy or interest to take under their protective wing. Like lepers begging for help, most people shun them, afraid of being burdened with yet another responsibility.

Soon enough, the survivors will band together into groups for protection, but until then, the camp is full of lonely individuals, wandering aimlessly, searching for a kind face or a compassionate hand. Anything to make them feel they're not entirely abandoned on this merciless planet. Most have dead eyes that look straight through you if you try to make contact, like the living dead in a desolate camp where even the smells of spring can't overpower the stench of urine and excrement hanging heavily in the air. There are days when I feel the stench has seeped into my pores, and no cold wash can re-move it. Days when hopelessness overwhelms me, and I won-der if life is even worth living anymore.

Those are the days I see my exhausted children, drained of the joy that children should have in abundance. But it's also on those days that I remind myself I can't give up. I owe it to them to be here, in the life they still have, no matter how bleak and pointless it may seem. We do what we do for them, even when it hurts the most.

When I reach my destination, I stand outside for a while, gathering my courage. My stomach growls, and I feel naus-eous. As a reminder of why I'm forced to carry out my task, my shrunken stomach suddenly seizes in a painful cramp, making me double over, crouching on the wet walkway. I gasp in pain, trying to take deep breaths and relax my abdom-inal muscles. But the cramps come from deep within, leaving me helpless to do anything but wait for them to pass. As I sit there, trying to gather my strength and as the cramps slowly subside, someone suddenly kicks me from behind, nearly sending me sprawling face-first onto the wet, dirty boards. I barely manage to catch myself with both hands when I hear Lars' vile, raspy laughter ring out around me.

"Well, well, it looks like we've got ourselves a guest," he crows loudly, addressing the small group of ragged men who always follow him around.

These are men whose status is still uncertain, but who try daily to win favor with Thomas' second-in-command, hoping to climb the ranks and secure enough food to survive comfort-ably. Their morals are dubious, and they'll stop at nothing. So when Lars orders them to grab me and drag me inside, I barely have time to react before I feel their hands all over me. They lift me off the ground and carry me into the tent, where they drop me from waist height onto the floor at Thomas' feet.

"This wench clearly can't get enough of our pleasant company," Lars laughs, addressing Thomas. "We found her just outside the entrance."

Thomas observes me silently as I try to gather myself into a sitting position.

I rub my sore elbow, which took a hard knock when I hit the ground. I'm scared and on the verge of regretting my decision, but I force myself to think of my hungry children and summon all the courage I need to say what I came to say.

When I open my mouth, though, my voice fails, and only a barely audible whisper escapes. Lars and his cronies burst out laughing, but abruptly stop when Thomas, irritated, raises a hand to silence them.

"Take your time," he says calmly.

I look at his greasy hair, clinging to his forehead, and the scruffy stubble that always seems to be the same length whenever I see him. Like an emperor on his throne, he watches me with curiosity, waiting patiently until I can muster the strength to explain my purpose. His breathing is heavy, clearly audible over the camp's dull murmur outside the tent.

The flu seemed to be relatively gentle on Thomas, no doubt thanks to his much better nutritional state than the rest of us. Despite his obesity, his immune system must be more resilient than mine, Magnus', and poor Nadja's, whose body could no longer muster the strength to fight off the illness. Her death still cuts deep, but it also gives me the courage I need to say what I came here for.

"I accept the offer," I say firmly, staring him directly in the eyes.

I try to project more strength than I actually possess, desperate to hide how weakened I've become. Under no circumstances can they get the impression that I'm no longer valuable to them, or the offer will vanish, and we'll be condemned to handing over Emilie's rations every week until we're no longer able to collect them ourselves.

Thomas' eyes widen in surprise.

"Excuse me?" he says, feigning confusion. "Can you repeat that? What offer are you accepting?"

My willpower is already starting to fade, so I quickly repeat myself.

"I'm accepting the offer. The one Lars made me a few weeks ago, when you were sick."

"Ah," he replies with mock forgetfulness. "Remind me again, which offer was that? You see, we get so many visitors, it's hard to tell you all apart. Especially when one has been ill. So, humor me—tell me again what offer Lars made to you?"

The humiliation weighs heavily on me as I hear myself answer faintly from somewhere distant. "I'm here to offer myself to your men in exchange for getting Emilie's ration back."

"Ah yes, it's coming back to me now," says Thomas, scratching at his stubble aggressively. "But that was weeks ago. You've lost weight since then, haven't you? And that makes you less valuable to my men, I believe Lars also mentioned that to you. 'Don't take too long to decide,' he said. 'Or you'll be nothing but skin and bones.' What do you think, Lars? Is she still worth anything to your men?"

Lars steps closer, examining me like I'm a mere piece of merchandise, which I suppose I am to them. He grabs my arms, feeling for any remaining muscle, then lets his hands slide over my breasts and down to my hips, where he notes, with a neutral expression, how my hip bones are starting to protrude.

He steps behind me and slides both hands under my jacket, around to the front, grabbing what's left of my emaciated breasts. Then he slips his hands into my trousers, groping my buttocks before suddenly stepping back.

"It's hard to say, Thomas. I think we'll need to see her without any clothes!"

"Of course," Thomas replies, ordering me to strip. "We need to know if the trade is still worth it, you understand? There are plenty of scarecrows here willing to screw for an extra handful of grain, so you'll have to offer something the others can't. Femininity is in high demand. So, let's see if you've still got it. Strip, sweetheart!"

I try to let my thoughts drift away from the degradation they're putting me through as I slowly undress. Piece by piece, I throw my clothing onto the floor in front of me, but no matter how hard I try to escape mentally, it doesn't help.

My muscles twitch as I let the sealskin trousers fall to the ground, the last piece of clothing, and step onto the floor beside them, wearing only a pair of knickers that are now far more stained with grey and yellow than white. The humiliation of allowing these repulsive men to see me naked is worse than I ever imagined when I made the decision to sacrifice myself in exchange for my family's survival. Naively, I had thought that by closing my eyes and letting my mind drift, I would be able to dissociate from what was about to happen. To float away from the act itself as the men, one by one, fulfill their desires using my body as a tool.

But now, standing here stark naked in front of them, it dawns on me that the humiliation of offering myself to be taken in turn far exceeds anything I had envisioned. Allowing a man I don't have feelings for to penetrate me is something I've experienced before, many times, before Magnus and I were together. But back then, there was the expectation of gaining something good from it—mutual sexual satisfaction. I had convinced myself that this wouldn't be so different, but as I stand here with so many eyes fixed on me, I realize it's not the same at all. There's a vast difference between having sex out of desire and having sex out of necessity. More than anything, I want to put my clothes back on and flee from the tent. Scream at them that I've changed my mind and they can keep Emilie's ration. But deep down, I know that option has long since passed.

Every man around me is staring lustfully at my breasts and backside. Some are already rubbing themselves through their trousers as they come closer, hands outstretched to grope me. Running now would surely lead to a gang rape, of that I have no doubt.

I let my gaze wander fearfully around the interior of the tent. How many men are there here? Fifteen? Twenty? Am I supposed to satisfy them all? I can't, I think in terror.

I feel Lars tugging down my knickers.

"We need to see it all," he laughs.

With a swift movement, he tears them off me, the decayed fabric falling apart completely.

I catch myself being painfully aware that I haven't trimmed my pubic hair in ages, now resembling an untamed wilderness. Then it hits me how irrational that thought is, and instead, I grow furious with myself. Why on earth am I worrying about my appearance down there when the men about to take turns using me are filthy, unkempt individuals who probably don't even brush their own teeth?

"Good!" Thomas suddenly roars, immediately silencing the crowd. With some effort, he stands and moves heavily towards me.

I can feel the floor give way beneath his weight.

"You've gotten thin," he says. "It's clear you've lost quite a bit of muscle, but I must say, it's been a long time since I've seen an ass as nice as the one you've got here."

He grabs one of my buttocks with a hand large enough to cover the whole thing. His hand slides between my legs.

"You're dry," he blurts out, referring to my vagina, which is bone dry and unreceptive to his inappropriate groping.

He looks around and spots Lars, who is curiously following every move Thomas makes.

"Lars," he says, "I think I'll test her out myself, but can you get her ready for me so it doesn't feel like I'm sticking it into a hole full of sand? Take her over to the corner and call me when she's ready."

"Of course, Big T," Lars responds promptly.

He obediently grabs my arm and begins dragging me away. Instinctively, I resist with the last of my strength. With a powerful jerk, I free myself from his grip and collapse onto the floor, gathering my clothes in my arms.

"Let's see if you're worth it," Thomas says, the beginning of a smile playing on his thick lips in stark contrast to the malicious gleam in his eyes.

A chill suddenly runs down my spine, a harbinger of what's to come.

Lars grabs me again and drags me to a corner at the back of the tent, where a camp bed stands, shielded from the rest. The blanket covering the mattress is a dark grey fleece, filled with dried white stains, a repulsive testament to what the camp bed is used for and why it's secluded from the rest of the tent.

"Welcome to the Romantic Cave," Lars laughs. "Lie down and get comfortable, and I'll make sure you're ready for Thomas."

He starts undressing, once again revealing his large member to me, though the first time I didn't see it—I only felt it. The size terrifies me, involuntarily bringing me back to the state of shock I left the tent in after he had taken me by force. I am paralysed, unable to move. I try to close my eyes but soon open them again, unable to take my gaze off that repulsive penis. The white buildup shows he hasn't bathed in a long time. The nauseating stench of week-old urine hits my nostrils, causing my stomach to churn.

Without warning, he dives between my legs, and before I can even process what's happening, I feel his tongue slide between my labia.

Once again, painfully aware of my own lack of hygiene, I feel, for a split second, the inexplicable shame I felt earlier, soon followed by intense anger at the absurdity of my feelings. My family and I have endured humiliation after humiliation, and now, as I'm forced to prostitute myself and let these vile men exploit my body, I'm embarrassed that I can't present a more well-groomed appearance. It makes no sense, but I can't stop the feeling of shame spreading through me as Lars's tongue eagerly explores my genitals.

I try to force myself to think of something else as I grip the blanket beneath me tightly.

Suddenly, he thrusts two fingers inside me, causing a painful spasm in my abdomen, which he mistakenly interprets as enjoyment.

"Yeah, not many women can resist my special treatment," he

chuckles crudely. "That's why Big T asks me to prepare the women for him."

He stands up between my legs, rubbing his erect member with one hand while trying to pull me closer to the edge of the bed with the other.

I begin to cry. The tears fall heavily from the corners of my eyes and down my cheeks, dripping onto the blanket and mixing with some of the dried semen stains.

Lars doesn't seem to notice. Or maybe he does but doesn't care. It's probably the latter, because once he's satisfied with my position on the bed, he proceeds without hesitation, thrusting his penis inside me. It feels far too big. Gigantic, even.

Unexpectedly, I find myself grateful that he at least took the time to prepare me with his spit first. But the gratitude is short-lived, for soon after, I feel his hard member slowly sliding into my vagina until it can go no further, at which point he begins to move violently back and forth. It hurts, but he doesn't stop, even as I beg him to. Instead, he grows more violent, thrusting harder and harder until, moments later, he explodes inside me with deep, heavy thrusts.

I let the tears flow freely. Helpless. Unable to move.

All I can think about is that his filthy, disgusting penis is still inside me, and I just want it out as soon as possible. But he doesn't move. He just stands there, staring at my tear-streaked face, seemingly enjoying the moment.

Two people, in the same place, in the same act, with two completely different sets of emotions.

I want to kick him away, scream, but I'm too afraid of the consequences if I do.

Finally, he pulls out.

"I'll get Big T for you now," he says. "I'd advise you to dry your eyes because he's known for getting rougher the more you cry."

He reaches out and, surprisingly tenderly, wipes the tears from my cheeks with a corner of the blanket.

"I don't really know why he's like that," he says into the air, shrugging. "Some kind of fetish, I suppose? Anyway, enough talking. I need to get him before he gets impatient, and we don't want that."

He pushes himself away, leaving me alone on the bed.

Naked. Abused. Sore. Full of guilt. Afraid.

Moments later, Thomas appears from behind the curtain. As soon as he sees my tears, he lashes out, slapping me so hard that my ears ring.

"Stop that crying, or I'll give you something serious to cry about."

He begins to undress. As he pulls off his shirts, revealing rolls of eczema-covered fat, a stench of stale sweat fills the air, so nauseating that my stomach threatens once again to empty its meagre contents all over. Not even the smell of the toilets, which I've somewhat gotten used to, surpasses the rank odour of decay surrounding me now.

It's obvious that big Thomas doesn't bathe often, and now he expects me to satisfy his repulsive desires.

The panic must be clear in my eyes, as he grabs my breasts roughly, squeezing them while hissing through his teeth, "If you want this to be painful, darling, just keep acting up. Otherwise, get it together and give me an unforgettable experience. Understood?"

His face is so close to mine that I can't avoid the toxic reek of his breath. I nod, terrified, unable to imagine how I'm going to survive this.

It's dawning on me that I'm making the biggest mistake of my life.

But we have to eat.

I don't feel like I have a choice. Just like with the frost, which threatened to kill us if we didn't act and flee south. We do what we must to survive, and right now, I'm forced to endure the worst humiliation of my life, just another trial in what our part of the world has become.

For my family's sake.

"Give me a hand," Thomas growls, positioning himself between my spread legs.

I lift my head and, horrified, catch sight of a yellow-spotted penis with a bluish-purple head poking out from under the enormous belly he's lifting with both hands. It looks insignificant under all the fat, but as my trembling hand grabs it and guides it into my vagina, I can't wrap my hand fully around it.

My mind explodes with images of disgusting coatings being scraped off against my vaginal walls as he pushes deeper and deeper. Bacteria and fungal spores implanting deep inside me, spreading, making me sick. Devouring me from the inside, while I try to survive by forcing in the few extra handfuls of nourishment, the reward for enduring all this degradation.

Thomas lets go of his belly as he thrusts fully inside me, and it flops down like a sweaty, foul-smelling, quivering mass over my lower abdomen and stomach.

The stench is unbearable, and I fight the urge to vomit all over myself and Thomas, who is already panting from the effort of moving in and out of me a few times. Sweat pours from his forehead and drips onto my breasts.

My stomach rumbles and contracts in the same spasms as

before. For a brief moment, Thomas smiles lustfully, feeling my abdomen tighten around his cock. But when the spasms are followed by a cascade of thin, slimy, foul-smelling vomit that sprays uncontrollably onto his eczema-ridden belly, his expression changes instantly. From lust, through surprise, to one of sadistic cruelty.

"So, you're determined to play games, are you?" he wheezes breathlessly, resuming his rhythm.

In and out. In and out.

I stare at him in terror.

"S-Sorry!" I manage to stammer. "I didn't mean to. Please forgive me. Please?"

I beg, pleading for forgiveness from the man who stands between my legs, abusing my body, while I watch the wicked thoughts swirl behind his cruel eyes.

Instead of replying, he delivers another quick slap to my face. "Shut up, bitch," he snarls. "Let me enjoy this pussy in peace. We'll play more later."

Blood trickles from one of my nostrils, down over my lips, mixing with the remnants of my vomit.

I'm dizzy. Dazed. Terrified of what he has in mind. I want to escape, but I'm trapped under the weight of the large man. I fumble blindly with my hands, searching for something to grab onto, something to pull myself free, but I find only empty air around the bed.

Thomas groans louder and louder.

I suddenly can't bear the thought of letting him release his seed inside me. My hands flail wildly until they suddenly grip a thin metal rod, part of the bed's frame. I pull and tug at it desperately as Thomas gets closer and closer to his climax. The rod is loosely screwed into the frame, but it doesn't immediately come free.

Thomas thrusts deeper. Faster. Harder.

I'm panicking. My brain is screaming at me not to let him finish, but I can't escape his hold. Suddenly, the rod gives way in my hand. With one final burst of strength, I yank it free, manoeuvring it out from beneath the mattress just as Thomas lets out a triumphant scream, ejaculating deep inside me.

I scream in despair and, without thinking, drive the rod into his throat as he leans exhausted over me.

His eyes widen in shock. He looks at me, first in surprise, then fury, followed by deep despair and panic as he realises he's been gravely wounded in a camp with no medical help. He staggers back a few steps, clutching at his throat.

I'm still gripping the rod, which slips out of his neck as he moves, allowing blood to spurt out of the gaping wound. I've hit his carotid artery.

He tries to call for help, but no sound comes from his mouth. Instead, he falls to his knees, grasping desperately at the air, trying to stay upright. I pull back, terrified, watching in frozen horror as he strug-gles for life, blood spraying over the bed and floor, turning everything a dark crimson.

With a crash, he collapses to the floor.

At last, I snap out of my daze. Instinct kicks in—I realise the danger I'm now in. Once the others find out that Thomas, their protector and provider, is dead, they'll come for me. I look around in panic and spot my clothes, tossed in a heap by the side of the tent wall. On shaky legs, I manage to stand and gather them, dressing as quickly as I can while keeping a fearful eye on Thomas, who now lies motionless, his breath a gurgling rattle.

I need to get out of here as fast as possible, but I can't just walk across the length of the tent and leave through the entrance without arousing suspicion from the other men.

I frantically search for another way out.

The canvas of the tent is bolted to a wooden frame about 20 centimetres above the ground. I try to force my way through with my body weight, but the fabric is too sturdy to give, no matter how hard I push. I look around for something to pierce the canvas with and spot the bloodstained rod on the bed. I grab it and, with all my strength, slam it into the canvas. When I pull it out, it leaves a small hole just big enough to poke a finger through. Soon, I manage to tear the fabric to create a hole large enough for me to squeeze through.

As I stick my head out, a small group of people is already standing there, watching me curiously. I must look terrible, but no one moves to help or stop me, so I quickly disappear into the crowd.

I feel so weak that I can barely walk upright. My whole body aches, and it feels like a fire is burning me from the inside. Confused and frightened, I stumble through the camp, attracting stares from everyone I pass. No one offers help. They're all too consumed with their own struggles.

We all have enough of our own to deal with.

● ● ●

Badly bruised and with dried blood in one nostril, I collapse sobbing onto mine and Magnus' bed when I finally make it back to the tent. It feels like an eternity since I left Thomas.

Like a small child, I curl up in the foetal position, clearly displaying my fragile state to anyone who might look. My mind seeks refuge somewhere far away from here, and I don't even notice Magnus or the children's presence until Magnus starts shaking me insistently.

"Freja! What happened?"

At first, I hear his voice as a distant echo, but it gets closer and closer as the question is repeated again and again.

"Freja, what happened? Come on, love! What happened to you?"

At last, the voice is so intrusive that I can no longer ignore it. I turn my head and catch a blurry outline of Magnus' face through my tear-soaked eyes. I can't make out his features clearly, but I can hear from his voice that he's worried.

"I've done something stupid," I stammer between sobs. "Something terrible. I never should have gone there."

"Gone where? What have you done?"

He strokes his hand gently over my close-cropped head. He sounds distraught.

"Thomas is dead. I killed him."

I can barely get the last sentence out before I burst into a high-pitched wail, which threatens to take over my entire body and rob me of any ability to draw life-giving air deep into my lungs. My whole body is seized by severe spasms, preventing me from speaking for the next five minutes until the muscles finally relax a little, and my sobbing subsides somewhat.

"Oh, God," Magnus repeats over and over. "What have you done, my love? Are you sure he's dead?"

"I went there to negotiate for Emilie's ration," I sob.

I can't bring myself to reveal that I let both Lars and Thomas do whatever they wanted with me. It's far too shameful. Instead, I invent a modified version of the truth, saying that the men started pushing me around, and that Thomas took me aside to rape me.

"I tried to get away and ended up stabbing him in the throat with a metal rod. He died almost immediately on the floor in front of me. I watched him die. Oh, God, what are we going to do, Magnus?"

"But isn't that good news?" Kristian interjects. "Now we won't have to hand over Emilie's ration anymore, right?"

"That's terrible news," Magnus replies sharply. "Firstly, it's never good to kill another person, no matter how much of a swine he was. Secondly, we have no idea what's going to happen now. My guess is that Thomas' whole gang is already searching for Freja with a vengeance. And it's not to congratulate her on taking down Thomas. No, it's much more likely they want revenge."

"What have I done?" I cry heart-wrenchingly. "I'm sorry, I'm sorry, I'm sorry."

"Besides the injuries I can see on your face, has anything else hap-pened to you?" Magnus asks gently. "Did he succeed in his plan? Did they rape you again?"

He looks at me with concern and begins to gently wipe the blood from my nose with a damp cloth that Emilie hands him.

I look away in shame and then nod so faintly it's barely visible. It's easier to let them believe that Thomas took me against my will than to admit that I let them do it willingly to get Emilie's rations back.

"That bastard," Magnus bursts out in fury. "If you hadn't killed him, I damn well would have! You can bet on that!"

"What are we going to do?" I ask quietly. "If they find me, I don't even want to think about the terrible things they'll do to me. And what about the children? And you? We can't stay here in the camp, Magnus. We just can't!"

Emilie starts crying, but I don't have the strength to comfort her, and Magnus doesn't notice. He's completely focused on me and my injuries. Eventually, Kristian leads her over to their own bed, where he sits holding her hand. Brother and sister. We are a family, and no matter what happens, we stand together.

"Let's hope that Zaid, Farhana, and Fatima haven't left yet," Magnus replies after a long pause. "Maybe it's not too late to go with them after all."

23 Magnus

It is still dark when, early one morning, just a few days after the murder, we crouch along the fence, keeping a close watch on the sludge trucks that tirelessly carry on their work around the clock. A dark green, dusty one is parked near the fence over by Zaid's camp. Once it finishes its job there, it will swing around and start emptying the latrines in our camp.

I squint, trying to make out the number painted on the front door. 57, I think. That's the one we need.

I scan for Zaid and his family, but everything seems quiet. I'm anxious. What if they can't get out of the camp? What will we do then? We have to try anyway. It's far too dangerous to stay here. The other day, Hans came back to our tent, flustered, saying that a large reward has been offered to anyone who brings Freja back to Lars, who has taken over leadership after the now-deceased Thomas. Everyone is looking for her, and it's only a matter of time before one of the people we share a tent with gives in to the temptation of a little extra food and reveals her hiding place. It's a miracle it hasn't happened yet.

We must leave as soon as possible, whether Zaid can escape with us or not.

"I can't see them," Freja whispers nervously.

She's hidden her face behind a scarf wrapped around her head to avoid being recognised, but it's a flimsy disguise. Dressed in her warm sealskin coat, she's as noticeable as a giraffe in a chicken coop.

The truck's diesel engine idles, its hum clearly audible above the low buzz of the camp, which never fully disappears, no matter the time of day.

I can't see what the driver is doing. He's probably busy handling the hoses on the far side of the truck, the ones that suck and then spray-clean the latrines.

Could Zaid and his family already be in the truck?

The uncertainty is unbearable.

I look around, but everything seems quiet.

Suddenly, two guards appear from the darkness. As they reach the truck, they stop and exchange a few words with the driver. I hold my breath, terrified they might suspect something. But soon enough, they continue down the road, turn around, and head back along the fence on our side.

I hear Freja exhale in relief as they move away. She's just as nervous as I am. So much could go wrong in the next few hours, it's best not to think too much about it.

As the guards come closer, we turn our backs and retreat into the shadows. No need to tempt fate.

Soon after, the truck's engine revs up. It's getting ready to leave.

I glance nervously over my shoulder.

Where are the guards now? Have they already passed us? What if they stop for a smoke break?

The truck approaches. There's no time to waste. We have to be ready when it gets here, or we won't make it. It won't wait for us if we're late. Zaid made that very clear in his letter, explaining the first part of his plan—how we'll escape the camp.

The rest, we'll only find out once we're out.

But what if Zaid, Farhana, and Fatima can't get out themselves? How will we know the rest of the plan, I wonder for the tenth time.

I push the thought away. There are so many unknowns in this plan that trying to fit all the pieces together is pointless.

I usher Freja and the children ahead towards the latrines. As we reach the entrance, the light momentarily blinds us until our eyes adjust.

We stick close together, which turns out to be a mistake. As we enter the building, we take up so much space that those trying to leave are forced to stop and press against the walls to let us pass. It gives them both the time and the incentive to lift their heads and study us as we hurry further inside. An old woman in tattered clothes reaches out enviously, running her fingers over the fur of our coats as we pass her one by one. Suddenly, a realisation dawns on her. She spins around with surprising agility and darts out of the door, no doubt convinced she's about to claim the greatest reward of her life.

"Damn," Kristian growls as he watches her disappear into the darkness. "She recognised us."

"There's no time to worry about that now," I reply, more confidently than I feel. "Hopefully, we'll be long gone before Lars and his cronies get here."

When we reach the latrine pits, we find Hans waiting for us. He smiles warmly when he sees us. I hadn't told him about our escape plans, so why he's here so early in the morning, when most are still in bed, is a mystery to me.

He must sense the questions on our faces because he quickly explains before we can say anything. "I'm coming with you. I heard you talking about it. I want to come. After Nadja died, there's nothing left keeping me here."

Freja stares at me in shock. I can clearly read her thoughts. He's not part of the plan.

Is there even room for him?

And the more people there are, the greater the risk of being caught.

Thoughts race through my mind as I hear the suction hose from the sludge truck being attached to the outside of the latrine tank. There's not much time left.

"My friend," I say urgently, placing a hand on his shoulder. "I'm sorry, but I don't know if there's space. This isn't our escape plan. Our friends in the neighbouring camp arranged everything. I don't even know what happens once we're outside."

"I have to take the chance," he replies. "I can't stand it here any longer. Not without my Nadja."

A tear escapes his eye and quickly rolls down his cheek, leaving a trail in the dirt. He wipes it away angrily with the back of his hand.

"I'm coming with you. If there's no room when we get out, I'll figure something else out. I promise I won't be a burden. But I have to get out of here. I need to! Everywhere I look, I see Nadja, but when the woman turns around, it's always someone else. I can't bear it any longer! I'll be the last one out. I promise. I won't take anyone's place."

Freja and I exchange worried glances. What should we do?

The truck has already emptied the tank, and now I can hear the driver getting ready to hose down the tanks. As soon as he's done, we'll have just a few minutes to get out before he drives off to empty the truck's contents, wherever that may be.

We have to be on that truck before it leaves.

The water starts gushing through the hoses. Quickly and efficiently, they spray the tanks clean. The noise is deafening, and it's nearly impossible to talk while it's happening. It gives me time to think.

Maybe it's a good thing Hans comes with us after all? As the last one out, he might be able to hold Lars off long enough for us to escape, should he arrive before we're out. Lars can't be far away.

I make a quick decision and nod to Hans.

He can come with us.

At that moment, the water stops, and Freja lowers herself into one of the latrine pits and into the tank below. As soon as she's down, Emilie follows.

Kristian uses the hole next to hers.

I look around, worried that Lars might be on his way, but he's nowhere to be seen yet. Instead, I notice several curious figures staring at us in disbelief as we disappear into the latrine tanks one by one.

As I land at the bottom of the tank, the sharp smell of ammonia hits me, burning my lungs and making my eyes water. Though the tanks have been somewhat cleaned, the fumes still linger.

I glance up briefly and see the curious faces staring back at me.

If Lars arrives now, we're trapped. There's no time to waste.

With a few long strides, I splash through the ankle-deep, brownish water that still lingers at the bottom after the cleaning, until I reach the watertight hatch, where the exhaust hose is attached from the outside. I hastily knock on it, hard enough that they should hear it outside.

I wait impatiently.

How long has it been?

Has he already left?

I knock again.

Only after the third knock does the hatch finally open, and a bearded face with a large red birthmark covering most of the left side peers in. The man waves impatiently.

"Con rapidez! Los guardias!"

Quickly. The guards.

I stick my head out through the opening and look around. Further up the road, I spot them—the guards. They are walking away.

The bearded man points to a large square hatch between the truck's cabin and the tank silo. He says something rapidly in Spanish, which I don't understand, but his gestures make it clear that we are to go in there.

With great effort, I manage to wriggle myself out through the round opening, just large enough to fit my shoulders and hips. If we had attempted this in the months right after we arrived, I would never have been able to squeeze through, but now I just manage. My hip wound scrapes painfully against the metal edge. It's still not healed.

Emilie quickly follows me. I take her hand and rush to open the hatch on the truck. When I look inside, it's pitch black, and for a moment, I feel disappointed when I don't spot our friends. But then I hear Zaid's familiar deep voice from the darkness.

"Hurry in. All three of us are here and safe."

Relieved, I help Emilie inside, followed quickly by Kristian.

Freja struggles to squeeze through the latrine hole as the last of our family. Her body is still suffering from the abuse inflicted by Thomas and his vile cronies. She hasn't yet told me the full details, but I have no doubt that what she went through surpasses my worst imagination. I'm furious with the helplessness I feel, but at the same time, proud of her courage when she killed Thomas—even though that act has now forced us to flee again. I hope and believe I would have done the same in her place.

Suddenly, a loud shout comes from the guards, now quite a distance away.

I'm in the middle of helping Freja into the cavity in the truck, where the hatch hides us from their view. They haven't seen us. It's Hans, the last person, still making his way through the latrine hole.

Our eyes meet. Fear is etched in his eyes.

I'm sure he sees the same in mine.

For what feels like an eternity, our gazes lock. Only when the guards shout again, much closer this time, is the connection broken.

He casts a quick glance toward the running guards.

I can see the guilt on his face. It's his fault if we're caught.

He looks at me again.

"Hurry inside and close the hatch," he whispers. "I'll distract them. I have nothing left to lose."

Before I can protest, he lets himself drop to the ground outside the tank, quickly standing up. With a curt nod—a mix of farewell, good luck, and apology—he suddenly sprints away from the truck, out into the open where the guards can clearly see him.

I watch him for a brief moment, grateful for the selfless act but deeply worried about what comes next.

Will we all be exposed despite his heroic sacrifice?

I rush into the cavity, where there's just enough space for me as well. As soon as I'm inside, the driver shuts the hatch behind me, slams the bolt shut, and locks it.

The darkness surrounding us is impenetrable, and I fumble

blindly for Freja's hand, squeezing it tightly when I find it. It feels limp, lacking the usual strength I've come to rely on.

I briefly recall Zaid's words back in Denmark, long before we had decided to flee south: *The camps aren't there to protect you. The camps are places where you're sent to die, while the hypocritical politicians can claim they're being humane, without anyone pointing fingers at them.*

Outside, we hear the soldiers shouting.

We all instinctively hold our breath in fear that even our breathing might give us away. Irrational, really, because the soldiers are so loud we could probably talk at normal volume without them hearing us.

The soldiers' footsteps draw closer, until they finally stop right outside the truck. A second later, two loud gunshots ring out in quick succession.

Freja squeezes my hand in fright, digging her nails into my skin so hard I feel it tear.

I listen intently to the sounds outside.

The camp stirs immediately after the gunfire, its usual hum rising like a swarm of grasshoppers suddenly taking flight, growing so loud it's impossible to hear what's happening outside the hatch.

Did they shoot Hans? Is he dead?

The uncertainty is unbearable, and if the driver hadn't locked the hatch from the outside, I'd probably be tempted to open it a crack to see if I could spot him—and thus endanger us all. But luckily, the hatch is locked, so all I can do is wait.

Soon after, three men begin shouting loudly over one another, just outside the hatch. It must be the driver arguing with the guards. I don't understand much of what they're saying, but it's clear the guards are accusing him of being involved in

Hans' escape attempt. Somehow, he manages to convince them otherwise, making it sound as though he was just as surprised as they were to see Hans fleeing through the latrine holes.

Then everything goes quiet again, but I can hear the soldiers' footsteps quickly moving away from the truck. Shortly after, the truck's front door slams, and the engine roars to life, slowly rumbling into motion. For a long time, we lie silent in the darkness, shoulder to shoulder, as the truck bumps over the uneven terrain, our heads knocking together every other moment.

The sound of the engine, right outside the wall of our hiding spot, is deafening. Each time the driver accelerates, it screeches shrilly in our ears. The heat from the engine, combined with our own body heat, quickly raises the temperature to the point where sweat begins to drip from our foreheads. The air around us becomes thick and stifling.

The truck stops briefly to empty the tanks before continuing for about 20 more minutes, until it finally comes to a complete stop and shuts off the engine.

The silence that follows is deafening.

The driver remains in the cabin while we silently struggle to pull the last bit of oxygen from the air around us.

I lie there for a long time, listening to the silence. Far off, I hear the faint sound of an engine growing closer and closer, until it stops just outside the hatch. Once it stops, the truck driver gets out. I hear him greet the newcomer quietly. Soon after, the hatch opens.

Cool, fresh air flows in, as welcome as the scent of freshly roasted seal meat, wrapping around my nostrils, caressing me for a moment, then moving effortlessly into my lungs. Only now do I realise how much my body craved oxygen.

Outside, the sun has risen. The light blinds me. I can't see the people outside the hatch as they reach in to help me out.

Outside, Zaid hugs the truck driver and kisses him on both cheeks before we all climb into the waiting military-green minibus. I stare nervously at the driver, dressed like a Spanish soldier, but Zaid reassures me that everything is as it should be.

"The truck driver is Farhana's cousin, and the soldier is his brother-in-law. It's family. We're in safe hands. They've lived here in Spain for many years."

The soldier gets behind the wheel, and soon the minibus starts moving, heading away from the camp, southward. For the first hour, Zaid sits next to the soldier, talking loudly in Arabic. I sit behind, holding Freja's hands in mine, while I secretly watch our friends, from whom we've been separated for so long.

Tears of reunion stream down the faces of both Farhana and Freja, and Kristian and Fatima can't stop staring at each other with fascination and curiosity. It's been so long since we last saw one another. I wonder if their love is still intact. Has it survived the long, painful separation? They've all changed so much. They've become thin, with hollow cheeks and muscles that have wasted away to almost nothing. It's clear they haven't had it any better than we have.

Farhana and Fatima are both wearing black niqabs, which would have covered most of their faces if they hadn't pulled them back. Farhana's usually radiant complexion is gone, and all that seems to remain is the greyish shadow of an emaciated and broken woman.

"We're being taken to the port in Algeciras," Zaid tells us as he sits down next to Farhana. "There, we'll board a cargo ship. The captain is a good friend of Ali's."

"Ali?" I ask, confused.

Zaid looks over at the soldier driving the minibus.

"That's Ali," he says. "He's a corporal in the Spanish army, and he says there's an empty container waiting for us on his friend's ship, which is sailing to Ceuta."

"Where's Ceuta?" Freja asks.

"It's a Spanish enclave in Morocco. We'll have to hide in the container throughout the crossing and until it's transferred from the ship onto the port. Tonight, another minibus will pick us up and drive us through Morocco and Algeria until we reach the Malian border."

For a moment, I stare blankly, letting the information sink in.

If we're discovered, we risk being shot on the spot. Or we'll just be sent back to the camp, where our fate is sealed anyway. Cynically speaking, we have nothing left to lose. But what do these people gain by helping us?

The driver with the red birthmark is Farhana's cousin. That's family. Okay, I can accept that. But what about this Ali? He's the brother-in-law of Farhana's cousin's wife, so not directly related to Farhana. And then there's the captain and the driver in North Africa?

"Why are these people helping us? They don't even know us," I ask Zaid.

"I don't know," Zaid admits. "That's what I was arguing with Ali about. I don't know if we can trust them, but he insists they're good people and that they've helped others before us."

"What do they expect in return? We've got nothing to offer."

"I don't know," Zaid repeats grimly. "Since the withdrawal

of US and European military forces from the Middle East, Morocco and Algeria have come under the rule of Caliph Omar Abu-Bakr. It's now part of a vast caliphate that stretches from Iraq in the east to Morocco in the west and includes Nigeria, Chad, and Sudan to the south. Smuggling us through the caliphate is extremely dangerous, not just for us, but equally for the driver who's sneaking unbelievers into the territory."

Zaid scratches his thick beard furiously and then looks me in the eye with a solemn expression.

"But do we have any other choice, my friend? Ali insists everything will be fine."

I meet his gaze for a long moment. I can see he's worried. But he's right. Do we really have any choice but to place our lives and fate in the hands of these people, whom none of us know and to whom we have absolutely nothing to offer in return?

Part IV

Caliphate

24 Freja

The container sways ominously as it hangs freely over the ship's railing, suspended by thin steel wires from the crane at the port in Ceuta. Seen from the waterfront, the movements would likely appear marginal and fully acceptable, but inside, unable to see what's happening outside, it's a terrifying experience.

I try to maintain my balance by pressing my back against the inner wall, spreading my arms and legs wide so that my body takes up as much surface area as possible. Even so, I barely manage to avoid toppling over when the container suddenly swings around.

Emilie is sitting between my legs, clinging tightly with her frail arms. She lets out a small scream at the moment it crashes down onto the ground with a thud that echoes in our ears long after.

Outside, we can hear the crane continuing for hours, unloading the remaining containers from the ship. One by one, containers are stacked on top of and beside ours. So many that I eventually fear that the one we're in will buckle under the weight of all the cargo above us.

The waiting is endless.

My thoughts keep drifting back to the tent with Thomas. I can't shake the image of the metal pipe buried deep in his throat, and all the blood spraying out, painting the floor dark red beneath him.

I've killed another human being.

I keep switching between blaming myself for his death and feeling relieved that he will never harm another woman again.

I try not to think about his filthy, disgusting cock inside me, but the darkness of the container is not my friend. With nothing to distract my mind, my thoughts keep circling around everything that threatens to drive me insane.

"The Muslims blame the Western world for climate change," Zaid suddenly says, as if he can read my mind.

His voice cuts through the thick tension in the container, where the air is so heavy it feels like you could slice it.

"They believe it's God's punishment upon the infidels, for having lived lives of sin for so many years, without honouring the holy Prophet Muhammad and His divinity. For them, climate change proves they've been right all along. It's strengthened their faith even more, and it hasn't been hard to bring the less devout back to a more radical interpretation of Islam in their efforts to build a vast caliphate to honour the one true God. A caliphate where the strictest form of Sharia law rules.

God has made the Western part of the world uninhabitable, while at the same time transforming their caliphate into a fertile oasis. A miracle that simultaneously proves God's existence, His presence, and His love for Muslims."

"If it proves God's love for Muslims, then why was there an entire camp in Spain full of Muslims?" Kristian interrupts. "They didn't seem to be living a life of luxury any more than we were. Why don't they just return to this fantastic caliphate instead of languishing in those dreadful camps?"

"That's a very good question, Kristian," Zaid answers, pausing for a moment. When he continues, I can hear sadness in his voice. "I had forgotten your ability to cut through all the makeup and get straight to the point. Because you're absolutely right. Why are those people there? Let me tell you: all the Muslims in the camps are Yazidi Kurds or Shia Muslims, like Farhana, Fatima, and myself. They were, like we were years ago, driven out of the caliphate by the Sunnis. However, that hasn't stopped them from following the strict Sharia laws that everyone now believes is the only way to ensure a place in Paradise after death. Shias and Sunnis each have their own way of interpreting the Quran and enforcing its teachings. For example, Imams don't have the same power among the Sunnis as they do among the Shias. After the Prophet Muhammad's death, the Sunnis chose his successor based on who they believed would be best suited to continue delivering God's important messages. For them, it's the caliph who alone ensures that the Quran's commands are followed by the people. The Imams' role is only to pass on the messages so they reach all His listeners.

Shia Muslims, on the other hand, believed that the Prophet's successor had to be a blood relative of his. The Imams are far more significant, and the most powerful are believed to be direct descendants of the Prophet Muhammad. A caliph's role is merely to unite the people, while the interpretation and spreading of God's word fall entirely under the Imams' responsibility.

These two views might seem insignificant to you and me, as long as they both worship the same God, but for radical Muslims, they are two very different interpretations that cannot coexist.

The Sunnis are the most powerful and the most numerous, and they've successfully established themselves under the strict leadership of Caliph Omar Abu-Bakr, who has a reputation as a harsh and particularly strict Muslim leader. Anyone who does not follow and acknowledge the caliph as the rightful successor to the Prophet Mu-hammad is considered either an infidel or a Rafida. All the Shia Mu-slims in the camps are Rafida. Deserters or apostates, if you will."

"What happens if they return to their homeland?" Kristian asks curiously. "What happens to you if someone finds out that you're Shia Muslims?"

Zaid's voice dies away as soon as the question is asked, and it hangs in the air, unanswered, for a long time until Farhana's voice breaks through the tense silence that has suddenly returned. Her voice is barely audible over the noise of the cranes outside.

"We would be executed on the spot. Men are beheaded if they're lucky, humiliated and mutilated first if they're unlucky. Women are stoned to death in a long and agonising process, where their whole body is buried underground, leaving only the head exposed. The stones used are not large enough to kill them individually. But after being struck by hundreds, the skull eventually becomes so damaged that it collapses, and the brain behind it so injured that death finally comes. By that point, death is a mercy for the poor woman, who has suffered unbearable pain for hours beforehand."

"Why do they do that to other people? What's the purpose? What do they gain from it?" Magnus asks.

The rage and indignation in his voice are so intense that Zaid feels compelled to try to explain their motives, though it's clear it doesn't come easily to him.

"It's hard for people like us to understand, where science takes precedence over religion. But for those who live in the shadow of Allah, it's their only way. They do it simply out of love for Muhammad, to whom they are so devoted that only by mutilating, humiliating, and ultimately killing His enemies can their inflamed hearts be calmed and healed after encountering such disturbing existences as ours. We, who do not share their narrow worldview. They feel obliged to do it, and they see nothing wrong with their actions. Now, feeling even more strengthened in their belief that Allah watches over them, they feel more compelled than ever to kill in His name. Why else would He have helped them create a great and fertile caliphate where they can live in harmony with their venerable Creator?"

A chill runs down my spine, and I can feel goosebumps rising on my arms and neck. I shudder at the thought that we are forced to cross this so-called caliphate. Our lives seem to be in danger no matter where we are. At home. In the camp. In the caliphate. And what awaits us on the other side of the caliphate? Will we be welcomed in Mali? Or will we once again have to flee for our lives?

I can't even begin to comprehend the thought.

I don't dare think about what will happen to us if we're caught on our journey through the caliphate. Farhana's words echo ominously in my ears, and I'm suddenly very grateful for the darkness, so neither Kristian nor Emilie can see how terrified I really am. I feel paralysed, in a way I can't even describe.

"This is insane!"

Magnus' voice explodes in my ears as he angrily expresses his unfiltered opinion. Each of those three little words hits a nerve deep in the back of my mind, slicing painfully through my brain.

"It's not madness," Kristian interrupts. "They've grown up

in a part of the world where religion governs every aspect of their lives. We can't relate to that at all. To us, it seems insane because we don't understand such a strong attachment to something divine, but even Christians have killed in the name of God. It was most clearly manifested during the Inquisitions, right up until the 1800s. Back then, Christians were as convinced of God's existence as Muslims are today. No matter what we in the Western world think of it, it's a part of their way of life, something we can neither change nor control. Christians abandoned that worldview as science slowly began to make inroads, but that only works as long as the results of science make life easier for people than religion does.

Climate change has now convinced many Muslims of the opposite. Their God has shown them, with absolute clarity, what happens when people turn their backs on Him, and conversely, the rewards that await those who faithfully hold onto their beliefs."

I listen to Kristian's words and can't quite grasp where this insight is coming from. He grew up under extraordinarily limited conditions, with only books, Magnus, and me to help him understand the world around him. Yet, he has developed a rare ability to see things from others' perspectives.

Fatima won't find a more perfect life partner, even if she searched the entire world, I think proudly. The two of them haven't let go of each other's hands since we boarded the minibus that took us from the camp to the ship. Even though they're still very young, I'm convinced they'll stay together for the rest of their lives. Their love, despite their age, is strong, even after being separated for more than six months. Six months where only the memory of each other has kept their love alive.

None of us feels like talking anymore, so we each lean back, lost in our own thoughts. I sit for a long time with my head resting against the cold steel wall of the container. At some point, I must have fallen asleep because I wake with a start when the container door suddenly clatters open, and the light from a powerful torch shines in my face, blinding my eyes.

A sharp, Arabic-speaking voice commands us outside into the dark night, where we're met by five weathered-looking Arabs with large, bushy black beards, dressed in dusty white robes and turbans of the same colour. In their hands, each one holds an AK-47 rifle, the barrels pointed menacingly at us.

● ● ●

"The plan has changed," Zaid explains as he returns to us. He had been loudly discussing something with the leader of the five Arabs for over 20 minutes. "They're going to split us up and transport us to two different buses that run on regular routes between Ceuta in the north and Bordj Badji Mokhtar, near the Malian border in the south of the caliphate."

We're standing close together just outside the container's opening. Around us, the port area is filled with containers stacked seven high, row upon row, forming a labyrinth that hides us well from the outside world. The five Arabs seem to be the only guards in the entire port; they seem fairly unconcerned about the risk of being discovered, and they make no attempt to lower their voices, even though their loud chatter echoes off the metal containers.

"But wasn't the plan to travel together in a private minibus?"

I cry out in distress. "How are we supposed to avoid being noticed if we're travelling on public buses? None of us can pass for Arabs! Look at us! Emilie and I are blonde with blue eyes. We'll be spotted immediately. Magnus and Kristian might get away with it because of their brown eyes and Magnus' dark stubble, but if anyone speaks to us, we're done for without you and Farhana to help us."

"That's true, Zaid," Magnus interjects. "We'll attract unwanted attention straight away. For God's sake, I don't even have a thick beard anymore. None of us can pass for Arabs or Muslims, for that matter."

Zaid watches us nervously as we let our emotions run wild. When we finally fall silent, his response takes the ground right from under me.

"They say that all private vehicles are stopped and checked by random patrols throughout the caliphate. They're looking for enemies of the Prophet. The risk of being caught is far too great if we travel by private minibus. They've provided clean burqas for the women and robes, turbans, and scarves to cover the men's faces. That way, we can probably blend into the crowd. The biggest problem is that it's not permitted for men and women to travel on the same bus. We'll have to split up and travel separately."

"Forget it," Magnus exclaims in shock, instinctively stepping backwards. "That's not happening. We're not splitting up." He waves his arms wildly in front of him as he tries to convince Zaid how wrong the plan is. "We only have each other. I can't let Freja and Emilie travel alone into the caliphate. It's irresponsible."

"Family is all we have," I protest, coming to Magnus' aid. "We only have each other in this world."

Zaid shakes his head gently and raises his hands in a calming gesture.

"There's no other way, I'm afraid. We can't stay here without being discovered, and if we are, they'll just send us back to the camps where the only certain fate awaiting us is death. If we drive into the caliphate in private vehicles, the chance of being stopped by a patrol is almost 100 percent, according to our Arab friends. The buses are only stop-ped sporadically because they know men and women travel separately, and they only stop them if they suspect illegal activity on board. This is our best chance."

"Can't we continue on foot?" Kristian asks. "We walked all the way from Denmark, so we can make it the rest of the way to Mali. That way, we wouldn't rely on anyone else."

"That's not an option either, Kristian. We have no food or money to buy any along the way. And don't forget, we'd have to cross a nearly 2,000-kilometre stretch of land that has remained one of the driest and most inhospitable areas in the world for the past 3,000 years. Climate change has left its mark, and parts of the desert have become fertile again—we already knew that before we froze in Denmark. But none of us knows how much of it is still barren desert. It's far too risky to venture out there alone and on foot."

Zaid pauses for a long moment, looking each of us deeply in the eyes. When he reaches me last, he holds my gaze tenderly before continuing in a tone that sounds far more confident than he likely feels.

"Freja, on buses in the caliphate, men and women aren't allowed to communicate. The male driver can't talk to the women, and they aren't even allowed to make eye contact. Hidden behind your burqas, no one will see your skin colour, or your eye or hair colour. Let Farhana do the talking if any women approach you. It's not uncommon for particularly oppressed women to avoid talking to others they don't already know. No one will find that suspicious. Just keep your head down and, for heaven's sake, avoid speaking Danish at all costs."

He pauses, turning his attention to Emilie, who stands listening with wide, fearful eyes.

"Do you understand, Emilie? Under no circumstances can you speak Danish, either on the bus or anywhere you risk being overheard in a foreign language. If they hear you, they'll report you to the driver immediately, and no one will be able to save you. No one. But if you keep a low profile, stay quiet, and avoid eye contact, and let Farhana lead the way, you'll be fine. You'll get through the caliphate unharmed. I promise you."

Emilie nods fearfully, unable to tear her eyes away from Zaid's bushy face. The fear is plain in her eyes. I wish I could hold her in my protective arms and tell her Zaid is just making up scare stories, but I can't. It's important she understands the seriousness of the situation. Because Zaid is right. We have no other choice. This *is* our only chance to get safely to Mali.

"The same goes for you two," Zaid continues, addressing Kristian and Magnus. "Keep your faces covered with your scarves, and try to avoid eye contact as much as possible. But don't show submissiveness either—submissiveness is seen as a weak character trait, and there's no room for that in Allah's kingdom. In Allah's kingdom, all men must be ready to fight to preserve the caliphate in honour of God, the Al-mighty. Only to Him can you show submission. If anyone looks directly at you, look back, but don't invite conversation by nod-ding or acknowledging them in any other way. Hold their gaze for a few se-conds, then slowly look away as if something else has caught your attention."

"What if someone still speaks to us directly?" Magnus asks. "What do we do then? Ignore them? Won't they get suspicious right away?"

"Let's pray to God that doesn't happen," Zaid replies quietly. "I can try to speak for you, but we won't get far if we encounter someone particularly talkative. You'll have to pre-tend you're asleep for the entire journey."

"It's over 2,000 kilometres!" Magnus exclaims skeptically. "How long will it take? A full day or more? No one can sleep that long without needing the toilet or something to eat or drink. People will get suspicious."

Zaid scratches his beard thoughtfully. I haven't had the chance to observe him closely in the past 24 hours, but now I suddenly notice that he, too, has lost a significant amount of weight. His beard hides his sunken cheeks, but his nose is nar-rower, and his eyes are deeply set in their sockets. His lips are pale, and I can see he's missing a couple of teeth in his lower jaw when he speaks. Clear signs of severe malnutrition.

I shudder at the thought of being sent back to the camps, whether it's the same one we came from or one of the many neighbouring camps.

I close my eyes and take a deep breath, followed by another. And yet another after that. I feel dizzy, and I can sense that if I give in to my inner demons, I'll collapse any moment now into an uncontrollable panic attack. I hear Zaid's voice speaking again, and I cling to it like an anchor in a storm.

"It's actually 2,500 kilometres, and the journey will take at least 36 hours. It's difficult to say exactly. But very few passengers are likely to travel the entire way, so I don't think you need to worry too much about people finding it suspicious if you sleep most of the journey."

"Except the bus driver," I hear myself say, still with my eyes closed.

There's a brief pause during which I can feel their gazes resting on me, before Magnus speaks again.

"What awaits us when we arrive at Bordj Badji Mokhtar?"

"It's less than 20 kilometres from there to the El-Khalil border crossing into Mali," Zaid replies.

"Is anyone waiting to help us with the last leg of the journey?"

"I don't think so. Once we're on the buses, we're on our own. From then on, we have to manage the rest of the journey by ourselves."

"How big is the town?" Magnus asks. "I mean, is it big enough for us to blend in, or will we stand out as strangers?"

"The town has long been a centre for human smuggling and illegal drug trafficking. Of course, this was before the caliphate was established, so I don't actually know if it's still happening. I don't know much about the area, apart from what I heard years ago. Back then, the town was mentioned as one of several crossings that human smugglers frequently used, but since it was in the opposite direction of our intended destination, I didn't bother to find out more details about it."

"We can expect a lot of military presence on both sides of the border," I state suddenly, opening my eyes again. "Mali has apparently managed to stay free from being swallowed up by the caliphate, and surely, that's only been possible because they've been able to fight back. Historically, Mali hasn't exactly been spared its share of jihadists. Why have they chosen to stay out of the caliphate? They, too, are predominantly Islamic."

I look up as two Arabs suddenly approach, arms full of clothing, which they dump onto the dusty ground in front of us. Our new attire. We all stand there for a moment, staring at the garments at our feet. No one moves to pick them up. It's as if the symbolism of the clothing brings reality too close, before we're fully ready for it.

"Islam in Mali has been shaped by a much more tolerant interpretation for many years," Zaid explains. "In fact, Islam in Mali has largely been adapted to the country's local tribal cultures, and women have been free to participate in the political aspects of society without having to wear veils. Islam in Mali was known as an inclusive religion, with room for everyone, whether you were Christian, Sunni, or Shia. However, as you mentioned, Freja, there were jihadists in northern Mali who fought to reinstate orthodox Sharia law. But it seems Mali succeeded in drawing a line in the desert, so the jihadists left the country and instead joined the fight to establish the vast caliphate under the leadership of Caliph Omar Abu-Bakr."

Zaid is interrupted by the Arab leader, who barks a few sharp sentences, sounding more like gunfire than words. He stands a few container lengths away, glaring angrily at us. Smoke streams from his nostrils as he speaks, and for a brief second, I wonder if we've struck a deal with the devil.

"We need to leave soon," Zaid translates. "It's time to put on the traditional garments."

He crouches down and begins handing out the clothing pieces, one by one. I reach out and take the black burqa as he passes it to me. It's heavier than I expected.

Farhana, Emilie, and I retreat into the container to change out of sight. Feeling somewhat wistful, I peel off my now extremely worn and foul-smelling sealskin jacket and toss it to the ground. The sealskin trousers follow. These two pieces have been with me for so long and have been so crucial to my survival that I hesitate to leave them behind. I shiver in the cold as I stand there in just a thin, sweat-stained pair of underwear and a long-sleeved wool sweater. While the temperature is nowhere near the extreme sub-zero conditions we survived in Denmark, and spring is starting to take hold, it still feels cold without the warmth of the sealskin against my slender frame.

I quickly pull the burqa over my head, the heavy fabric draping over my shoulders. The garment is one large piece of cloth that sits atop my head, falling in loose folds around the rest of my body, with only a small mesh opening for my eyes. The burqa instantly brings a feeling of shame and oppression, but just as quickly, the feeling lifts when Farhana and I step outside the container, and Magnus can't tell which of us is which.

Maybe this could actually work?

A faint hope stirs deep inside my chest. The otherwise oppressive symbolism of the burqa might very well end up being our saving grace.

I turn my head and find Emilie through my limited field of vision—a small, black, anonymous figure.

Magnus pulls us back inside the container. "In a moment, we'll be split into two different cars and driven to separate buses that will take us all the way to Bordj Bardji Mokhtar in the southwestern part of the caliphate. If all goes well, we'll meet again in 36 hours."

He tries to find an opening in the fabric to pull it back and see my face, but he quickly realises it's impossible without taking off the entire burqa.

"I really don't feel good about splitting up," I say. "I don't know what I'll do if something happens to you."

He places his hands on the soft folds around my face.

I ache to kiss him, but the fabric is in the way, and I also don't dare to show that kind of affection here, where the five Arabs are probably watching us. Who knows if such a simple act could be enough to make them reconsider helping us.

Magnus kisses the part of the fabric that covers my forehead. "Keep a low profile and stick close to Farhana. You'll be fine."

"I hope you're right," I whisper back. "I'm more worried about you and Kristian. You don't have a burqa to hide behind."

I try to sound braver than I feel. In truth, I'm a bundle of nerves. Whatever we've survived together so far, it's nothing compared to the challenge we're facing now. Crossing a caliphate full of religious fanatics so deeply devoted to their beliefs that they'd be willing to torture, maim, or kill us on the spot, without trial, if we're discovered.

And we're forced to do it alone, separated.

I'm, of course, grateful to have Farhana by my side, but Magnus is my rock. He's the one who gives me the strength to keep going when I'm consumed by fear or doubt. When my inner demons threaten to overpower my common sense.

"What about passports?" Kristian suddenly asks, bringing up a new problem. "How are we going to enter the caliphate without passports?"

25 Magnus

The first raindrops begin to fall just as I sink heavily into the back seat of the bus, where it's easier to hide from curious eyes. Kristian has positioned himself by the window to my left, and Zaid now sits on the other side of me, legs stretched out into the aisle.

I try to appear calm, as though I'm not terrified to the point of shaking, but truth be told, my heart is racing, and sweat is pouring from my forehead under the scarf that covers most of my face.

The next few hours will pass in silence, but the questions are already pushing to the forefront of my mind. The moment I boarded the bus, one of the smugglers handed me a slip of paper stamped with a date and text written in Arabic. I'm holding it now, trying to decipher the script, but it makes no more sense to me than if it were written in hieroglyphics.

Is this our ticket into the caliphate?

What does it say?

Is this slip of paper meant to replace our missing passports?

I simply don't know.

Zaid notices me turning the paper over in confusion and, sensing my uncertainty, discreetly places a hand over mine, giving a thumbs-up to signal that everything is as it should be. Gratefully, I tuck the paper away without looking up.

Two men board the bus and sit across from each other at the front. Both are wearing the same dusty robes as us, their faces partly covered by black-checkered scarves. Seeing them makes my heart calm a little.

Maybe we really can blend into the crowd.

I glance out of the window toward the women's bus on the other side of the parking lot. A small group of eight black-clad figures stand outside its closed doors, waiting to be let in.

The rain is now falling more heavily, blurring my view through the window. I can't distinguish one woman from another, no matter how hard I try. I attempt to pick out features that would tell me which one is Freja, but the burqas hang so loosely on their bodies that it's impossible. The only difference is in their heights, and even then, there's not much variation, except for one of the black-clad figures who stands about a head shorter than the rest.

I assume that must be Emilie.

I picture her beautiful face hidden beneath that horrible garment, which is both her salvation and her curse. Suddenly, a wave of anxiety hits me. How will she recognise her own mother among the other women without calling her name and risking exposure? But then it strikes me that Freja will surely recognise Emilie by her smaller height alone.

I keep watching until I spot one of the women next to Emilie, slightly taller than the others. That must be Freja. The Danish, blonde-haired, blue-eyed woman who must now pass as an Arab.

I can hardly bear to think of the consequences of what we're about to undertake. My family, which I've fought so hard to keep together these past few years, is now divided. We are each other's lifelines. None of us would have survived these years without each other. It's only out of loyalty to family that none of us have given up long ago, that we've taken every blow life has thrown at us with our heads held high. Family makes us strong and gives us a deeper purpose, even though life itself seems almost meaningless these days.

But now we've been split up, divided in half, heading into a part of the world where we are not welcome. Where death is the likely outcome should we be discovered.

I don't know what I will do if I lose them. I don't know if I could survive such a loss.

My stomach knots up at the thought, and I feel an over-whelming urge to reach for Kristian's hand beside me, to feel his warmth and tell him I love him. But for fear of being dis-covered, I don't. Instead, I continue staring out the window until the bus coughs into motion, slowly pulling out of the parking lot, leaving Freja and Emilie still standing outside, waiting.

We head onto the road, turning south, towards the caliphate just a few kilometres away. The landscape around us is lush, green, and rolling. Under different circumstances, I would have considered it breathtakingly beautiful. I would have longed to leap off the bus, feel the grass under my bare feet, breathe in the scents of the Mediterranean, and rejoice that the days of bitter cold are behind us. But instead of joy, cold sweat drips from my forehead. It runs down my back, soaking my clothes. I only hope we won't be forced to leave the bus when we reach the border, because it's certain that someone will no-tice the sweat stains and become suspicious.

Before long, I spot the barbed wire fence that marks the bor-der between the new caliphate and Ceuta. Once, it marked the border with Morocco and had been erected by Spain to pre-vent the influx of illegal migrants from the south to Europe. Now, it stands as a physical barrier, guarded by Islamist sol-diers to stop the illegal flow of people going the other way.

From Europe to the south.

The world truly is changing.

The only thing that never seems to change is humanity's intolerance towards one another, I think sadly.

The bus stops, and the doors hiss open. Border guards with loaded AK-47s step inside, casting stern looks over the few passengers.

I shrink back as the gaze of one particularly fierce-looking guard lands on me, and he starts walking down the aisle. He stops right in front of Zaid's outstretched legs and gives a short command in Arabic.

Without a word, Zaid hands him the pass slip, which the man takes without a change of expression. A few seconds later, he returns it. All clear.

Kristian and I also hand over our slips, and after a quick glance at them, the guard turns and leaves the bus.

That's all it took. We've been cleared to enter the caliphate.

I let out a breath of relief, leaning my head back against the seat as the bus grumbles back to life. I cross my fingers that things go just as smoothly for the women.

After a few hours of driving, we enter the Atlas Mountains, stretching 2,500 kilometres from Morocco in the west to Tunisia in the east. They are home to millions of Sunni Berbers, living in small towns scattered across the mountain ranges and on the vast plains between them.

Every few hours, the bus stops, and passengers get on and off, some carrying baskets of fruit and vegetables, others with bags of freshly baked bread. The smells are wonderful, and they make my stomach growl loudly. The sound reminds me of how long it's been since I last ate. Not to mention how long it's been since I tasted freshly baked bread. Or any bread at all.

A tall, lean man with a grey beard that tapers to a point halfway down his chest sits in the seat in front of Kristian. On the seat beside him, he places an open basket filled with ripe dates and oranges, their sweet fragrance filling the air around us.

I yearn to reach out, grab an orange and a couple of dates to satisfy my gnawing hunger, but I restrain myself for fear of being noticed. No one, however, seems particularly interested in us, and as we travel deeper into the caliphate, I get the impression of a population living well and in harmony. Without the internal conflicts and tensions I had imagined before coming here. A civilisation that, despite differences in the depth of their religious beliefs, may not be so different from our own. They are simply trying to get through life in the best way they can.

But the glaring absence of women on the bus speaks volumes and strongly undermines any illusion of harmony. We are not tourists in their land, and any romantic idea of being welcomed as such and helped along the way by the locals is naive. That may have been the case once, but not anymore. Climate change and the belief in divine favour have changed everything. We are enemies, and if we are discovered, there will be no rescue from anywhere.

As evening falls and the sun begins to set behind the horizon, I hear Kristian's breathing grow heavier. Until now, the fear of being discovered has kept us both in a tense state of alertness, preventing us from truly falling asleep despite our best efforts to appear as if we have. But now, I can hear that his body has finally given in. We've been awake for nearly a day and a half, and after our time in the camp, our bodies are in no state of health to go without the rest they so desperately need.

The wound on my hip constantly reminds me of my deteriorating condition as sharp pains relentlessly shoot through my ravaged body. If it isn't treated soon, I'm afraid I might end up with gangrene.

The thirst is becoming unbearable too. We haven't brought any water with us, and we have no money to buy any. Twelve hours into the journey, without food or drink, my thirst has reached the point where my lips are starting to crack.

I glance at Zaid and can see he's suffering as well.

We need something to drink before we collapse and draw unwanted attention. We've barely drunk anything since leaving the camp, and 36 hours without water is far too long, especially in our condition.

I nudge Zaid in the side with my elbow. He looks at me questioningly, and when I point to my dry lips, he nods in understanding. But, like me, he has no idea where we'll get water, so he simply leans his head back and closes his eyes.

There's nothing else to be done.

Near the middle door of the bus, there's a small fridge, from which several passengers have taken turns grabbing a cold bottle of water. I secretly watch one of my fellow passengers, a middle-aged man with an unnaturally large, crooked nose. He drops a few coins into a plastic container on the outside of the fridge door, grabs a bottle, and lets the cool, soothing liquid flow into his mouth.

I can almost feel the water myself. I can smell it. Teasing, it embraces my senses, playing with them until my thirst becomes so overwhelming that I have to force myself to look away.

Afraid of letting my guard down and realising too late if someone becomes suspicious of us, I struggle to keep sleep at bay, even though it's what my body craves. Aside from water. I glance at Zaid again. I can't tell if he's asleep or not, but his face looks tense, so I assume he's awake, frantically wondering how things are going for Farhana and Fatima.

I'm doing the same.

Freja and Emilie never leave my thoughts. One small mistake, and they're doomed. Forgiveness is not a word often used by those who devote themselves to the most fundamentalist interpretations of the Quran.

The darkness outside the bus windows has now become so impenetrable that the driver dims the lights inside to a softer glow. Soothed by the bus's gentle rocking, I slowly begin to slip into a relaxing state of false security. Soon, my eyelids grow heavy, and I fight with all my might to resist the sleep I so desperately need. But it's not long before, in the heart of enemy territory and surrounded by people who wouldn't hesitate for a second to report me, I fall into a deep sleep, from which I only awaken when Zaid gently shakes my arm a few hours later.

The glowing numbers on the digital clock at the front of the bus tell me it's three in the morning. I've slept for six hours. The ceiling lights in the bus are now completely off, and only a strip of lighting along the aisle glows faintly.

Suddenly, I feel Zaid press a cold, full bottle of water into my hands. I glance at him in surprise, but I can't make out his face in the dark. I can, however, hear him drinking quietly from another bottle, and immediately my thirst returns with renewed force.

With my head full of unanswered questions, I gratefully unscrew the cap and drain half of the bottle in one long gulp. The rest is for Kristian, who eagerly gulps down the precious drops as soon as I wake him and hand him the bottle.

• • •

"Reggane," Zaid mutters to himself as the bus passes through a crumbling city gate somewhere in the desolate, barren stretches of Algeria's desert landscape.

Even though the amount of rain falling in the Sahara Desert has increased significantly since climate change began to take hold, it's still not enough to settle all the eroded sand and dust that have gathered over thousands of years of extreme heat. The dust swirls in the wind, creating a light haze that stretches as far as the eye can see.

The Sahara wasn't always this dry, barren place with extreme temperatures and scant rainfall. Just 10,000 years ago, it was covered in forested steppes, with rivers and lakes teeming with life, along with a rich variety of flora and fauna. Around the same time that the Northern Hemisphere was beginning to emerge from the last ice age, which had gripped it for more than 13,000 years, humans lived in the Sahara. Up until a few thousand years before our time, the Sahara was described as a fertile landscape, abundant with animals and plants. But then, for reasons unknown, the landscape dried up. Animals and people disappeared, and for many years it has been home primarily to the Tuareg nomads, except for a few small towns that have sprung up around the natural gas and oil fields in Algeria and Libya.

We've been travelling for a little over a day.

The bus signals and pulls in to refuel at a yellow-painted petrol station along the main road, just inside Reganne's city gate.

We haven't seen much traffic since we entered the desert, so the sight of a queue of five cars and three pickup trucks in front of the station immediately stirs a sense of unease in me.

I crane my neck to get a better view out the window.

Just as I spot the seven or eight armed jihad fighters along the north side of the building, the bus doors swing open, and six men, shouting loudly and with black-checkered scarves covering their faces, storm inside. They hold their machine guns menacingly in front of them, clearly ready to shoot anyone who dares stand in their way. Two of them gesture wildly for us to leave the bus, while they aggressively yank at the sleeves of the nearest passengers to make them stand.

Terrified, I watch helplessly as an elderly passenger collapses in the aisle and is brutally kicked in the back as punishment.

Following Zaid out of my seat, I quickly glance over my shoulder and lock eyes with Kristian. Fear is etched across his face.

What's happening?

If only I could say or do something to ease his fear, but anything I can think of would only make things worse. I can't hold him in my arms. I can't whisper reassurances, telling him that everything will be alright if we just stay calm. I can't, because deep down in my bones, I can feel that our time as refugees is about to take a terrifying turn, far worse than anything we've experienced so far.

A man grabs my sleeve and yanks hard, urging me to move faster. I lose my balance and stumble into Zaid, but somehow manage to stay upright. As I step down the bus's three steps, I'm kicked hard in the back, sending me sprawling onto the cracked, rough asphalt outside. I barely manage to get my hands up in time to protect my face, scraping them painfully as they make contact with the ground.

Dazed, I get to my feet, blood running down my arms in dark red streaks, staining the sleeves of my now filthy tunic.

The men give me no time to recover. They continuously drive me forward, like a sheep to slaughter, towards the waiting jihadists I had seen by the northern wall of the building.

I try to spot Kristian among the other passengers.

I can't see him.

My thoughts whirl in panic.

Where is he?

I need to protect him.

Did he manage to slip away in the confusion? Why can't I see him?

I'm shoved forward again, pulled, kicked, until, along with the other passengers, I'm forced to kneel against the wall in front of the waiting fighters.

How many of us are there? Twelve, thirteen?

Someone yanks off my head covering and scarf, revealing my beardless face.

I spot Kristian.

There are two men between us, and their head coverings have also been ripped off.

Kristian stares at me with wide eyes, terror written across his face, tears streaming down his young cheeks. I try to hold his gaze, but every time I turn my head, I'm struck hard at the back of my skull.

The jihadists shout incessantly.

The atmosphere is chaotic, and it's impossible not to feel the stress. Perhaps that's their aim?

I still don't dare speak.

Where is Zaid? I can't see him!

I try to turn my head in the opposite direction and am rewarded with another blow that makes my ears ring.

We need Zaid. He's supposed to speak for the three of us. That's the plan. Does Zaid remember the plan? He has to. Without him, we're doomed.

A thin fighter steps forward in the square before us. He's pulled his scarf away from his face, revealing a bright red scar running from the outer edge of his right eye, down his cheek, disappearing into his thick, grey-streaked beard. He holds a large, rusted machete in one hand.

The sight of it makes my blood run cold.

Flanked by two fighters with their faces hidden behind checkered scarves, both gripping dusty black AK-47s, he raises his free arm in the air, bringing an abrupt silence.

The sudden quiet is a relief, but it doesn't last long.

The man speaks, his voice sharp and clear, cutting through the air as he addresses the crowd in a language I don't understand. Occasionally, he's interrupted by a loud, passionate *Allahu Akbar!* from the fighters around us, as well as from the other bus passengers kneeling by the wall, just like me.

I try to mimic the act, but I have no sense of timing, and each time I chant "Allahu Akbar," I do so too late.

I draw unwanted attention.

The man's eyes bore into me as he speaks. He holds my gaze, clearly noticing that my praise is forced, not natural.

When he finishes, the bus driver suddenly steps forward. He's holding two empty water bottles and points angrily at Zaid. Before I can even process what's happening, the two fighters who had flanked the leader grab Zaid and drag him out into the open space in front of the rest of us. They force him

452

down onto his knees again. The leader says a few words, and the square erupts into a cacophony of screams and shouts, stopping only when Zaid's left hand lies severed on the ground in front of him.

The leader raises his arm again, restoring silence.

Blood drips from the machete in his right hand.

I stare in shock at the scene before me.

I try to process what's happening, but my brain can't work fast enough, and it's only when the leader holds up the two water bottles that it dawns on me: Zaid must have stolen them from the bus's fridge while everyone was asleep. The bus driver must have seen him take them and alerted the jihadists. Theft is punished by amputation under Islamic law.

I stare, frozen, at the blood flowing from Zaid's arm where his hand had been cut off. If they don't stop the bleeding soon, he'll die, I think, horrified, as I see the fighters grab his other arm. They hold it out between them, about a metre off the ground.

The machete glints in the sunlight as it slices through the air, once again severing flesh and bone, separating the right hand from the rest of Zaid's body.

One of the fighters bends down and picks up both severed hands from the ground, then triumphantly holds them up in the air.

The crowd erupts in cheers.

Two bottles, two hands.

That's the punishment.

My eyes fill with tears. I see Zaid through a blurry veil of grief. He's hunched forward on his knees, his head to the ground, both arms hidden beneath his body.

I can't tell if he's screaming.

The noise around me drowns everything out.

Suddenly, for the third time, the jihadists fall silent.

The leader, the executioner, points at me with the machete. Before I know what's happening, I'm dragged forward and positioned in front of Zaid, my back to Kristian.

I can hear my son calling desperately for me.

I try to turn and meet his eyes, but the fighters hold me in an iron grip. I'm convinced I'm about to die, and I can't even look at my son one last time.

"You enter the Caliphate, God's kingdom, thinking you can get away with it!" the executioner declares in perfect English. "Almighty Allah informed us long ago that you were coming. Do you really believe Allah would allow three infidel dogs to roam freely in His own backyard? What are you doing here, enemies of Islam?"

I look up at him nervously.

I don't know what I'm expected to say.

"We just want to get to Mali," I say hoarsely. "Can't we just be allowed to continue to Mali? We're not enemies of Islam, I swear!"

"You're from the camps!" he replies harshly. "The camps are full of enemies of Islam!"

How does he know that?

The question forms like a seed in the back of my mind, but he doesn't give me time to let it grow.

"Infidel dogs who for years have tried to fight Allah's children and the true faith. You are worthless. Allah has punished you for your blasphemy."

He spits out the last words, rewarded by a chorus of storming *Allahu Akbar* from the jihadists around us.

"Him," he continues, pointing at Zaid, who still lies on the ground before me. "A Shia thief! He's worse than a dog. A pig, that's what he is. An apostate pig who thinks he can get away with mocking Allah's message. He doesn't deserve to live."

I can hear Kristian sobbing, calling my name over and over again.

"This is what we do to pigs!"

The executioner bends over Zaid and grabs a fistful of his hair. He pulls his head back far enough that I make eye contact with him. I see the despair and pain in his deeply set brown eyes. My friend, who has endured so much, has given up! The fight is lost.

I stare at him in anguish, realising that our wives will never know what happened to us. When they step off the bus, and we aren't there waiting for them. When we never show up.

"Pigs are slaughtered!"

With one long, smooth motion, he mercilessly slashes Zaid's throat. Blood instantly gushes from the wound, extinguishing the last flicker of life in him.

I watch the light fade from his eyes as the ground turns red in front of my knees.

"The boy can still be saved," says the executioner, releasing Zaid's head.

His lifeless body collapses into the pool of blood in front of me.

I stare at him, confused.

Saved? Who can be saved?

"To give your son to a life in Allah's holy kingdom and raise him in His great wisdom is the greatest gift a man can give his child. To offer that gift to a boy who has grown up among infidels is his only salvation. *Allahu Akbar.*"

Is he talking about Kristian?

I look questioningly at the executioner, who speaks again.

"Will you give your son to Allah? To be raised among His chosen children, to learn to honour His will and defend His kingdom? As a jihadist among like-minded believers?"

The executioner crouches down, staring at me, clearly waiting for an answer. His white robe is stained red with Zaid's blood. He's stuck the tip of his machete into the sand in front of him, resting his hands on the handle.

"The boy's life is in your hands. Only you, as his father, can give him to Allah. So answer me now. Will you give him to the one true God, and to a life of defending and rebuilding the Caliphate?"

My thoughts swirl like a tornado, snatching fragments of information from everywhere.

Is there really a way out?

Is he offering to spare Kristian's life if I say yes to giving him to the jihadists? To a life under strict control, where sharia dictates his every step? Where science is only considered valid because the Almighty Creator chooses to give us glimpses of His vast universe?

"Last chance, you infidel dog!"

The executioner is growing impatient.

"Will you give your son to a life in Allah's service?"

Do I even have a choice?

If I say no, will he suffer the same fate as Zaid?

I can't bear the thought of him dying. We—he—has fought so long to stay alive. Do I even have the right to deny him the chance to live, even if it's under a different life than the one he's known?

I nod faintly, defeated.

"You must say it aloud, so your son hears you. He must

know that you're giving him the greatest gift of all, so he can focus entirely on his sacred duties."

I swallow with difficulty.

Distantly, like an echo, I hear my own voice repeating the executioner's demand. "I give my son Kristian away to a life in Allah's wisdom and to the defence of the Caliphate."

The words barely make it past my lips. Words that seal Kristian's fate. The question is whether that fate is better or worse than death, the thing we've fled from for so long.

The executioner nods in approval. Then he rises and gives a subtle nod to one of the guards behind me.

I hear someone scream.

Kristian?

Then I feel a hard blow to the back of my head, and everything goes black.

When I come to, the area around the petrol station is empty.

No cars.

No bus.

No people.

No Kristian.

In front of me, only Zaid's bloated body lies baking in the sun.

Flies crawl all over it in a thick, glistening layer. They swarm aggressively when I move but settle again soon after.

I squint against the sun.

Am I alive?

26 Freja

The landscape around Bordj Badji Mokhtar surprises with its green oases, appearing like bright islands amidst the dry desert sand. Increased rainfall has resulted in a lush landscape not seen here for thousands of years. A light green carpet of grass stretches across vast areas, as if deliberately laid out for the large herds of goats that roam freely across the desert plains. Every now and then, I spot a solitary goat standing on its hind legs, stretching its neck to reach some of the fresh shoots on one of the many small bushy trees that have also sprung up.

Despite the enormous size of the goat herds and the vast grazing areas, I can't see many shepherds. When I do spot them, they rarely stray far from the dilapidated huts near the main road, which are presumably their homes while they stay with the goats. I use my eyes carefully, for we must pass through the goat herds to reach Mali.

I am getting used to the mesh in front of my eyes and the limited view it provides. At first, it made me dizzy, but I appreciate the anonymity the clothing gives me. Gives us. Emilie, Farhana, Fatima, and myself. So far, the journey has gone smoothly. No one has shown us the slightest interest, and despite the heat under the thick, black cloth of the burqa, I am starting to relax more.

The male bus driver indeed sits alone at the front, separated from the women by a partition with no window. The female passengers who board and exits again along the route either keep to themselves or remain within their own small travel group.

The anonymity applies to all of us, it seems, and I'm beginning to think that many Muslim women might actually appreciate it, given the circumstances. With it, they can keep their identities hidden from the outside world and only reveal themselves when directly asked. In a male-dominated world, where their every move is watched, the burqa may be their only refuge. Beneath it, men can't criticise their appearance, how they chew their food, whether they wear makeup, or whether they wear jewellery. Under the burqa, there is room to be oneself—something they otherwise have no right to be.

We arrive in Bordj Badji Mokhtar just as the sun is setting. It spreads its orange-red colours over the dusty city streets and dilapidated buildings, giving a romantic first impression, despite the fact that I am fully aware of the danger in our situation. Once we leave the bus, we step into a male-dominated world, completely subject to their whims and wishes.

The bus passes a roundabout with a statue in the centre. The statue depicts a jihadist wearing a blue robe and a white headscarf. In one hand, he holds an AK-47 assault rifle, and in the other, a black flag with white Arabic text. The flag is likely that of the caliphate, and the statue is an unabashed reminder that the holy warrior is regarded as a hero here, not a terrorist.

As we pull into the bus station, I immediately spot the blue bus that Magnus, Kristian, and Zaid boarded a day and a half ago. It left Ceuta three hours before ours, so they must be eager to receive us so we can continue southward, out of hostile territory.

After our encounters with France and Spain, Denmark's close allies for so many years, I am not optimistic that our meeting with Mali will go much better though. If the climate crisis has shown anything, it's how quickly friends can become enemies when resources are scarce.

With my heart in my throat and butterflies in my stomach, I step off the bus with Farhana and the children. I'm relieved to see Emilie gripping my burqa tightly, terrified of a repeat of our adventure in the snowstorm. It feels like a distant memory, even though it was only about a year ago. I'm so proud of all the courage she's shown throughout the journey from Denmark. And not once during the bus ride did she give in to the temptation to speak to me in Danish, risking exposing us.

My emotions are a rollercoaster, constantly shifting between joy and relief at the prospect of seeing Magnus and Kristian again, and fear of the final part of our journey. We've come so far, but my gut tells me something terrible is looming, and I've learned to trust it. That instinct has saved us several times in recent years, and right now, as I step down from the bus and into the warming rays of the evening sun, it's on high alert.

I look around the square but can't see anything alarming, aside from the obvious fact that we're in the heart of one of the caliphate's strongholds. Men in white robes and colourful headscarves, with burqa-clad women trailing obediently behind, move purposefully down the streets away from the bus station. Across the street, there's a café. Outside, a few men enjoy a hookah together, watching the traffic pass by.

I can't see Magnus or Zaid.

Farhana stops and looks around once we're a good 50 metres away from the bus and its other passengers. "Can you see them?" she asks quietly once we're out of earshot. "Their bus is parked right over there, so they must be around here somewhere. They can't be far. Zaid would never leave me alone here. He knows it's far too risky."

"No, I can't see them. Where could they have gone?" I whisper ner-vously. "Maybe they're arranging transport further south to Mali?"

"Maybe. But if that's the case, I hope they're here soon because if a patrol finds us outdoors without them after the sun sets, we'll be in serious trouble."

"They'll come," I say, trying to sound calm.

But my stomach screams that something has gone terribly wrong, and we need to get out of here fast.

"They would never abandon us. Neither Magnus nor Zaid. They'd both walk through fire for us. I'm sure they'll be here any minute."

"We can't just stand here," Farhana says. "We're drawing attention to ourselves." She glances around the streets for a refuge. After a moment, she moves. "Come on! Let's hide in that collapsed building over there. From there, we can watch the square."

The building is little more than a few bare walls, silently standing alone after the roof long ago gave up and collapsed. Before we step inside, we make sure no one is watching us. Then, we cross the thres-hold, taking shelter from the everpresent eyes of the town, as darkness quickly descends over its potholed streets.

Where are they?

We take turns watching the bus station throughout the night.

Hunger and thirst are constant companions, which, when they become overwhelming, can almost push the fear of what's happened to the men into the background.

What would we do without them?

I can't live without Magnus. Or Kristian.

Has something happened to them? It must have, or they wouldn't have left us like this. But the bus is right there. The one they were on.

As the hours pass, the town falls quieter and quieter. The streets lie deserted, and the only sound is the song of cicadas. At one point, a sand-coloured desert fox casually strolls down the main road. It stops and sniffs the air. Then, it glances briefly in our direction before suddenly bolting between the buildings, scared off by the sound of a night patrol's rattling pickup truck.

The truck, with four jihadists sitting on the bed, each with an AK-47 resting carelessly on their laps, passes the collapsed building.

I hold my breath as it drives by slowly.

The men on the truck's bed scan the darkness, looking for anything that defies their strict interpretation of the Quran's teachings. At one point, I feel as though I have direct eye contact with one of them, but he seemingly doesn't see me in the protective darkness of the building, and they continue their patrol through the town's streets with-out showing any sign of stopping.

Where are Magnus and Kristian?

I don't understand.

The pain in my stomach is unbearable. Hunger and anxiety are tearing my insides apart.

Magnus, where are you? You can't abandon us. What's happened to you?

Beneath my burqa, tears stream from my eyes.

Something terrible has happened.
I can feel it.

● ● ●

The next day drags on slowly.

We remain in hiding, praying that no one enters the building and stumbles upon us by chance. All day, we keep a sharp eye on the square outside, but there's still no sign of Magnus, Kristian, or Zaid anywhere.

The sun beats down on the rooftops, and although temperatures in this part of the world, indeed across the globe, no longer reach the extreme highs they once did, it's still hot enough that sweat starts pouring early in the morning. We're not used to the heat. The contrast to the extreme cold we've endured for the past few years is stark. My eyes sting as sweat constantly drips into them. I try to wipe it away with the fabric of my burka, but it doesn't take long before it's so soaked through that it can no longer absorb it.

My throat tightens. I'm dizzy, and my tongue feels like it's been dipped in sand. All four of us are suffering from the onset of dehydration. None of us has had anything to drink since we boarded the bus more than two days ago, and Emilie has hardly moved all morning. I'm worried about how much longer she can hold out.

Magnus. Where are you?

Out on the street, the day continues as normal. Men tend to their work in shops and stalls. Women do their shopping for the evening meal. Everything proceeds peacefully and uneventfully until, late in the afternoon, three pickup trucks full of jihadists suddenly speed into the square. The jihadists shoot wildly into the air while shouting loudly.

"Allahu Akbar."

The cries of praise to Allah blare constantly from a loud-speaker on the roof of the lead vehicle.

Burka-clad women scatter in all directions, desperate to get out of the way. The fear of the jihadists seems to be great, even among the town's own residents.

Behind me, I suddenly hear footsteps crunching on the rubble from the collapsed roof. The sound startles me, and I spin around quickly, my heart racing. A burka-clad woman, seeking shelter from the jihadists, is making her way through the door. She hesitates when she sees us.

Farhana quickly murmurs *"Allahu Akbar,"* which seems to reassure the woman.

"Allahu Akbar."

The magical words, repeated over and over as reassurance that everything is as it should be, as God wills it. The woman sits down on a pile of rubble along the wall, opposite the door-way, away from the windows. She remains silent. If she notices the sweat stains on our burkas, she'll know we've been here a long time. It wouldn't take much to figure out that we've been hiding here all day, and that women who hide do so from their husbands. That's the only reason.

Will she report us once the jihadists have gone and she's able to return home? To her husband?

The woman leaves without a word shortly after the jihadists have left the street. Darkness is already starting to fall. She needs to get home before the curfew for women comes into effect.

After she's gone, Farhana comes over and sits close beside

me. "We need to leave before she tells on us," she whispers hoarsely.

"Yes, but where?" I reply. "We have to wait for Magnus and Zaid."

"Something's happened to them," she says hesitantly. "They wouldn't have left us like this unless they were prevented from reaching us."

"What do you think happened? The bus was here when we arrived."

"I don't know. I only know that we can't stay here. That woman, if she doesn't report us and reveal our hiding place to her husband, then we'll still die of thirst before tomorrow is over. The girls can't last much longer."

"What do you suggest?" I ask, feeling a growing sense of dread.

"We have to try to make it to Mali on our own. Tonight."

"But we can't just leave the meeting place," I protest. "What if Magnus and Zaid turn up and we're not here? What then?"

"What if they turn up and we're already dead from thirst? Or have been stoned to death? What if they never show up? Something has happened to them. I can feel it deep in my gut. I know it," Farhana whispers, her voice breaking as she holds back tears, careful not to let the girls hear us. "We have a duty to the girls, don't we? Even if something has happened to the men, it's our responsibility to get the girls to safety. We can't stay here; that much is certain. If we do, we'll all die—there's no doubt about that. Both Zaid and Magnus will understand and know that we had no choice but to try to reach the border on our own if they do show up here eventually. And they'll follow us as soon as they can."

I listen, frozen in thought. I know she's right. We have to

keep going on our own.

But what if Magnus can't find us in Mali? It's a vast country. What if we end up in different refugee camps? I can't bear the thought of living without him, but I also can't leave Emilie in the hands of the jihadists, subject to their barbaric lifestyle and methods of execution. She's still just a child who deserves a chance at life. Isn't that why we fled Denmark in the first place? Because the children deserve a chance at life? I have to be strong once again. For Emilie's sake.

"Let's go," I say, finally agreeing. "You're right. We have to move on."

● ● ●

Once we reach the outskirts of the city, it's simply a matter of continuing due south on foot. We avoid following the main road towards Mali, opting instead to cut straight across the desert sand, where herds of goats wander in large groups.

I'm grateful that Magnus insisted we all learn how to navigate by the stars, as out here in the dark, the only landmarks are the stars in the night sky. Once again, the burkas help us on our way. Like four black ghosts, we slip through the shadows of the night. I make sure Emilie and Fatima hold our hands, as when clouds cover the moon for long periods, we can't even see each other, even though we walk only a few metres apart.

So, we don't notice we are in the middle of a large herd of goats until they suddenly start bleating loudly from all sides, nearly scaring the life out of all four of us. In the silence of the night, every sound seems much louder. The noise from the goats is deafening, and I'm convinced it travels swiftly through the darkness, reaching the ears of the goatherds and alerting them that something is amiss. It can't be long before they get into their trucks and come to investigate, so we hurry onwards, but the goats are all around us. The noise follows us, as the goats all react the same way, bleating in alarm as our black silhouettes glide silently through their flocks.

At long last, we reach the edge of the herd. The herders haven't arrived yet. Perhaps they're not coming at all, but I still breathe a sigh of relief once the herd is behind us. It's probably not so unusual for the flocks to get agitated by something during the night. Desert foxes or lynx are likely common visitors in the dark.

Thirst, however, is an unbearable companion. Farhana taught us to suck on a small stone as we walk to trick our bodies into producing a bit of saliva, easing the burning dryness in our mouths. But our bodies are starting to give up. We stumble along on shaky legs, like babies who've just learned to walk.

I don't know if I can make it all the way to Mali. I ask Emilie if she's alright, but she doesn't answer. Did she not hear me? Maybe no sound is coming out of my mouth? I don't know. I'm disoriented. Is Emilie still here? Where is she? I can't have lost her too.

"Emilie?" I call out into the night, but I can't even hear my own voice.

Then I realise she's still holding my hand. She's still here. I breathe a sigh of relief.

What does dehydration feel like? Suddenly, my feet feel wet and cold. Is that normal? The sensation creeps further and further up my legs until it reaches my waist.

"Mum?" I hear Emilie's voice, and I stop abruptly.

"Mum, it's too deep!"

What is she saying? Deep?

"Mum?"

I look down but can only see dark shadows through the burka's mesh, yet I suddenly sense a swaying mass all around me.

Water?

My brain slowly begins to function properly again. Water? In my disoriented state, we've wandered straight into an oasis in the desert, formed from heavier rainfall over a longer period. I hadn't considered it before, but of course, there must be several of them scattered around to provide water for the goats during the hot days. Otherwise, they wouldn't survive out here in the desert.

At last, we can fill our bodies with the life-giving liquid they so desperately crave. I don't care that the water tastes foul or that the goats likely trample through the pool daily. For me and my parched body, it tastes wonderful. All four of us drink until our stomachs are full and we can feel the water reaching the furthest parts of our exhausted bodies. Then we take a short break before drinking again.

The headache that's been with me for days starts to ease, allowing me to think more clearly. How much further do we have to go? I look around. It's dark in every direction. I can't even see the lights of the city behind us. The darkness is a blessing, keeping us hidden from prying eyes, but it's also a frustrating companion, preventing us from gauging how far we have left or avoiding holes, ravines, or thorn bushes along the way. But we have no choice but to keep going. It's vital to put as much distance between ourselves and the city—and the jihadists—as possible before the revealing rays of the sun peek over the horizon to the east.

Revitalised by the water we've consumed, we continue undeterred. We know the border is about 20 kilometres from the city. With a pace of three kilometres an hour through the desert sand, we should reach it by early morning.

From time to time, we come across another noisy herd of goats, but the herders either seem unconcerned by the commotion or too far away to hear it. We carry on with a bit more peace of mind, even though the goats bleat indignantly as soon as they spot us.

As the sun begins to rise and its rays turn the horizon dark blue, a foul smell suddenly reaches my nose. The burka effectively blocks most scents, so I'm startled by the stench that manages to seep through its tightly woven fabric. What is that smell? It reminds me of something familiar, but I can't place it until we've walked for another half-hour.

The Gaza Strip!

It stinks like the camp around the Gaza Strip.

A shiver runs down my spine. Is this really our destiny? To replace one camp with another? My shoulders sag as if a massive weight has been placed upon them. I won't survive another camp—I know that much. And how will Magnus ever find us if we end up there?

"Farhana," I say. "Can you smell that too?"

"Yes," she replies. "What is it?"

"Another camp," I answer grimly.

"It smells different!"

"Does it?"

"I think so." Farhana lifts her burka over her head to better identify the smell. She inhales deeply.

"It doesn't smell like people."

"What else could it be?" I ask dejectedly. I still can't come to terms with the idea of adjusting to life in another camp. The memories of Thomas and his cronies hit me like a punch in the gut. So much has happened since I stabbed him in the neck. It feels like an eternity, even though only a few days have passed.

As we approach the border and the light fully replaces the night, the stench grows stronger, so intense now that it burns our eyes and lungs. We stop abruptly and stare in disbelief at the scene before us, unable to comprehend what we're seeing. As far as the eye can see, in both directions on the other side of the barbed-wire fence marking the border between Mali and the caliphate, the land is teeming with pigs. Pink and black-spotted pigs.

● ● ●

"They're keeping the jihadists from crossing the border." The officer lets out a loud laugh, a contagious cackle that would have impressed even Nadja.

I can't help but smile, but the memory of the woman who welcomed us so warmly into the camp brings tears to my eyes. She's gone, killed by a virus that under normal circumstances would have required nothing more than a week in bed. Nadja died from a combination of malnutrition, poor hygiene, and lack of medical care.

No, there's not much left to smile about in this world any-more.

I have nothing left to smile about.

My thoughts drift back to Denmark and the friends we left

behind. How many of them are still alive after the last winter? Spring might not have reached that far north yet. Maybe they're still trapped inside their houses, watching their supplies dwindle day by day. Or maybe they've already died—frozen to death during the unbearably cold and increasingly long winter storms that grow more severe each year?

What about Mikkel and Anna? And Kasper? Where are they now? Are they still alive?

We've lost so many friends along the way that it's almost too much to bear. My soul is an open wound, and if it were visible, it would look like a bush attacked by caterpillars—wrapped in a thick layer of web-bing and full of larvae, gorging themselves on every open sore, which never has the chance to heal before another is added.

Where are Magnus, Kristian, and Zaid?

I try not to dwell on it too much, because if I give in to my worst fears, I won't be able to stay strong for Emilie. And I *have* to be. Right now, I'm all she has left. *She's* all I have left.

The officer doesn't seem to notice the tears in my eyes, even though my face is visible again after removing the full head covering. Or maybe he does and just chooses to ignore them.

We live in a terrible time, where everyone suffers in one way or another, and everyone has a story to tell. We're certainly not the first to show up on his doorstep with scars on our souls, and we certainly won't be the last.

"Aside from the obvious benefit that the pigs form an effective barrier, apparently stopping those filthy devils from invading our country, they've also become Mali's golden calf. After the collapse of pig farming in northern Europe, our president, Oumar, saw a unique opportunity to establish pig farms here and take over the supply for all the export markets suddenly left without providers—especially China.

We don't eat them ourselves, of course. Most of us are Muslims, as you probably know, and while we're not quite as fanatical as those devils over there in that so-called caliphate, there are still certain commandments from the Quran that we follow. Abstaining from pork is one of them. But we have no issue handling the pigs or their meat, which would be unthinkable for the inhabitants of the caliphate. The entire production is exported, and within just a few years, it has made Mali a very wealthy nation."

The man continues talking for a while, but I find it hard to focus.

Our lives have been uprooted. We no longer have a country to return to. I've lost most of my friends. My family has been torn apart, and I have no idea if my husband or son are still alive. My daughter has barely spoken a word since we left the camp, except for the moment when I almost led her into the deep water where she could no longer stand. I fear that her mind has been permanently damaged and that she'll never again be the sweet, joyful girl she once was back home.

"We've also had our share of refugees," the officer continues. "Many of them we have to house in camps around the country. But those who can work and help rebuild the new Mali are given that opportunity before being sent to the camps. That includes you, of course."

He stares at us for a long time with eyes as black as woodland lakes, which I can't read at all.

I feel like I need to respond. "I'd like to wait here for my husband and my son."

My voice is hoarse and barely audible. The officer hands me

a bottle of water, which I accept reluctantly. But I don't drink it. He turns to look north, toward the caliphate on the other side of the border fence. The land lies desolate. Aside from the dark green bushes scattered a-cross the ground, there's little sign of life. The goat herds don't seem to come this far south.

"Are they still out there?" he asks after a long pause.

I nod sadly. "Them and Zaid."

The officer looks at Farhana. "Zaid is your husband?"

Farhana nods.

He turns his face back north, absentmindedly picking at his nose.

There's a light breeze from the west, just enough to sweep away the worst of the pig stench in the direction of the caliphate.

I've never seen so many pigs before. There must be millions of them if they stretch all along the border. Pen after pen, packed with pigs biting each other's tails and ears, squealing frantically when they get into fights.

Everywhere, there are people working to feed them, clean the pens, and drive pigs to slaughter. Men, women, and older children working side by side, while the sun beats down on their backs. It's hard work, but they are free, and they look healthy.

The officer speaks again, though it sounds more like he's talking to himself than to us. "Rumour has it the caliph has ordered all enemies of the caliphate killed as soon as they set foot in their land. And it seems that order is being carried out with great zeal, because it's been a very long time since anyone has come here from that direction." He turns his head back to us, looking at us with what I interpret as tenderness in his eyes. "But then, you suddenly appear. Against all odds. Two women and two girls. Normally, you wouldn't be allowed to move two feet on your own without being accompanied by your husbands or fathers, and yet here you are, standing on my doorstep after crossing the entire caliphate from north to south all alone."

The man turns and starts walking slowly towards some long, thatched buildings. He doesn't seem to mean us any harm, but we still follow him reluctantly. Over the past year, our trust in others has been shattered.

As we approach one of the buildings, he points to the door at the far end. "You can stay in there. The section leader is named Bintou. She'll take good care of you. Room and board are included, as long as you help with the daily tasks. On the farm. In the kitchen. In the houses. You can sort that out with her. She's a good woman."

Epilogue Magnus

The sun hangs low on the horizon, casting long shadows over the desert sands and painting the sky a fiery orange in a vibrant explosion of warm hues. A yellow deathstalker scorpion, out early, scurries across a clearing between the protective bushes. It usually emerges only when the moon replaces the sun, and darkness takes over, hunting insects and spiders through the night.

I shudder at the sight of it. I hate those little beasts, their venom potent enough to kill a fully grown man past his prime. Too many times to count, I've woken up in terror to the sound of one of them rustling near my ears, or because one had crawled over my hand while I slept beneath the open desert sky.

It took me nearly a month and a half to cover the more than 600 kilometres from where Kristian disappeared and Zaid was murdered, to the border fence separating Mali from the caliphate south of Bordj Badji Mokhtar. I don't know why my life was spared. I suspect the jihadists needed to convince Kristian that I had handed him over to them willingly, that it was my desire for him to be trained in the true faith. Had they killed me in front of him, it would have been impossible to convert and mould him into their twisted hands.

That had been their vile plan all along. Ever since they helped us escape the camp in Spain. I'm certain of it.

I instinctively touch my hip as my thoughts drift back to the camp.

Today, there is a hollow the size of a fist where the pressure sore, day by day, ate away at my healthy tissue, all the way down to the bone. The pain was unbearable. One night, I woke up screaming, unable to stifle the cry, jihadists or not. I was convinced I had been stung by a scorpion in my sleep, but it was the wound that had finally gnawed its way down to the bone, exposing an area the size of a one-euro coin.

It's healed now, but it nearly killed me, as I wandered delirious through the desert for weeks, fevered and disoriented, until I finally collapsed along the border fence near Bordj Badji Mokhtar.

It took almost a year in Bintou's skilled nursing care for the infection to clear and for the skin to close over the exposed bone. A whole year in which I couldn't bear to look either Freja or Farhana in the eye, ashamed of having abandoned both Kristian and Zaid. A whole year in which every waking minute, I thought of nothing else but when I'd be well enough to go out and search for my missing son and wrench him from the clutches of the damned jihadists.

Five years have passed since then.

This is my 18th trip into the caliphate to search for him.

The first many times, I was fumbling blindly, not knowing where to look, and each time I returned empty-handed, the distance be-tween Freja and me grew wider. I don't know if she blames me for his disappearance, or if it's because she sees him every time she looks at me. We've barely been able to speak since we were reunited in Mali.

We still share a room, of course, when I'm home at the pig farm, though that's rarely for long. But whenever I step inside, she sighs heavily and turns away from me. The longing is too much, and the knowledge that he's out there somewhere, with no way to reach him without risking our lives, is eating us up inside.

But then something changed last year. I started hearing stories about a Nordic jihadist, who, along with his gang of young fighters, roams the border further northwest, taking potshots at the pigs on the farms there.

A new hope sparked within me. Could it possibly be Kristian?

Now, I stand atop a low rock formation along the border fence, at the crossroads where Mauritania, Mali, and the caliphate meet.

A cloud cover hides the moon, and with the sun now set, it's too dark to see anything on the other side.

This is where the jihadist operates, and it's not the first time I've spent days here watching the caliphate for any sign of him. But so far, he's managed to elude me.

I sit down and rest my head against the rock behind me. I'll try to get some sleep before I head back in tomorrow.

As I have many times before, I wonder whether Farhana's cousin knew all along when he helped us escape through the latrines. Was he part of the plan? The cunning scheme to help families with sons escape from the camps, only to kidnap the boys as soon as they entered the caliphate.

How many times had I asked Zaid why those people were helping us when we had nothing to offer them in return?

I was wrong. We had plenty to offer them. Kristian was their price. Kristian and others like him. Boys they could train to become proud jihadists, to defend the caliphate from invaders like Zaid and me.

The next morning, I'm jolted awake by the sound of gunfire and the roar of an engine. Startled, I leap to my feet and stare over the border fence. There, about 100 metres into the caliphate, a battered pickup truck revs its engine. Clouds of sand billow around it. On the back sit four jihadists, firing shots at the pigs below the cliff I stand on.

I shield my eyes against the sun, but I can't make out their faces from this distance.

Could it be Kristian?

Enjoyed reading MALI?

3 Degrees Celsius is the second book in the Victims of Hothouse Earth series. *3 Degrees Celsius* focuses on the threat of Islamic extremism during the climate crisis and will be released in English during 2025.

Climate migration is one of the major challenges the world is facing. The World Bank estimates that up to 216 million people will be forced to leave their homes due to climate change by 2050. The UN fears that the situation could easily become a recruitment ground for Islamic extremist groups.

About the book:
The global temperature rise has reached 3 degrees Celsius. Africa is burning, and life has become a daily struggle for survival, with hundreds of millions of people starving across the continent.

Somewhere in Central Africa, the tribal girl Bintou must dig deep to find a remarkable inner strength, as both Mother Nature and the Islamist militant group Ansaru seem determined to hold her in an iron grip.

Further north, the orphaned boy Muhammad finds himself in a ghost town in Algeria, with little hope for the future. An impulsive action leads him on a fateful journey that will change his life forever.

Printed in Great Britain
by Amazon

57168667R00273